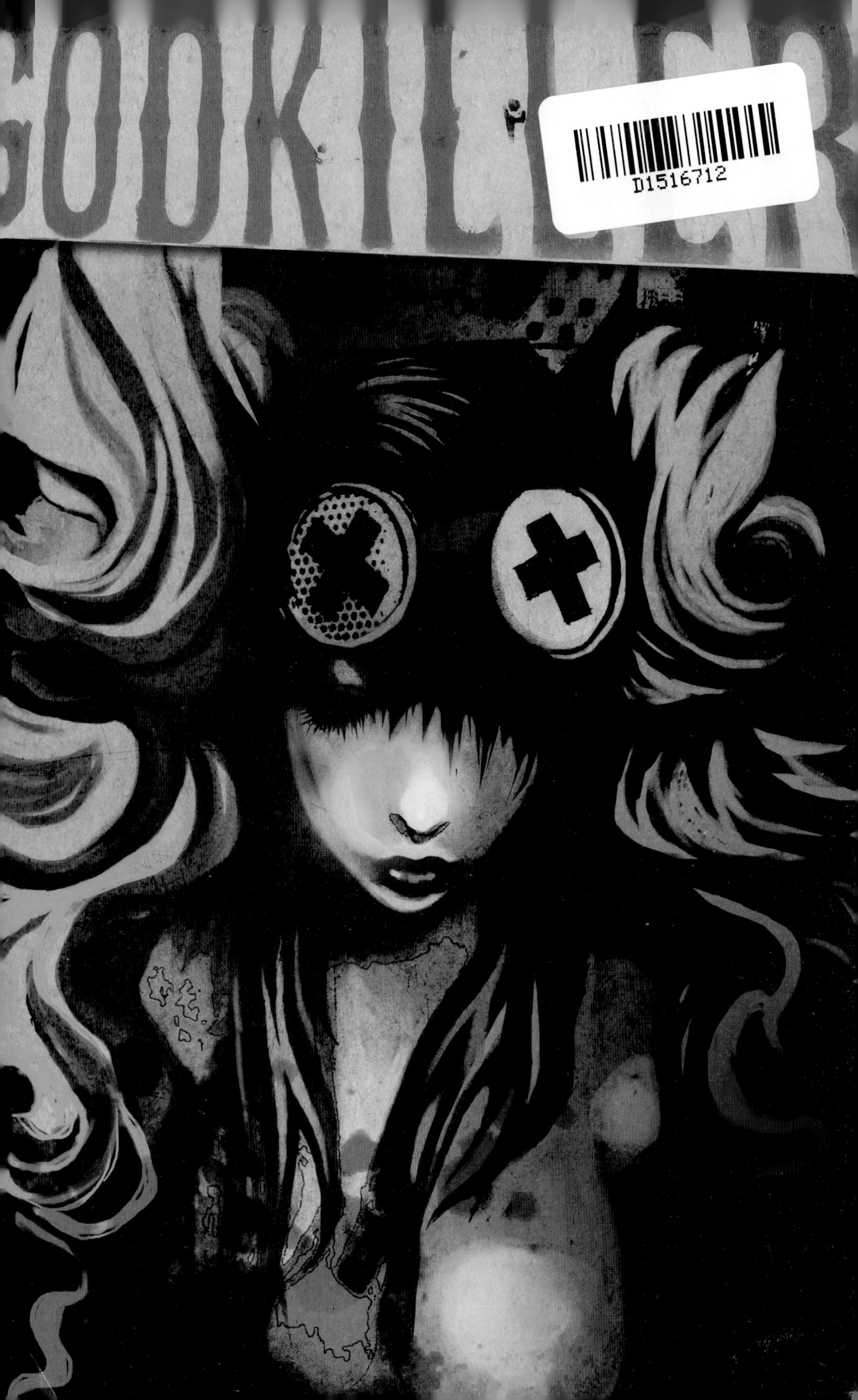

GODKILLER
Book One
Walk Among Us, Vol 1

Written by Matt Pizzolo

Illustrated by Anna Muckcracker Wieszczyk

Cover by Ben Templesmith

Production Artists Vincent Kukua, Matt Harding

Additional Illustrations by
Anna Muckcracker Wieszczyk
Ben Templesmith
Tim Seeley
Amancay Nahuelpan

Published by Black Mask Studios LLC
Brett Gurewitz | Matt Pizzolo | Steve Niles

First Edition 2015 | Printed in the USA

10 9 8 7 6 5 4 3 2 1

WHEN FREE WILL IS OUTLAWED
ONLY OUTLAWS WILL HAVE FREE WILL

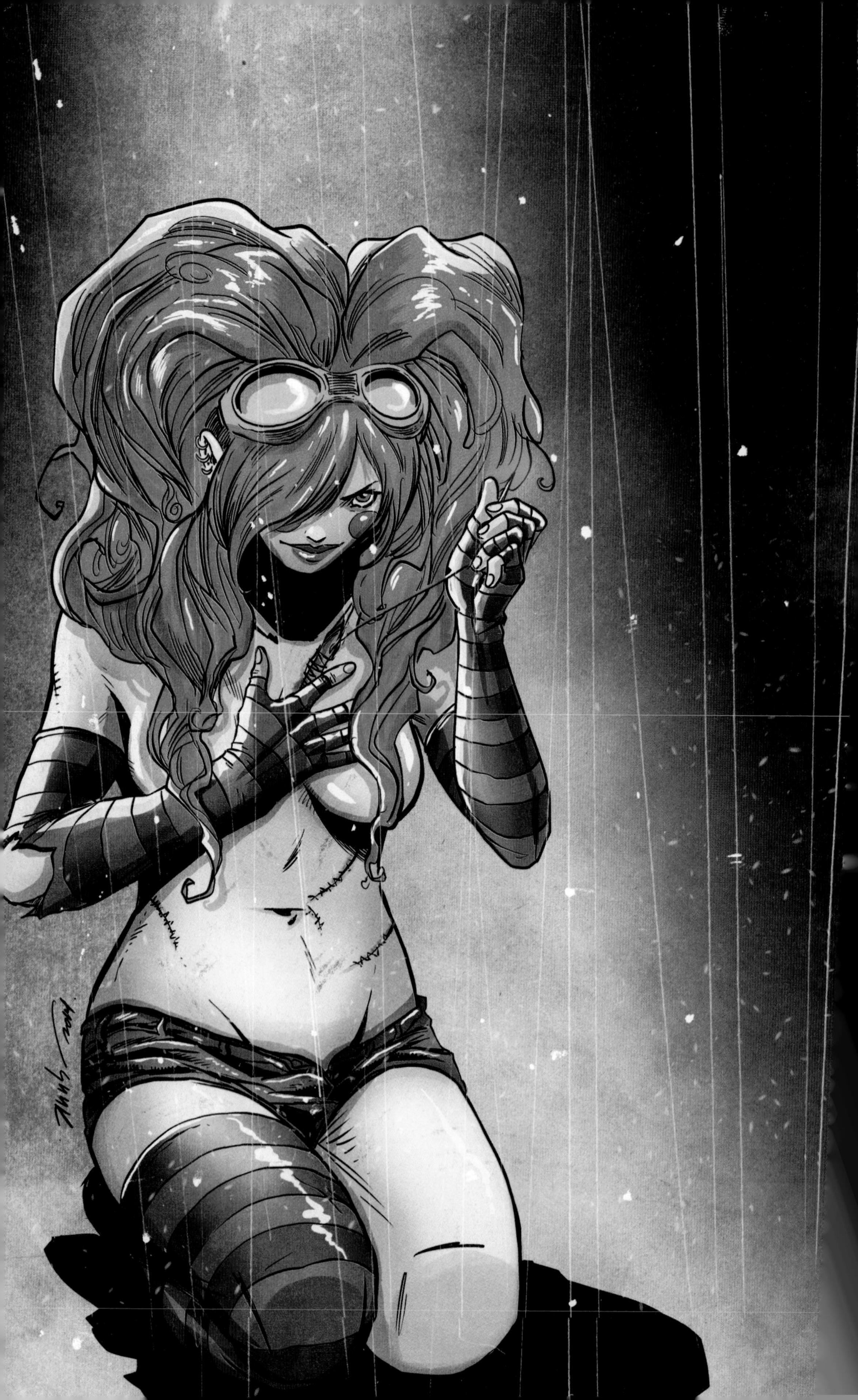

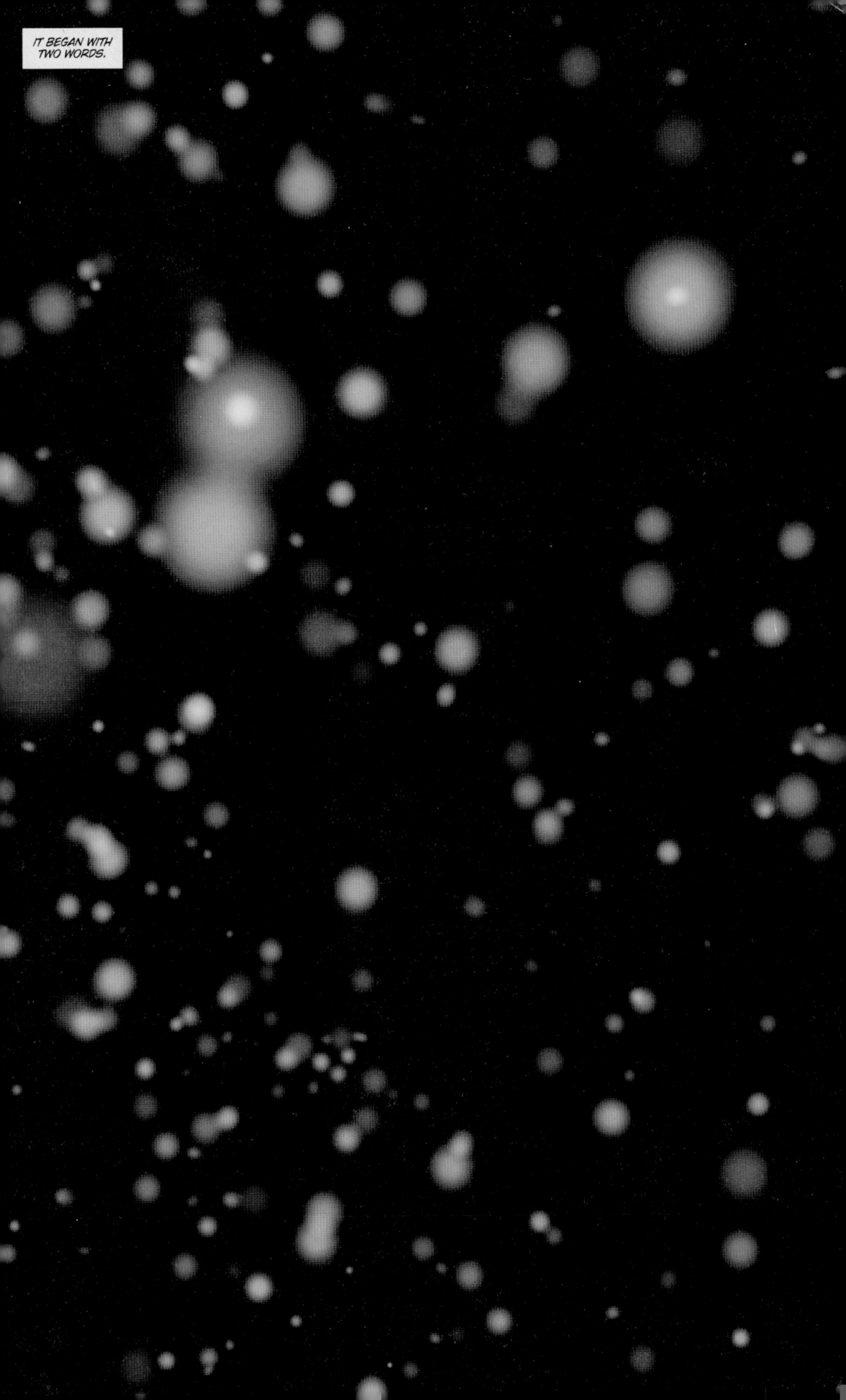
IT BEGAN WITH TWO WORDS.

NON SERVIAM

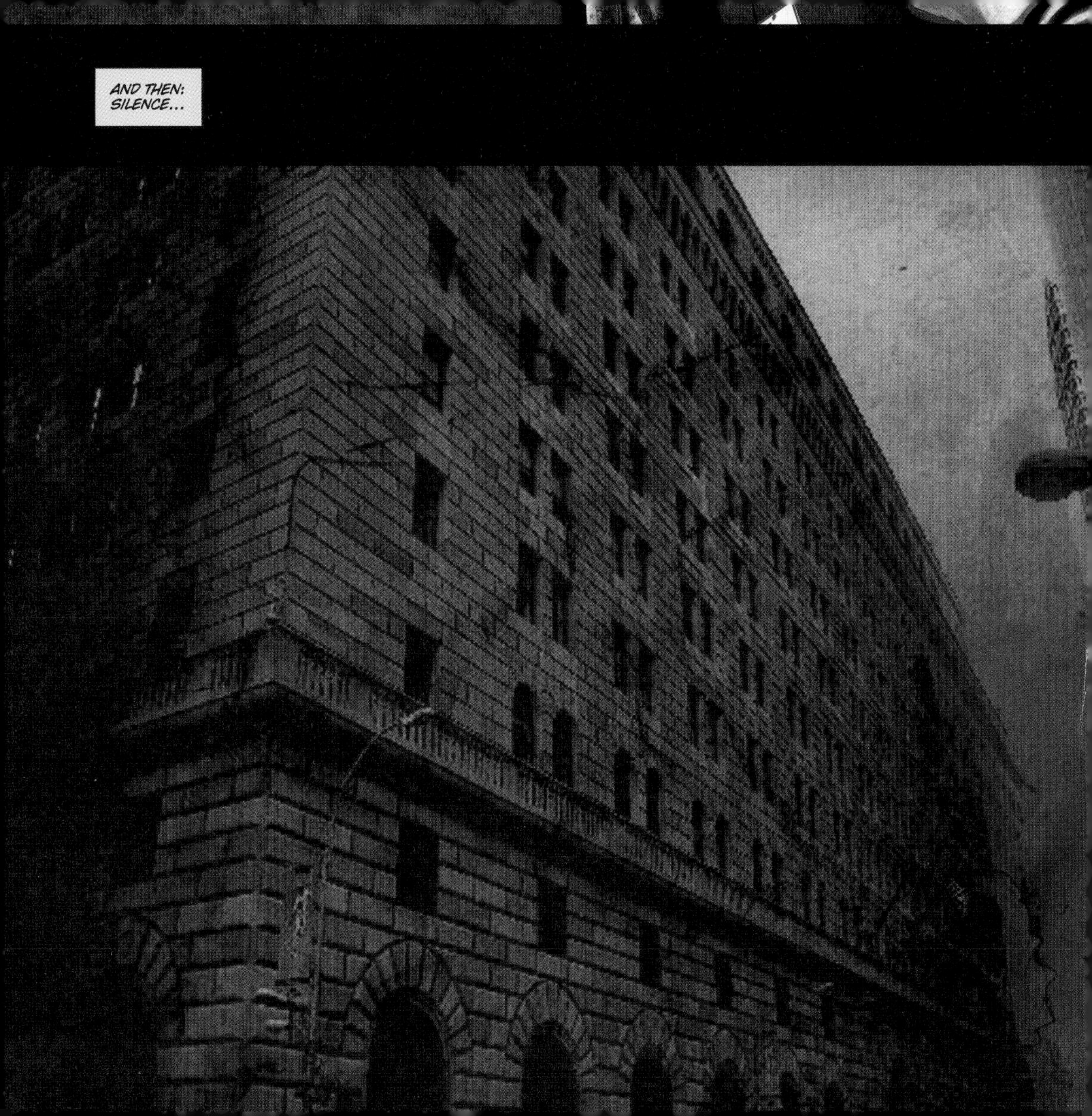
AND THEN:
SILENCE...

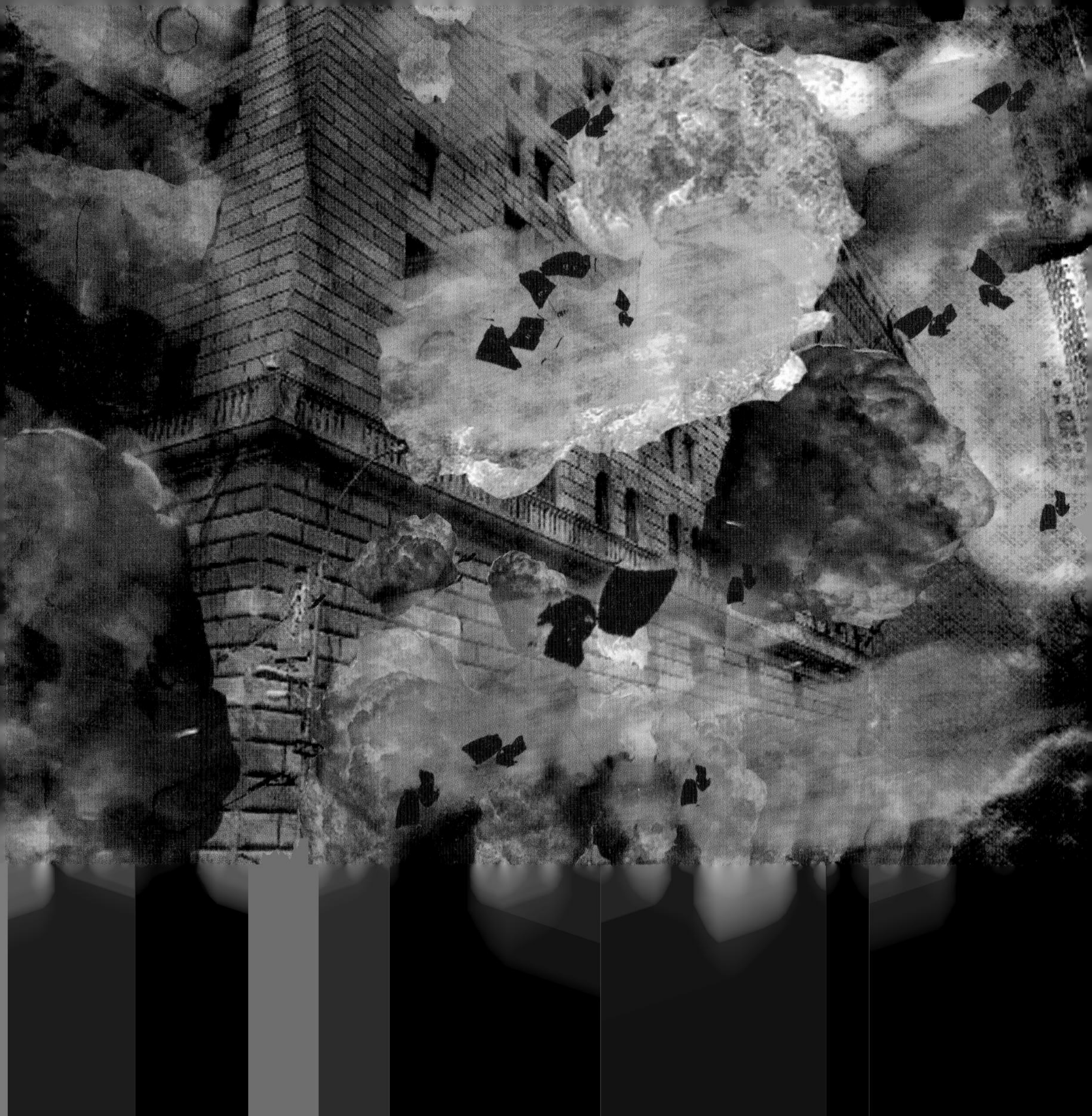

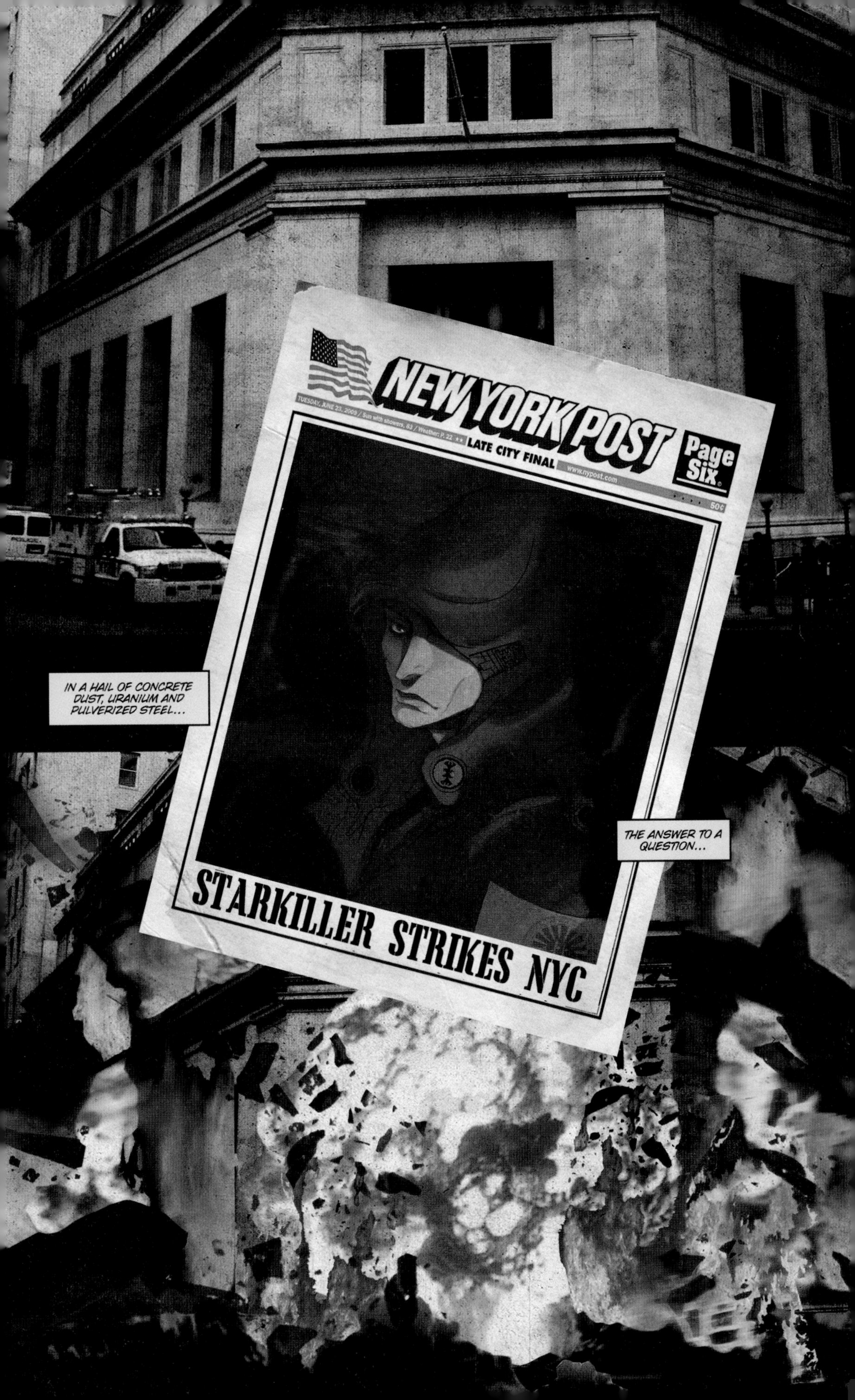
NEW YORK POST
TUESDAY, JUNE 23, 2009 / Sun with showers, 83 / Weather: P. 22
LATE CITY FINAL
www.nypost.com
Page Six
50¢
IN A HAIL OF CONCRETE DUST, URANIUM AND PULVERIZED STEEL...
STARKILLER STRIKES NYC
THE ANSWER TO A QUESTION...

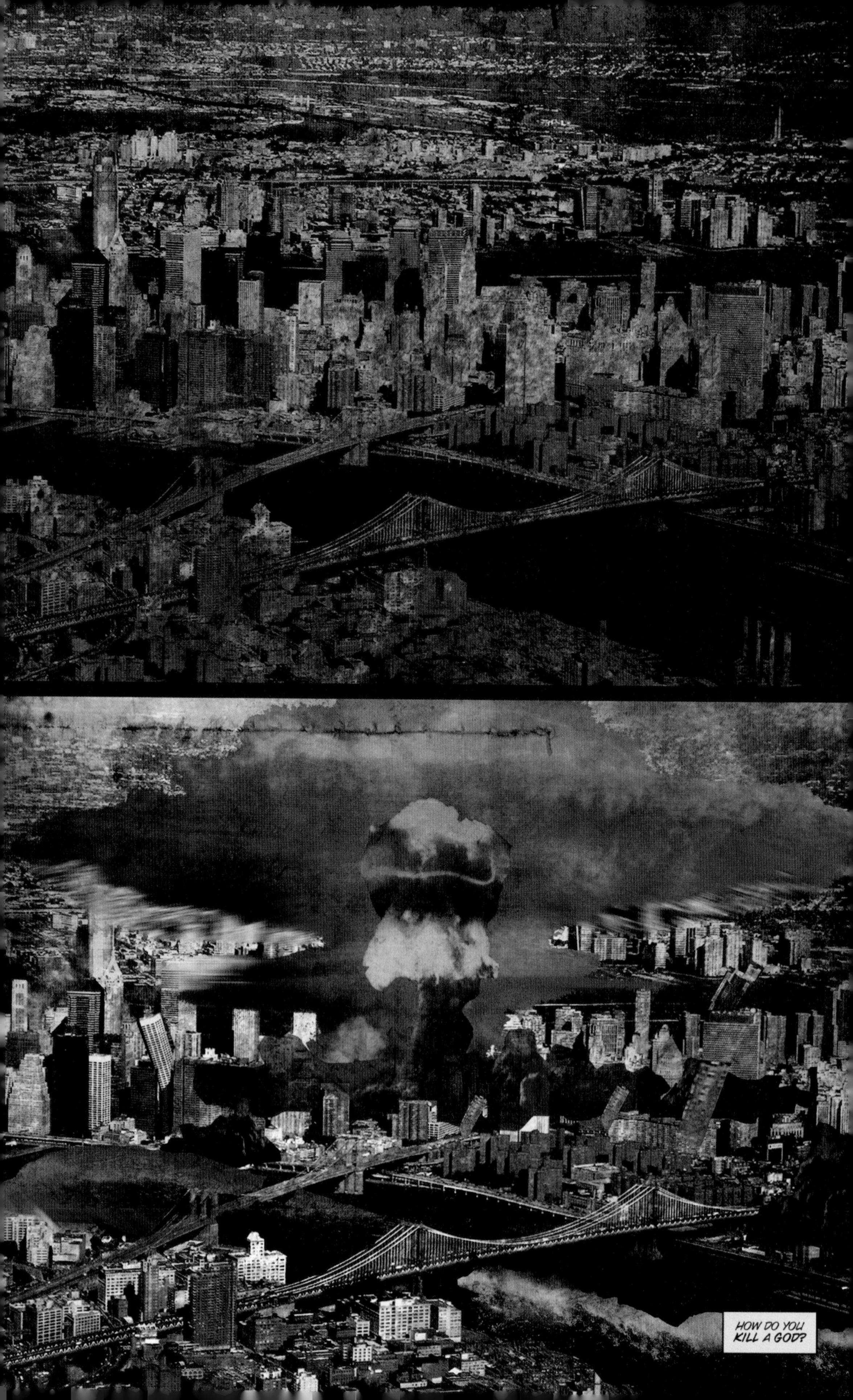
HOW DO YOU KILL A GOD?

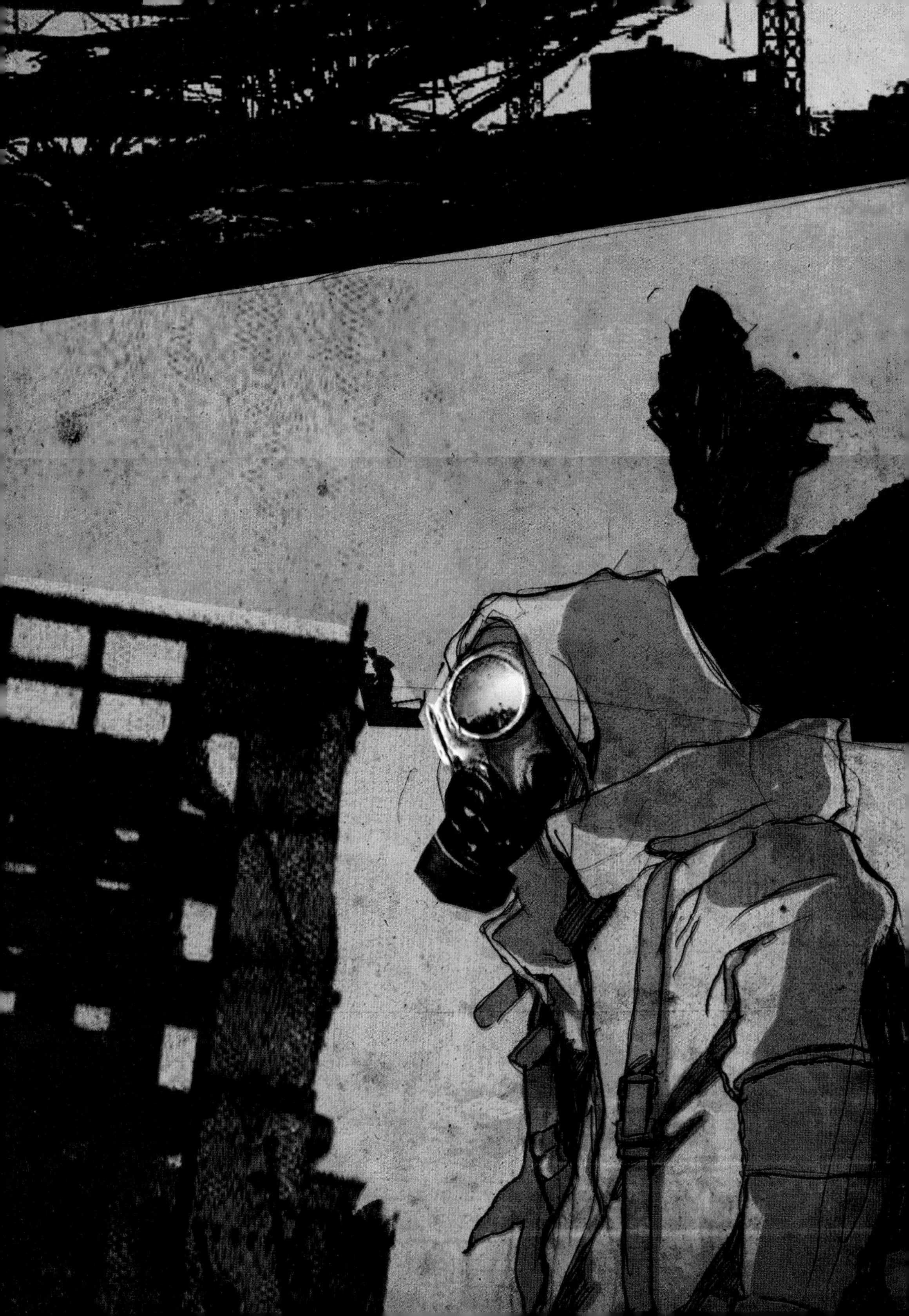

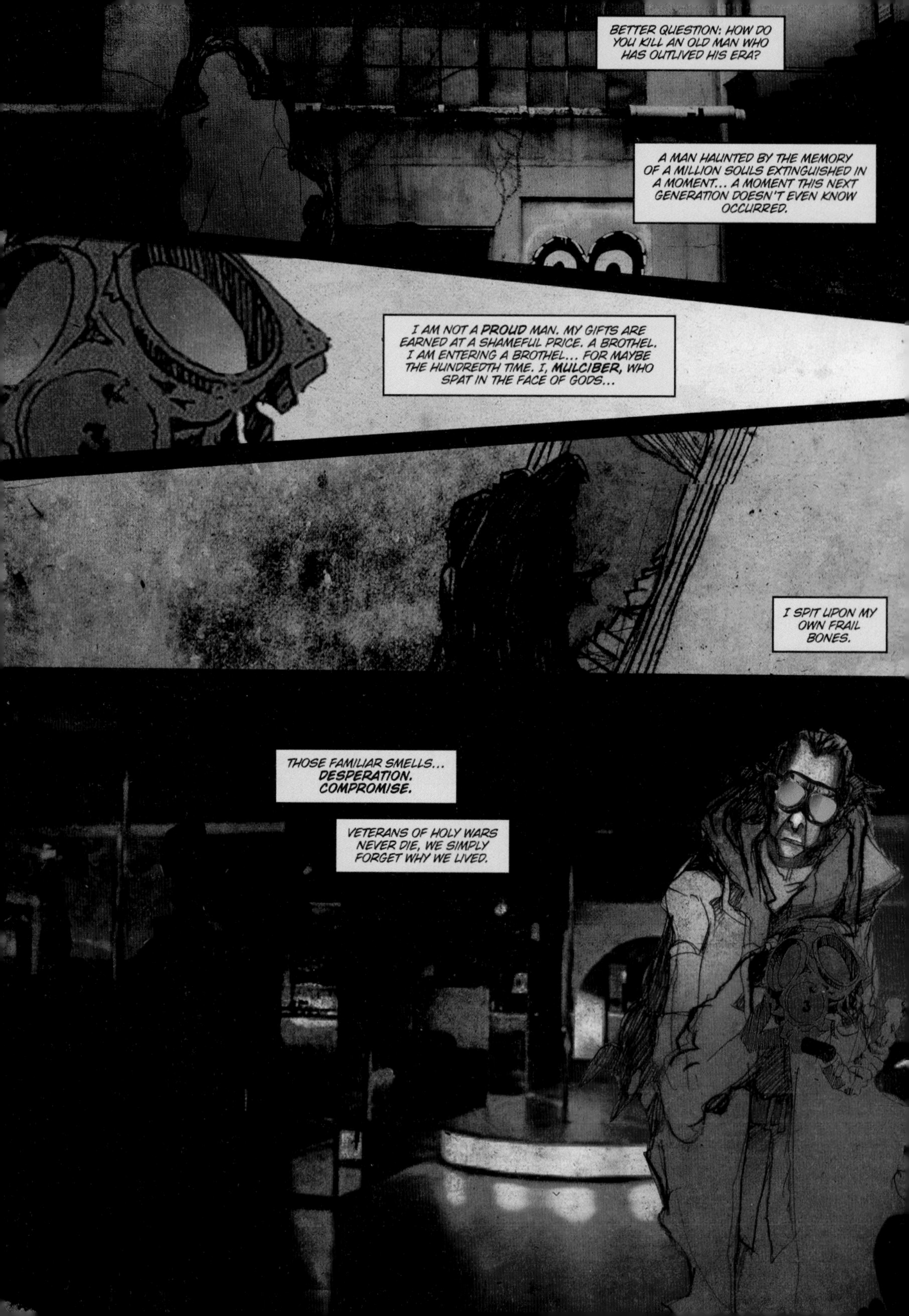
BETTER QUESTION: HOW DO YOU KILL AN OLD MAN WHO HAS OUTLIVED HIS ERA?
A MAN HAUNTED BY THE MEMORY OF A MILLION SOULS EXTINGUISHED IN A MOMENT... A MOMENT THIS NEXT GENERATION DOESN'T EVEN KNOW OCCURRED.
I AM NOT A **PROUD** MAN. MY GIFTS ARE EARNED AT A SHAMEFUL PRICE. A BROTHEL. I AM ENTERING A BROTHEL... FOR MAYBE THE HUNDREDTH TIME. I, **MULCIBER,** WHO SPAT IN THE FACE OF GODS...
I SPIT UPON MY OWN FRAIL BONES.
THOSE FAMILIAR SMELLS... **DESPERATION. COMPROMISE.**
VETERANS OF HOLY WARS NEVER DIE, WE SIMPLY FORGET WHY WE LIVED.

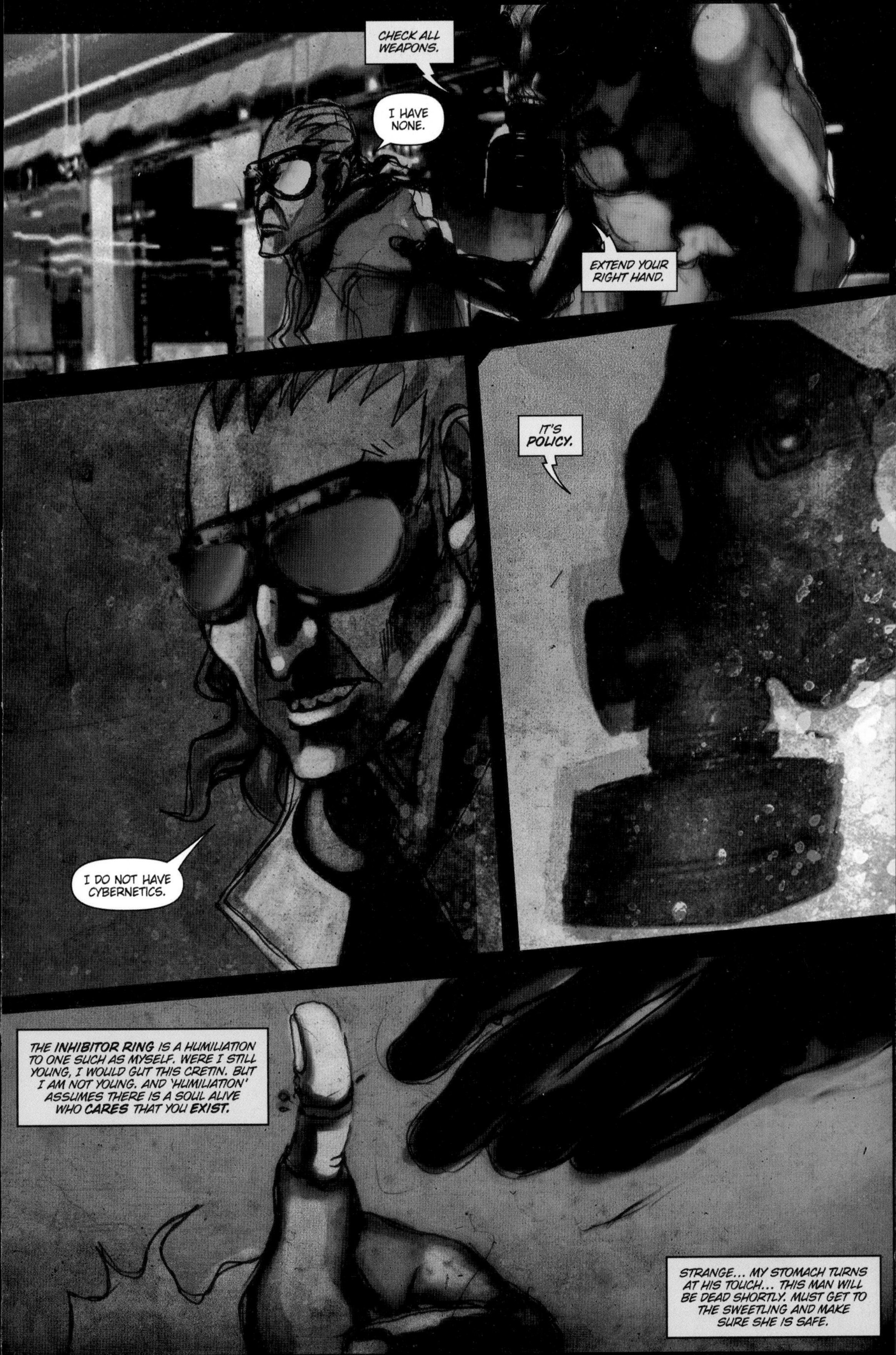
CHECK ALL WEAPONS.
I HAVE NONE.
EXTEND YOUR RIGHT HAND.
I DO NOT HAVE CYBERNETICS.
IT'S POLICY.
THE INHIBITOR RING IS A HUMILIATION TO ONE SUCH AS MYSELF. WERE I STILL YOUNG, I WOULD GUT THIS CRETIN. BUT I AM NOT YOUNG. AND 'HUMILIATION' ASSUMES THERE IS A SOUL ALIVE WHO CARES THAT YOU EXIST.
STRANGE... MY STOMACH TURNS AT HIS TOUCH... THIS MAN WILL BE DEAD SHORTLY. MUST GET TO THE SWEETLING AND MAKE SURE SHE IS SAFE.

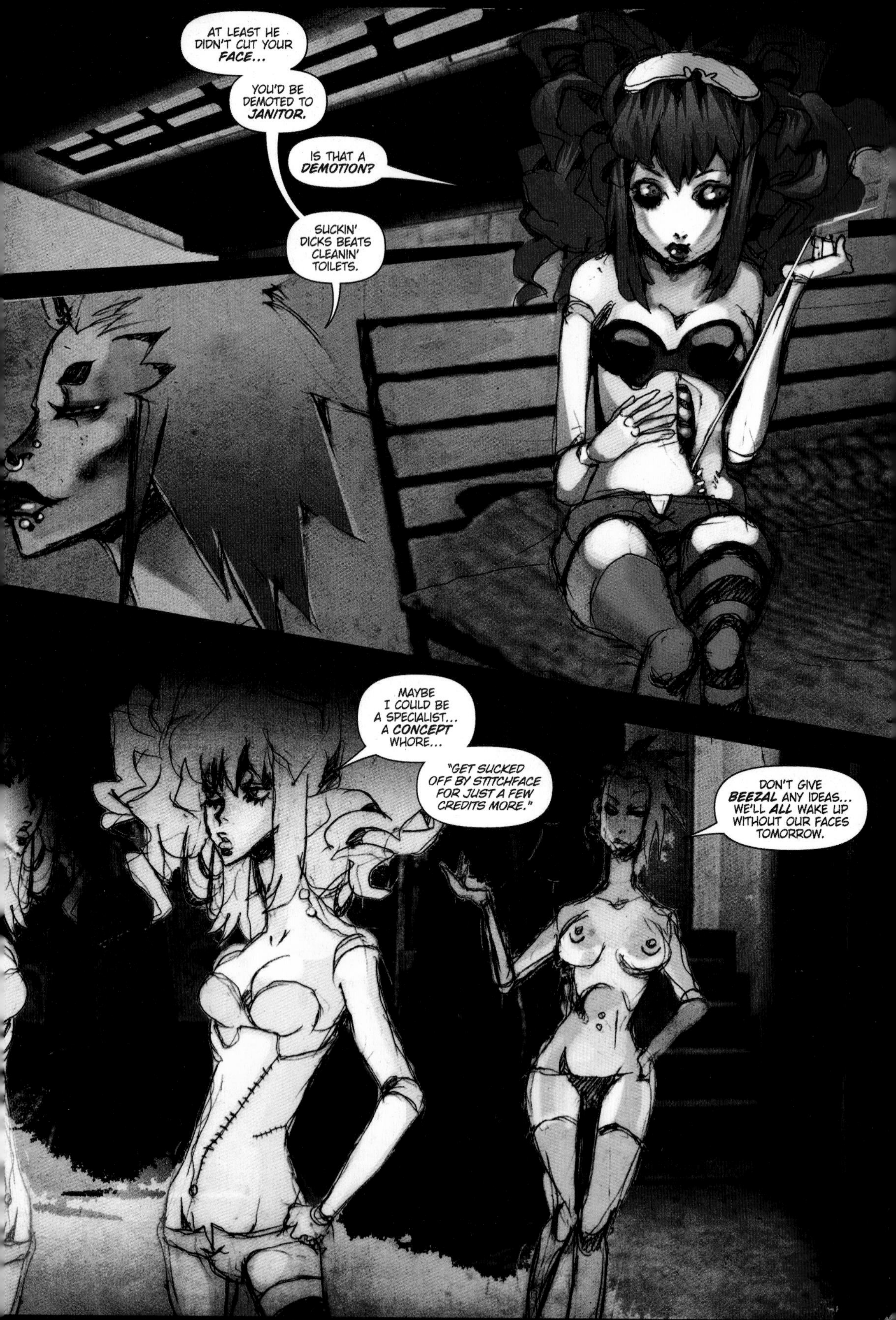
AT LEAST HE DIDN'T CUT YOUR **FACE...**
YOU'D BE DEMOTED TO **JANITOR.**
IS THAT A **DEMOTION?**
SUCKIN' DICKS BEATS CLEANIN' TOILETS.
MAYBE I COULD BE A SPECIALIST... A **CONCEPT** WHORE...
"GET SUCKED OFF BY STITCHFACE FOR JUST A FEW CREDITS MORE."
DON'T GIVE **BEEZAL** ANY IDEAS... WE'LL **ALL** WAKE UP WITHOUT OUR FACES TOMORROW.

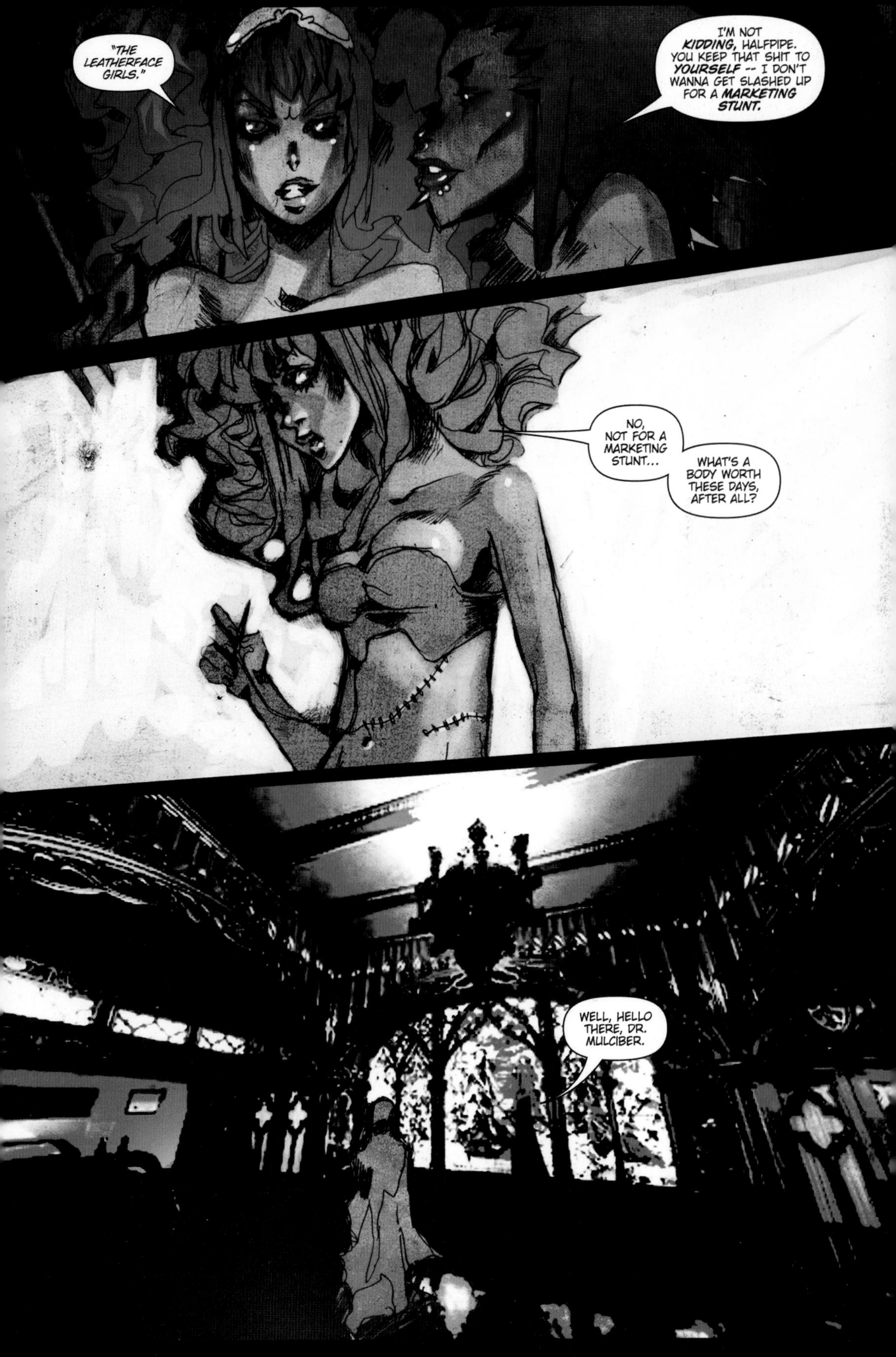
"THE LEATHERFACE GIRLS."
I'M NOT KIDDING, HALFPIPE. YOU KEEP THAT SHIT TO YOURSELF -- I DON'T WANNA GET SLASHED UP FOR A MARKETING STUNT.
NO, NOT FOR A MARKETING STUNT...
WHAT'S A BODY WORTH THESE DAYS, AFTER ALL?
WELL, HELLO THERE, DR. MULCIBER.

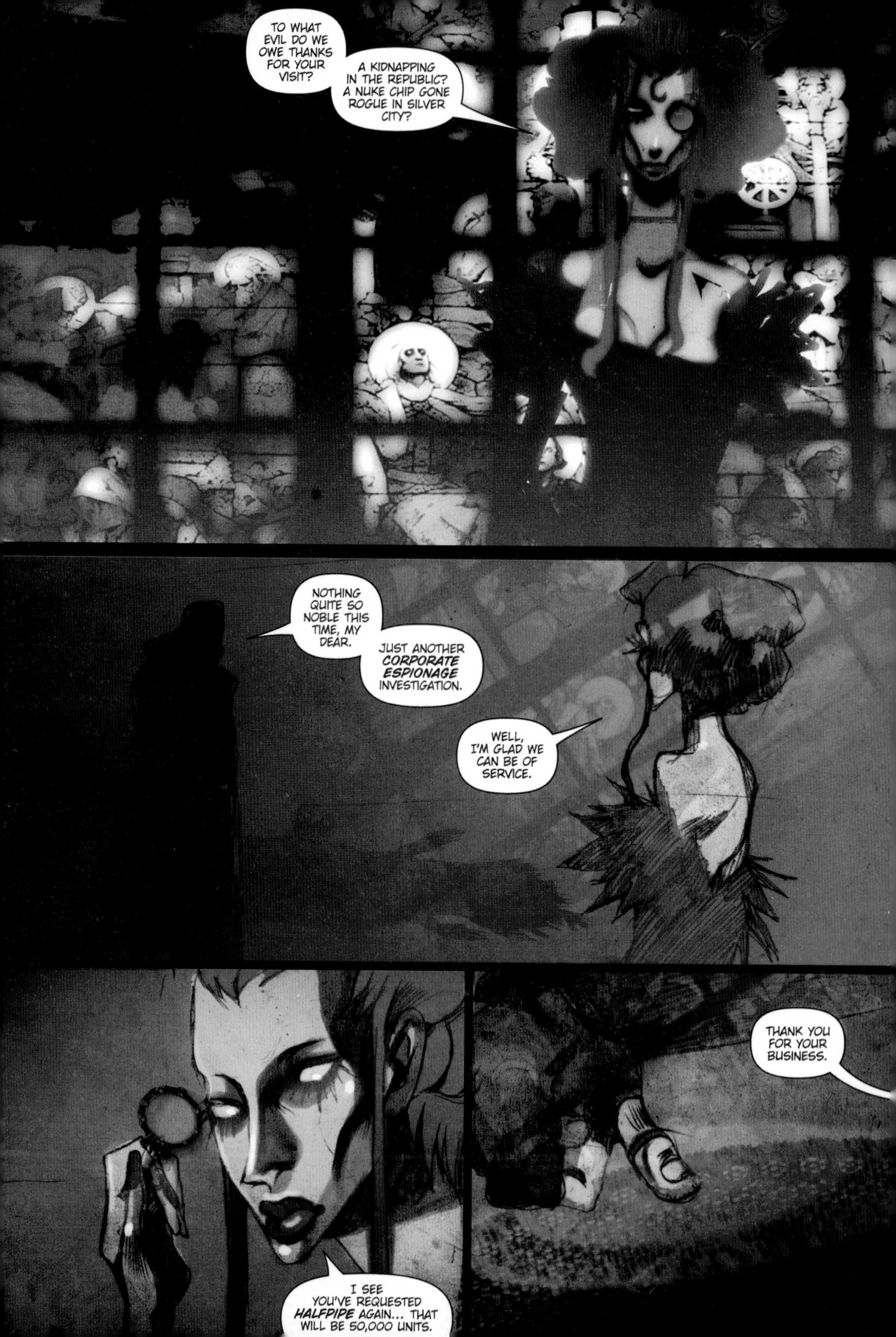

TO WHAT EVIL DO WE OWE THANKS FOR YOUR VISIT?
A KIDNAPPING IN THE REPUBLIC? A NUKE CHIP GONE ROGUE IN SILVER CITY?
NOTHING QUITE SO NOBLE THIS TIME, MY DEAR.
JUST ANOTHER *CORPORATE ESPIONAGE* INVESTIGATION.
WELL, I'M GLAD WE CAN BE OF SERVICE.
I SEE YOU'VE REQUESTED *HALFPIPE* AGAIN... THAT WILL BE 50,000 UNITS.
THANK YOU FOR YOUR BUSINESS.

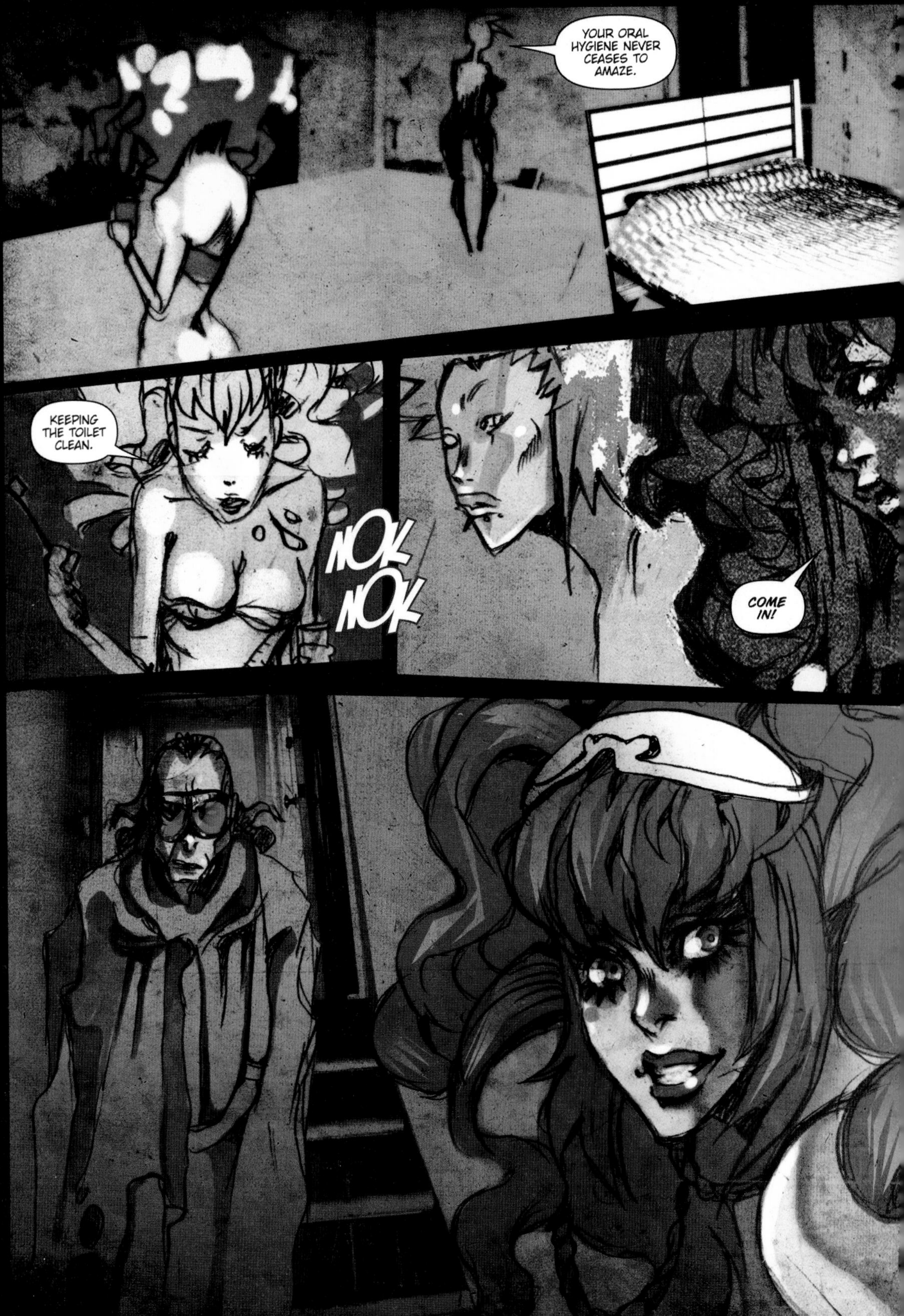
YOUR ORAL HYGIENE NEVER CEASES TO AMAZE.
KEEPING THE TOILET CLEAN.
NOK NOK
COME IN!

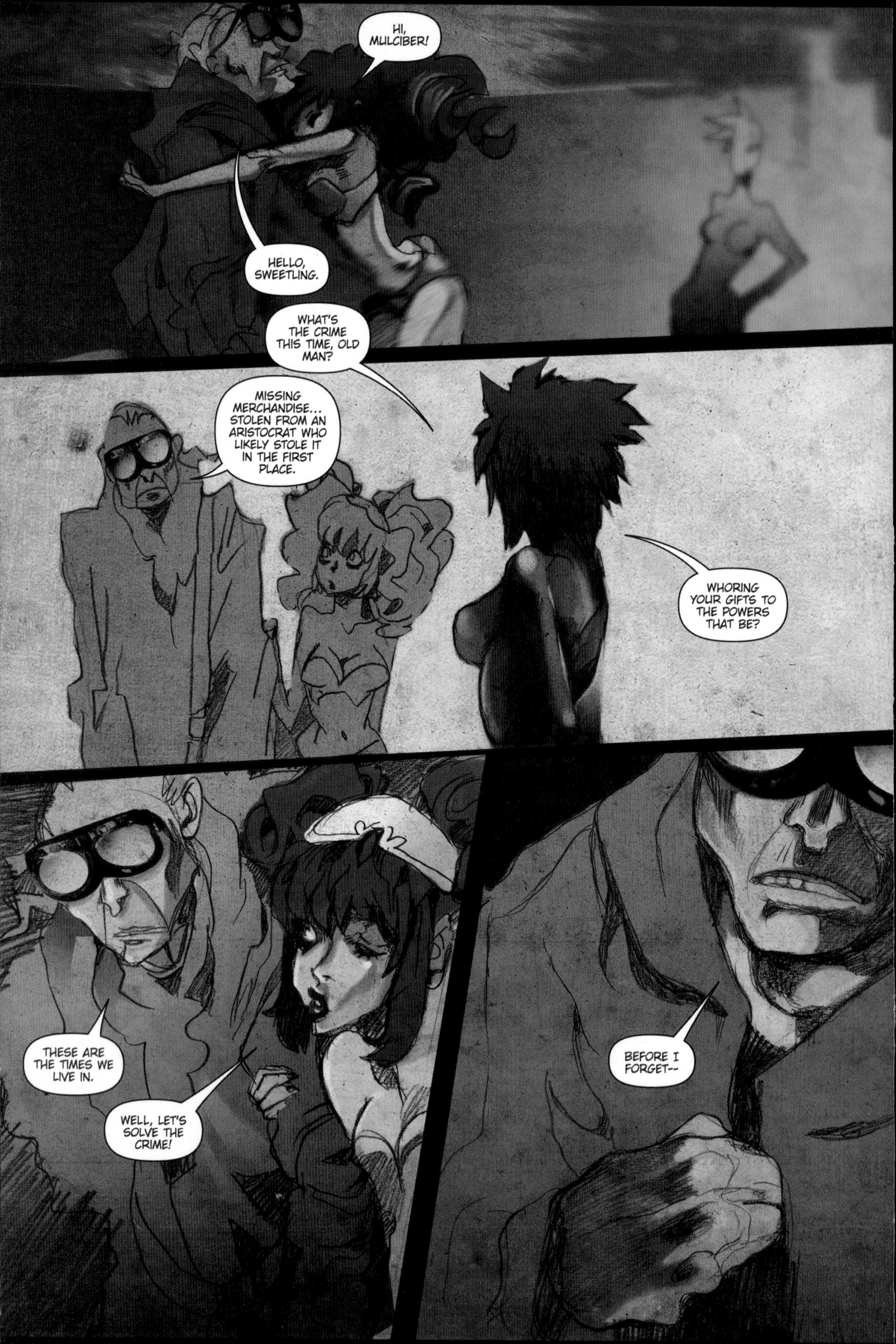
HI, MULCIBER!
HELLO, SWEETLING.
WHAT'S THE CRIME THIS TIME, OLD MAN?
MISSING MERCHANDISE... STOLEN FROM AN ARISTOCRAT WHO LIKELY STOLE IT IN THE FIRST PLACE.
WHORING YOUR GIFTS TO THE POWERS THAT BE?
THESE ARE THE TIMES WE LIVE IN.
WELL, LET'S SOLVE THE CRIME!
BEFORE I FORGET--

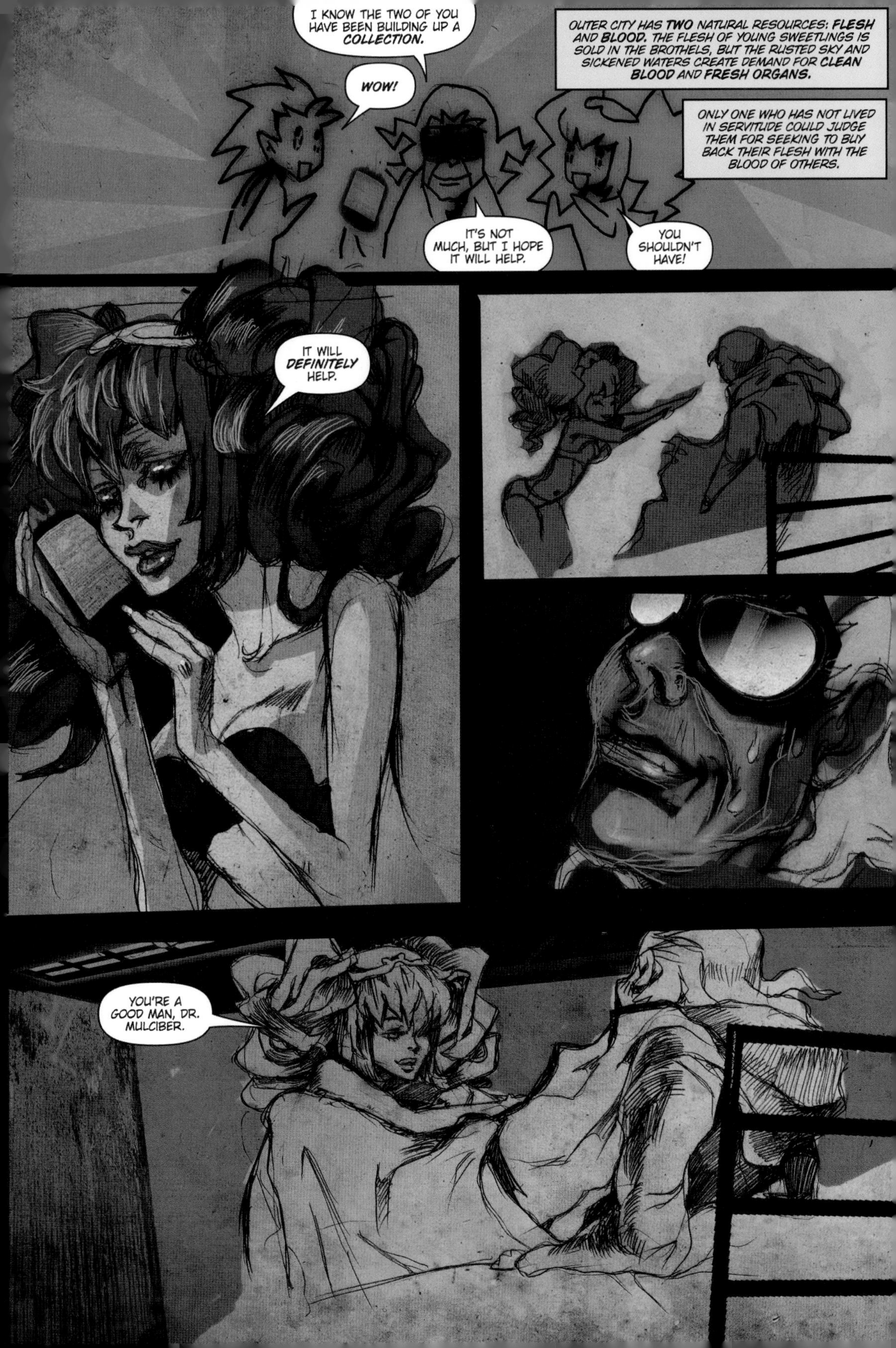

OUTER CITY HAS TWO NATURAL RESOURCES: FLESH AND BLOOD. THE FLESH OF YOUNG SWEETLINGS IS SOLD IN THE BROTHELS, BUT THE RUSTED SKY AND SICKENED WATERS CREATE DEMAND FOR CLEAN BLOOD AND FRESH ORGANS.
ONLY ONE WHO HAS NOT LIVED IN SERVITUDE COULD JUDGE THEM FOR SEEKING TO BUY BACK THEIR FLESH WITH THE BLOOD OF OTHERS.
I KNOW THE TWO OF YOU HAVE BEEN BUILDING UP A COLLECTION.
WOW!
IT'S NOT MUCH, BUT I HOPE IT WILL HELP.
YOU SHOULDN'T HAVE!
IT WILL DEFINITELY HELP.
YOU'RE A GOOD MAN, DR. MULCIBER.

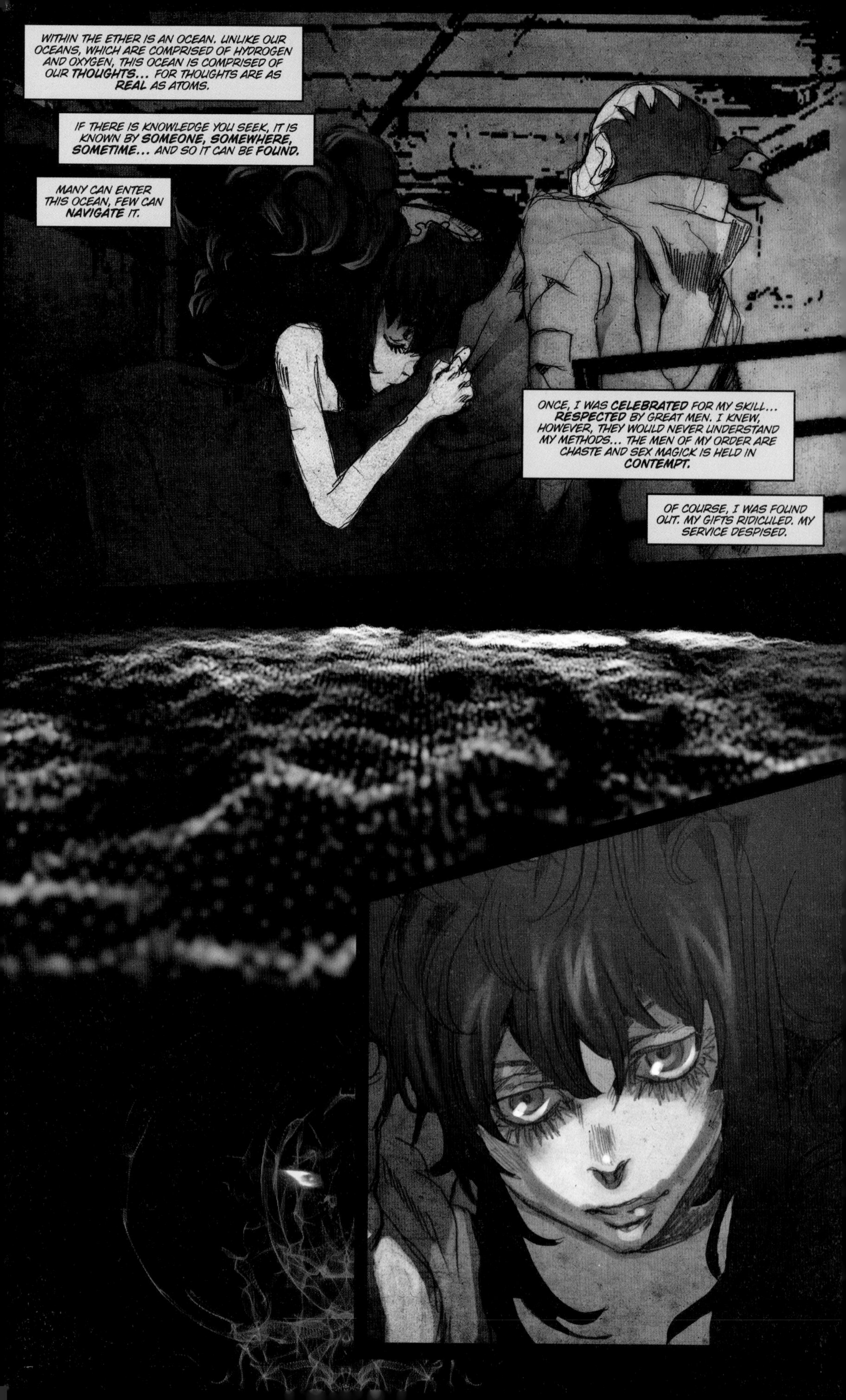
WITHIN THE ETHER IS AN OCEAN. UNLIKE OUR OCEANS, WHICH ARE COMPRISED OF HYDROGEN AND OXYGEN, THIS OCEAN IS COMPRISED OF OUR THOUGHTS... FOR THOUGHTS ARE AS REAL AS ATOMS.
IF THERE IS KNOWLEDGE YOU SEEK, IT IS KNOWN BY SOMEONE, SOMEWHERE, SOMETIME... AND SO IT CAN BE FOUND.
MANY CAN ENTER THIS OCEAN, FEW CAN NAVIGATE IT.
ONCE, I WAS CELEBRATED FOR MY SKILL... RESPECTED BY GREAT MEN. I KNEW, HOWEVER, THEY WOULD NEVER UNDERSTAND MY METHODS... THE MEN OF MY ORDER ARE CHASTE AND SEX MAGICK IS HELD IN CONTEMPT.
OF COURSE, I WAS FOUND OUT. MY GIFTS RIDICULED. MY SERVICE DESPISED.

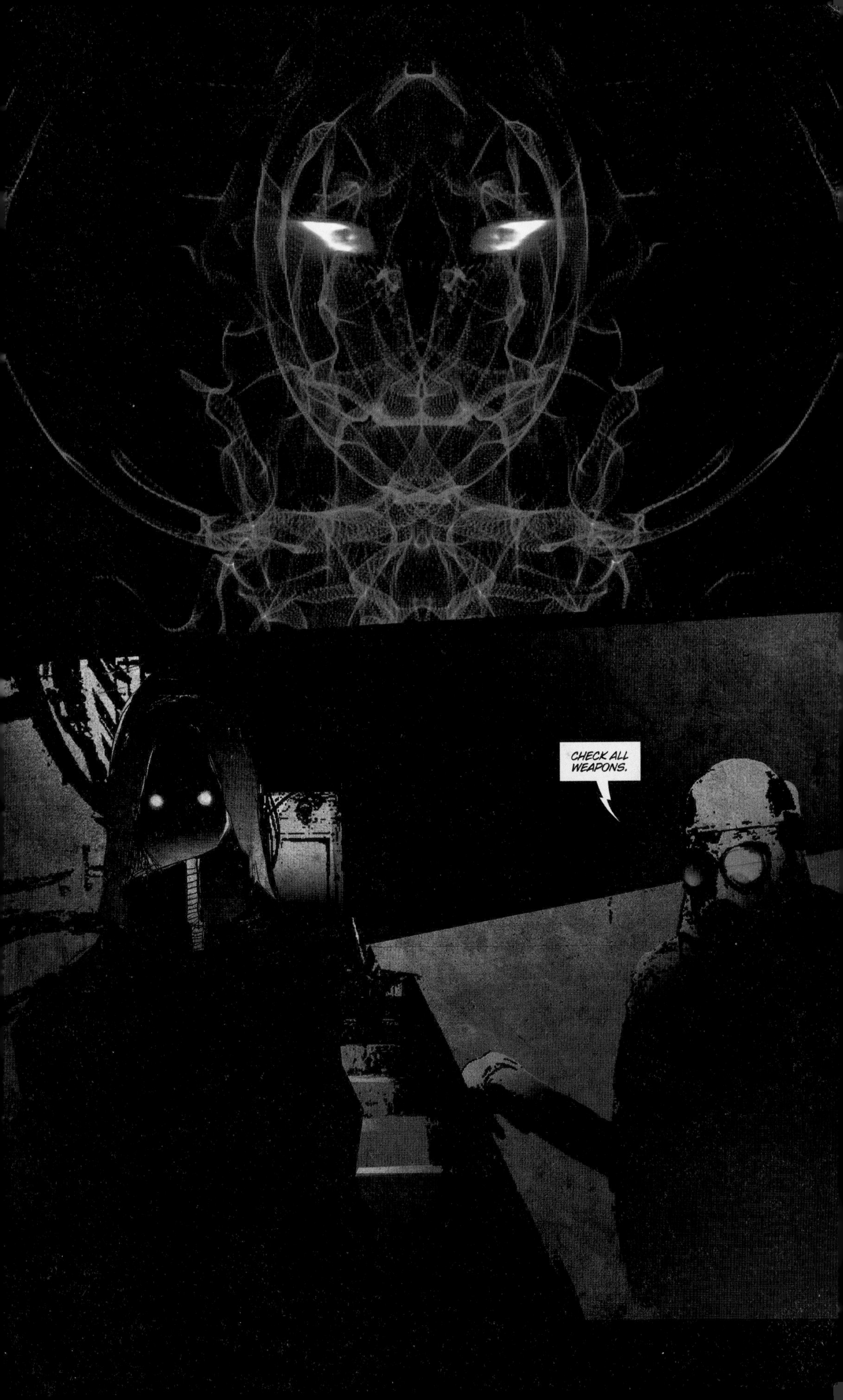
CHECK ALL WEAPONS.

EXTEND YOUR RIGHT HAND.
TIK TIK
TIK TIK
THE ETHER IS FIERCE, SCREAMING DANGER -- ANSWERING QUESTIONS I DID NOT ASK.
I AM NO LONGER NAVIGATING THIS OCEAN. I AM DEEP IN THE UNDERTOW! DROWNING IN VISIONS -- FIRE IS AT THE DOOR. PESTILENCE, FEAR!
DRAGOS!

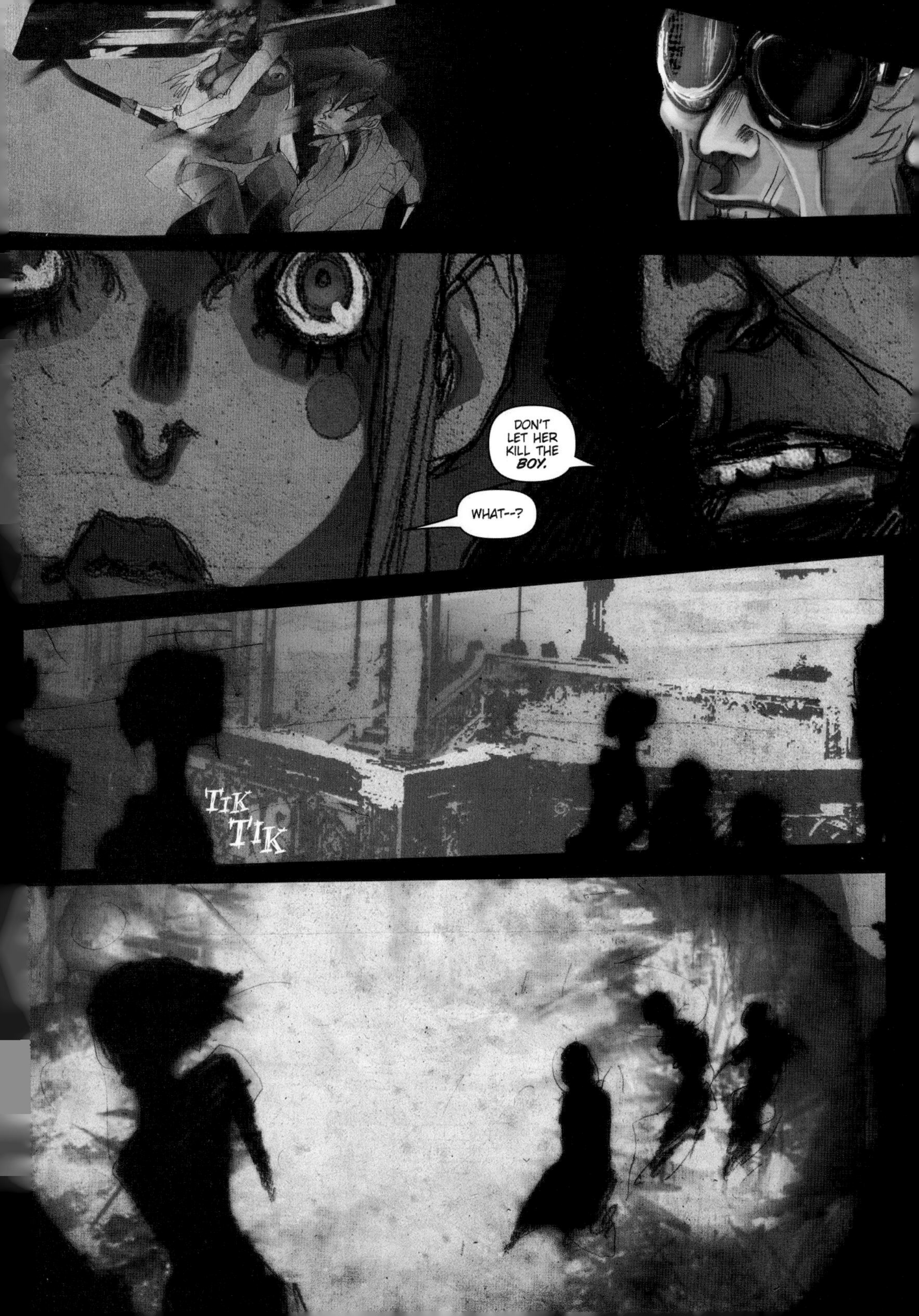
DON'T LET HER KILL THE *BOY.*
WHAT--?
TIK TIK

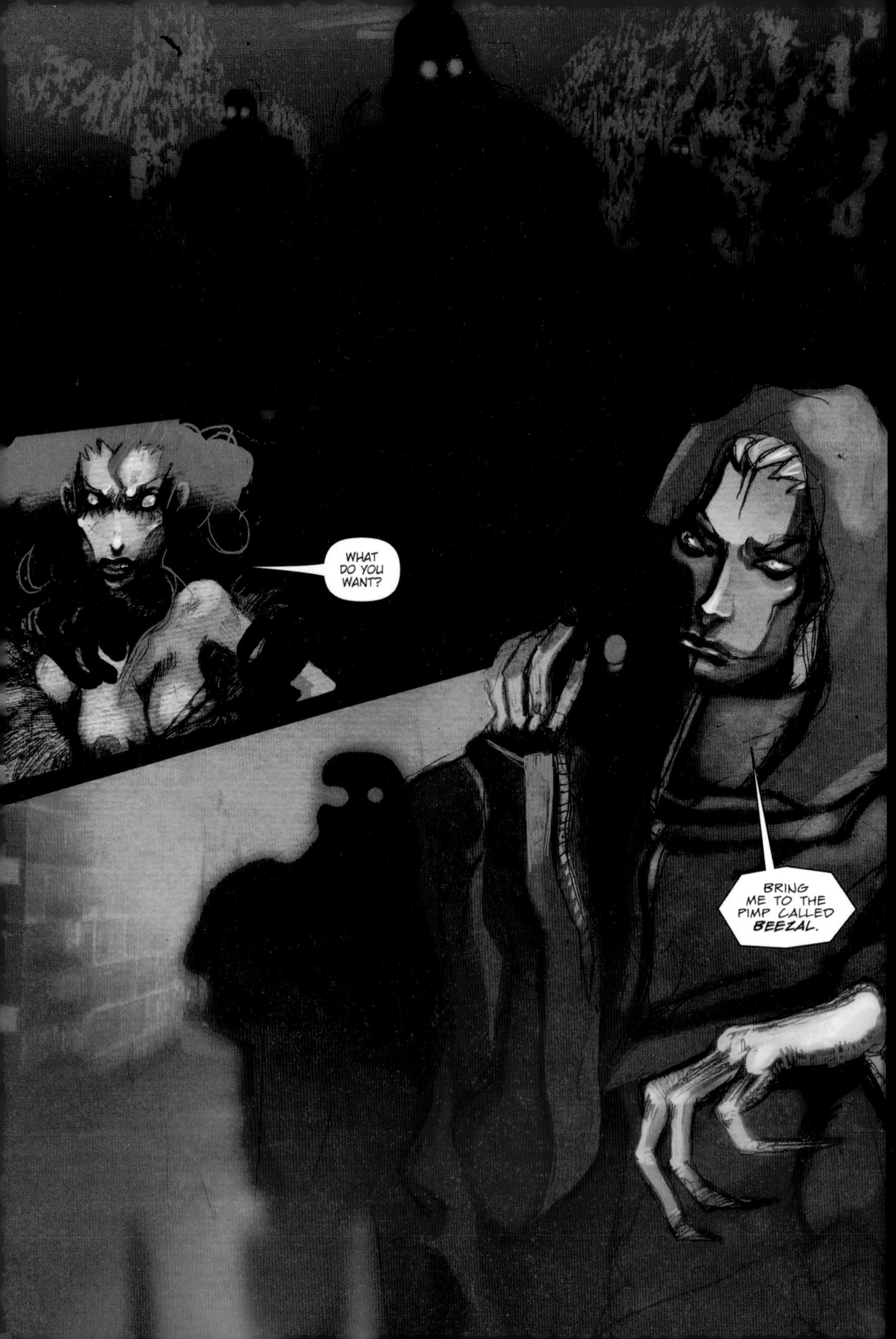
WHAT DO YOU WANT?
BRING ME TO THE PIMP CALLED BEEZAL.

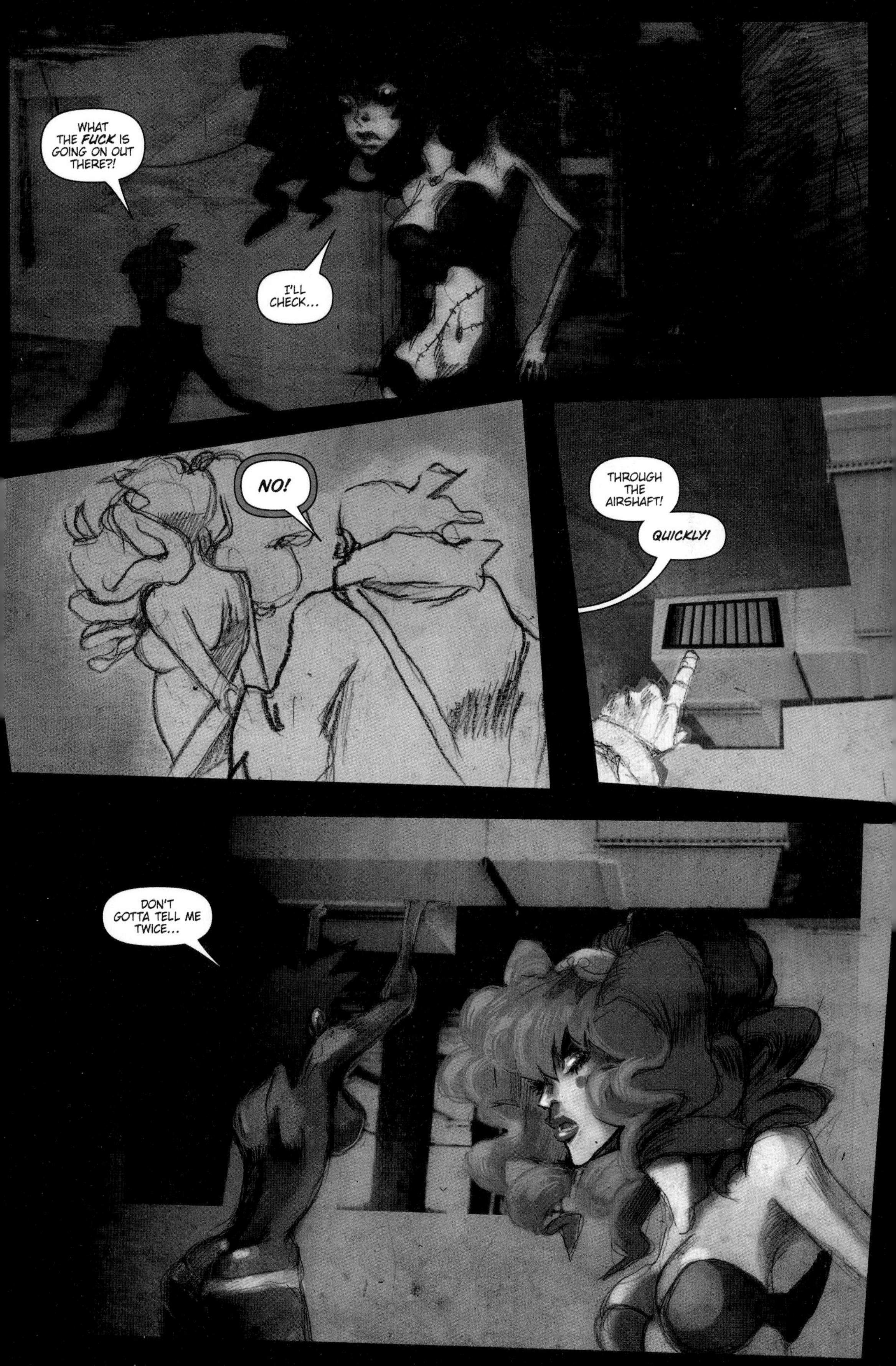

WHAT THE FUCK IS GOING ON OUT THERE?!
I'LL CHECK...
NO!
THROUGH THE AIRSHAFT!
QUICKLY!
DON'T GOTTA TELL ME TWICE...

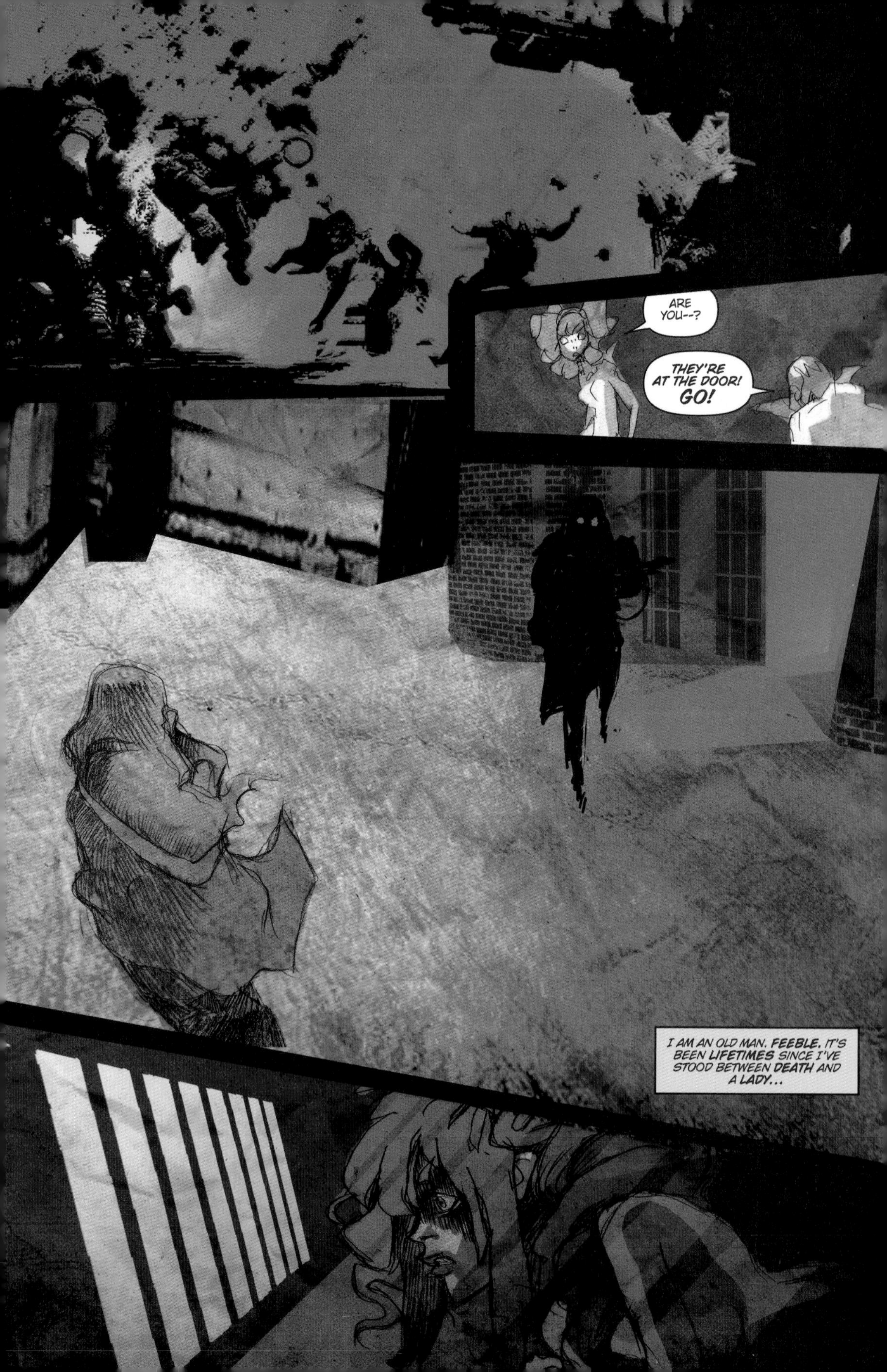
ARE YOU--?
THEY'RE AT THE DOOR! GO!
I AM AN OLD MAN. FEEBLE. IT'S BEEN LIFETIMES SINCE I'VE STOOD BETWEEN DEATH AND A LADY...

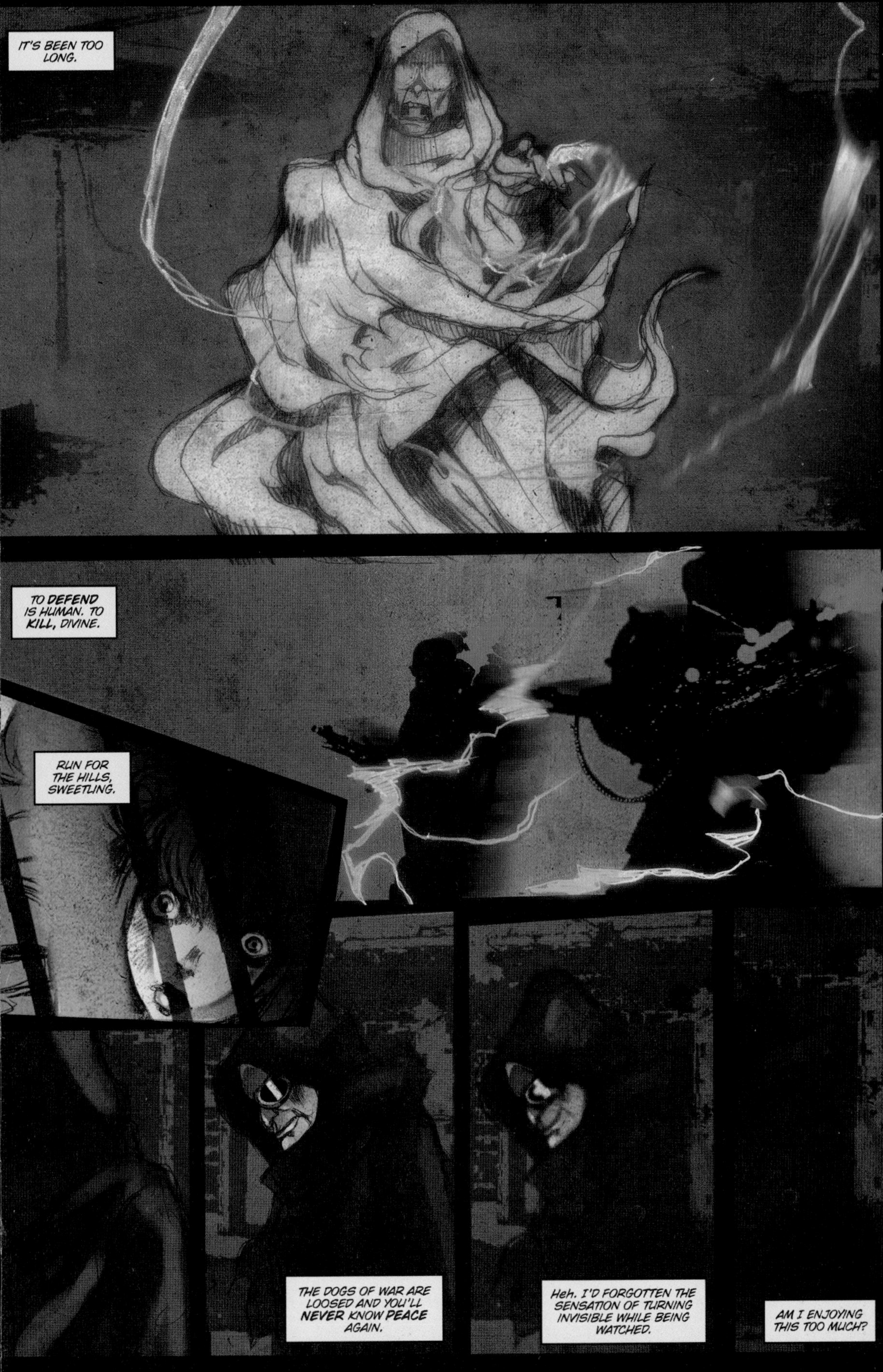
IT'S BEEN TOO LONG.
TO DEFEND IS HUMAN. TO KILL, DIVINE.
RUN FOR THE HILLS, SWEETLING.
THE DOGS OF WAR ARE LOOSED AND YOU'LL NEVER KNOW PEACE AGAIN.
Heh. I'D FORGOTTEN THE SENSATION OF TURNING INVISIBLE WHILE BEING WATCHED.
AM I ENJOYING THIS TOO MUCH?

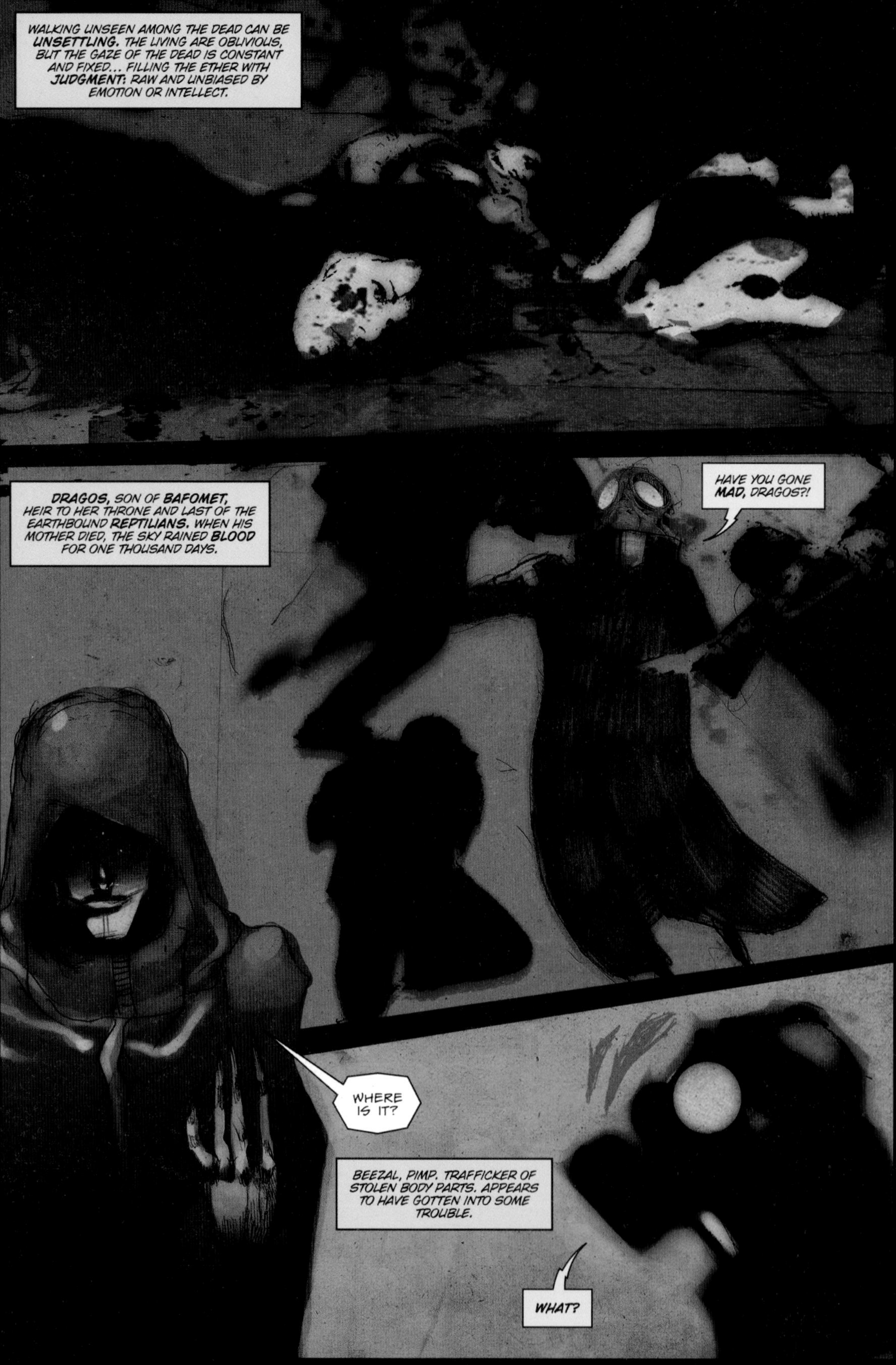
WALKING UNSEEN AMONG THE DEAD CAN BE UNSETTLING. THE LIVING ARE OBLIVIOUS, BUT THE GAZE OF THE DEAD IS CONSTANT AND FIXED... FILLING THE ETHER WITH JUDGMENT: RAW AND UNBIASED BY EMOTION OR INTELLECT.
DRAGOS, SON OF BAFOMET, HEIR TO HER THRONE AND LAST OF THE EARTHBOUND REPTILIANS. WHEN HIS MOTHER DIED, THE SKY RAINED BLOOD FOR ONE THOUSAND DAYS.
HAVE YOU GONE MAD, DRAGOS?!
WHERE IS IT?
BEEZAL, PIMP. TRAFFICKER OF STOLEN BODY PARTS. APPEARS TO HAVE GOTTEN INTO SOME TROUBLE.
WHAT?

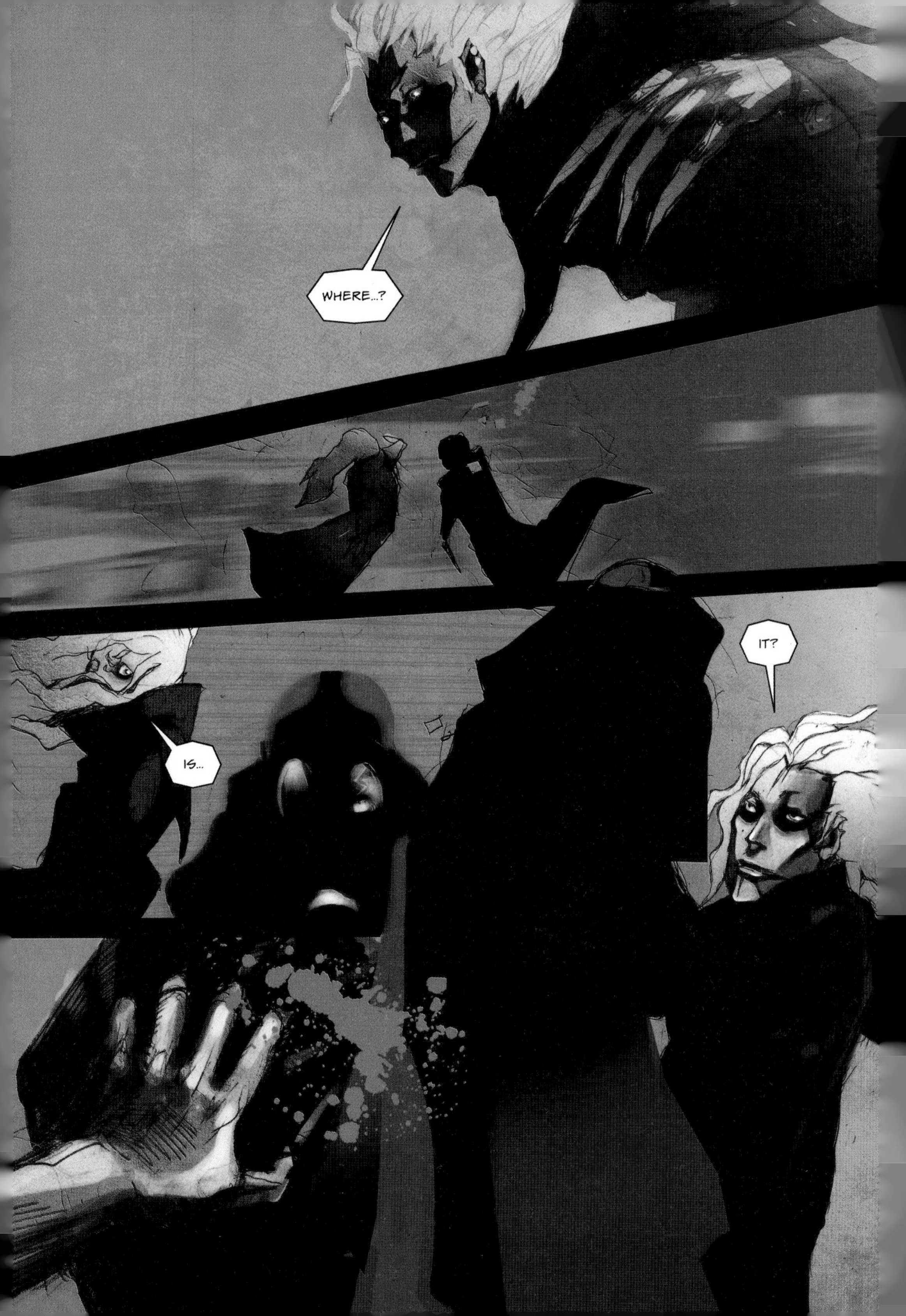
WHERE...?
IS...
IT?

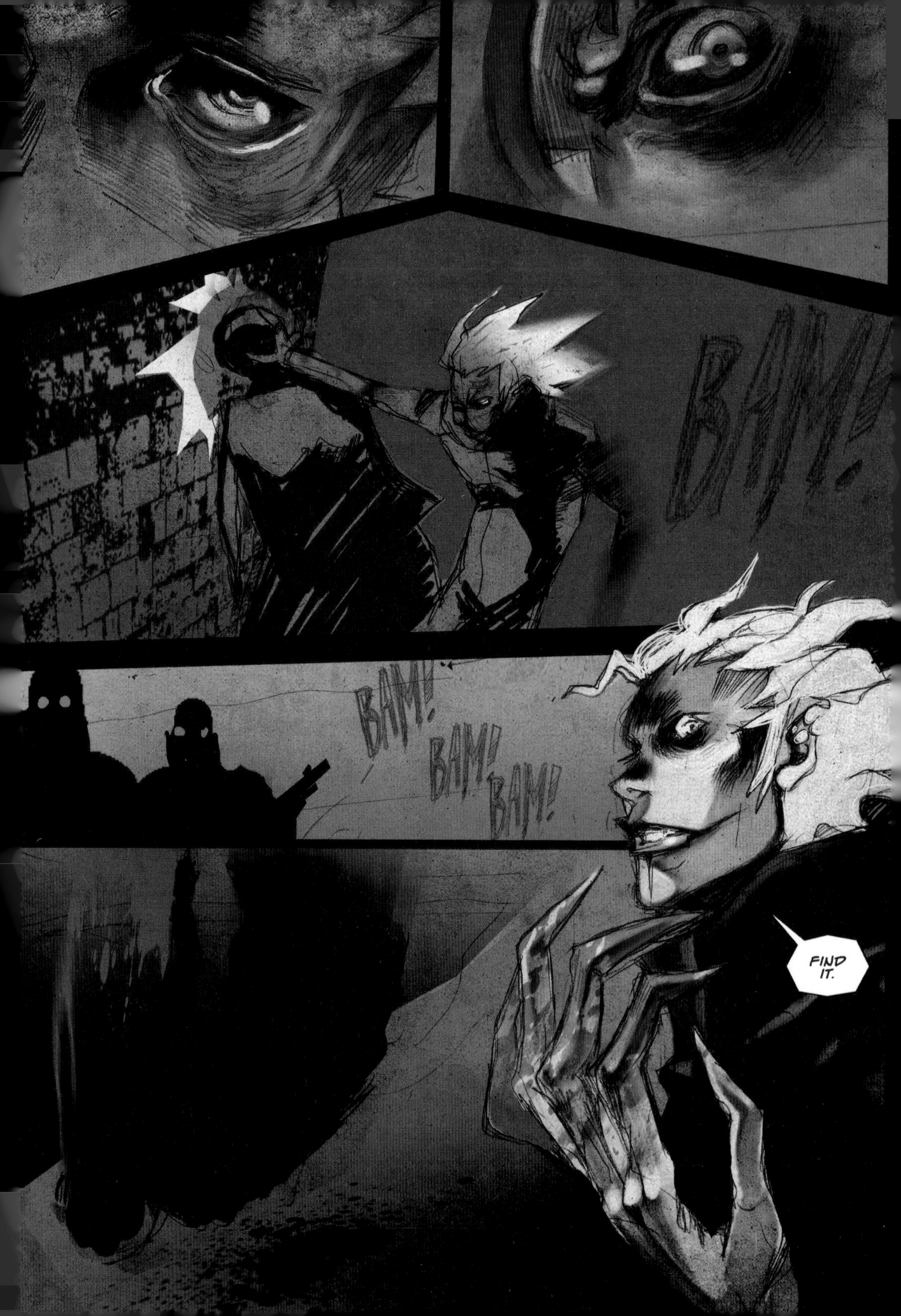
BAM!
BAM!
BAM!
BAM!
FIND IT.

C'MON, WE GOTTA GET THE FUCK OUTTA HERE.
THIS IS **SO** FUCKED UP.
IT HURTS ME TO DO THIS TO YOU.
URGH...
SQUIRCH
MASTER. I FOUND IT.

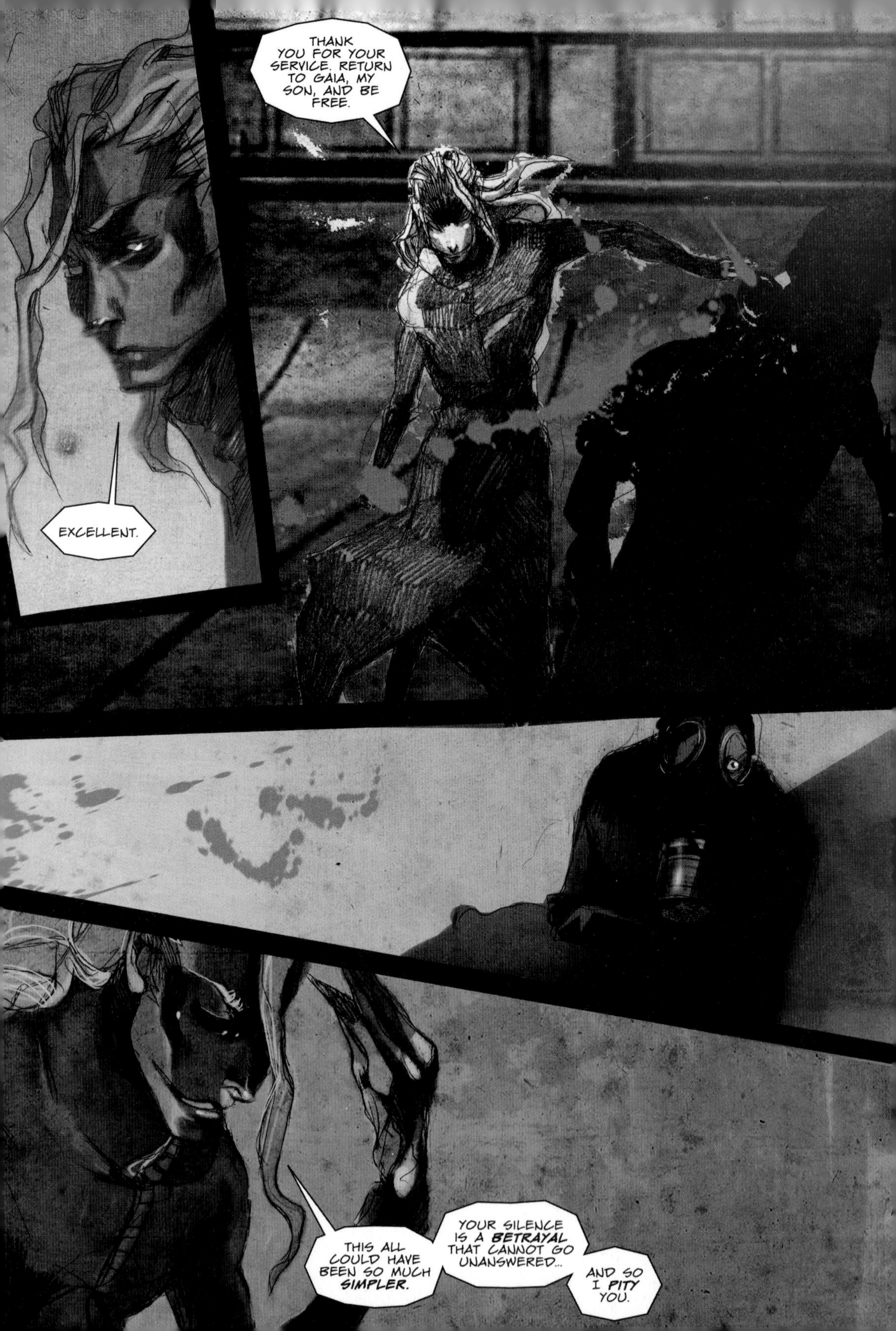

EXCELLENT.
THANK YOU FOR YOUR SERVICE. RETURN TO GAIA, MY SON, AND BE FREE.
THIS ALL COULD HAVE BEEN SO MUCH SIMPLER.
YOUR SILENCE IS A BETRAYAL THAT CANNOT GO UNANSWERED...
AND SO I PITY YOU.

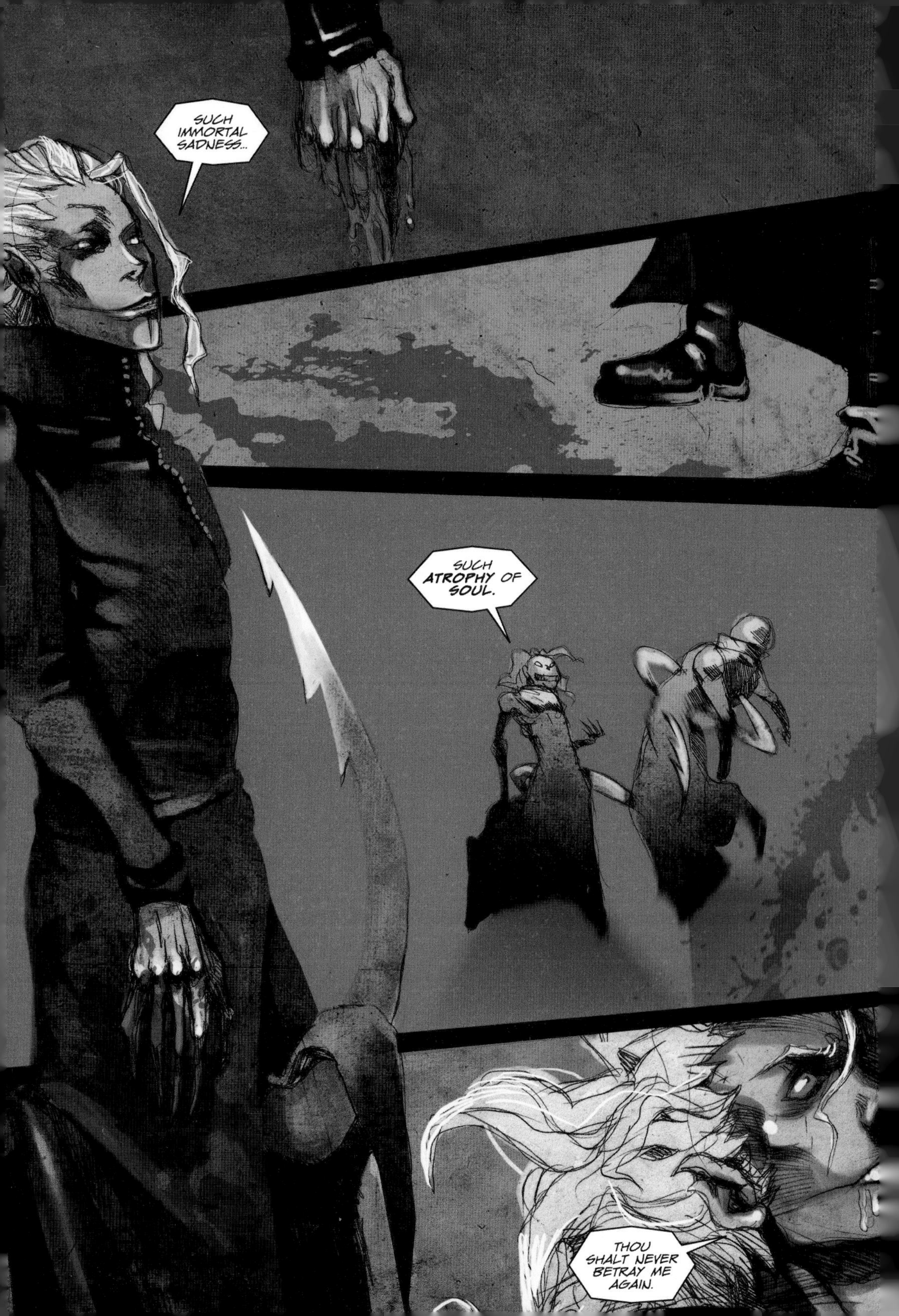
SUCH IMMORTAL SADNESS...
SUCH ATROPHY OF SOUL.
THOU SHALT NEVER BETRAY ME AGAIN.

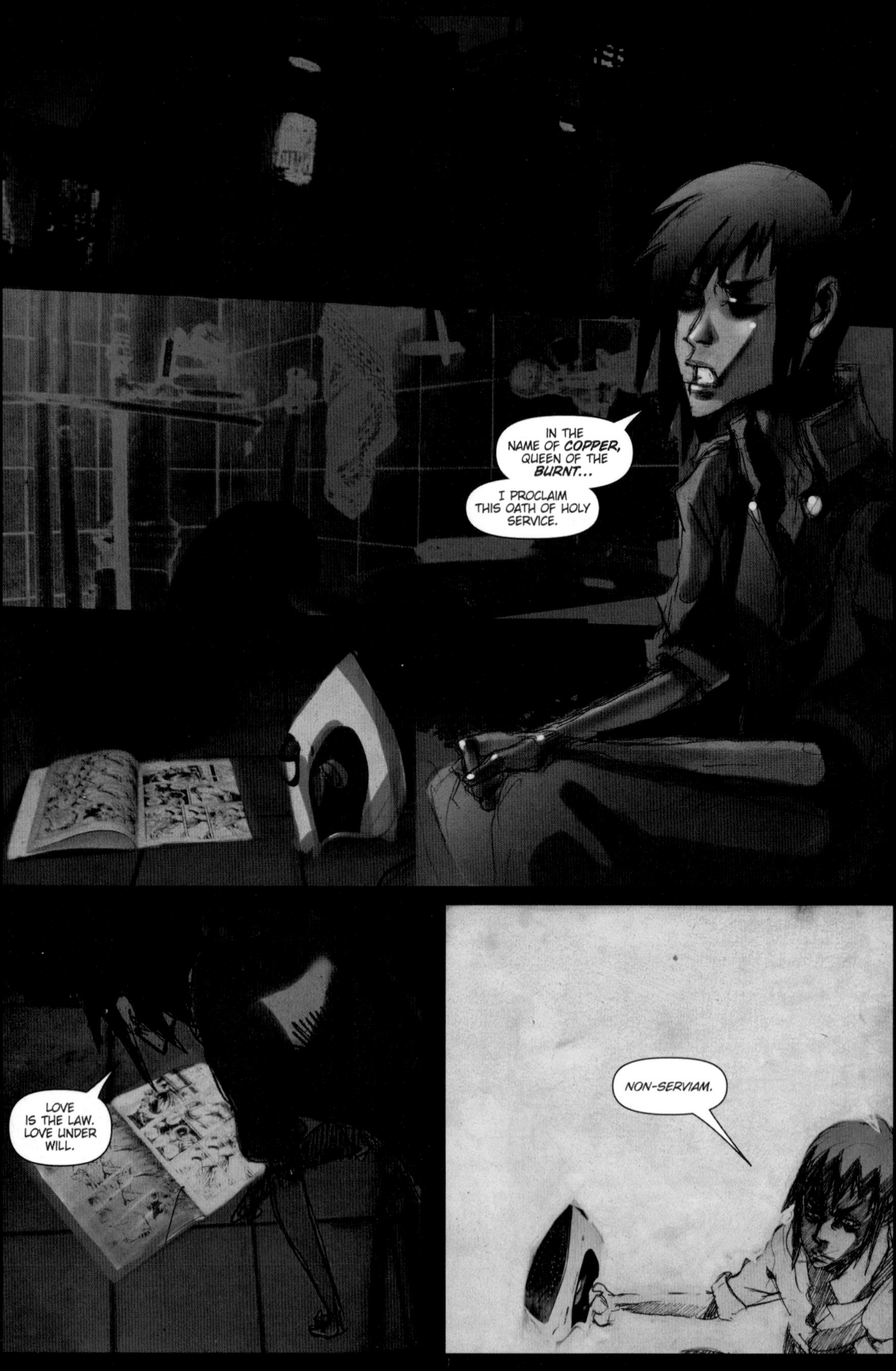
IN THE NAME OF COPPER, QUEEN OF THE BURNT...
I PROCLAIM THIS OATH OF HOLY SERVICE.
LOVE IS THE LAW. LOVE UNDER WILL.
NON-SERVIAM.

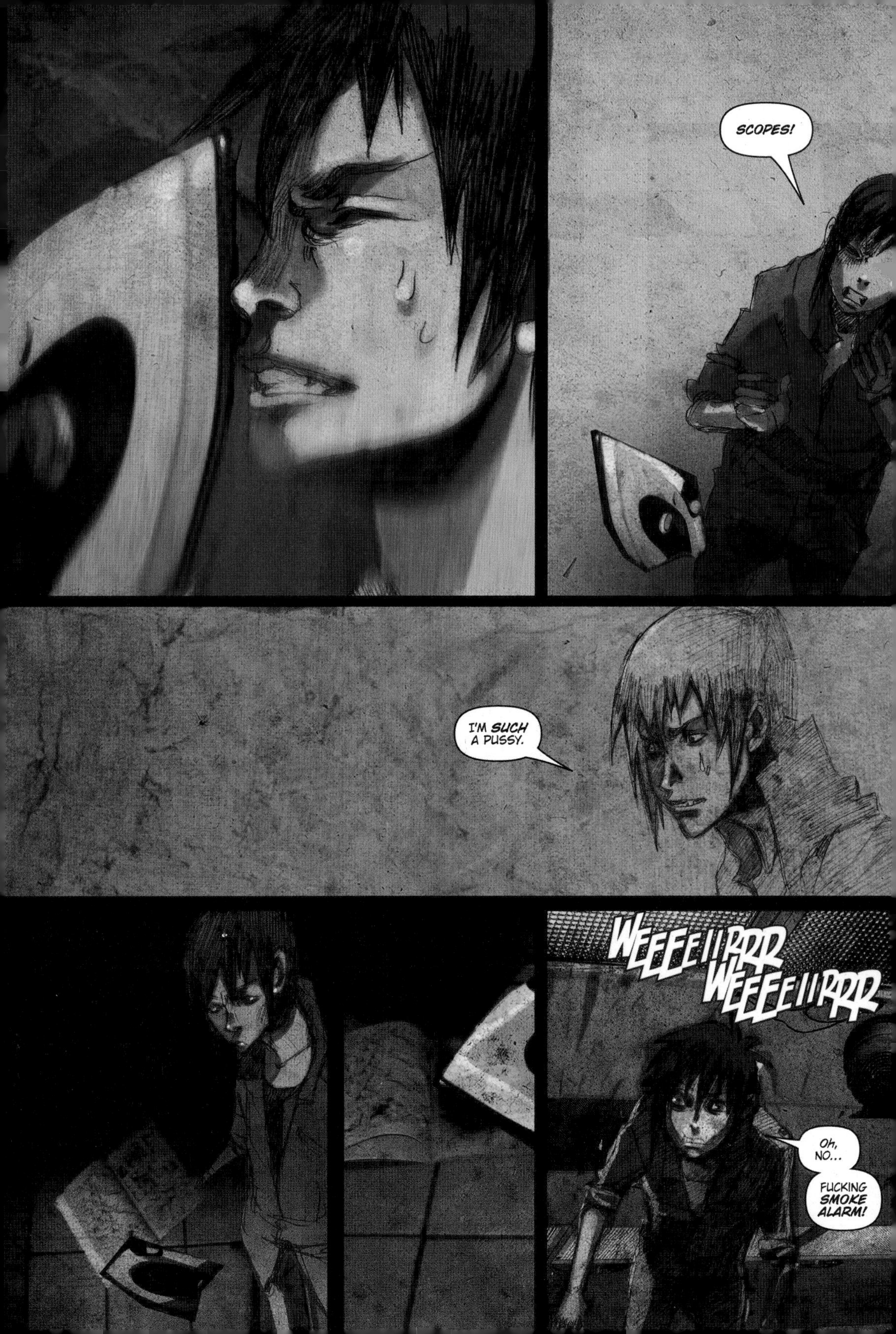
SCOPES!
I'M SUCH A PUSSY.
WEEEEIIRRR WEEEEIIRRR
OH, NO...
FUCKING SMOKE ALARM!

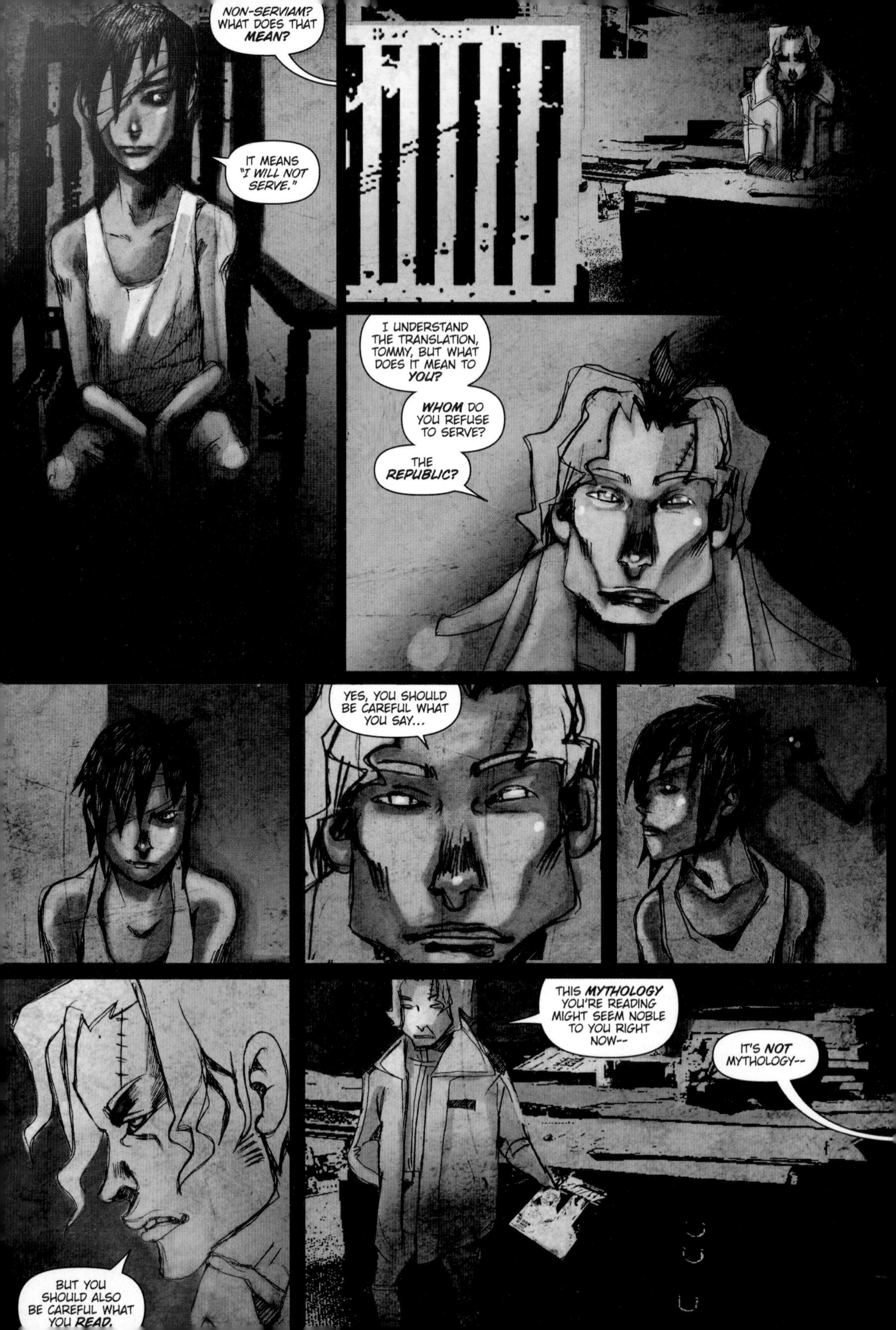
NON-SERVIAM? WHAT DOES THAT MEAN?
IT MEANS "I WILL NOT SERVE."
I UNDERSTAND THE TRANSLATION, TOMMY, BUT WHAT DOES IT MEAN TO YOU?
WHOM DO YOU REFUSE TO SERVE?
THE REPUBLIC?
YES, YOU SHOULD BE CAREFUL WHAT YOU SAY...
BUT YOU SHOULD ALSO BE CAREFUL WHAT YOU READ.
THIS MYTHOLOGY YOU'RE READING MIGHT SEEM NOBLE TO YOU RIGHT NOW--
IT'S NOT MYTHOLOGY--

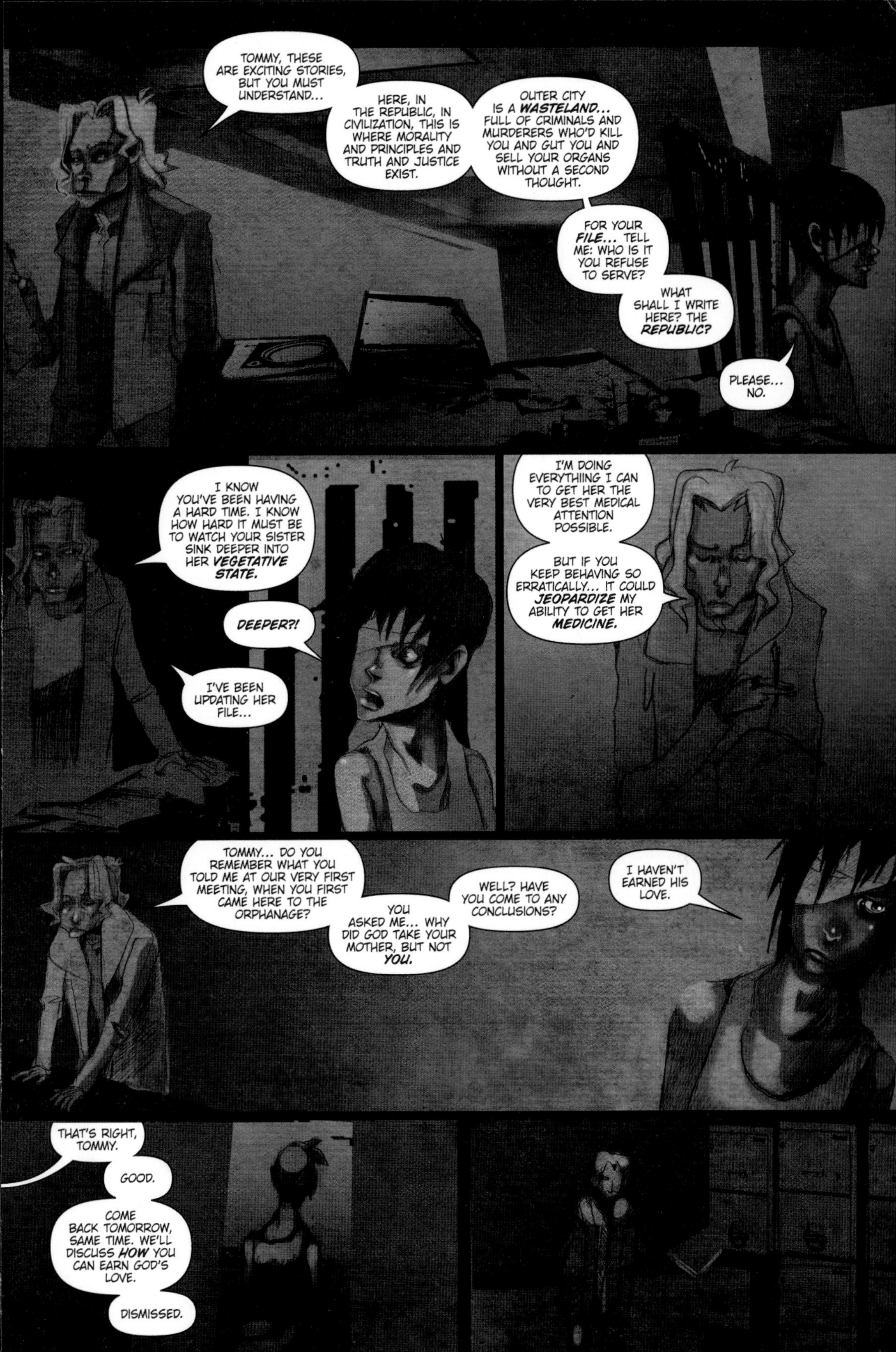
TOMMY, THESE ARE EXCITING STORIES, BUT YOU MUST UNDERSTAND...
HERE, IN THE REPUBLIC, IN CIVILIZATION, THIS IS WHERE MORALITY AND PRINCIPLES AND TRUTH AND JUSTICE EXIST.
OUTER CITY IS A WASTELAND... FULL OF CRIMINALS AND MURDERERS WHO'D KILL YOU AND GUT YOU AND SELL YOUR ORGANS WITHOUT A SECOND THOUGHT.
FOR YOUR FILE... TELL ME: WHO IS IT YOU REFUSE TO SERVE?
WHAT SHALL I WRITE HERE? THE REPUBLIC?
PLEASE... NO.
I KNOW YOU'VE BEEN HAVING A HARD TIME. I KNOW HOW HARD IT MUST BE TO WATCH YOUR SISTER SINK DEEPER INTO HER VEGETATIVE STATE.
DEEPER?!
I'VE BEEN UPDATING HER FILE...
I'M DOING EVERYTHIING I CAN TO GET HER THE VERY BEST MEDICAL ATTENTION POSSIBLE.
BUT IF YOU KEEP BEHAVING SO ERRATICALLY... IT COULD JEOPARDIZE MY ABILITY TO GET HER MEDICINE.
TOMMY... DO YOU REMEMBER WHAT YOU TOLD ME AT OUR VERY FIRST MEETING, WHEN YOU FIRST CAME HERE TO THE ORPHANAGE?
YOU ASKED ME... WHY DID GOD TAKE YOUR MOTHER, BUT NOT YOU.
WELL? HAVE YOU COME TO ANY CONCLUSIONS?
I HAVEN'T EARNED HIS LOVE.
THAT'S RIGHT, TOMMY.
GOOD.
COME BACK TOMORROW, SAME TIME. WE'LL DISCUSS HOW YOU CAN EARN GOD'S LOVE.
DISMISSED.

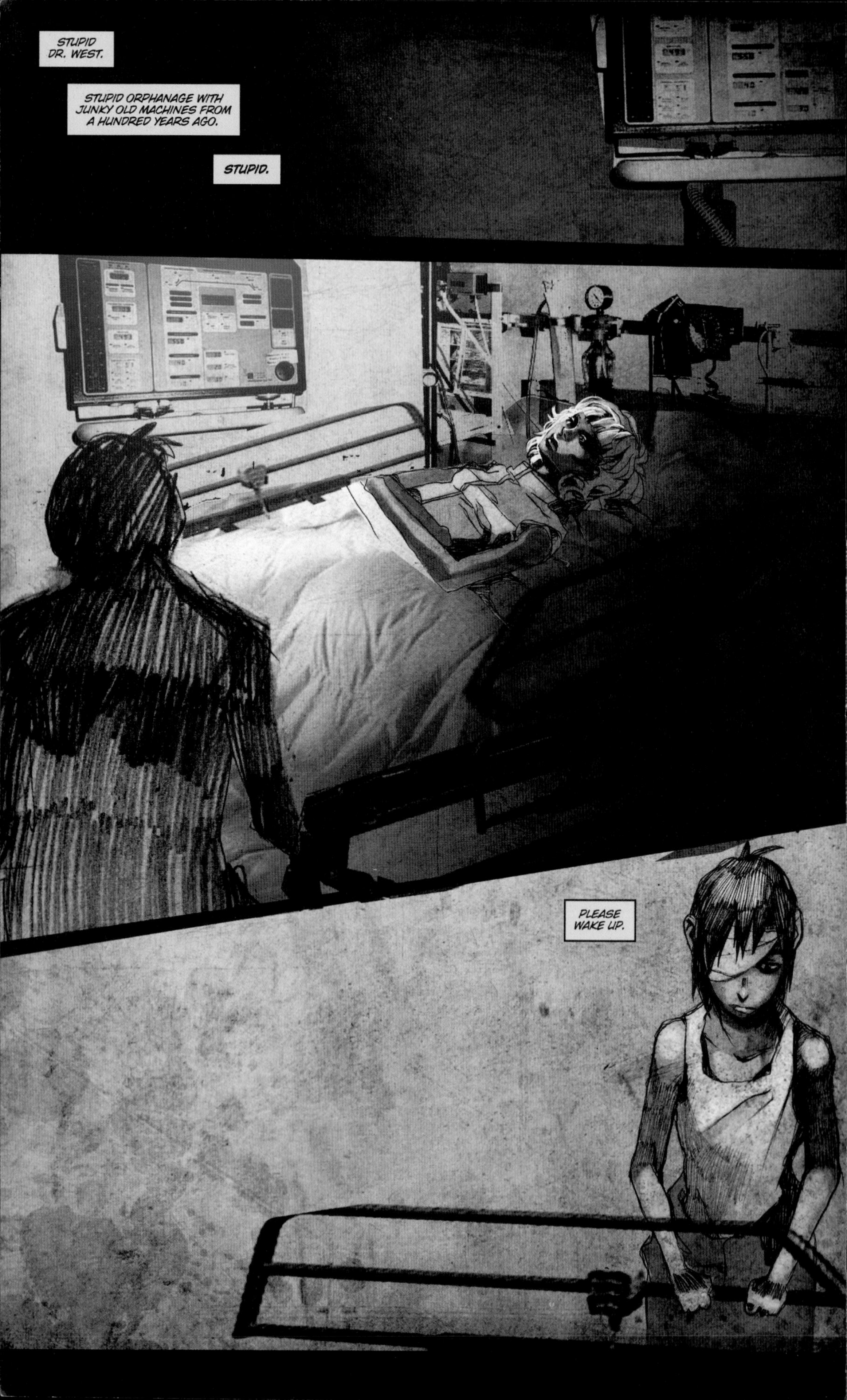
STUPID DR. WEST.
STUPID ORPHANAGE WITH JUNKY OLD MACHINES FROM A HUNDRED YEARS AGO.
STUPID.
PLEASE WAKE UP.

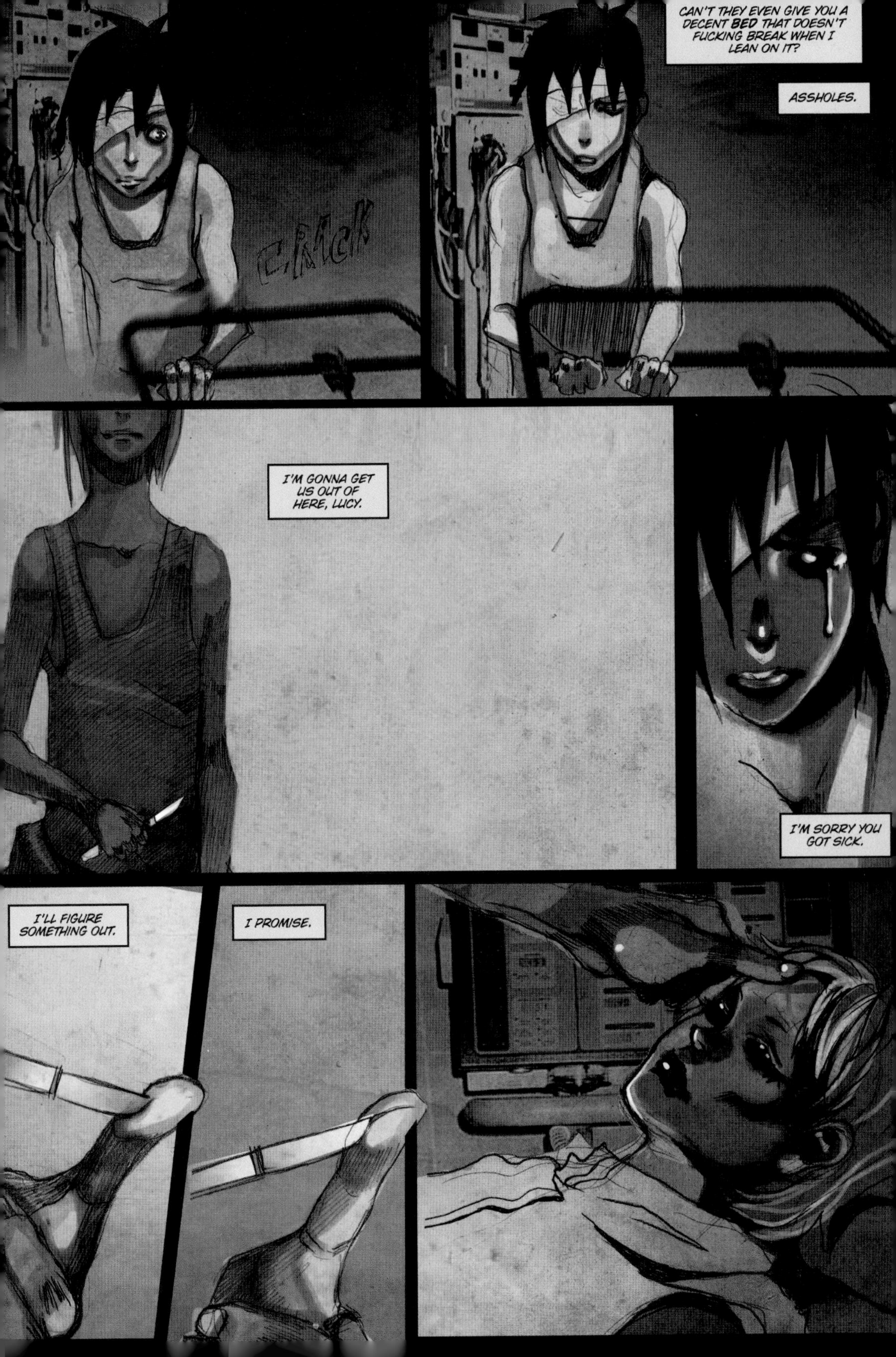
CAN'T THEY EVEN GIVE YOU A DECENT BED THAT DOESN'T FUCKING BREAK WHEN I LEAN ON IT?
ASSHOLES.
I'M GONNA GET US OUT OF HERE, LUCY.
I'M SORRY YOU GOT SICK.
I'LL FIGURE SOMETHING OUT.
I PROMISE.

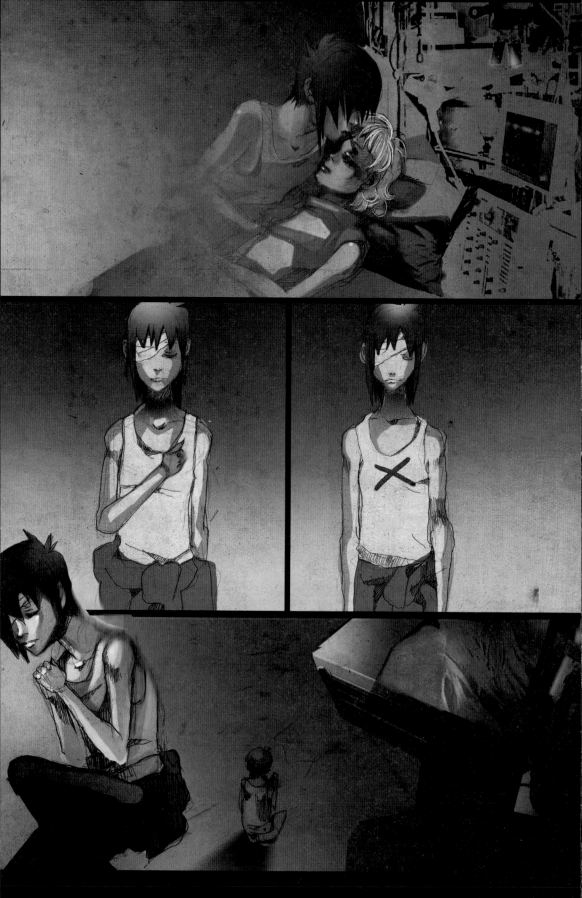

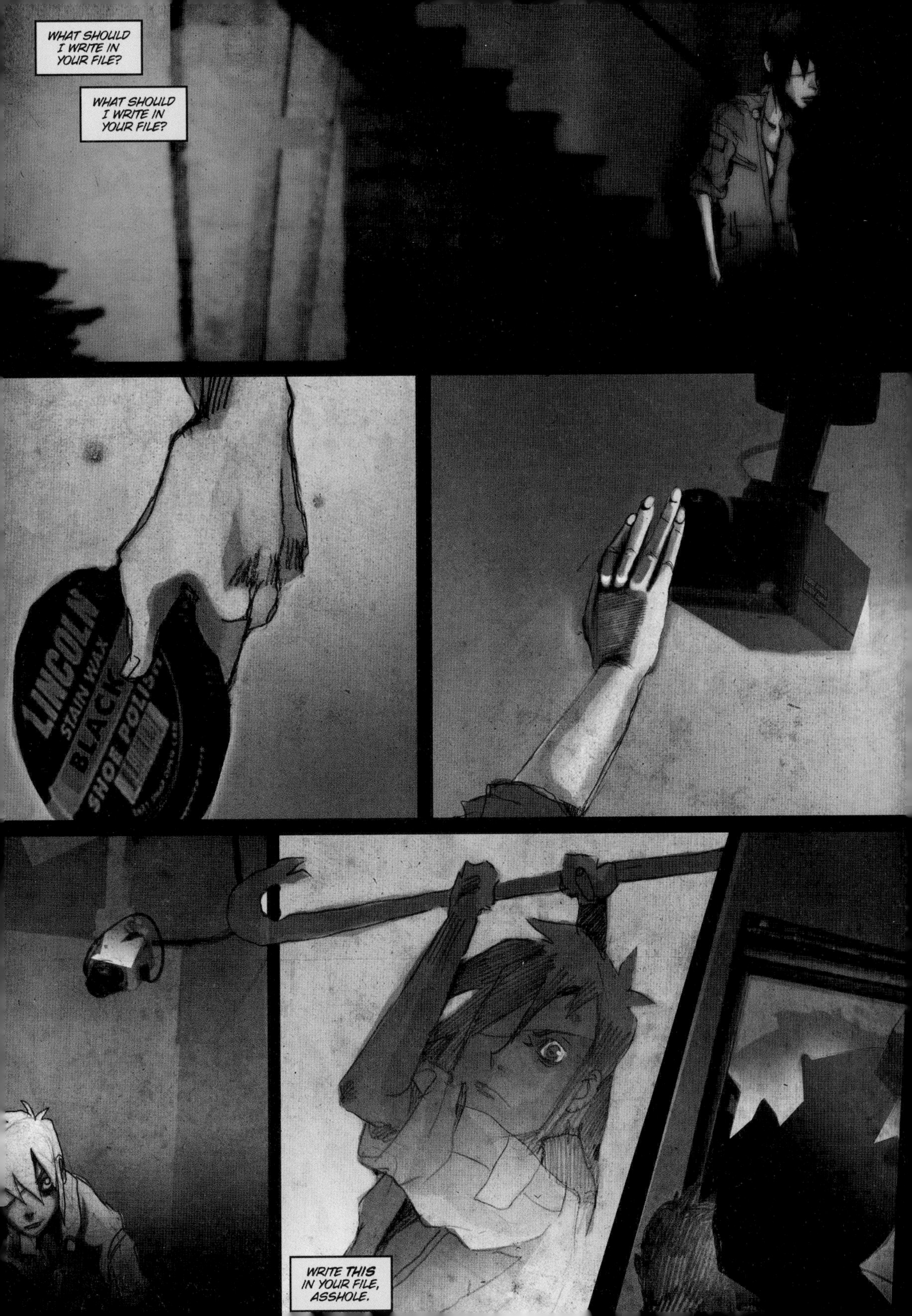
WHAT SHOULD I WRITE IN YOUR FILE?
WHAT SHOULD I WRITE IN YOUR FILE?
LINCOLN
STAIN WAX
BLACK
SHOE POLISH
WRITE THIS IN YOUR FILE, ASSHOLE.

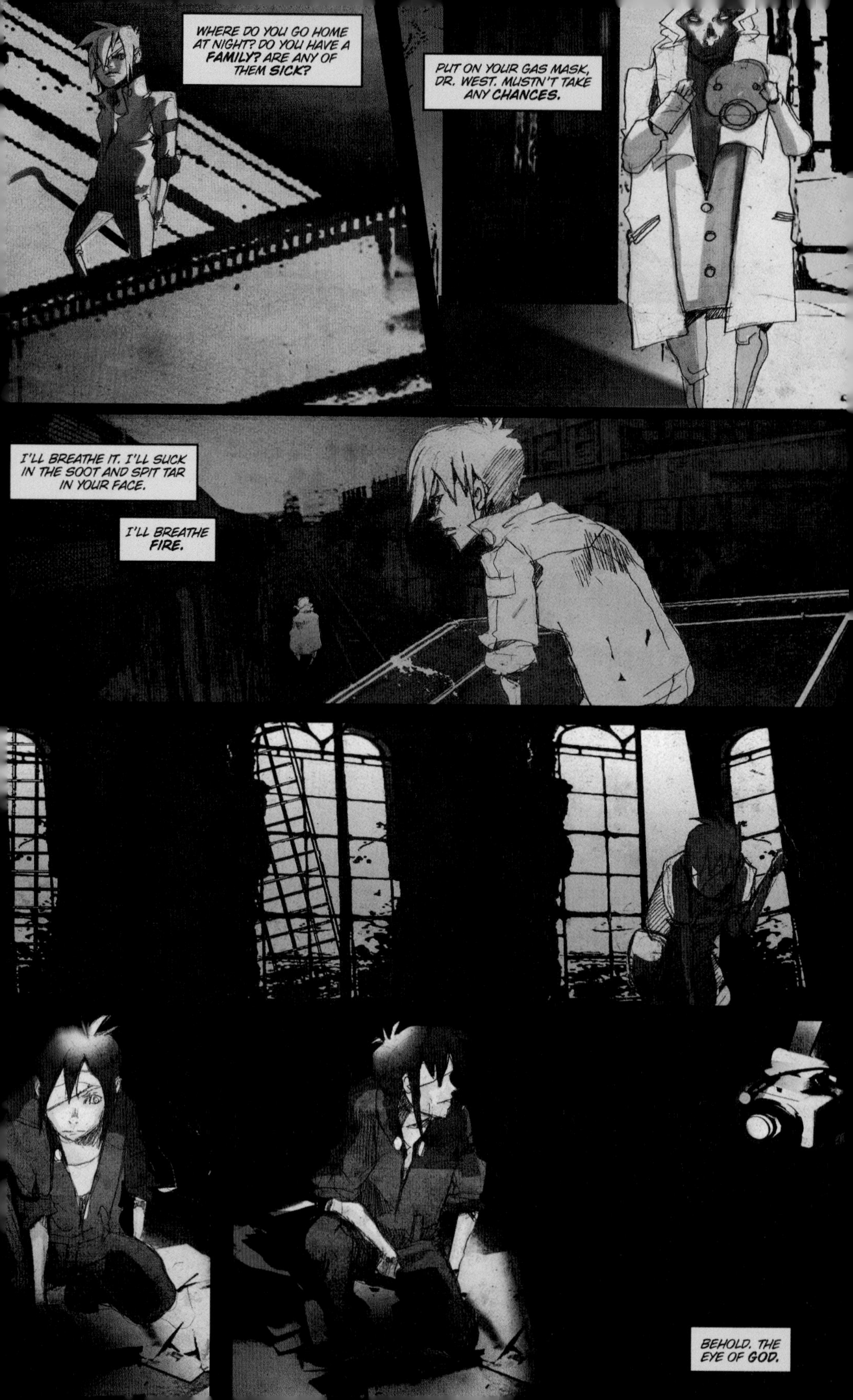

WHERE DO YOU GO HOME AT NIGHT? DO YOU HAVE A FAMILY? ARE ANY OF THEM SICK?
PUT ON YOUR GAS MASK, DR. WEST. MUSTN'T TAKE ANY CHANCES.
I'LL BREATHE IT. I'LL SUCK IN THE SOOT AND SPIT TAR IN YOUR FACE.
I'LL BREATHE FIRE.
BEHOLD. THE EYE OF GOD.

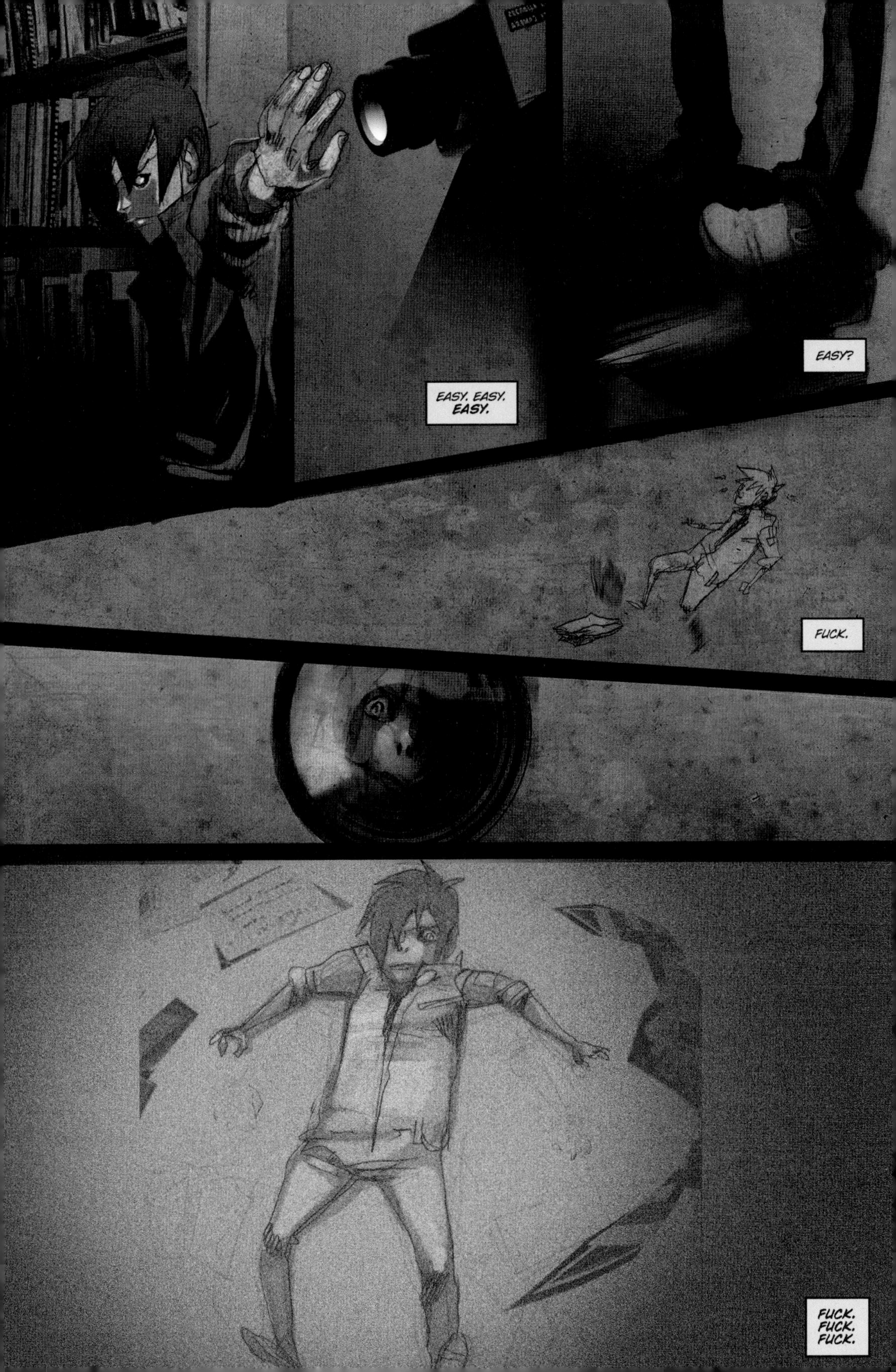
EASY. EASY. EASY.
EASY?
FUCK.
FUCK. FUCK. FUCK.

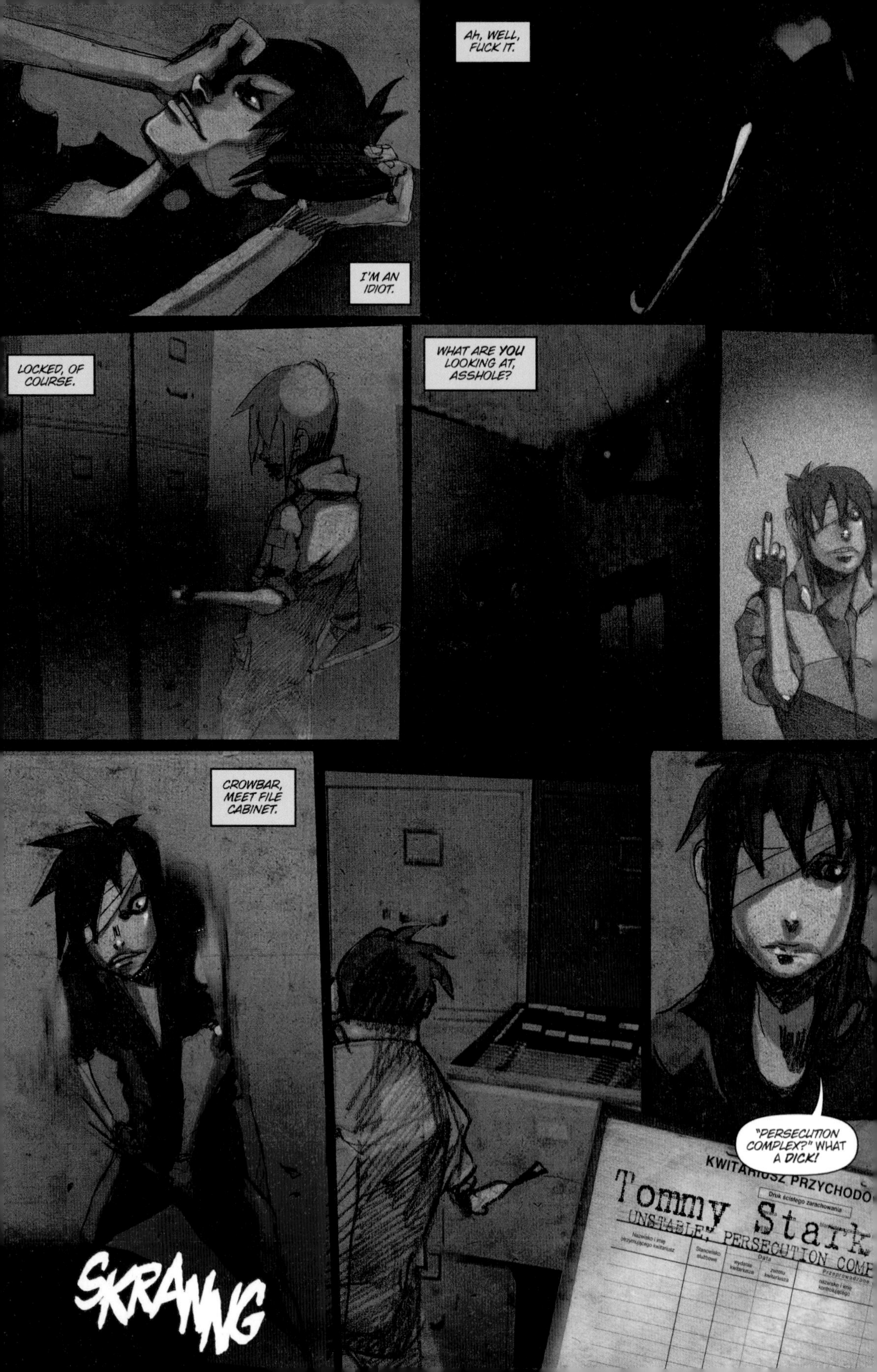
I'M AN IDIOT.
Ah, WELL, FUCK IT.
LOCKED, OF COURSE.
WHAT ARE YOU LOOKING AT, ASSHOLE?
CROWBAR, MEET FILE CABINET.
SKRANNG
"PERSECUTION COMPLEX?" WHAT A DICK!
KWITARIUSZ PRZYCHODO
Druk ścisłego zarachowania
Tommy Stark
UNSTABLE, PERSECUTION COMP

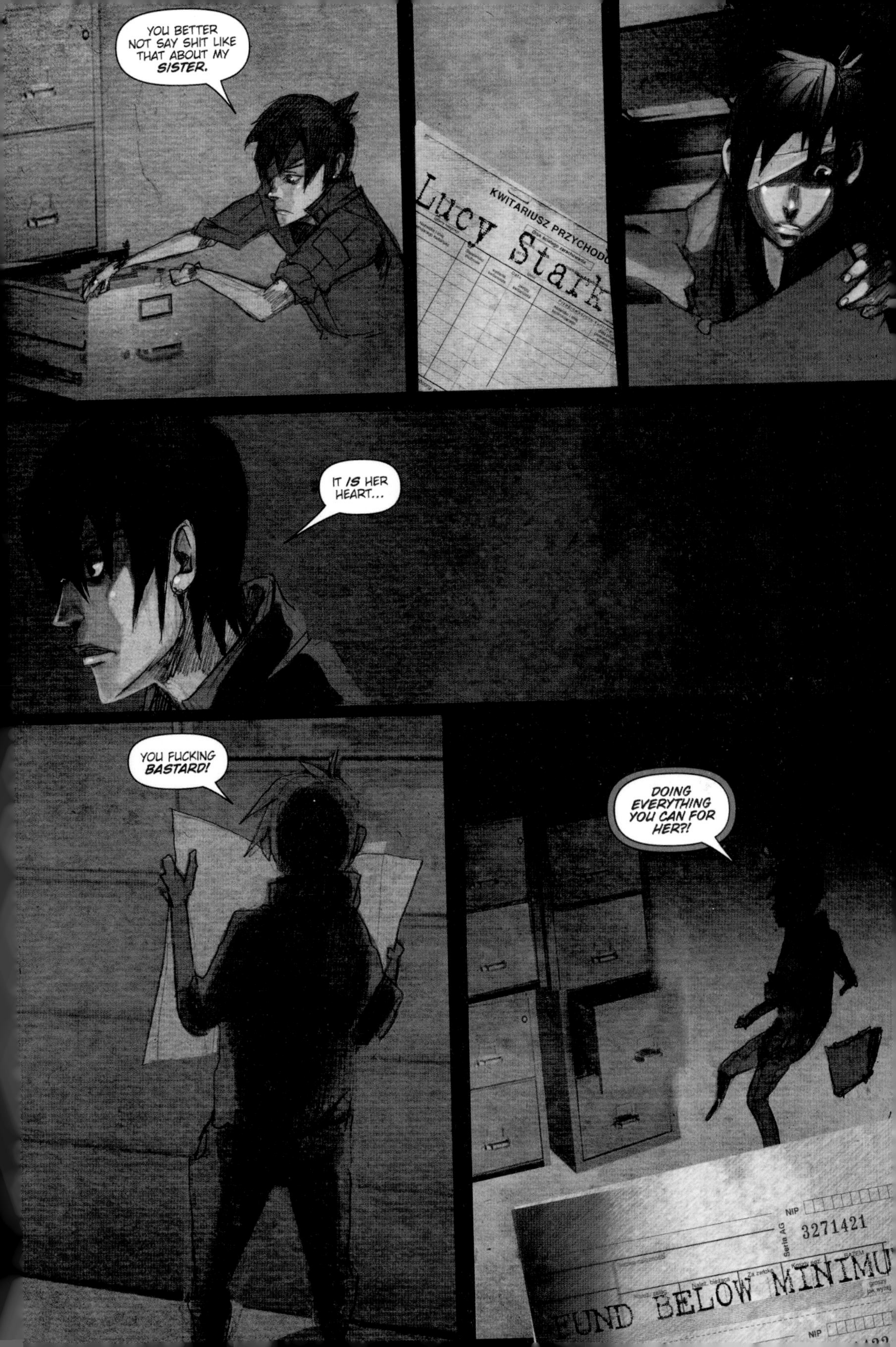
YOU BETTER NOT SAY SHIT LIKE THAT ABOUT MY SISTER.
Lucy Stark
IT IS HER HEART...
YOU FUCKING BASTARD!
DOING EVERYTHING YOU CAN FOR HER?!
3271421

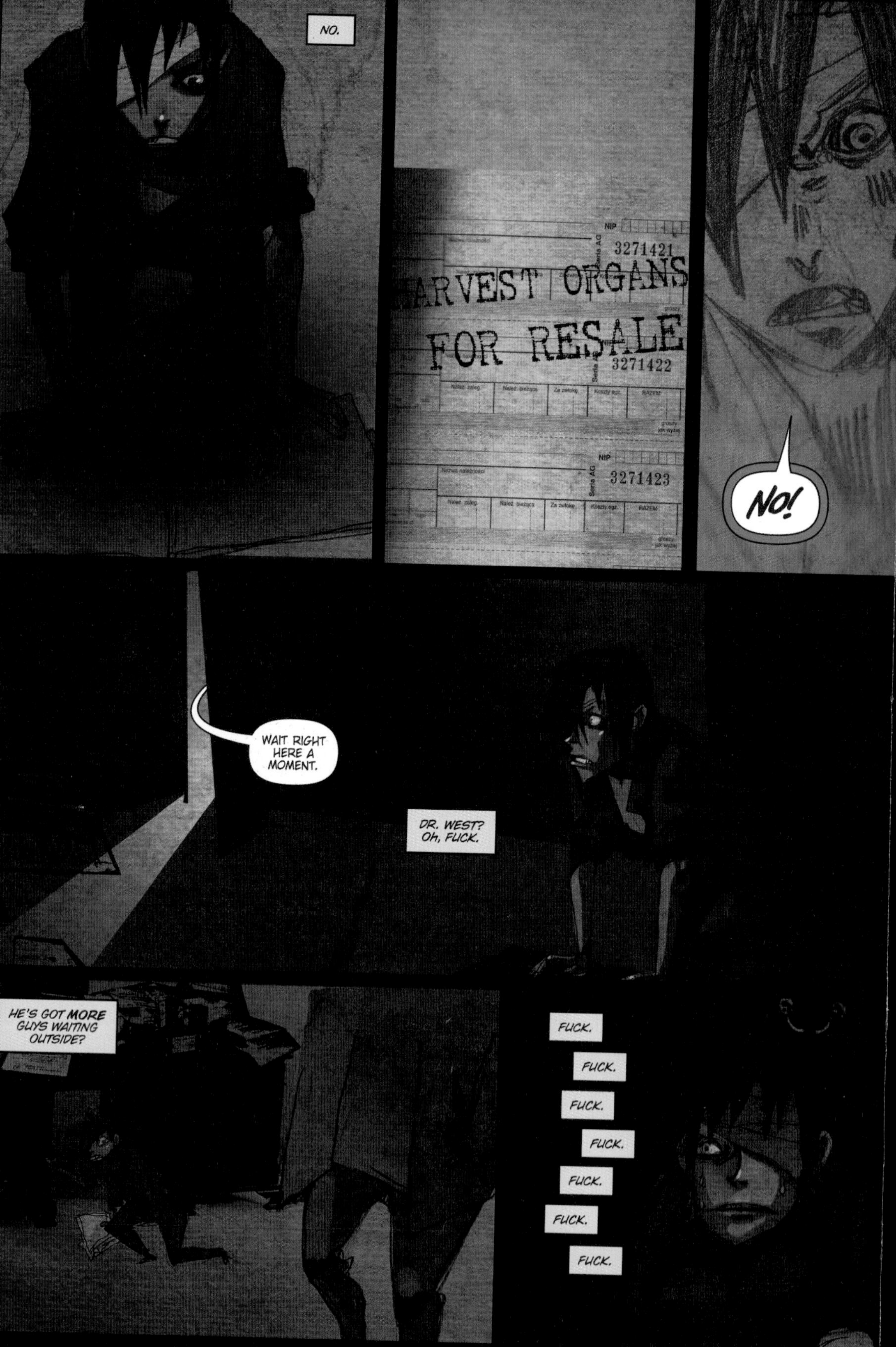
NO.
NIP
3271421
HARVEST ORGANS
FOR RESALE
3271422
NIP
3271423
NO!
WAIT RIGHT HERE A MOMENT.
DR. WEST? Oh, FUCK.
HE'S GOT **MORE** GUYS WAITING OUTSIDE?
FUCK.
FUCK.
FUCK.
FUCK.
FUCK.
FUCK.
FUCK.

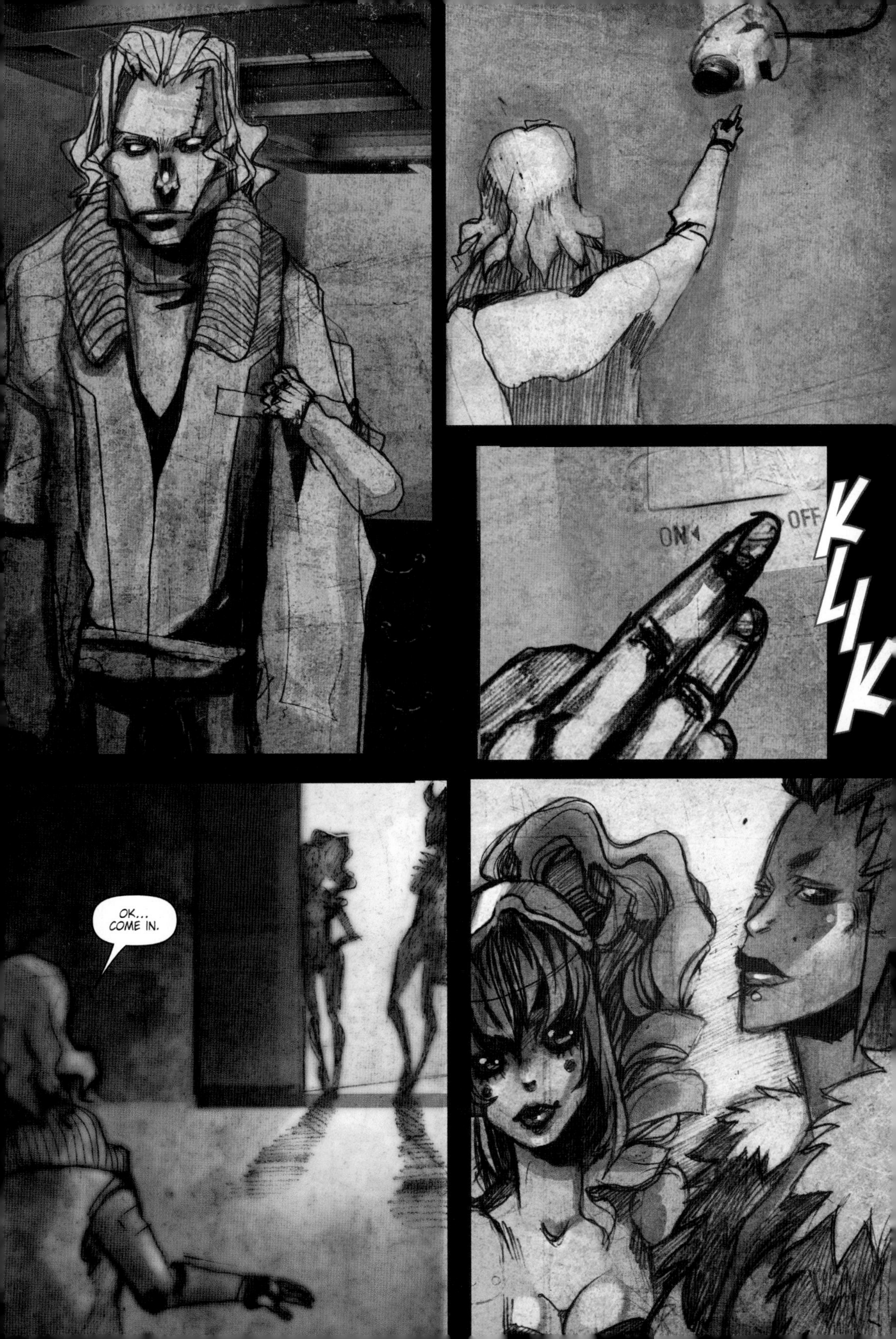
ON
OFF
KLIK
OK... COME IN.

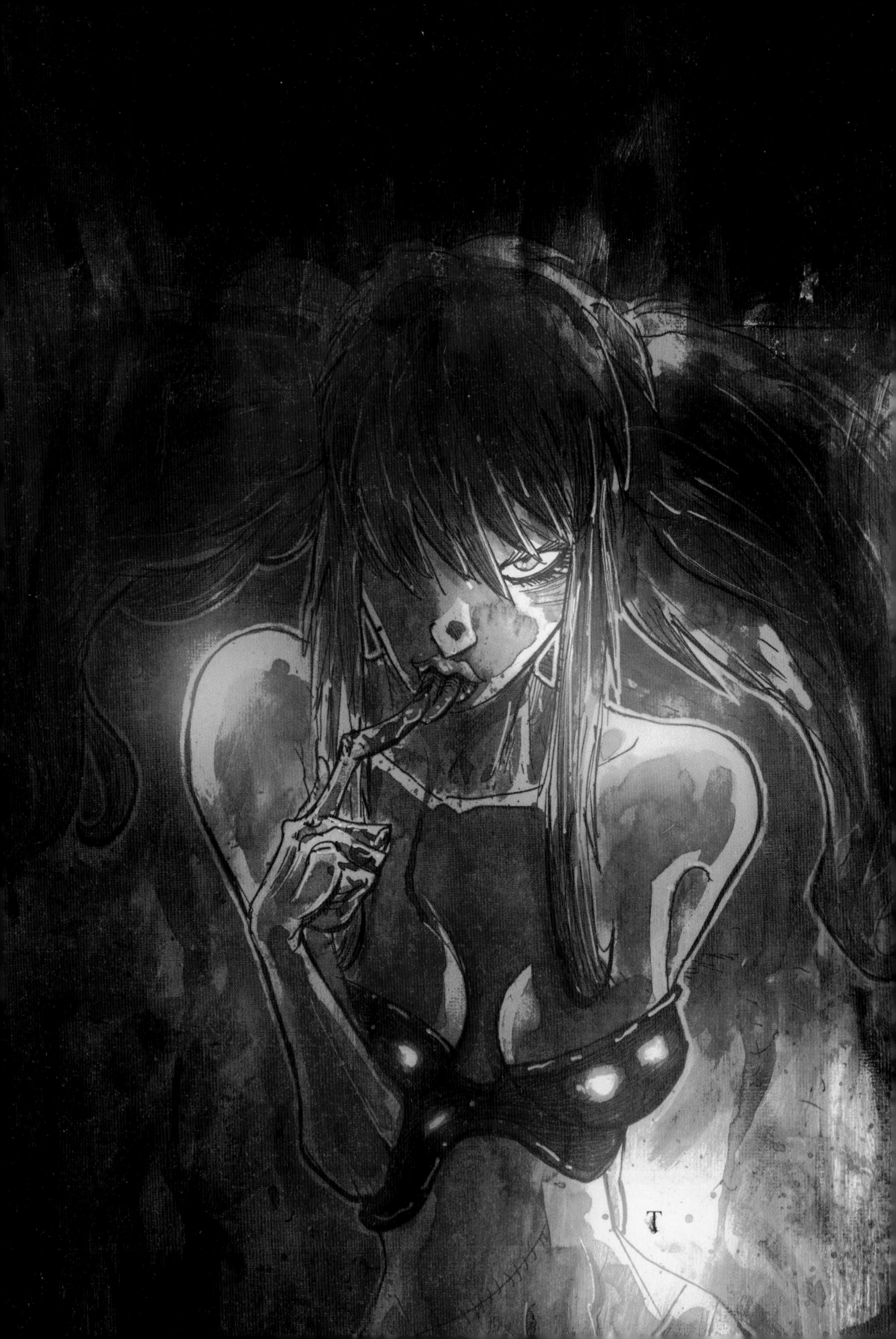

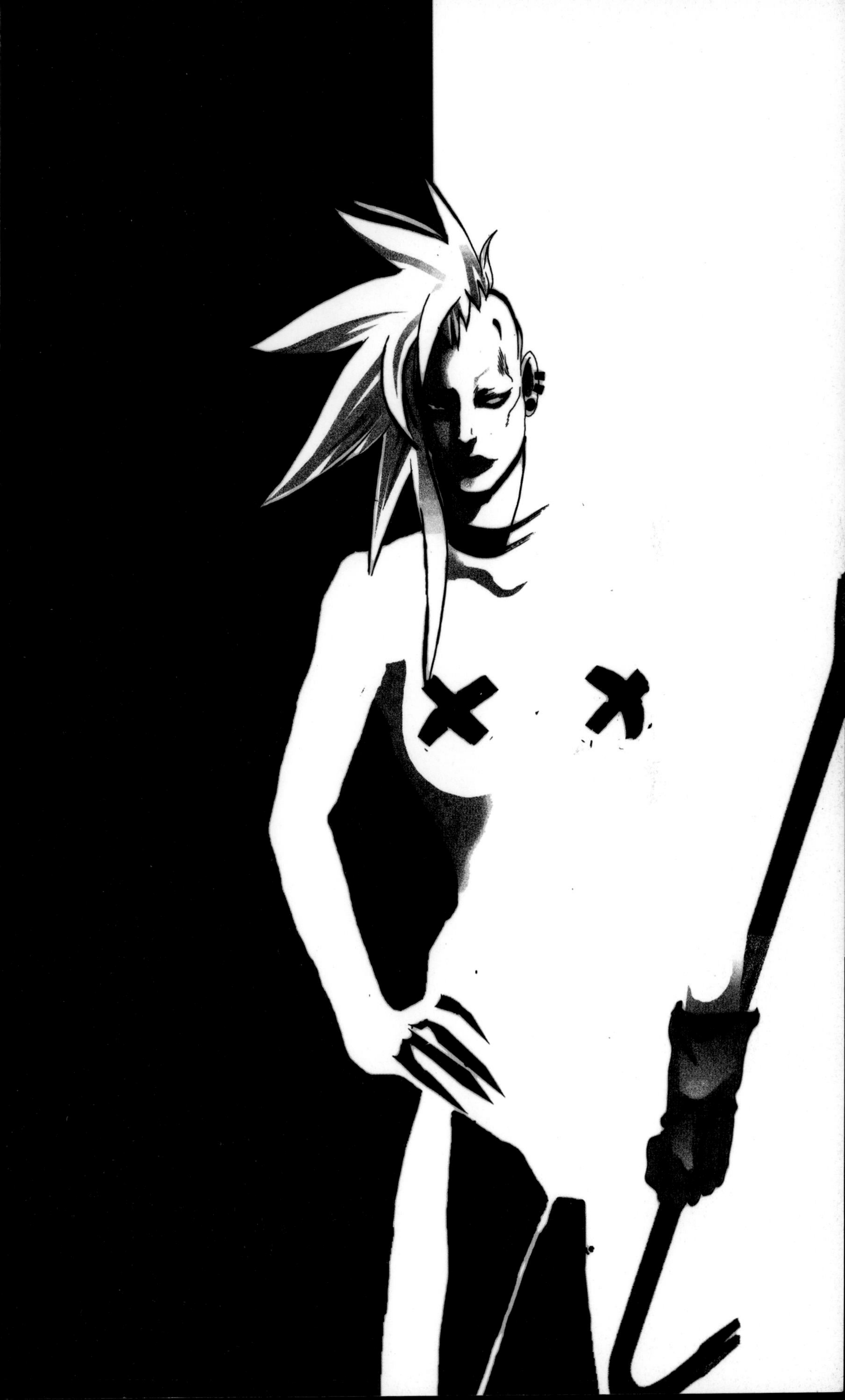

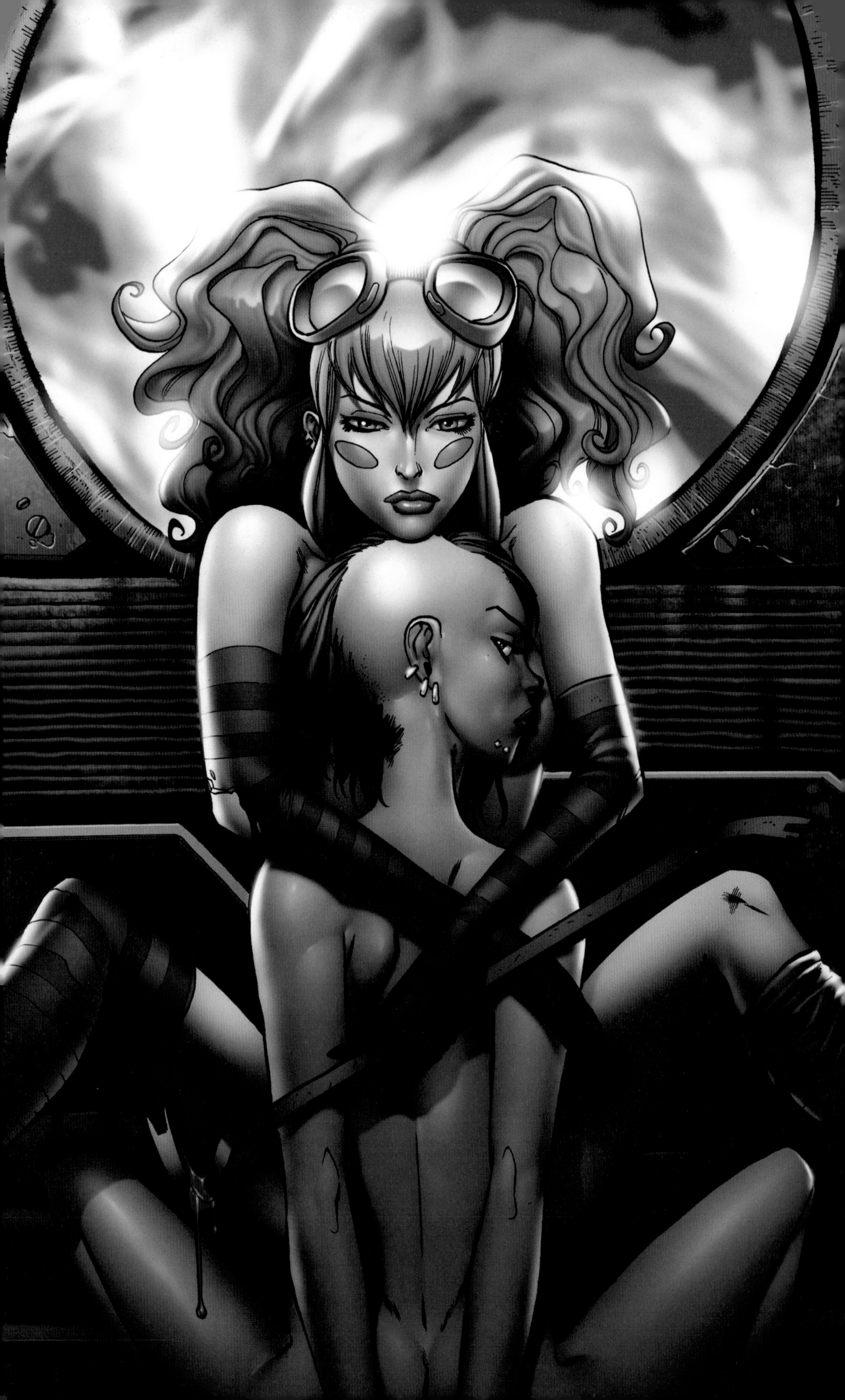

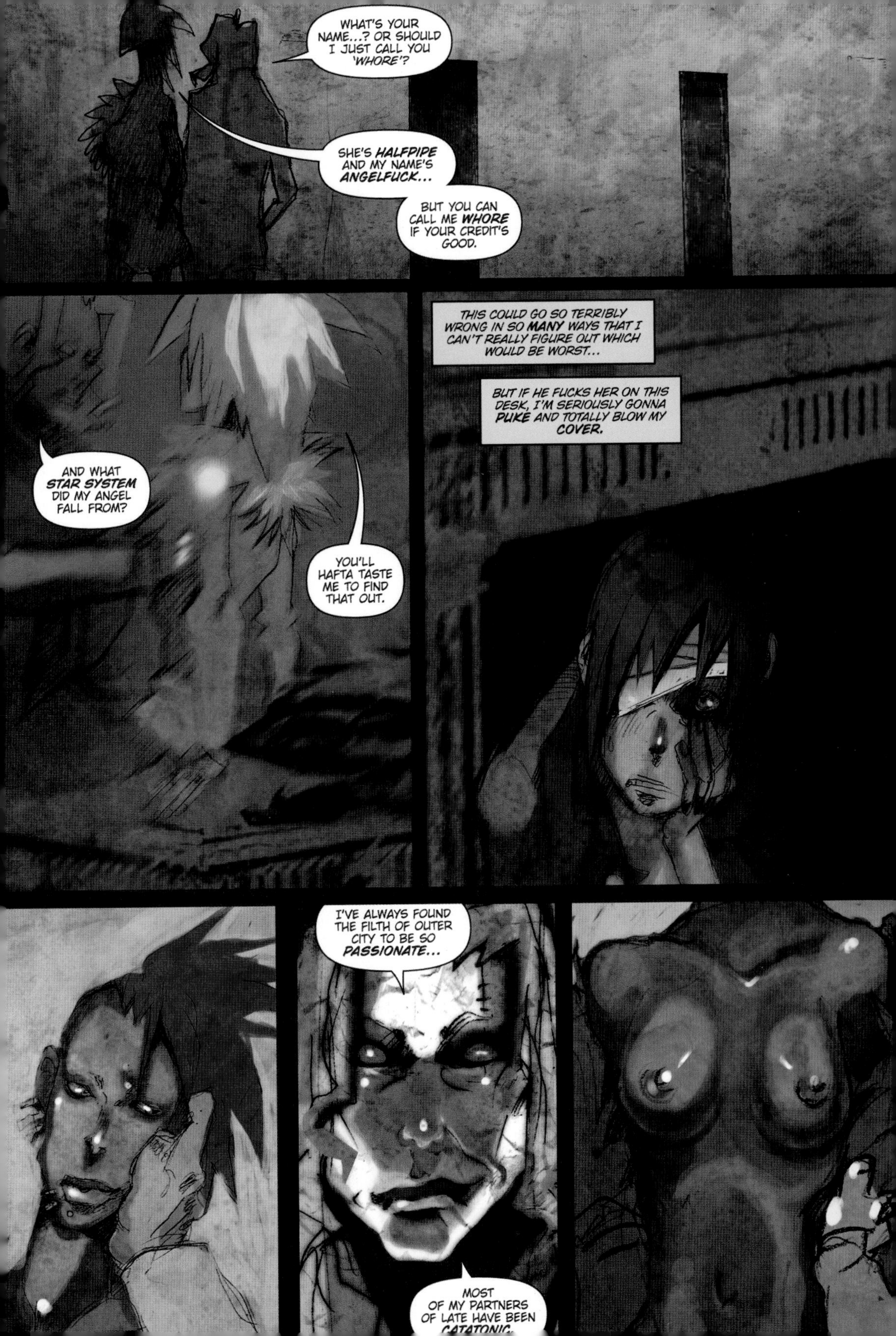
WHAT'S YOUR NAME...? OR SHOULD I JUST CALL YOU '*WHORE*'?
SHE'S ***HALFPIPE*** AND MY NAME'S ***ANGELFUCK...***
BUT YOU CAN CALL ME ***WHORE*** IF YOUR CREDIT'S GOOD.
AND WHAT ***STAR SYSTEM*** DID MY ANGEL FALL FROM?
YOU'LL HAFTA TASTE ME TO FIND THAT OUT.
*THIS COULD GO SO TERRIBLY WRONG IN SO **MANY** WAYS THAT I CAN'T REALLY FIGURE OUT WHICH WOULD BE WORST...*
*BUT IF HE FUCKS HER ON THIS DESK, I'M SERIOUSLY GONNA **PUKE** AND TOTALLY BLOW MY **COVER.***
I'VE ALWAYS FOUND THE FILTH OF OUTER CITY TO BE SO ***PASSIONATE...***
MOST OF MY PARTNERS OF LATE HAVE BEEN ***CATATONIC.***

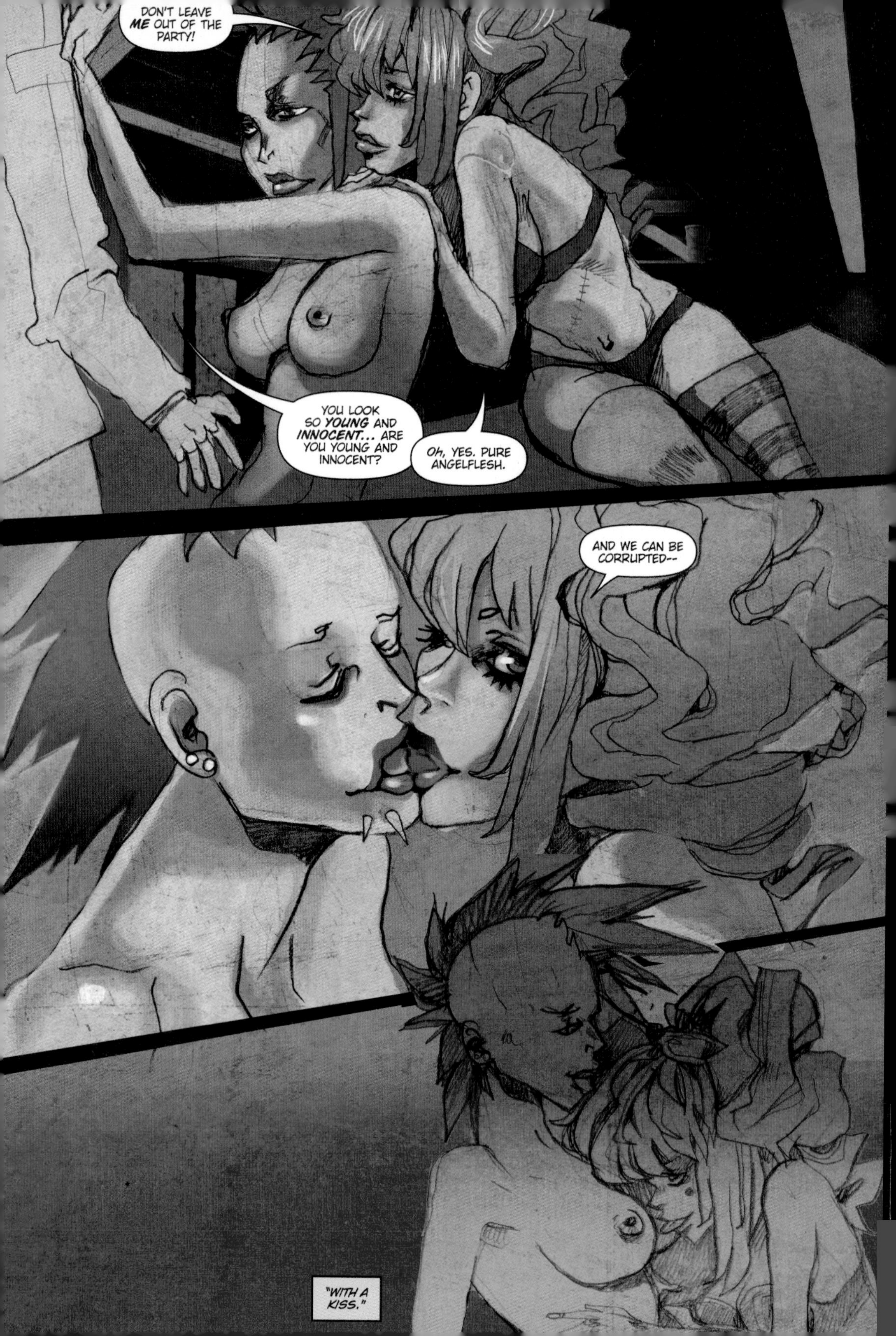
DON'T LEAVE ME OUT OF THE PARTY!
YOU LOOK SO YOUNG AND INNOCENT... ARE YOU YOUNG AND INNOCENT?
Oh, YES. PURE ANGELFLESH.
AND WE CAN BE CORRUPTED--
"WITH A KISS."

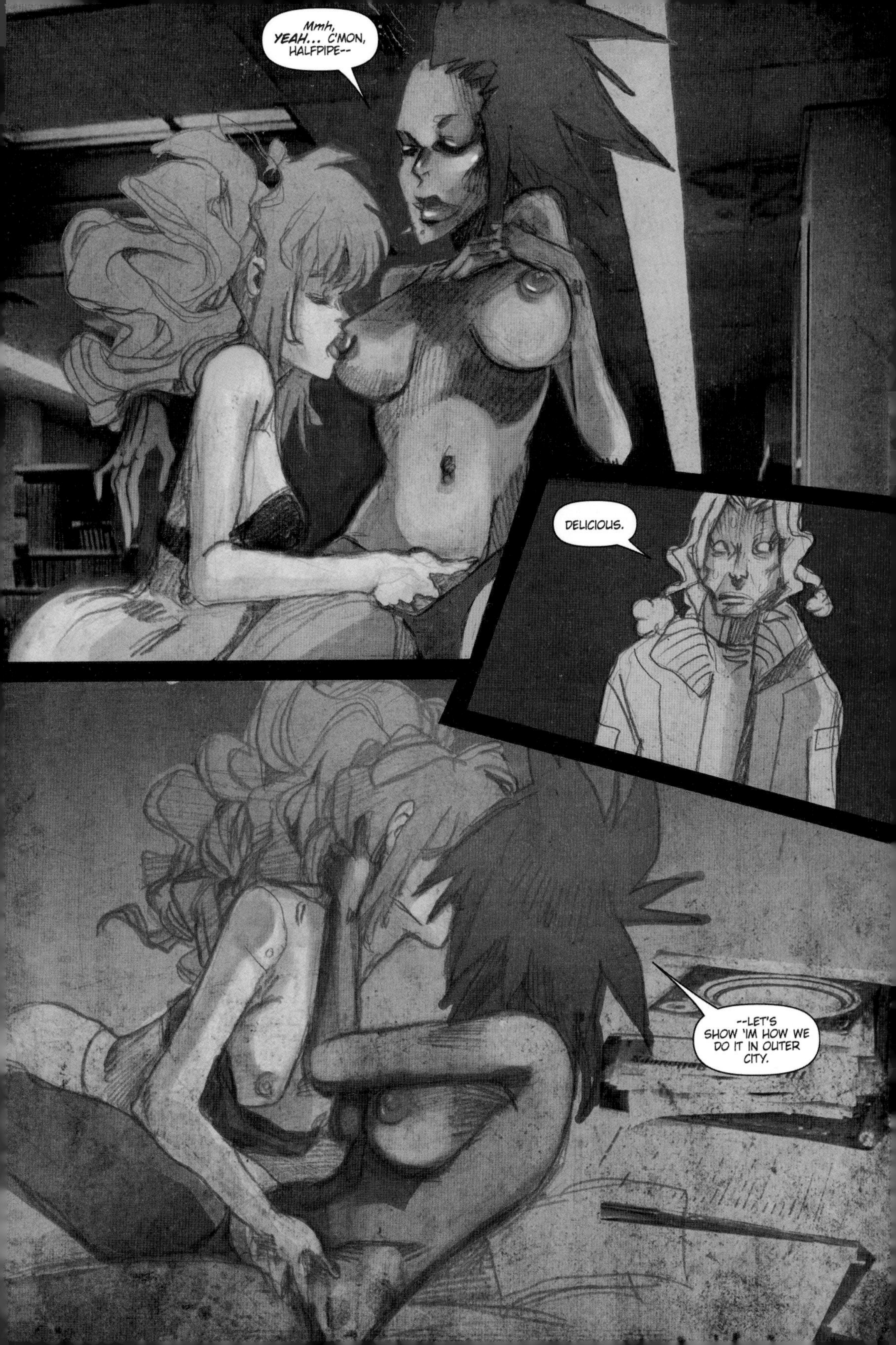
Mmh, YEAH... C'MON, HALFPIPE--
DELICIOUS.
--LET'S SHOW 'IM HOW WE DO IT IN OUTER CITY.

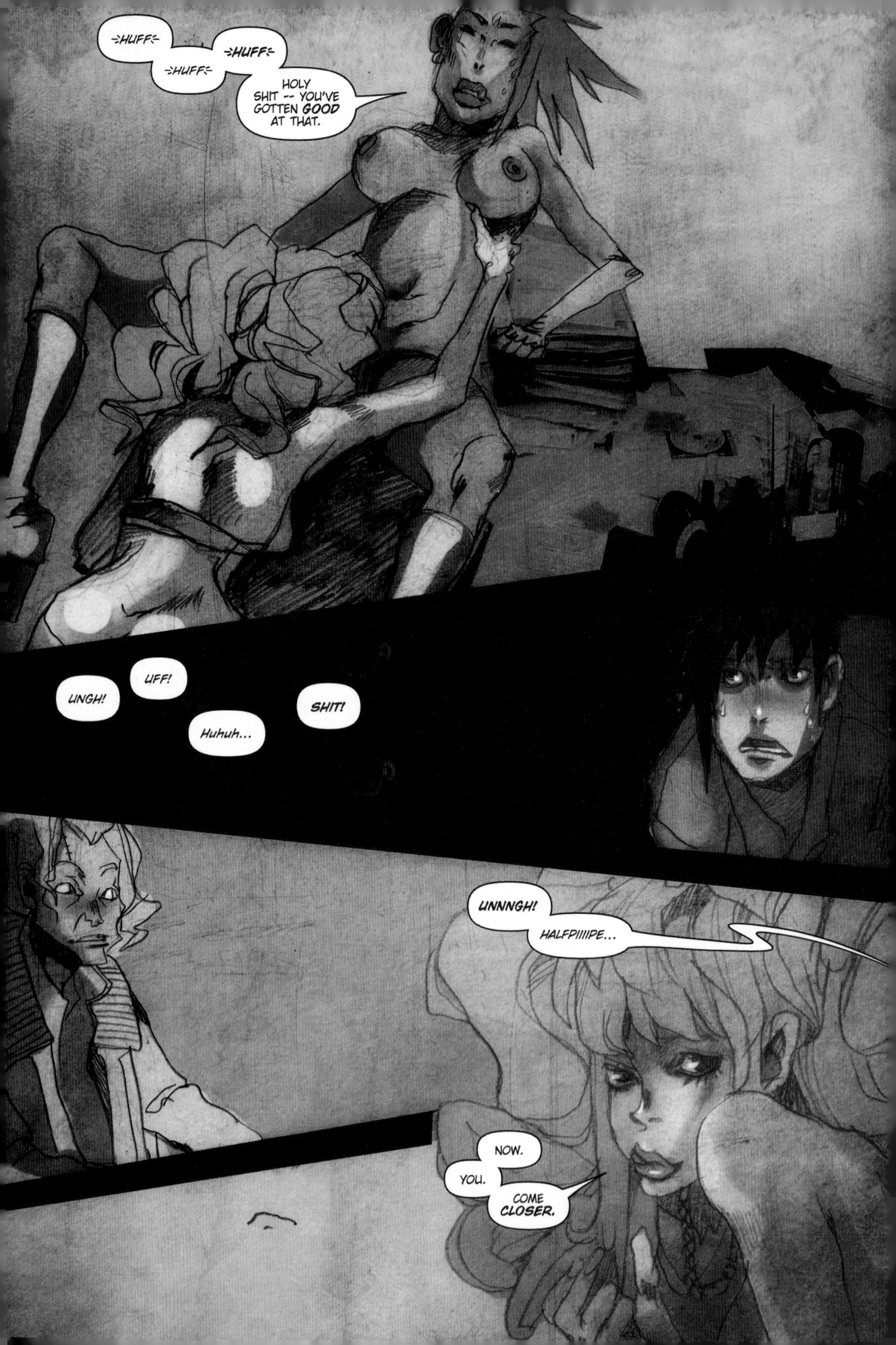

=HUFF=
=HUFF=
=HUFF=
HOLY SHIT -- YOU'VE GOTTEN **GOOD** AT THAT.
UNGH!
UFF!
Huhuh...
SHIT!
UNNNGH!
HALFPIIIIPE...
NOW.
YOU.
COME **CLOSER.**

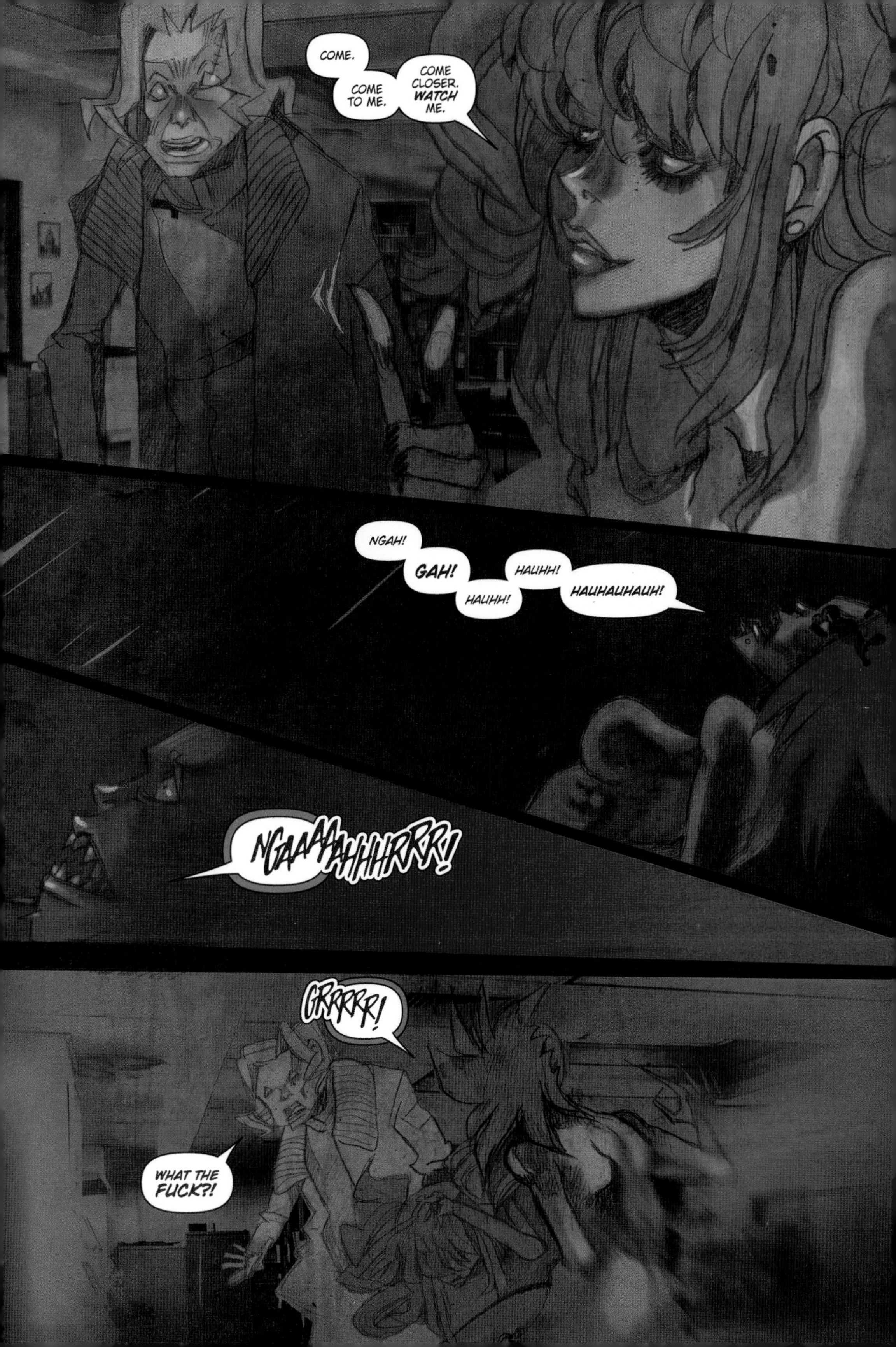
COME.
COME TO ME.
COME CLOSER. WATCH ME.
NGAH!
GAH!
HAUHH!
HAUHH!
HAUHAUHAUH!
NGAAAAAHHHRRRR!
GRRRRR!
WHAT THE FUCK?!

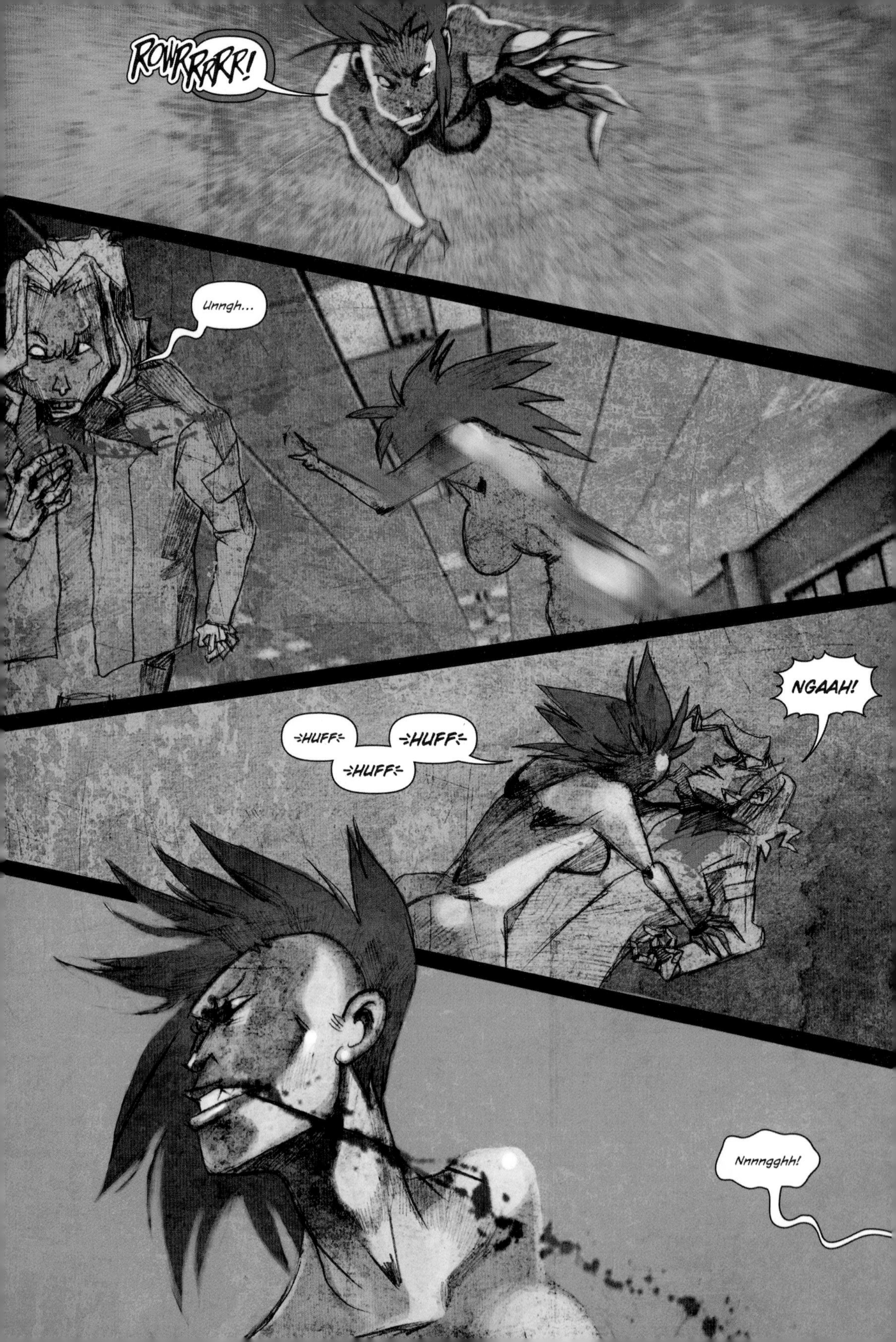
ROWRRRRR!
Unnngh...
NGAAH!
=HUFF=
=HUFF=
=HUFF=
Nnnngghh!

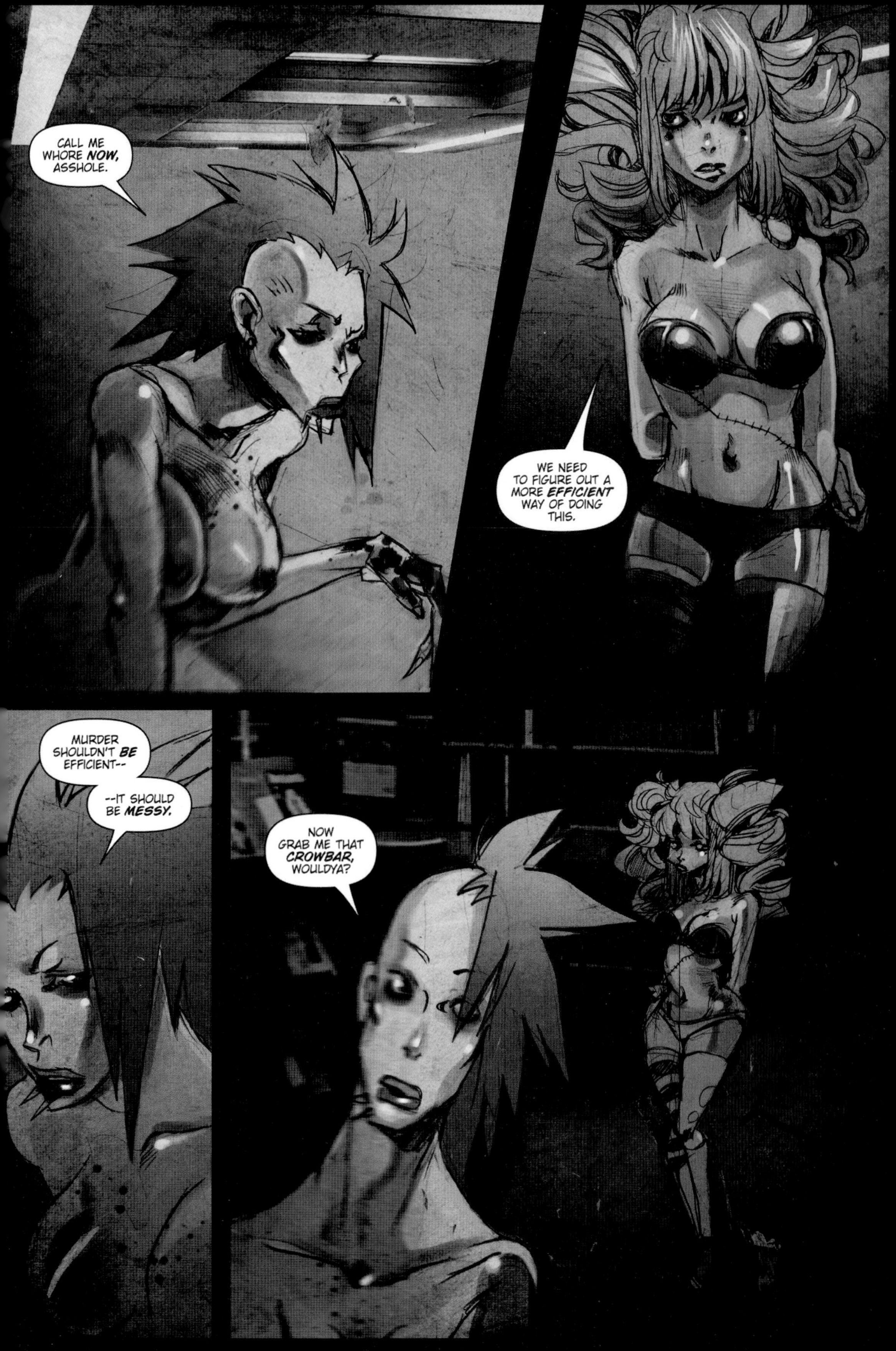
CALL ME WHORE **NOW,** ASSHOLE.
WE NEED TO FIGURE OUT A MORE **EFFICIENT** WAY OF DOING THIS.
MURDER SHOULDN'T **BE** EFFICIENT--
--IT SHOULD BE **MESSY.**
NOW GRAB ME THAT **CROWBAR,** WOULDYA?

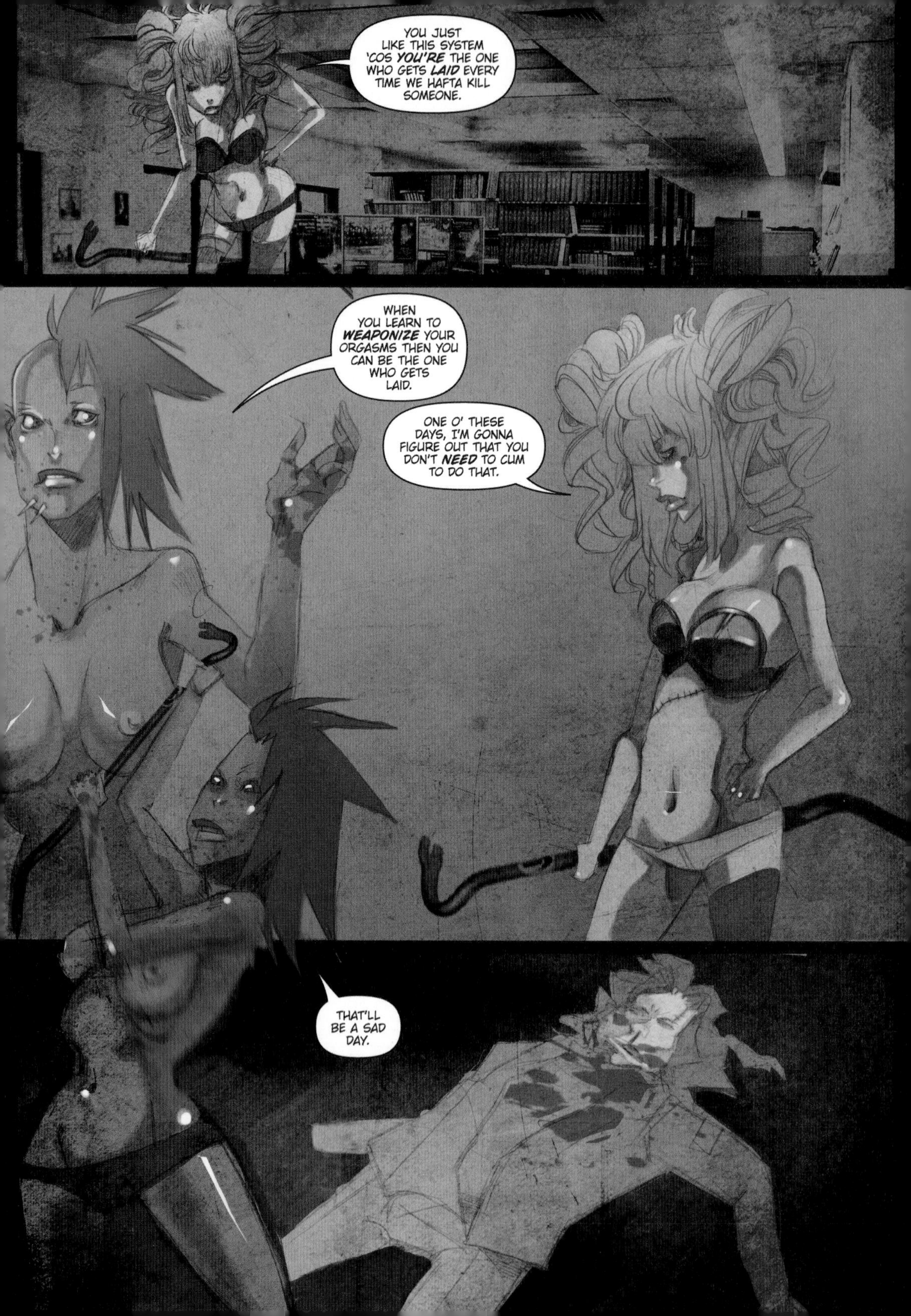
YOU JUST LIKE THIS SYSTEM 'COS *YOU'RE* THE ONE WHO GETS *LAID* EVERY TIME WE HAFTA KILL SOMEONE.
WHEN YOU LEARN TO *WEAPONIZE* YOUR ORGASMS THEN YOU CAN BE THE ONE WHO GETS LAID.
ONE O' THESE DAYS, I'M GONNA FIGURE OUT THAT YOU DON'T *NEED* TO CUM TO DO THAT.
THAT'LL BE A SAD DAY.

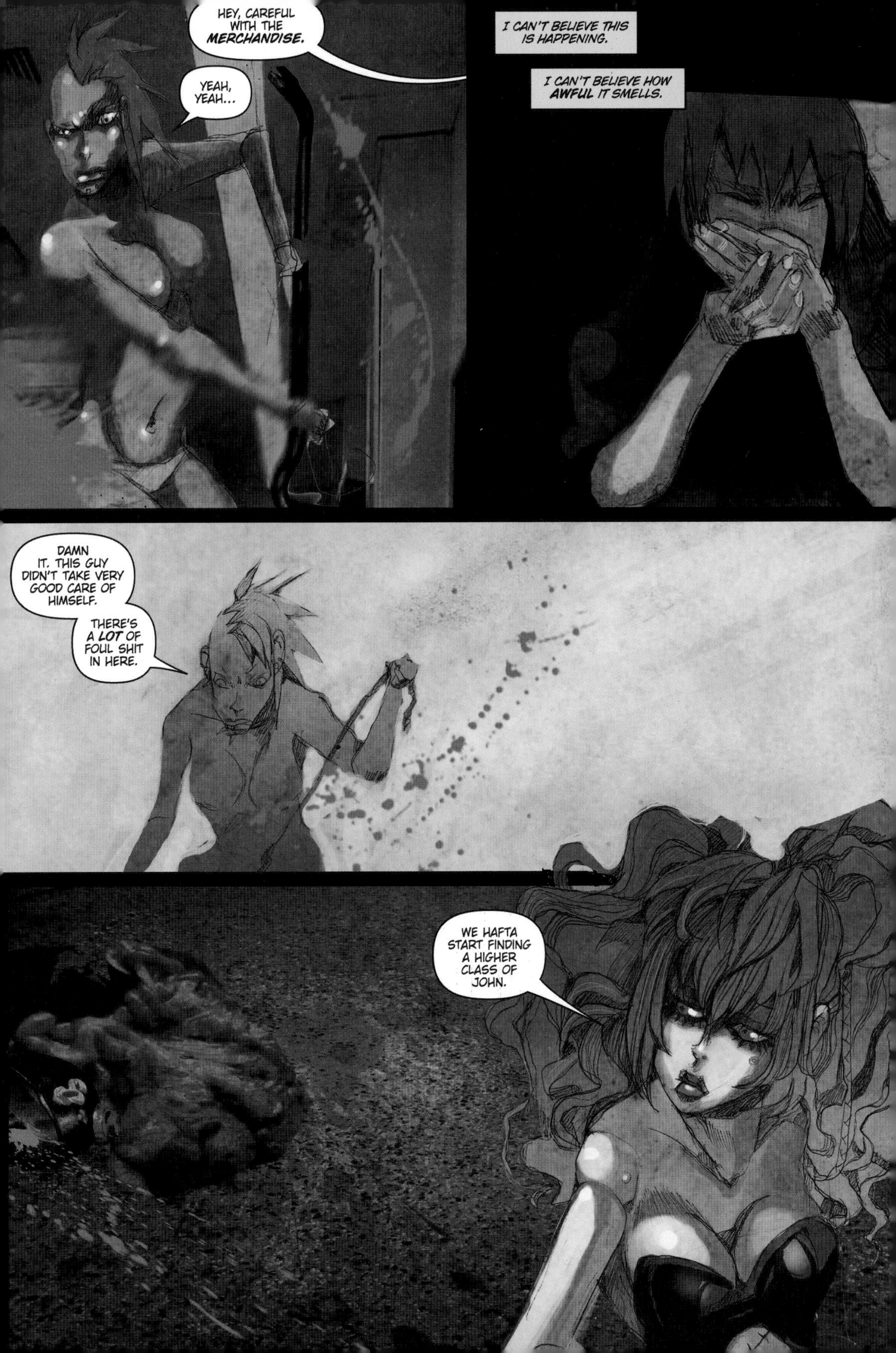
HEY, CAREFUL WITH THE MERCHANDISE.
YEAH, YEAH...
I CAN'T BELIEVE THIS IS HAPPENING.
I CAN'T BELIEVE HOW AWFUL IT SMELLS.
DAMN IT. THIS GUY DIDN'T TAKE VERY GOOD CARE OF HIMSELF.
THERE'S A LOT OF FOUL SHIT IN HERE.
WE HAFTA START FINDING A HIGHER CLASS OF JOHN.

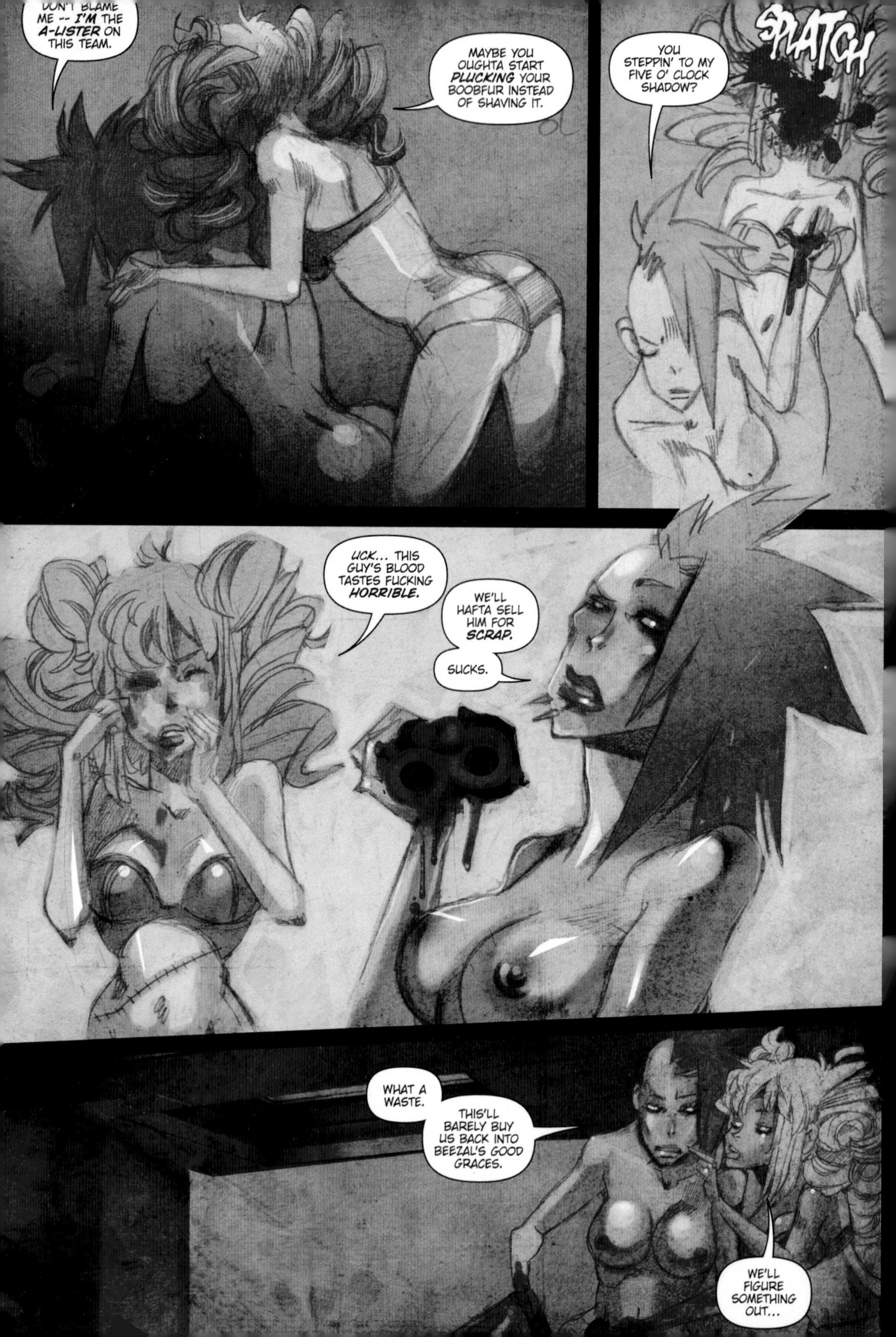
DON'T BLAME ME -- I'M THE A-LISTER ON THIS TEAM.
MAYBE YOU OUGHTA START PLUCKING YOUR BOOBFUR INSTEAD OF SHAVING IT.
YOU STEPPIN' TO MY FIVE O' CLOCK SHADOW?
SPLATCH
UCK... THIS GUY'S BLOOD TASTES FUCKING HORRIBLE.
WE'LL HAFTA SELL HIM FOR SCRAP.
SUCKS.
WHAT A WASTE.
THIS'LL BARELY BUY US BACK INTO BEEZAL'S GOOD GRACES.
WE'LL FIGURE SOMETHING OUT...

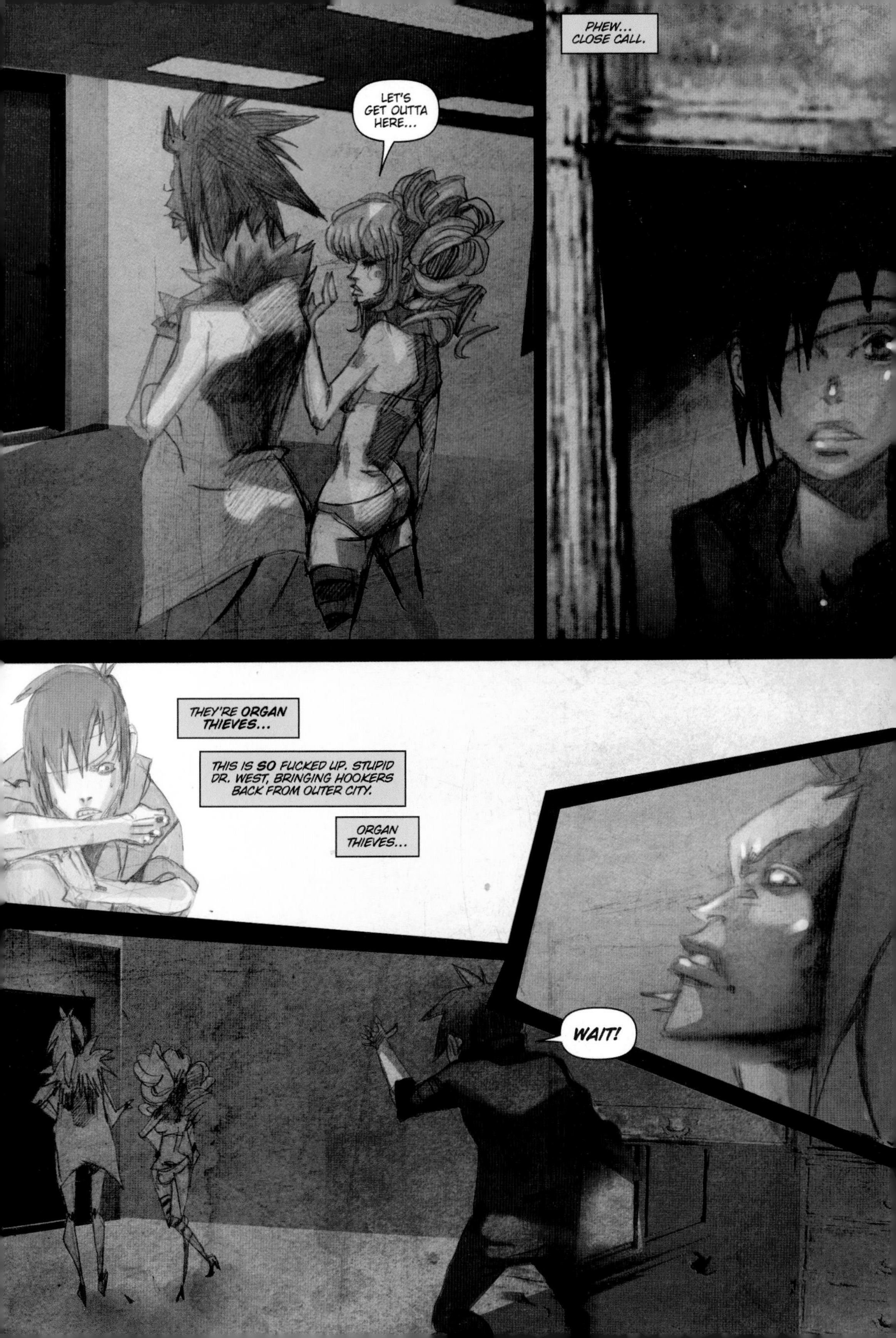
LET'S GET OUTTA HERE...
PHEW... CLOSE CALL.
THEY'RE ORGAN THIEVES...
THIS IS SO FUCKED UP. STUPID DR. WEST, BRINGING HOOKERS BACK FROM OUTER CITY.
ORGAN THIEVES...
WAIT!

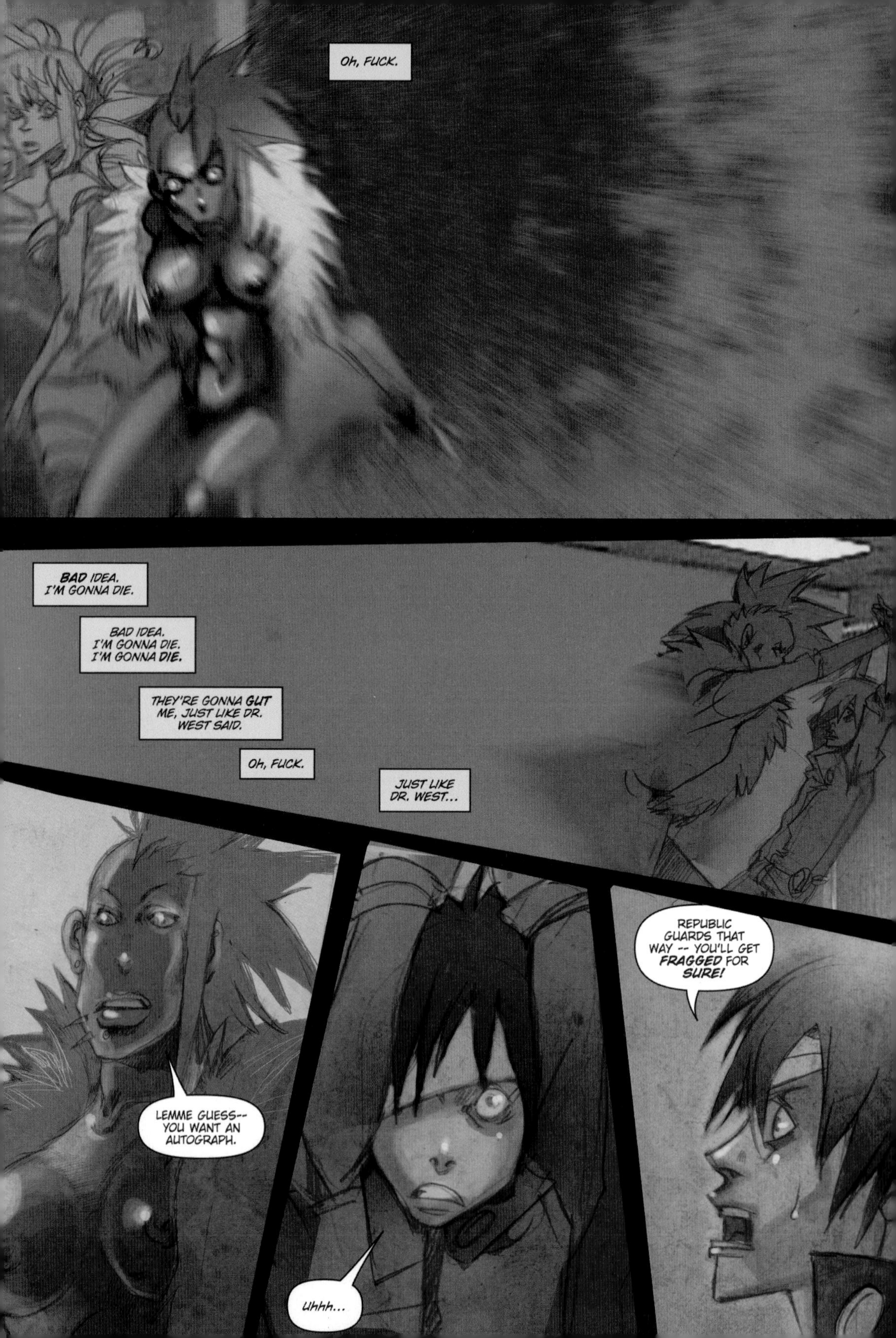
Oh, FUCK.
BAD IDEA. I'M GONNA DIE.
BAD IDEA. I'M GONNA DIE. I'M GONNA DIE.
THEY'RE GONNA GUT ME, JUST LIKE DR. WEST SAID.
Oh, FUCK.
JUST LIKE DR. WEST...
LEMME GUESS-- YOU WANT AN AUTOGRAPH.
Uhhh...
REPUBLIC GUARDS THAT WAY -- YOU'LL GET FRAGGED FOR SURE!

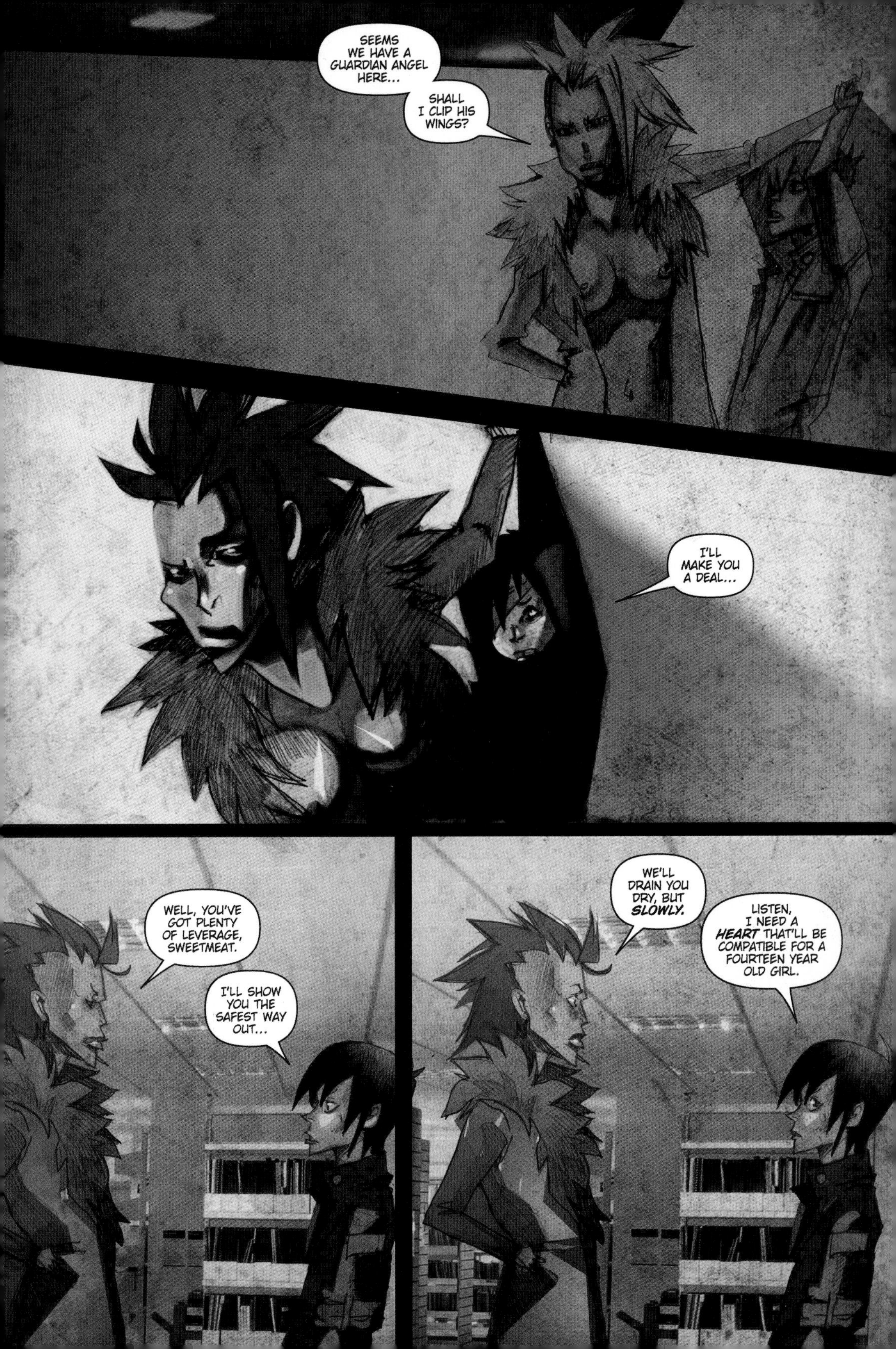
SEEMS WE HAVE A GUARDIAN ANGEL HERE...
SHALL I CLIP HIS WINGS?
I'LL MAKE YOU A DEAL...
WELL, YOU'VE GOT PLENTY OF LEVERAGE, SWEETMEAT.
I'LL SHOW YOU THE SAFEST WAY OUT...
WE'LL DRAIN YOU DRY, BUT SLOWLY.
LISTEN, I NEED A HEART THAT'LL BE COMPATIBLE FOR A FOURTEEN YEAR OLD GIRL.

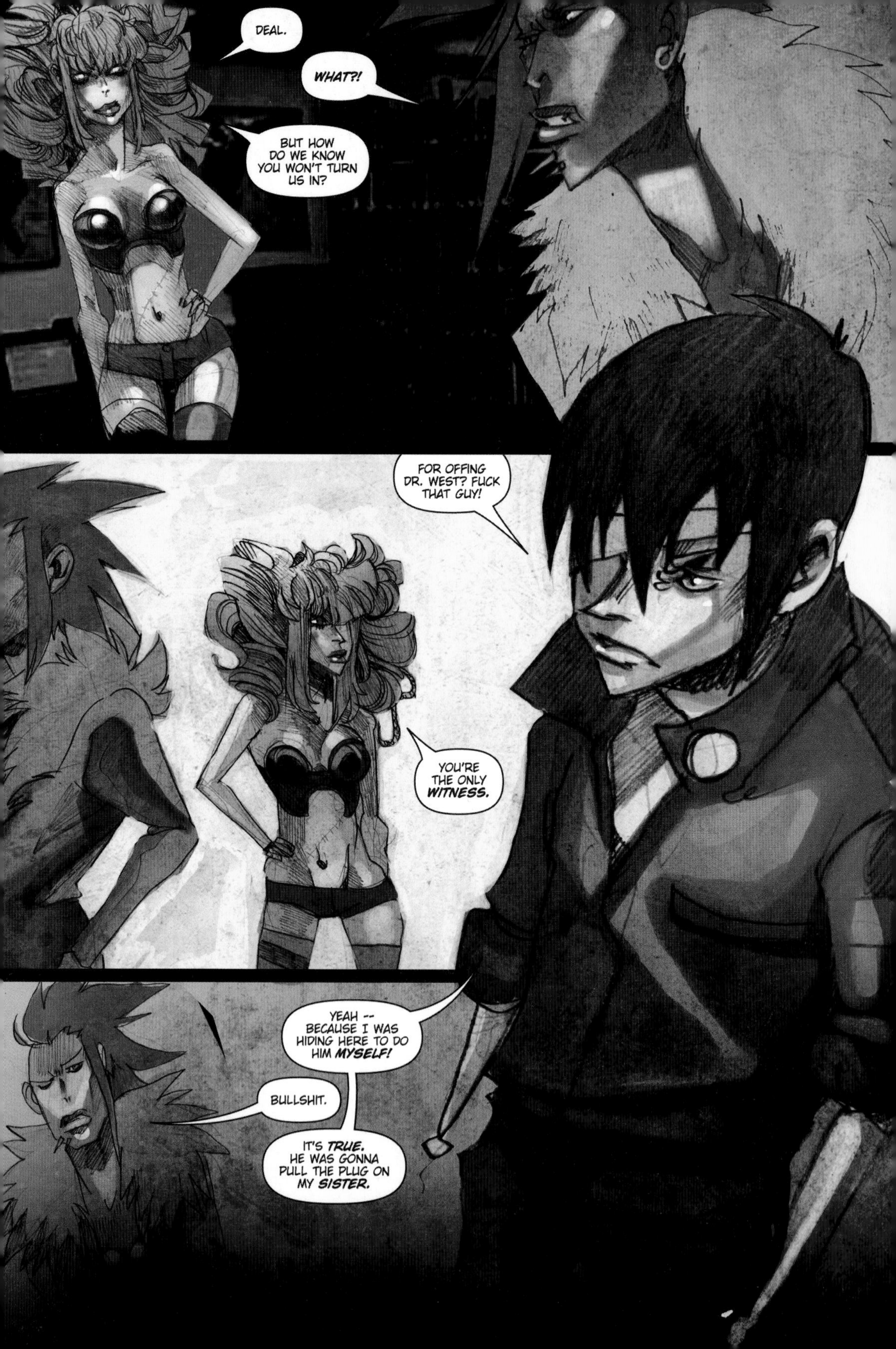
DEAL.
WHAT?!
BUT HOW DO WE KNOW YOU WON'T TURN US IN?
FOR OFFING DR. WEST? FUCK THAT GUY!
YOU'RE THE ONLY WITNESS.
YEAH -- BECAUSE I WAS HIDING HERE TO DO HIM MYSELF!
BULLSHIT.
IT'S TRUE. HE WAS GONNA PULL THE PLUG ON MY SISTER.

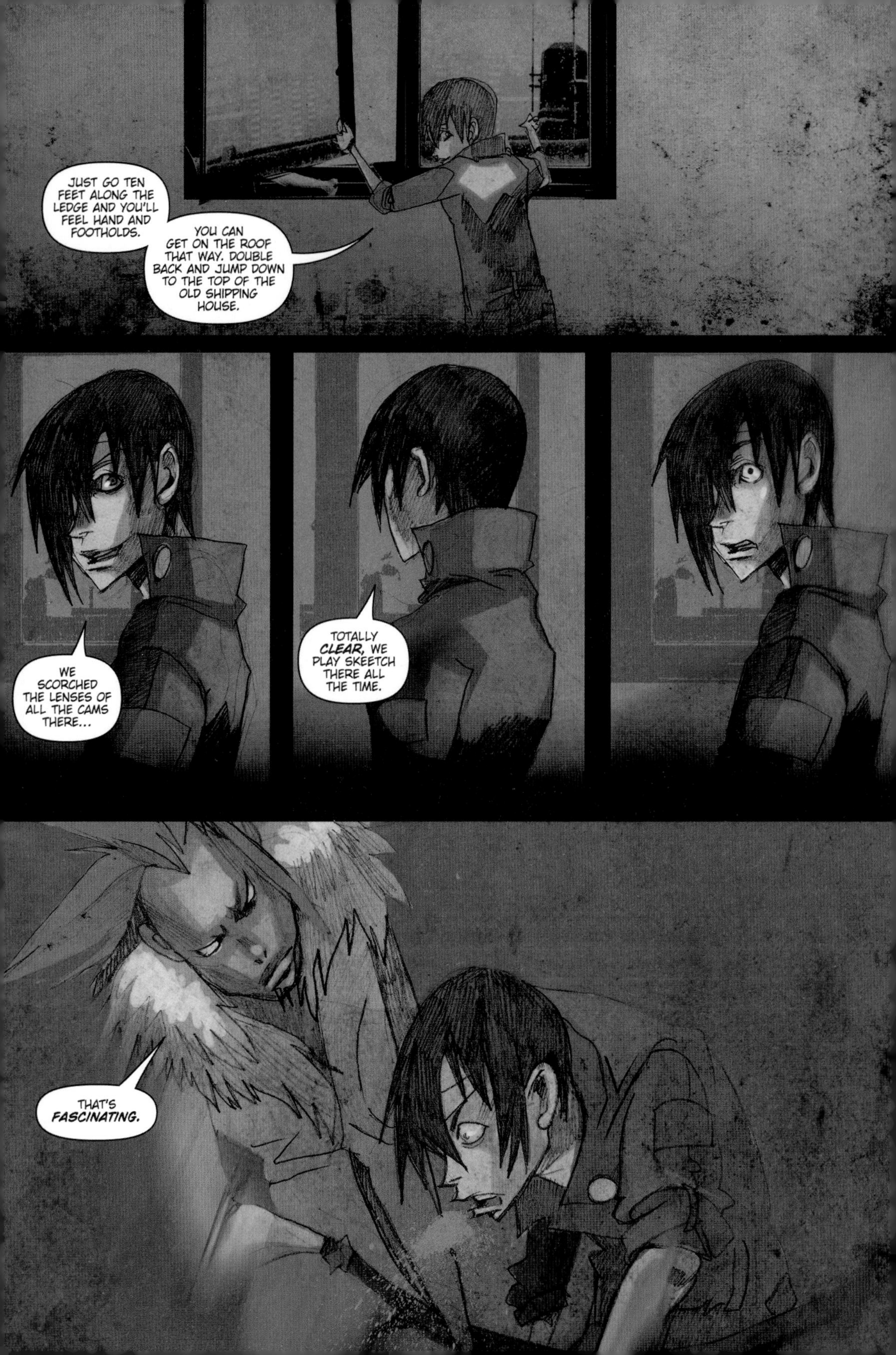
JUST GO TEN FEET ALONG THE LEDGE AND YOU'LL FEEL HAND AND FOOTHOLDS.
YOU CAN GET ON THE ROOF THAT WAY. DOUBLE BACK AND JUMP DOWN TO THE TOP OF THE OLD SHIPPING HOUSE.
WE SCORCHED THE LENSES OF ALL THE CAMS THERE...
TOTALLY *CLEAR,* WE PLAY SKEETCH THERE ALL THE TIME.
THAT'S *FASCINATING.*

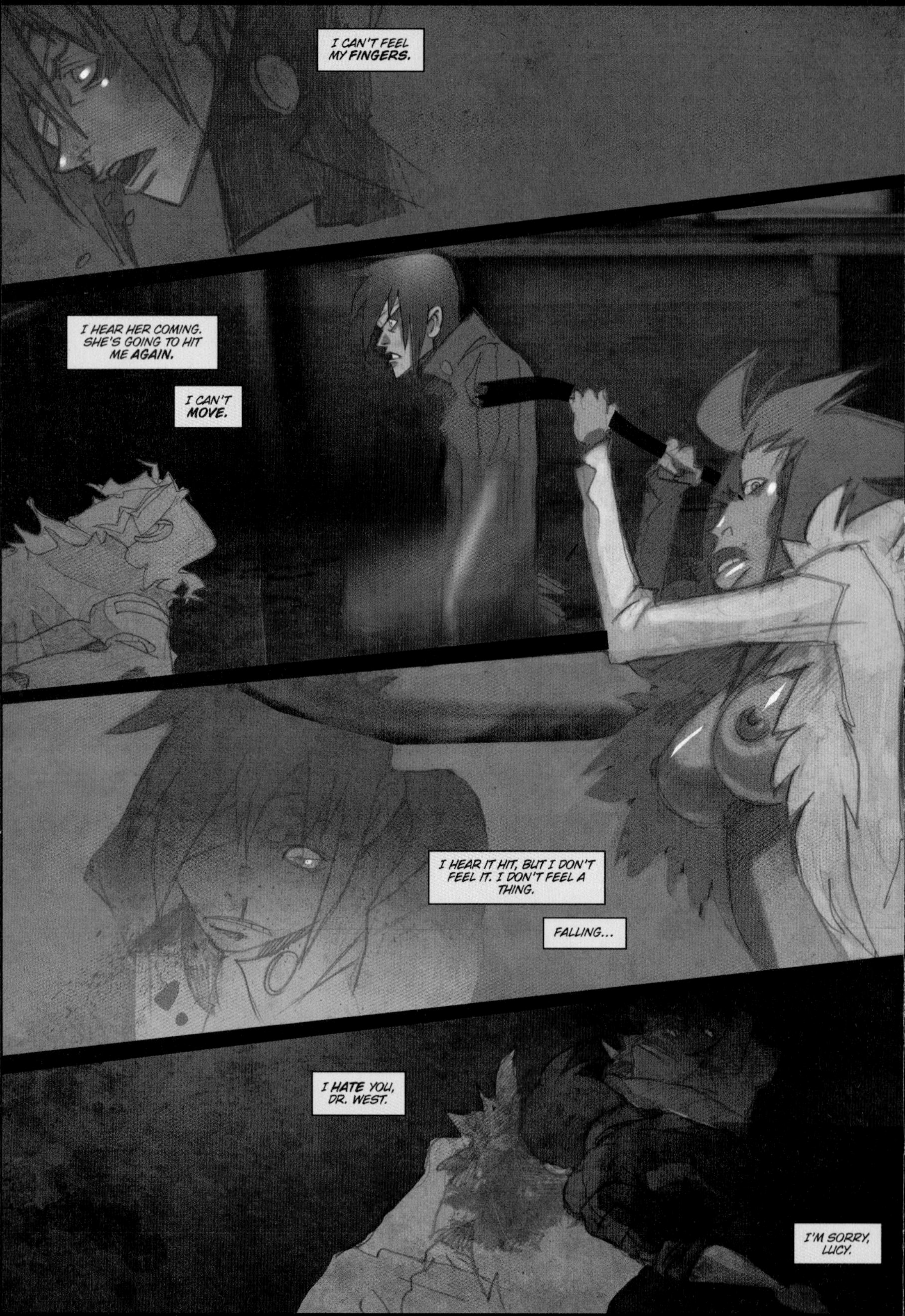
I CAN'T FEEL MY FINGERS.
I HEAR HER COMING. SHE'S GOING TO HIT ME AGAIN.
I CAN'T MOVE.
I HEAR IT HIT, BUT I DON'T FEEL IT. I DON'T FEEL A THING.
FALLING...
I HATE YOU, DR. WEST.
I'M SORRY, LUCY.

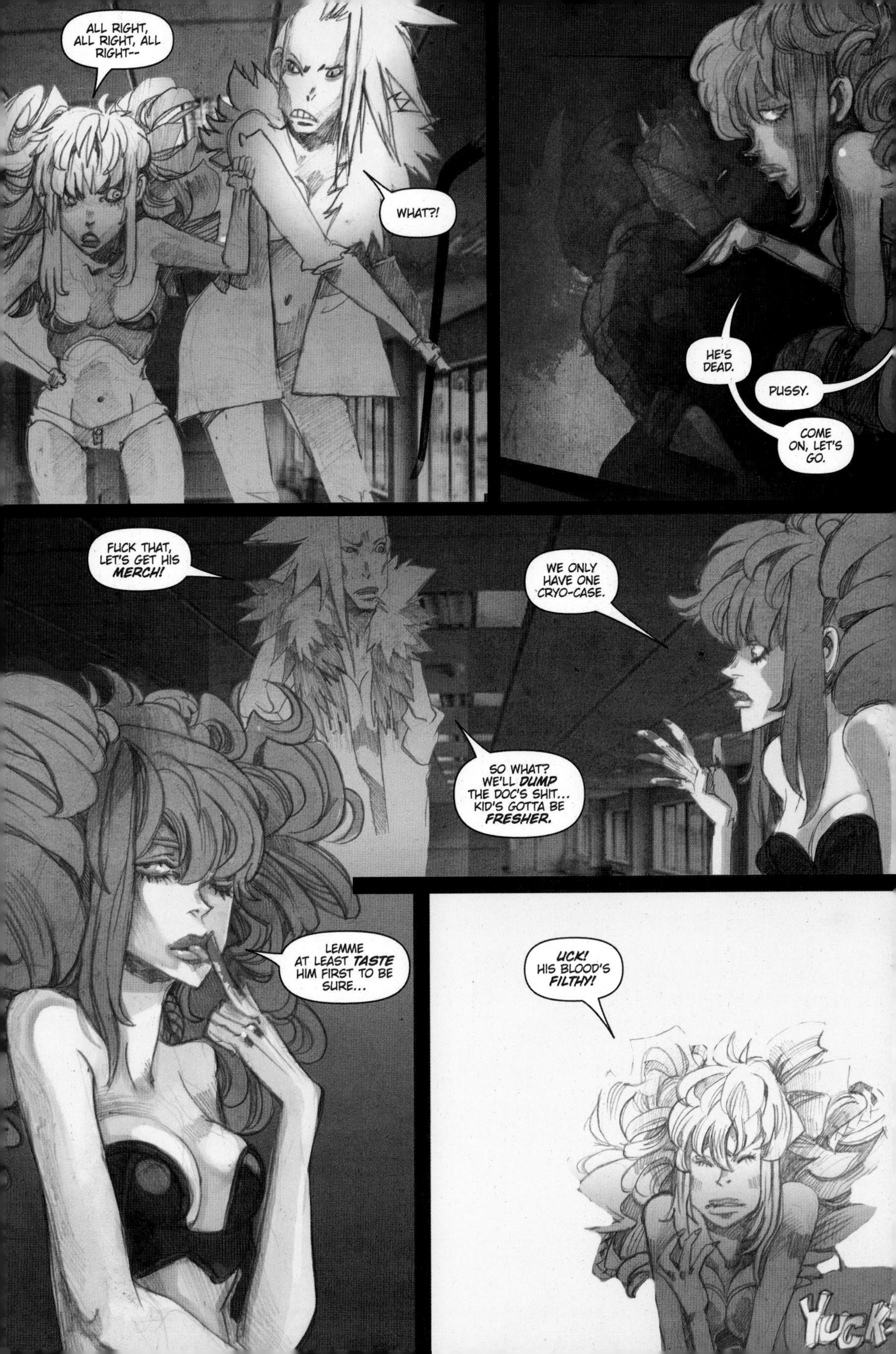
ALL RIGHT, ALL RIGHT, ALL RIGHT--
WHAT?!
HE'S DEAD.
PUSSY.
COME ON, LET'S GO.
FUCK THAT, LET'S GET HIS MERCH!
WE ONLY HAVE ONE CRYO-CASE.
SO WHAT? WE'LL DUMP THE DOC'S SHIT... KID'S GOTTA BE FRESHER.
LEMME AT LEAST TASTE HIM FIRST TO BE SURE...
UCK! HIS BLOOD'S FILTHY!
YUCK

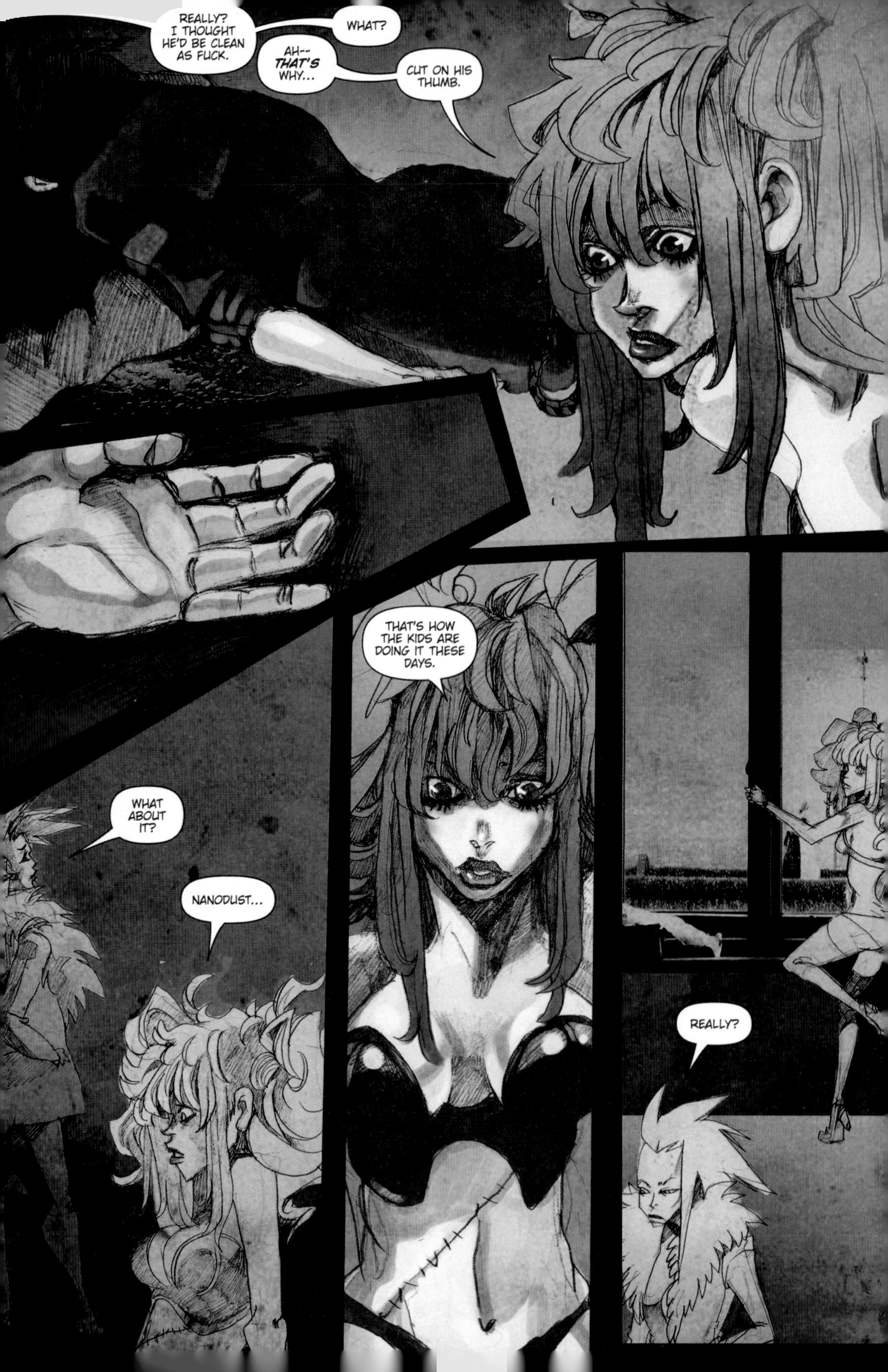
REALLY? I THOUGHT HE'D BE CLEAN AS FUCK.
WHAT?
AH-- THAT'S WHY...
CUT ON HIS THUMB.
THAT'S HOW THE KIDS ARE DOING IT THESE DAYS.
WHAT ABOUT IT?
NANODUST...
REALLY?

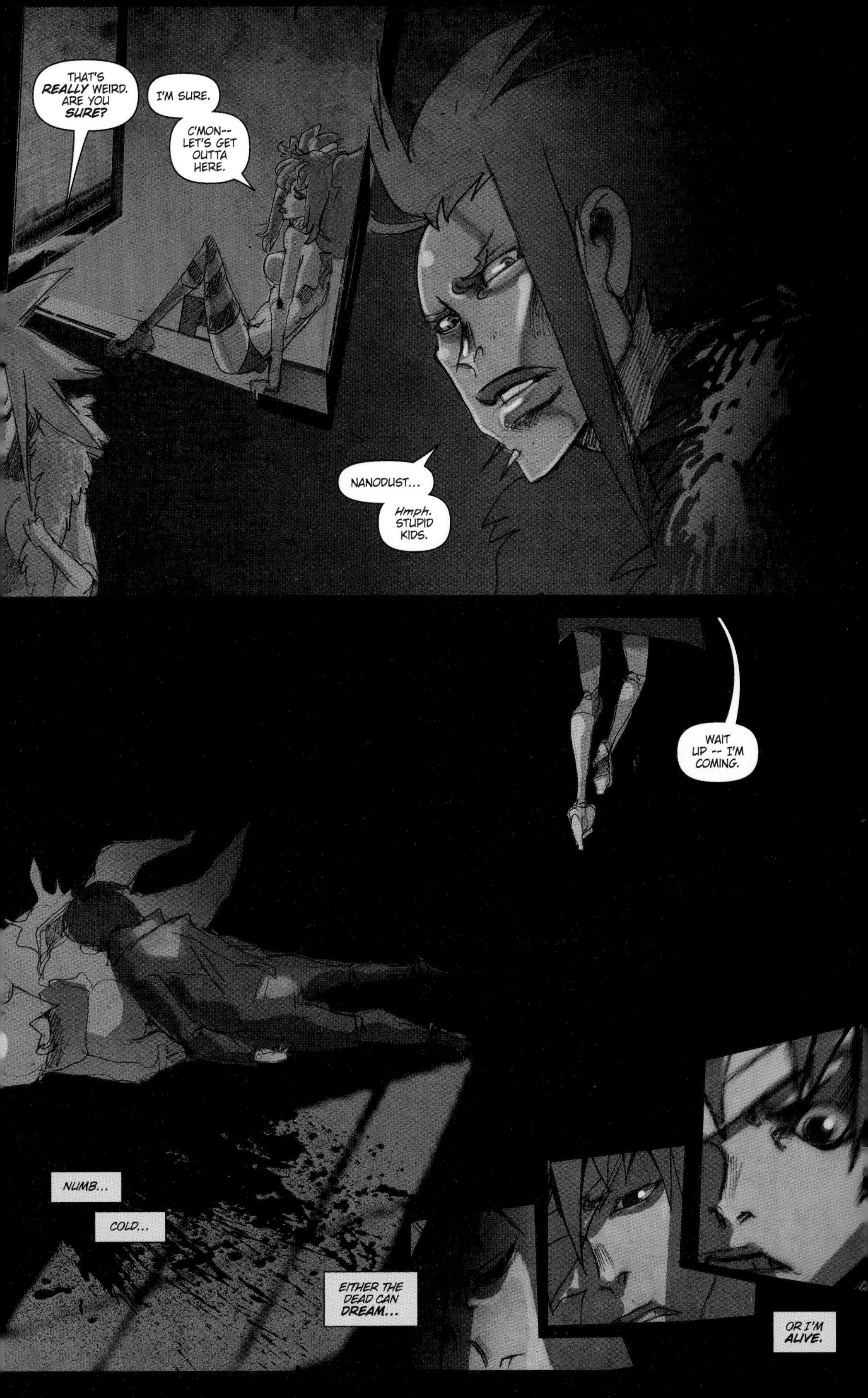
THAT'S *REALLY* WEIRD. ARE YOU *SURE?*
I'M SURE.
C'MON-- LET'S GET OUTTA HERE.
NANODUST...
Hmph. STUPID KIDS.
WAIT UP -- I'M COMING.
NUMB...
COLD...
EITHER THE DEAD CAN *DREAM...*
OR I'M *ALIVE.*

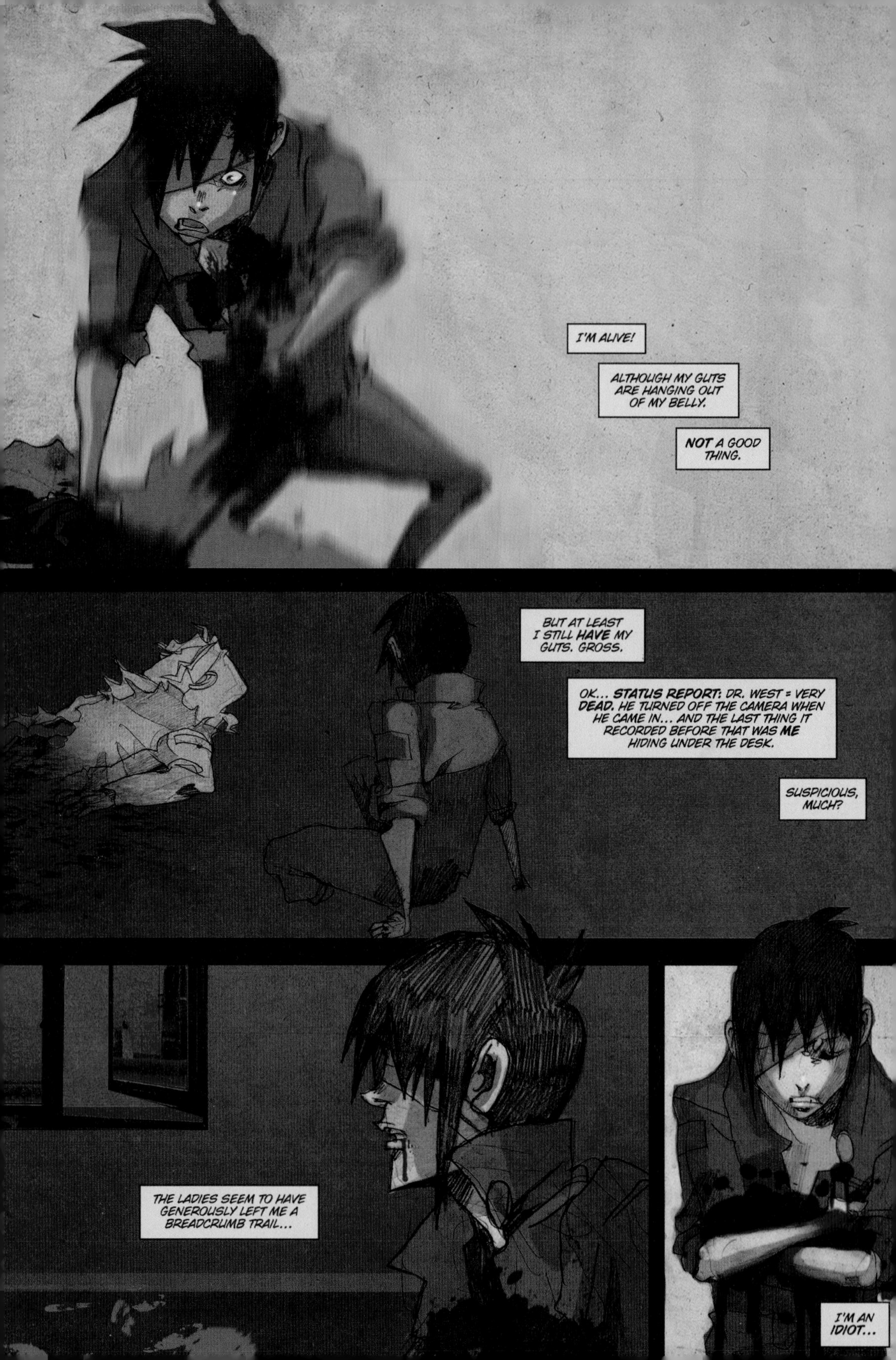
I'M ALIVE!
ALTHOUGH MY GUTS ARE HANGING OUT OF MY BELLY.
NOT A GOOD THING.
BUT AT LEAST I STILL HAVE MY GUTS. GROSS.
OK... STATUS REPORT: DR. WEST = VERY DEAD. HE TURNED OFF THE CAMERA WHEN HE CAME IN... AND THE LAST THING IT RECORDED BEFORE THAT WAS ME HIDING UNDER THE DESK.
SUSPICIOUS, MUCH?
THE LADIES SEEM TO HAVE GENEROUSLY LEFT ME A BREADCRUMB TRAIL...
I'M AN IDIOT...

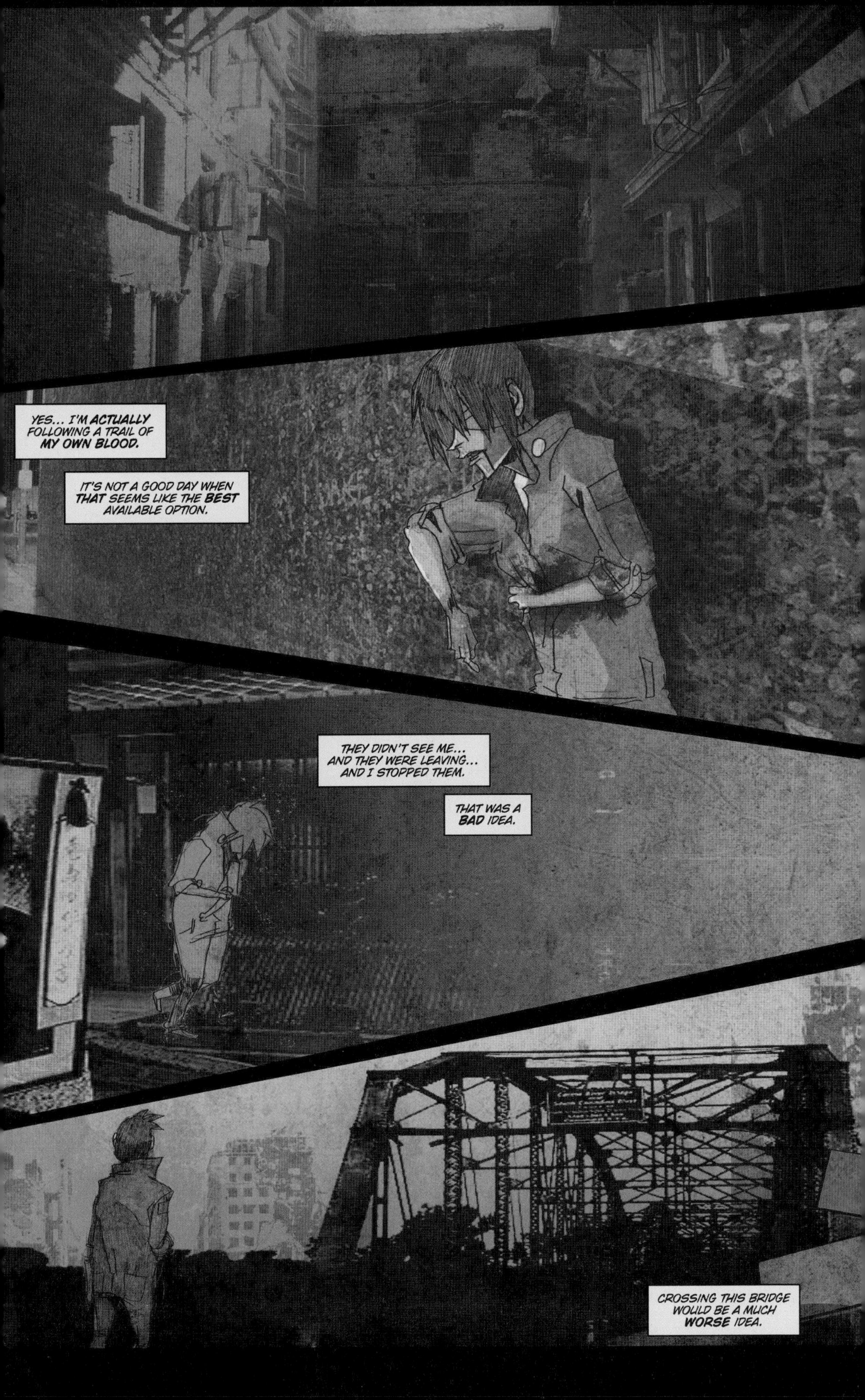

YES... I'M ACTUALLY FOLLOWING A TRAIL OF MY OWN BLOOD.
IT'S NOT A GOOD DAY WHEN THAT SEEMS LIKE THE BEST AVAILABLE OPTION.
THEY DIDN'T SEE ME... AND THEY WERE LEAVING... AND I STOPPED THEM.
THAT WAS A BAD IDEA.
CROSSING THIS BRIDGE WOULD BE A MUCH WORSE IDEA.

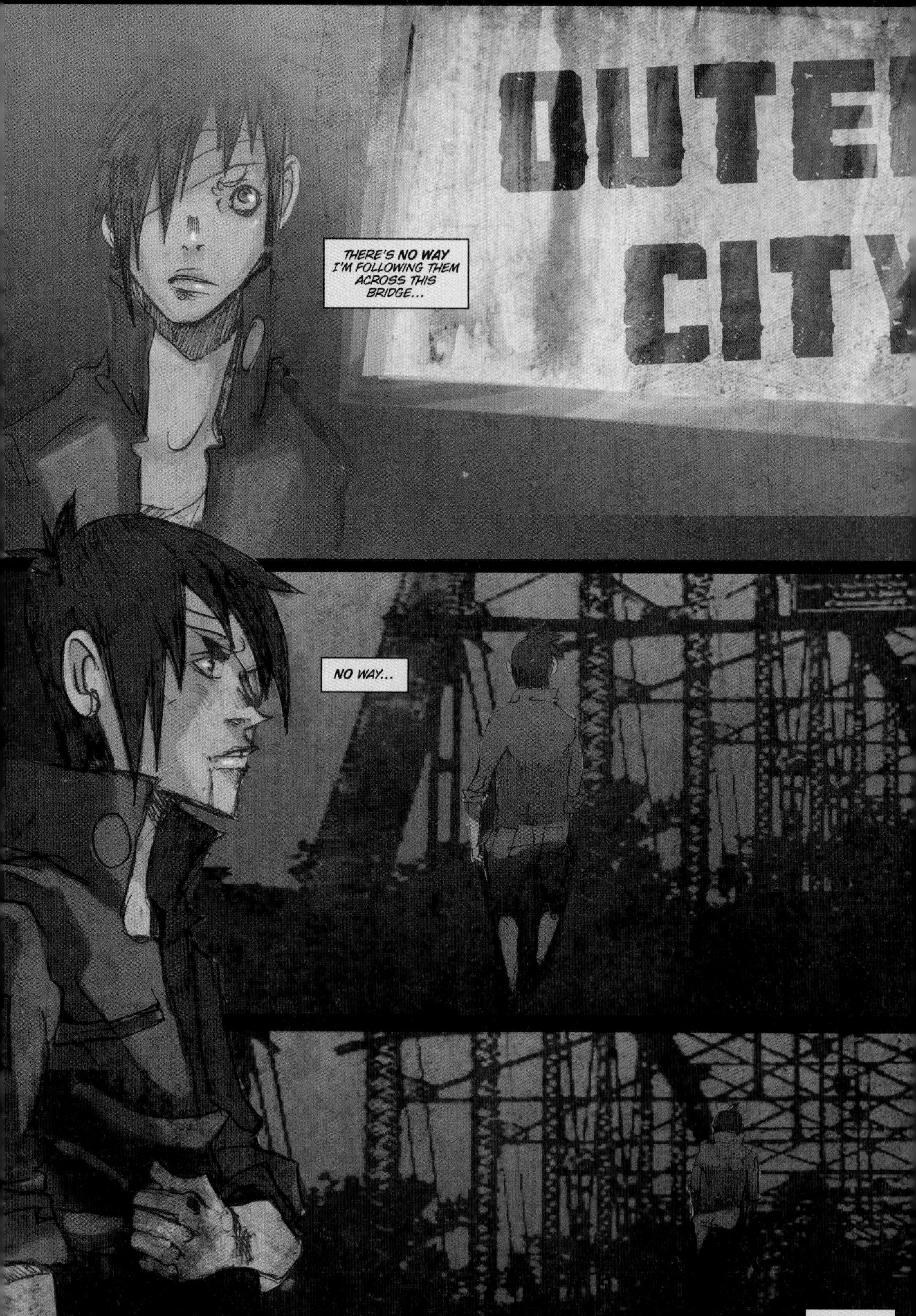
OUTE
CITY
THERE'S NO WAY I'M FOLLOWING THEM ACROSS THIS BRIDGE...
NO WAY...
THIS IS A TERRIBLE IDEA.

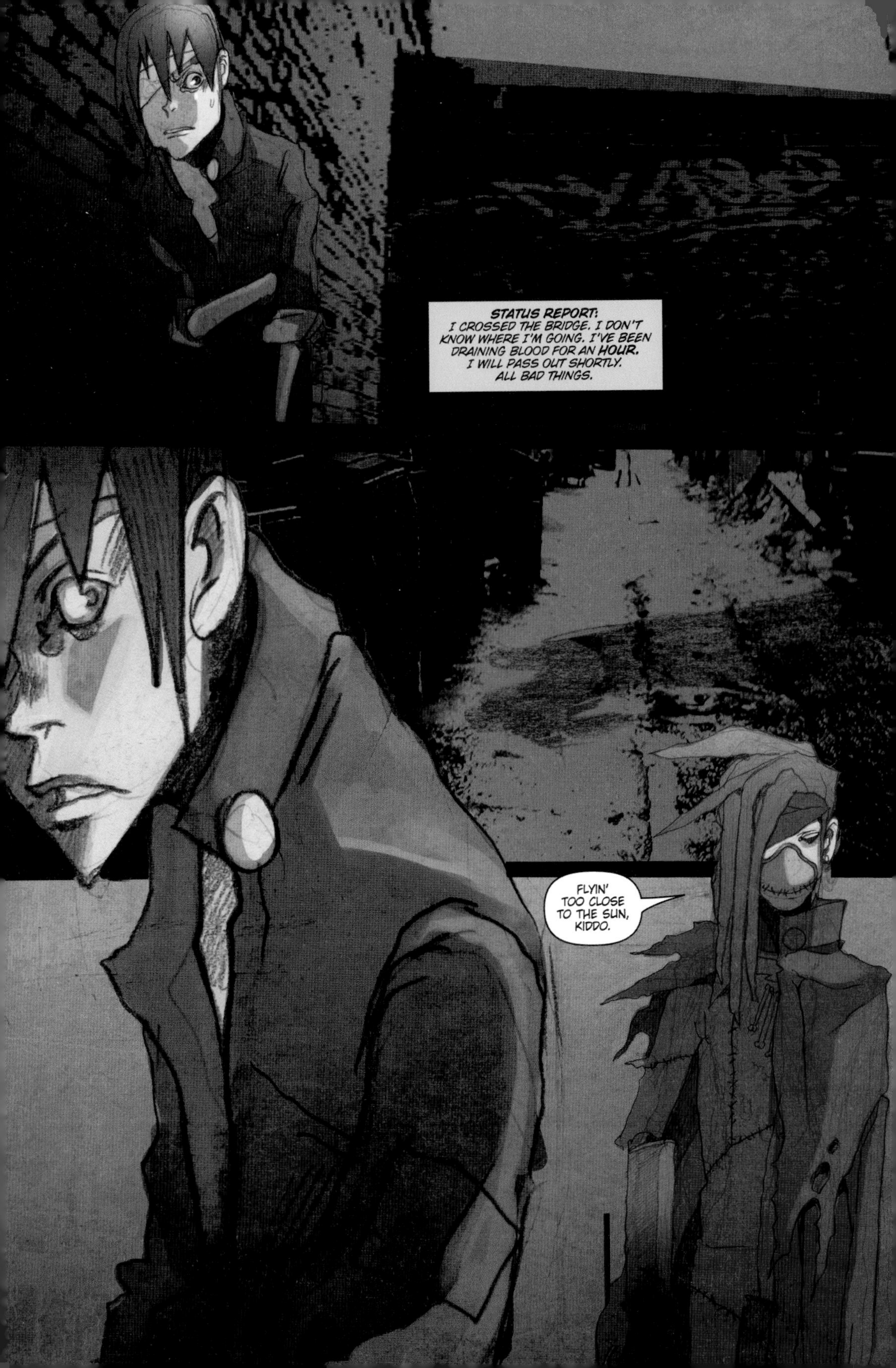
STATUS REPORT:
I CROSSED THE BRIDGE. I DON'T KNOW WHERE I'M GOING. I'VE BEEN DRAINING BLOOD FOR AN HOUR. I WILL PASS OUT SHORTLY. ALL BAD THINGS.
FLYIN' TOO CLOSE TO THE SUN, KIDDO.

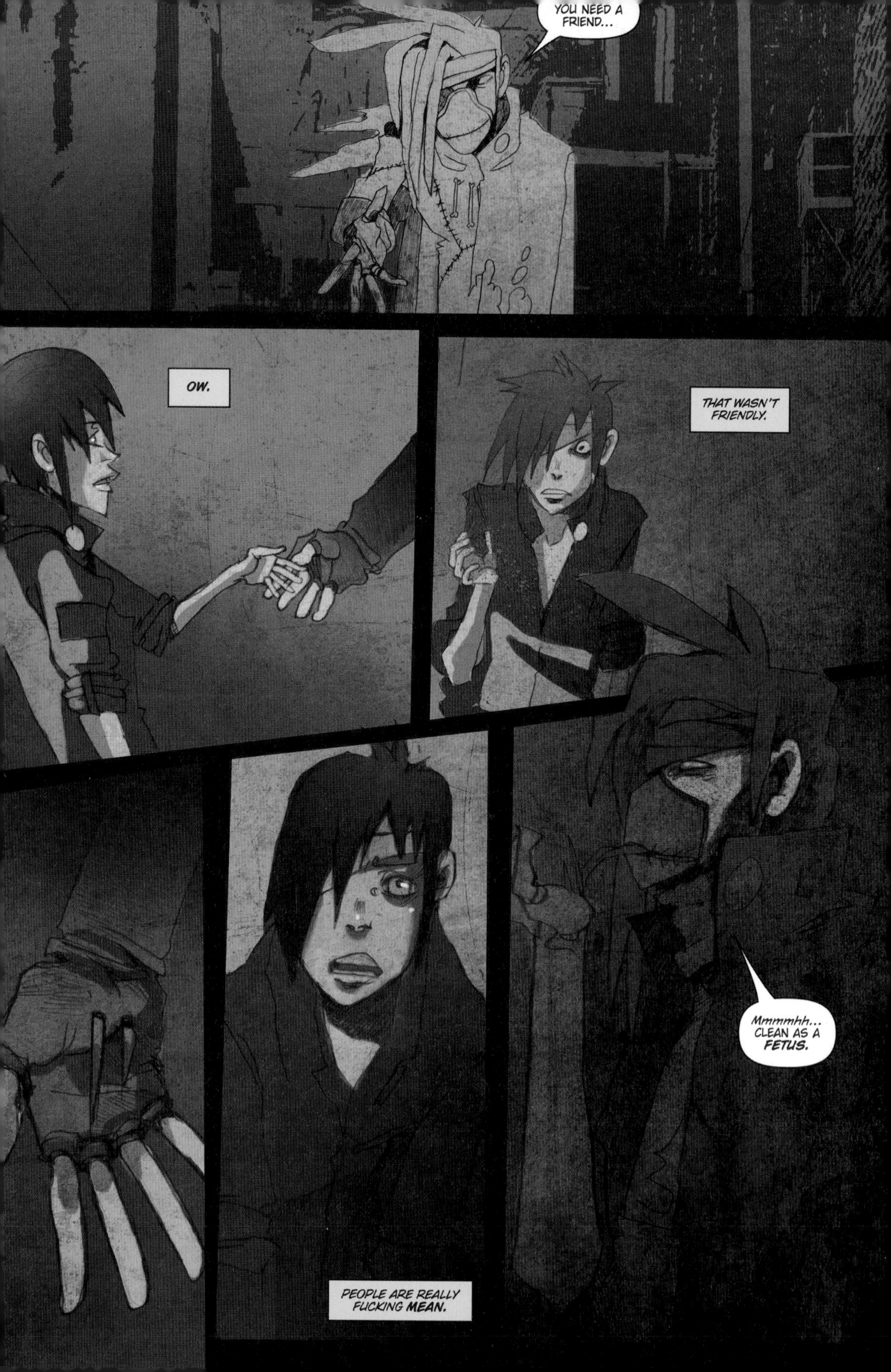
YOU NEED A FRIEND...
OW.
THAT WASN'T FRIENDLY.
Mmmmhh... CLEAN AS A **FETUS.**
PEOPLE ARE REALLY FUCKING **MEAN.**

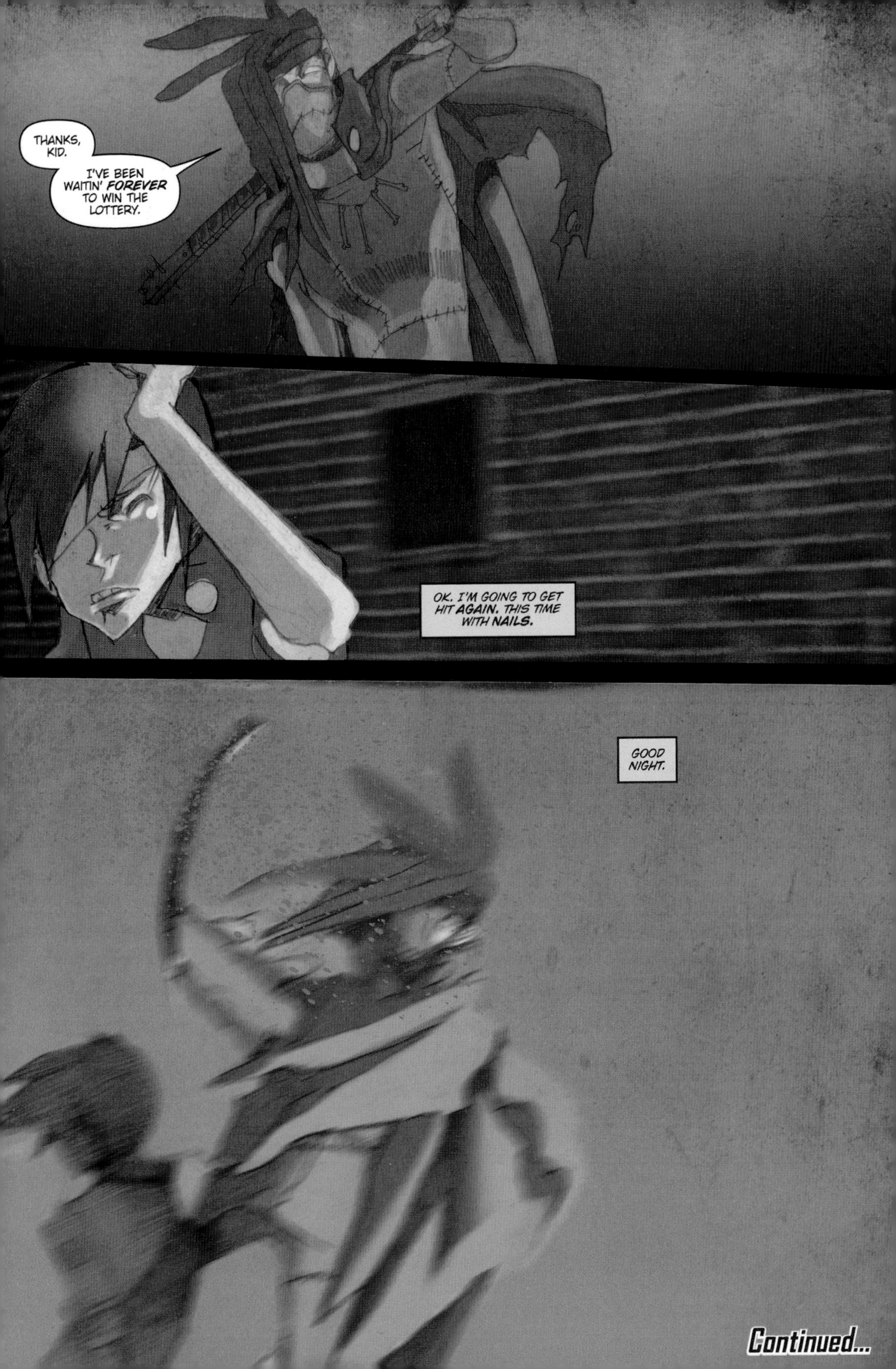
THANKS, KID.
I'VE BEEN WAITIN' FOREVER TO WIN THE LOTTERY.
OK. I'M GOING TO GET HIT AGAIN. THIS TIME WITH NAILS.
GOOD NIGHT.
Continued...

NOTHING
IS
TRUE

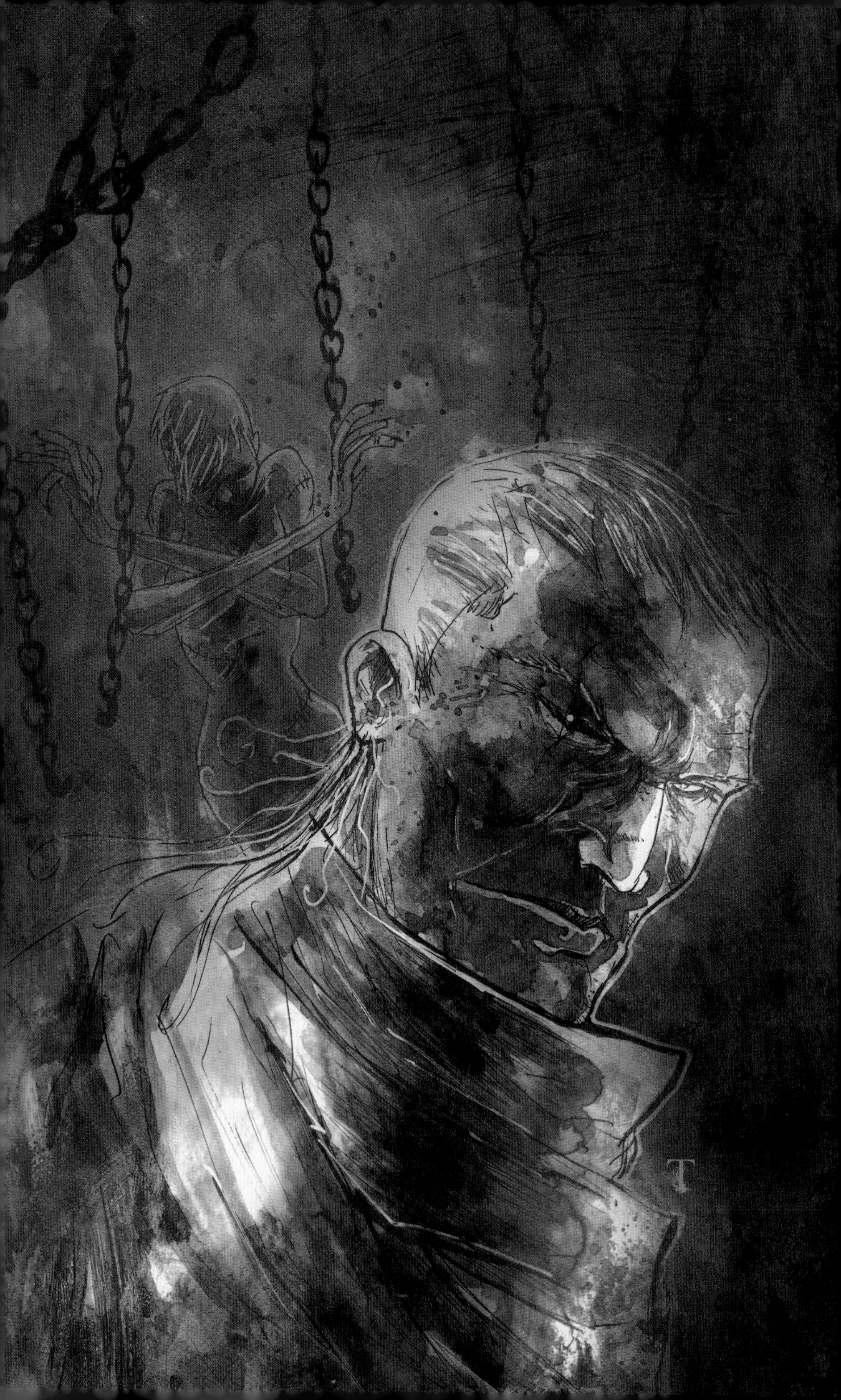

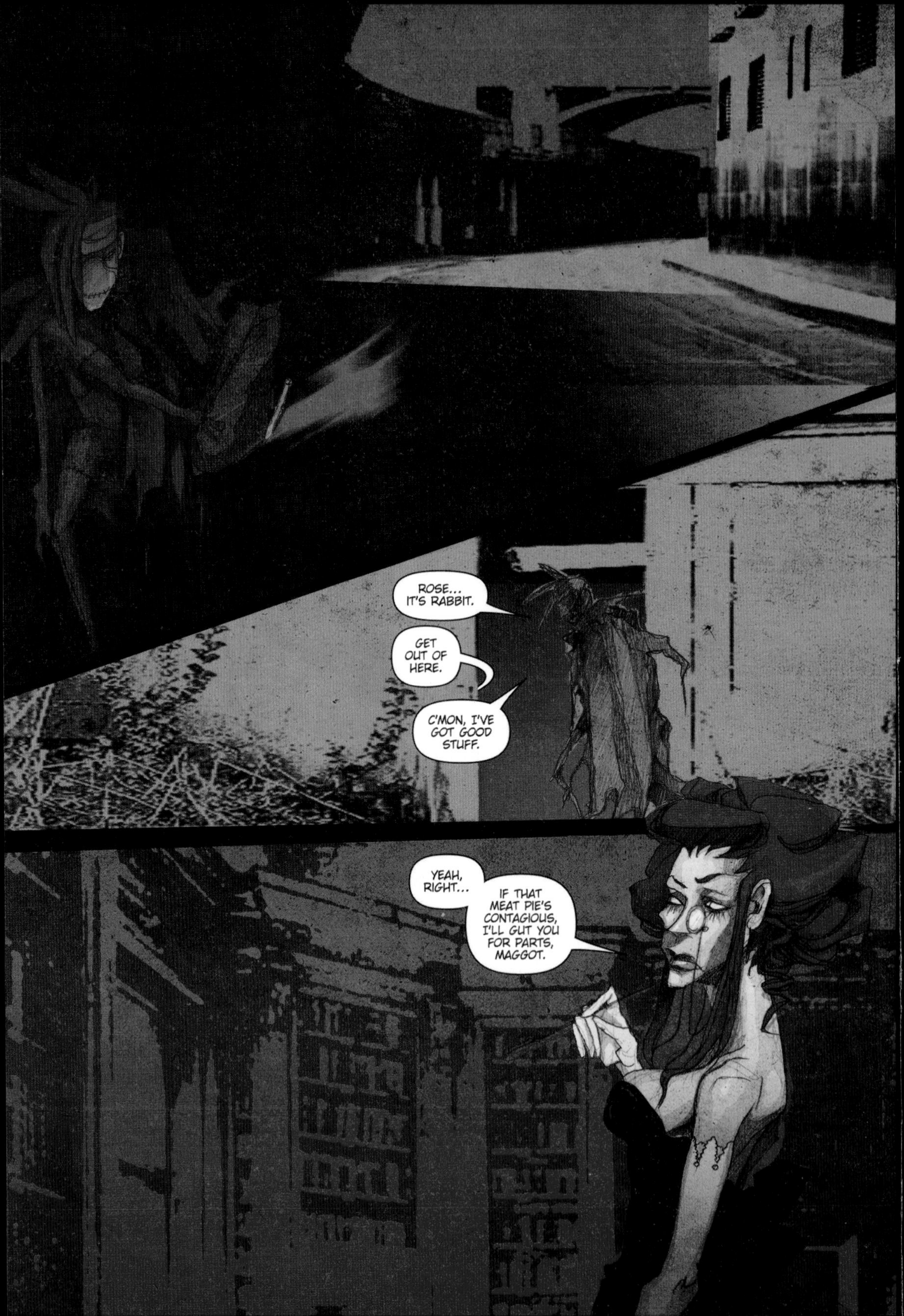
ROSE... IT'S RABBIT.
GET OUT OF HERE.
C'MON, I'VE GOT GOOD STUFF.
YEAH, RIGHT...
IF THAT MEAT PIE'S CONTAGIOUS, I'LL GUT YOU FOR PARTS, MAGGOT.

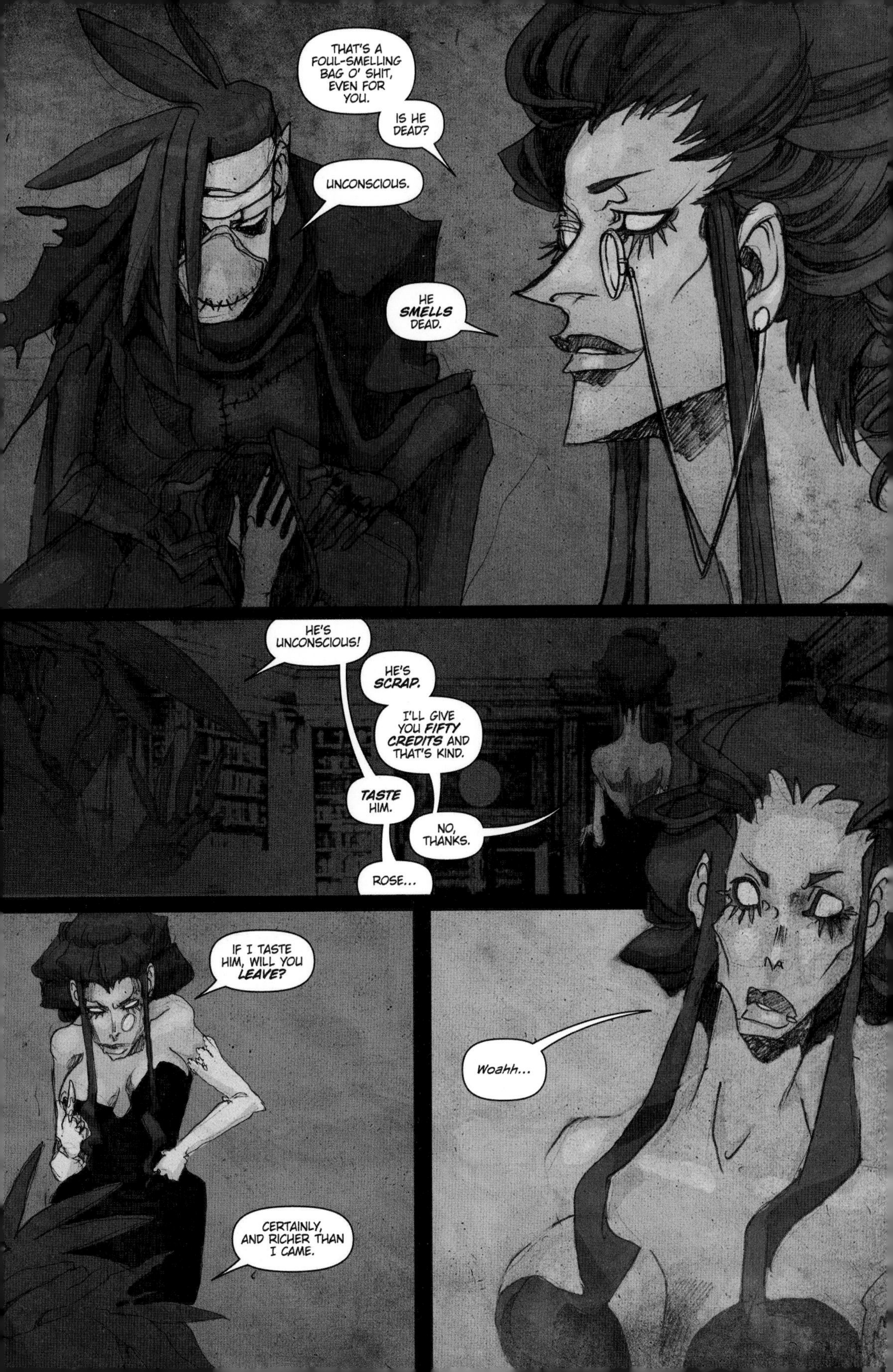
THAT'S A FOUL-SMELLING BAG O' SHIT, EVEN FOR YOU.
IS HE DEAD?
UNCONSCIOUS.
HE *SMELLS* DEAD.
HE'S UNCONSCIOUS!
HE'S *SCRAP.*
I'LL GIVE YOU *FIFTY CREDITS* AND THAT'S KIND.
TASTE HIM.
NO, THANKS.
ROSE...
IF I TASTE HIM, WILL YOU *LEAVE?*
CERTAINLY, AND RICHER THAN I CAME.
Woahh...

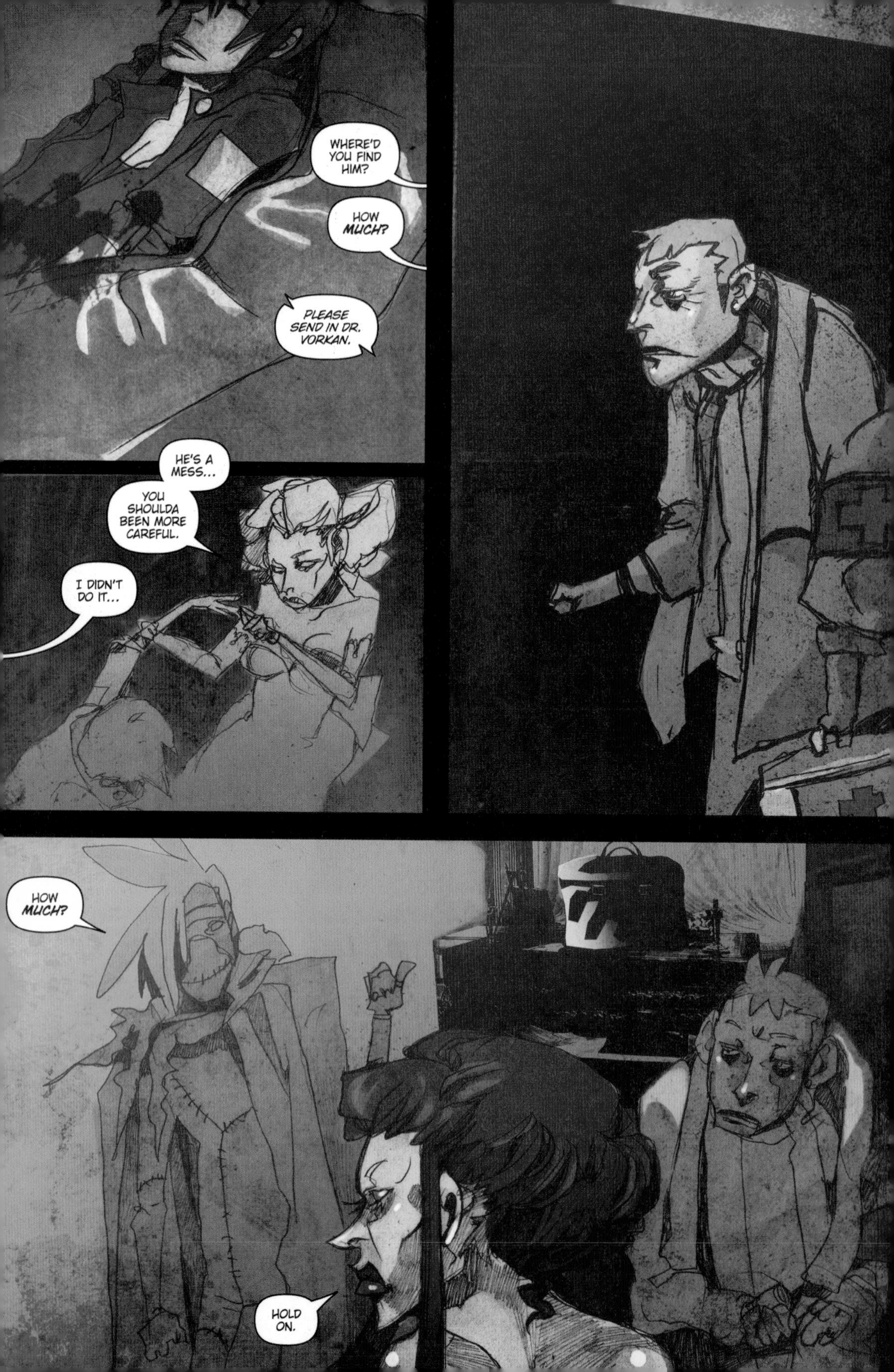
WHERE'D YOU FIND HIM?
HOW MUCH?
PLEASE SEND IN DR. VORKAN.
HE'S A MESS...
YOU SHOULDA BEEN MORE CAREFUL.
I DIDN'T DO IT...
HOW MUCH?
HOLD ON.

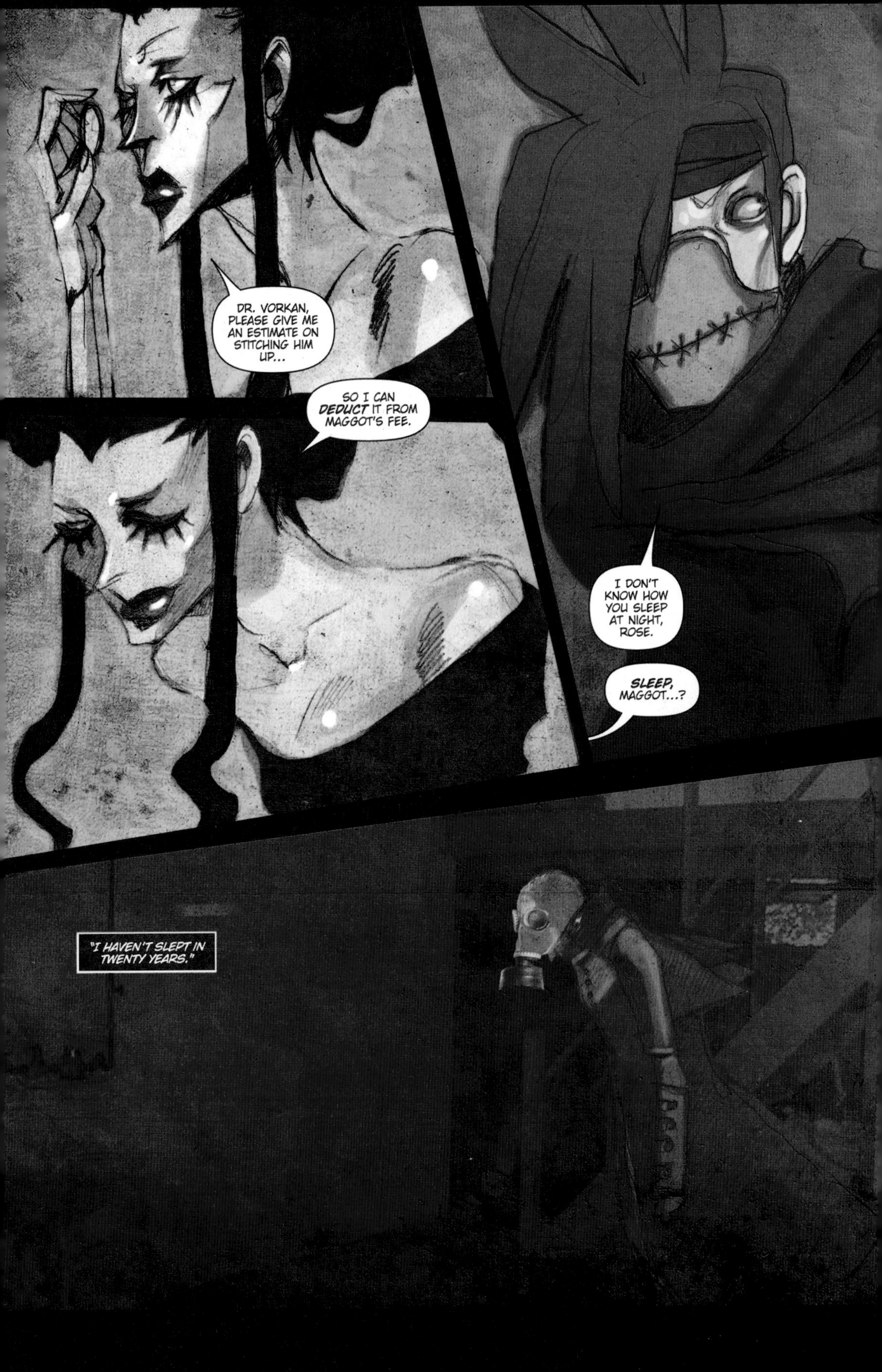
DR. VORKAN, PLEASE GIVE ME AN ESTIMATE ON STITCHING HIM UP...
SO I CAN DEDUCT IT FROM MAGGOT'S FEE.
I DON'T KNOW HOW YOU SLEEP AT NIGHT, ROSE.
SLEEP, MAGGOT...?
"I HAVEN'T SLEPT IN TWENTY YEARS."

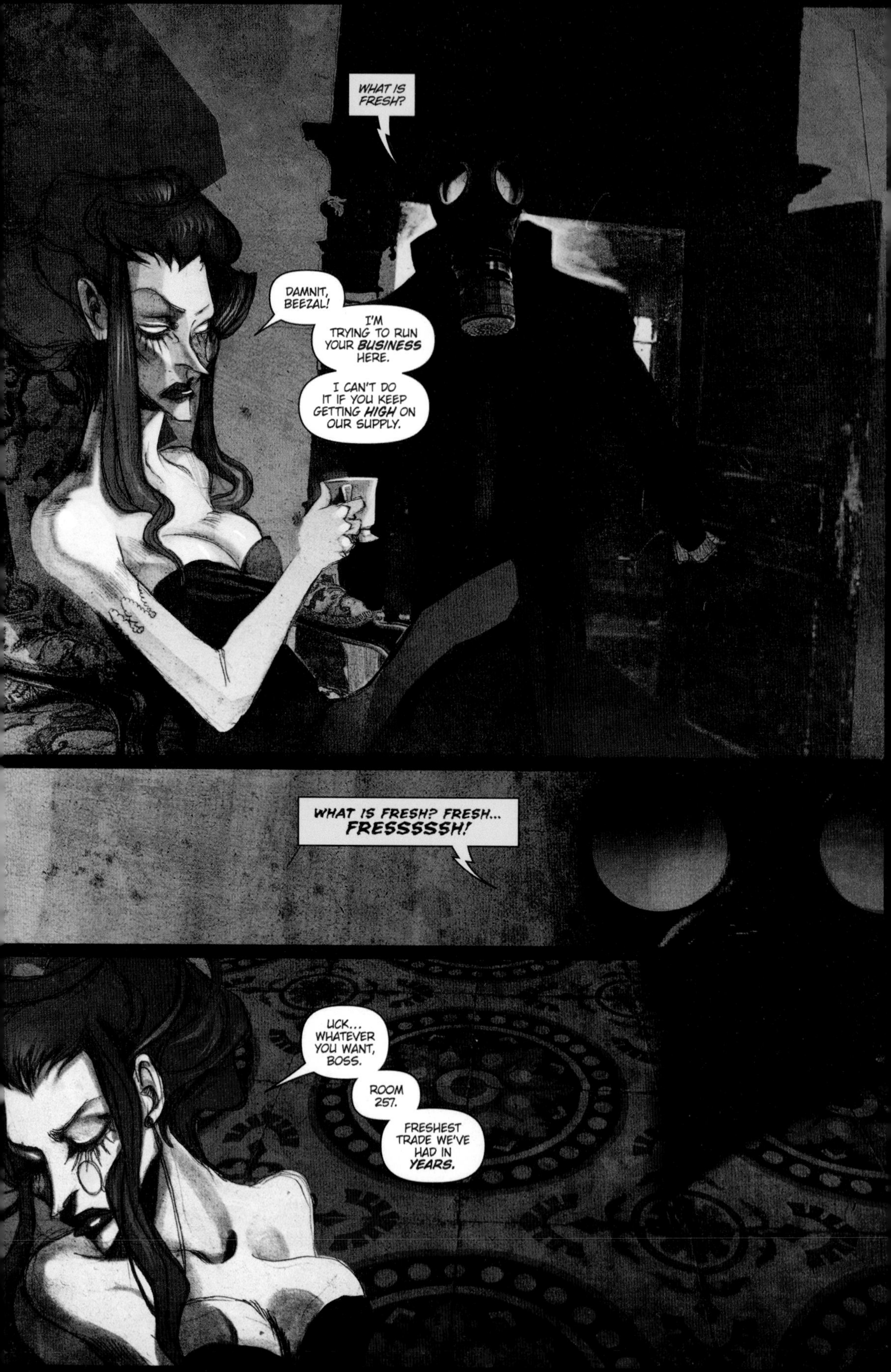
WHAT IS FRESH?
DAMNIT, BEEZAL!
I'M TRYING TO RUN YOUR BUSINESS HERE.
I CAN'T DO IT IF YOU KEEP GETTING HIGH ON OUR SUPPLY.
WHAT IS FRESH? FRESH... FRESSSSSH!
UCK... WHATEVER YOU WANT, BOSS.
ROOM 257.
FRESHEST TRADE WE'VE HAD IN YEARS.

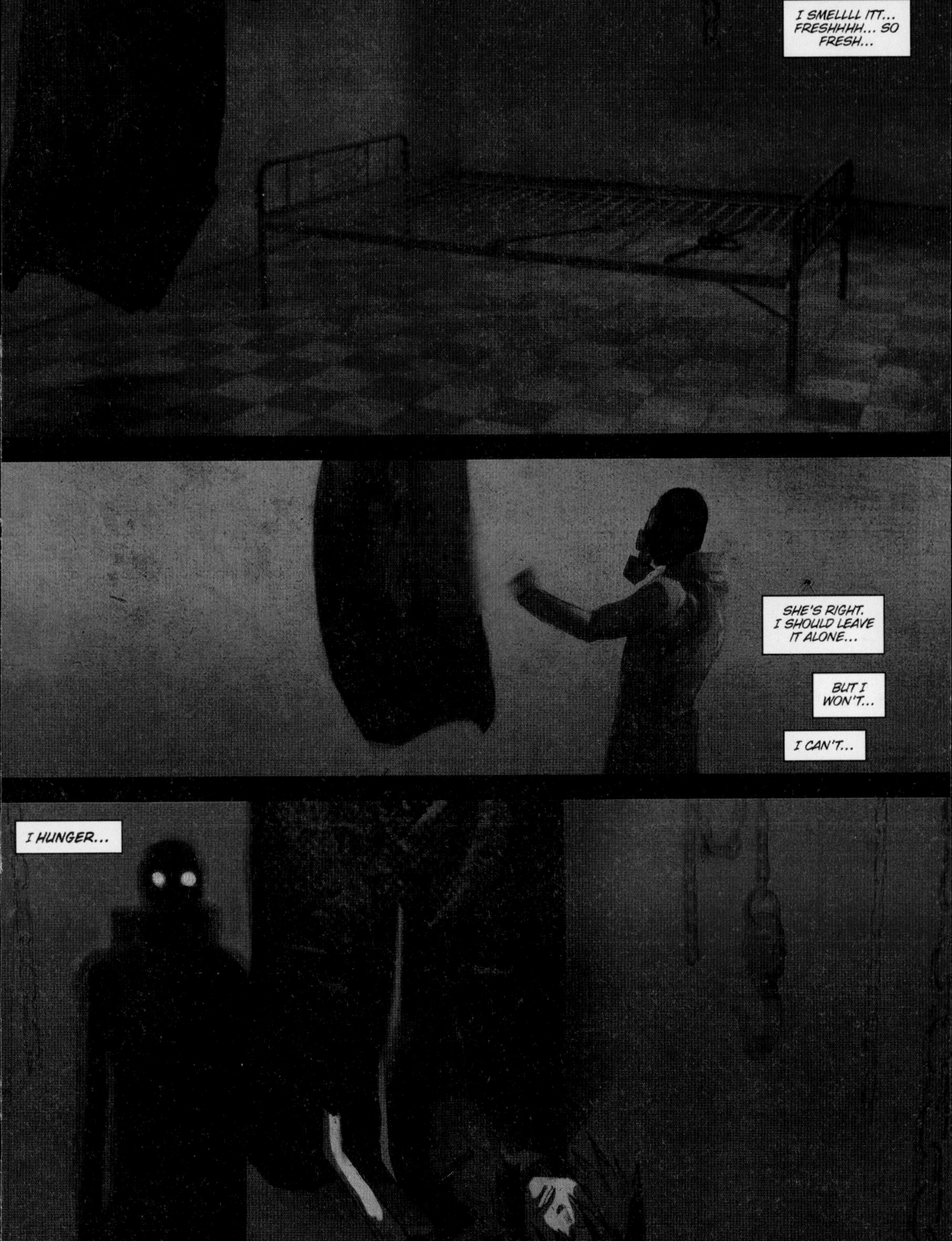
I SMELLLL ITT... FRESHHHH... SO FRESH...
SHE'S RIGHT. I SHOULD LEAVE IT ALONE...
BUT I WON'T...
I CAN'T...
I HUNGER...

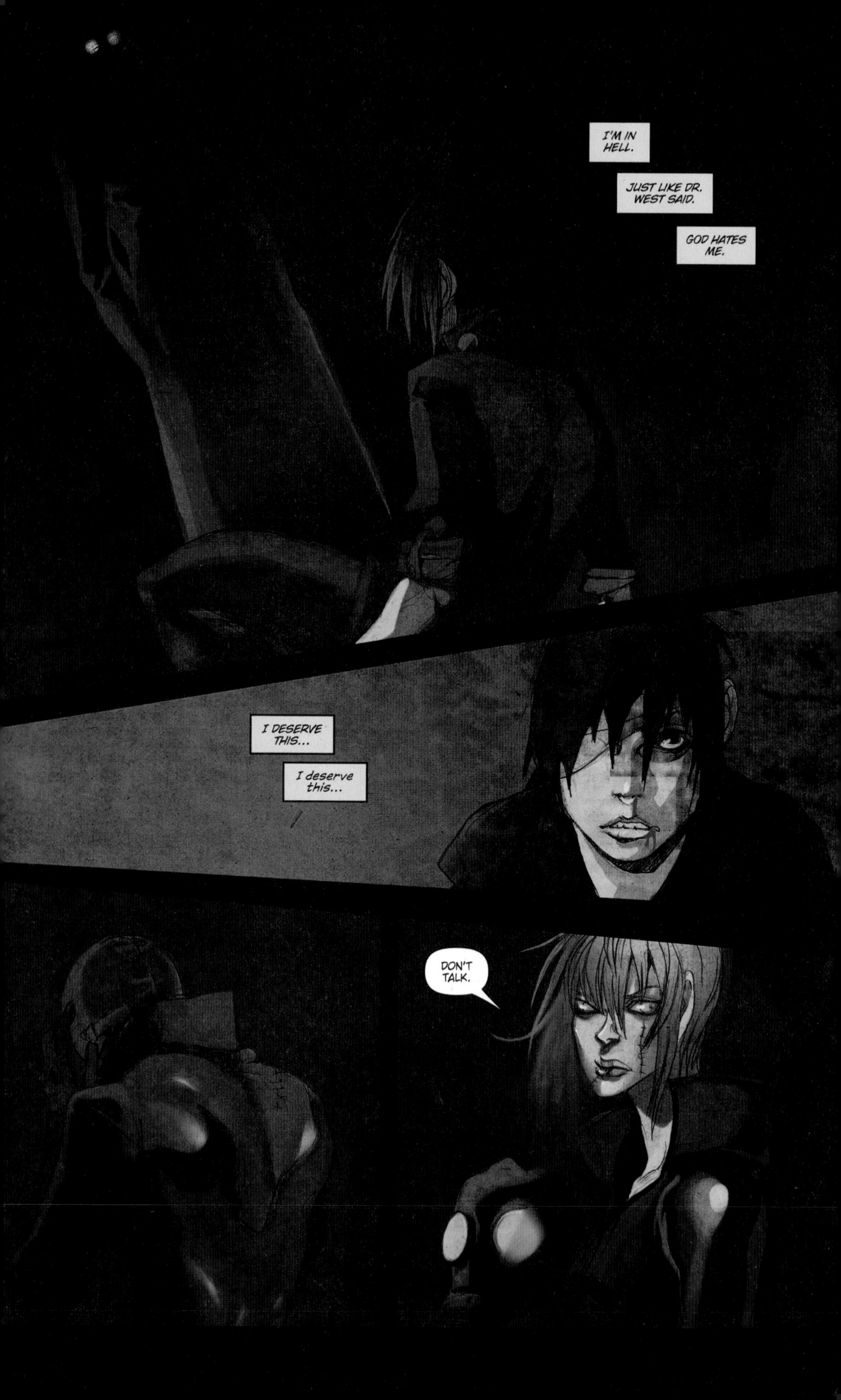
I'M IN HELL.
JUST LIKE DR. WEST SAID.
GOD HATES ME.
I DESERVE THIS...
I deserve this...
DON'T TALK.

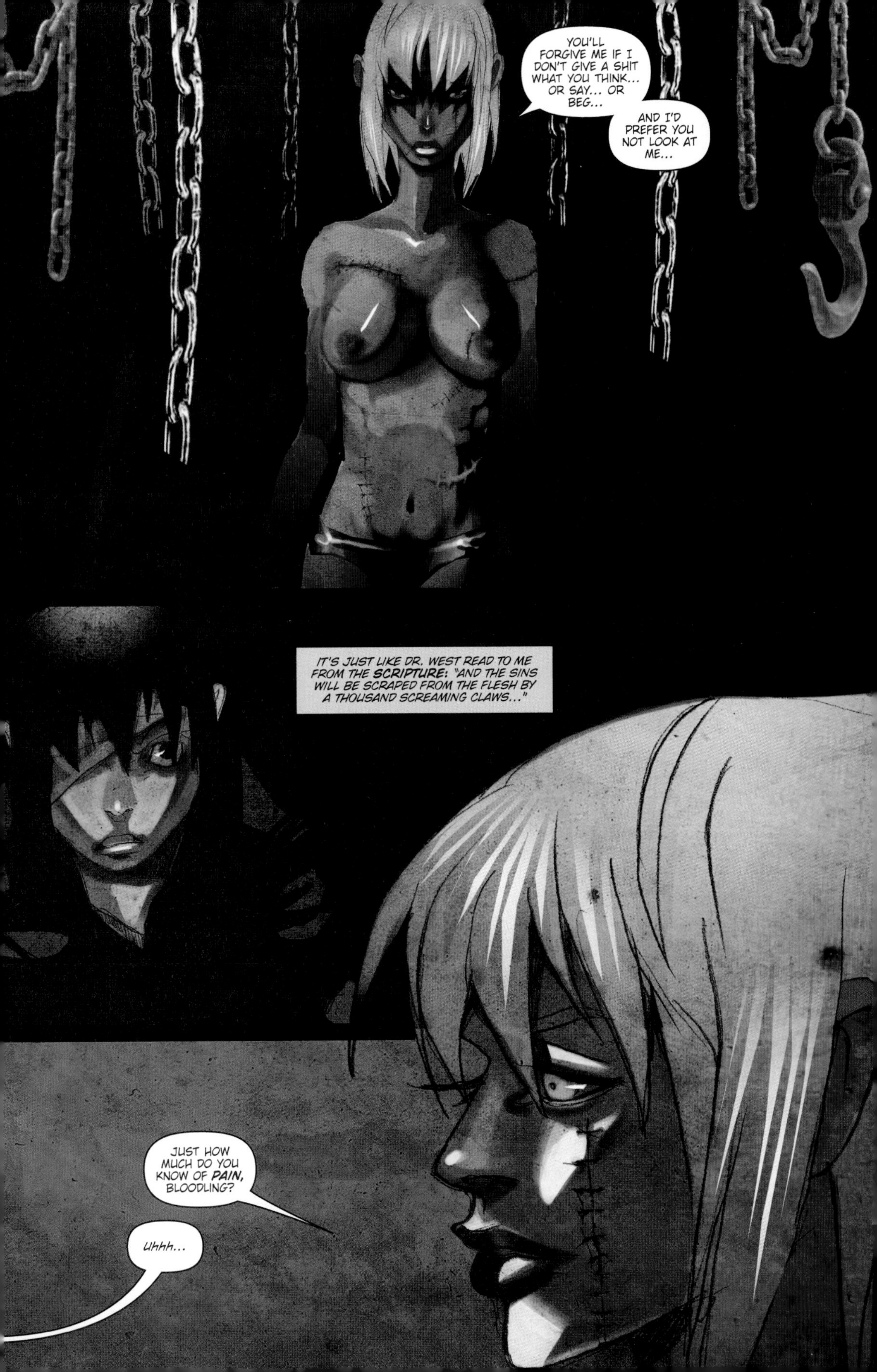
YOU'LL FORGIVE ME IF I DON'T GIVE A SHIT WHAT YOU THINK... OR SAY... OR BEG...
AND I'D PREFER YOU NOT LOOK AT ME...
IT'S JUST LIKE DR. WEST READ TO ME FROM THE SCRIPTURE: "AND THE SINS WILL BE SCRAPED FROM THE FLESH BY A THOUSAND SCREAMING CLAWS..."
JUST HOW MUCH DO YOU KNOW OF PAIN, BLOODLING?
uhhh...

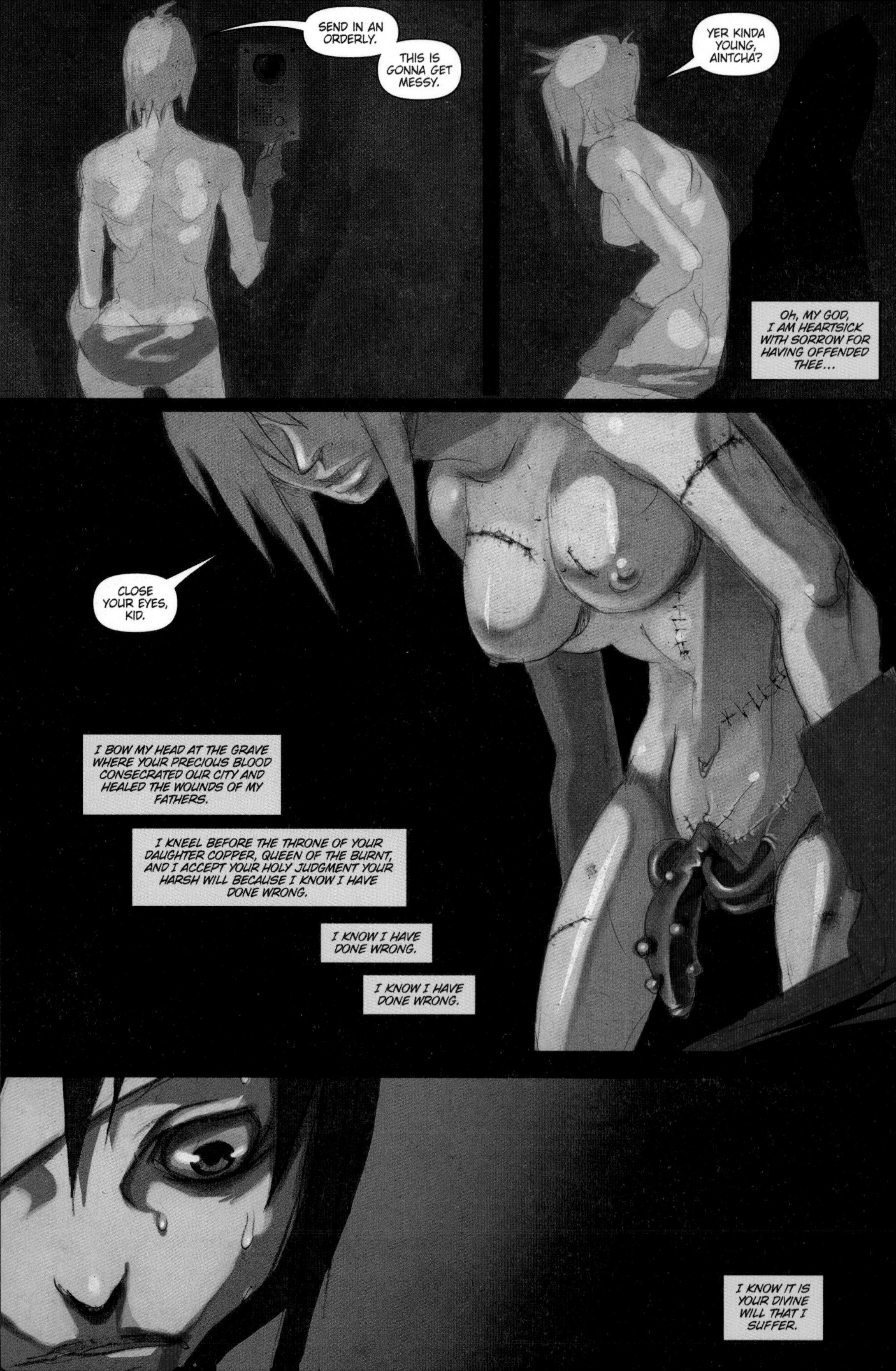
SEND IN AN ORDERLY.
THIS IS GONNA GET MESSY.
YER KINDA YOUNG, AINTCHA?
OH, MY GOD, I AM HEARTSICK WITH SORROW FOR HAVING OFFENDED THEE...
CLOSE YOUR EYES, KID.
I BOW MY HEAD AT THE GRAVE WHERE YOUR PRECIOUS BLOOD CONSECRATED OUR CITY AND HEALED THE WOUNDS OF MY FATHERS.
I KNEEL BEFORE THE THRONE OF YOUR DAUGHTER COPPER, QUEEN OF THE BURNT, AND I ACCEPT YOUR HOLY JUDGMENT YOUR HARSH WILL BECAUSE I KNOW I HAVE DONE WRONG.
I KNOW I HAVE DONE WRONG.
I KNOW I HAVE DONE WRONG.
I KNOW IT IS YOUR DIVINE WILL THAT I SUFFER.

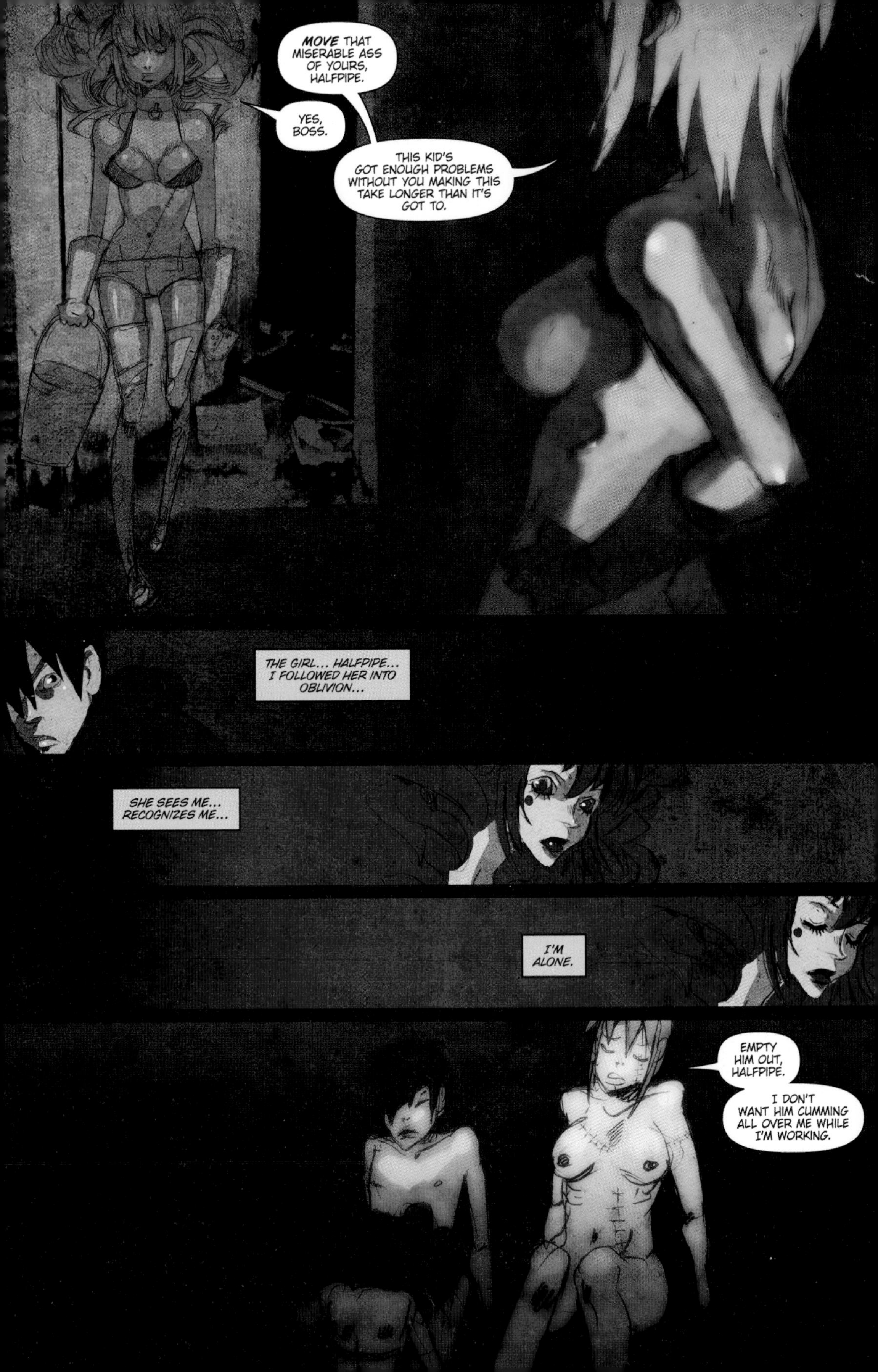
MOVE THAT MISERABLE ASS OF YOURS, HALFPIPE.
YES, BOSS.
THIS KID'S GOT ENOUGH PROBLEMS WITHOUT YOU MAKING THIS TAKE LONGER THAN IT'S GOT TO.
THE GIRL... HALFPIPE... I FOLLOWED HER INTO OBLIVION...
SHE SEES ME... RECOGNIZES ME...
I'M ALONE.
EMPTY HIM OUT, HALFPIPE.
I DON'T WANT HIM CUMMING ALL OVER ME WHILE I'M WORKING.

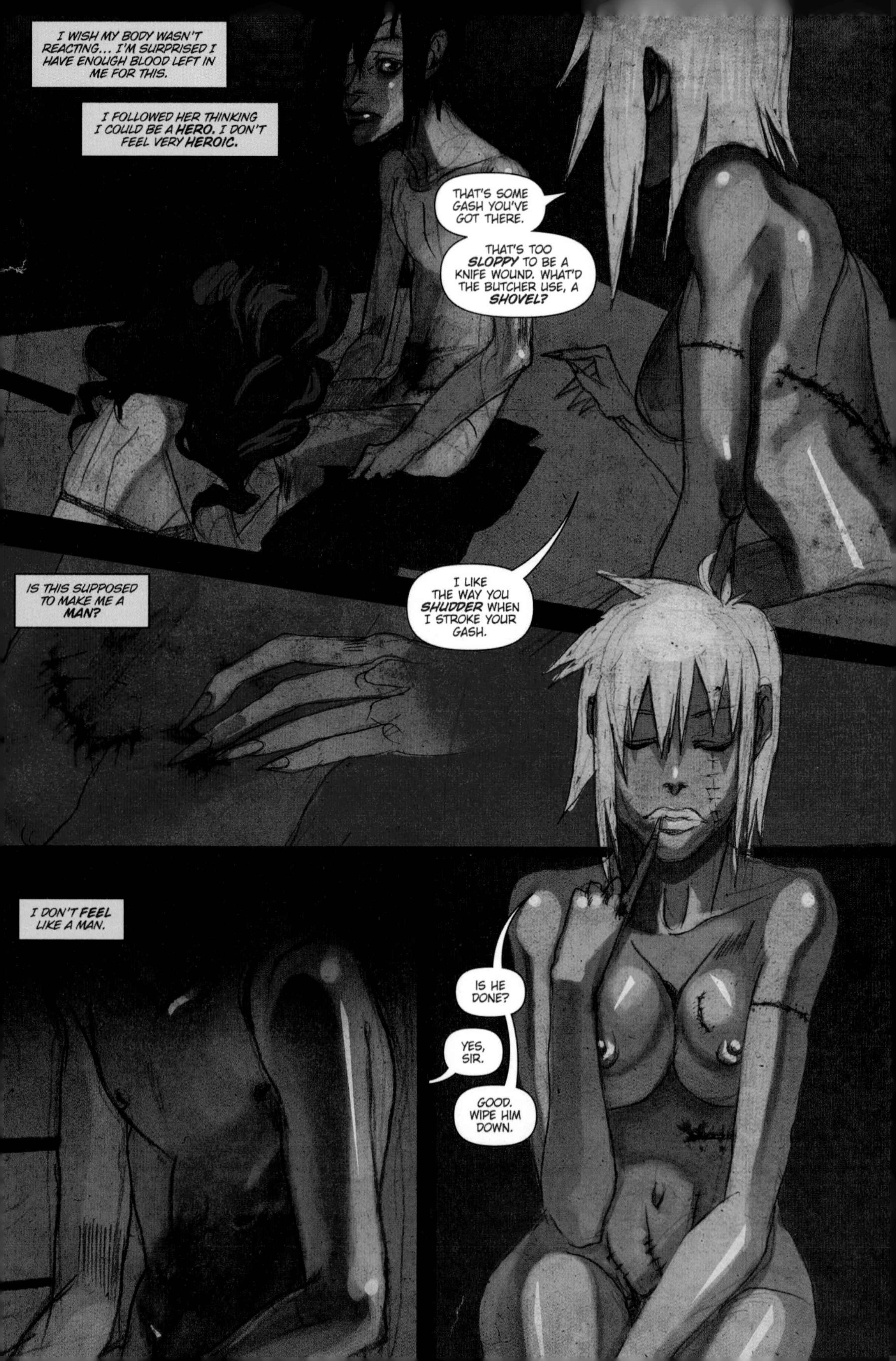
I WISH MY BODY WASN'T REACTING... I'M SURPRISED I HAVE ENOUGH BLOOD LEFT IN ME FOR THIS.
I FOLLOWED HER THINKING I COULD BE A HERO. I DON'T FEEL VERY HEROIC.
THAT'S SOME GASH YOU'VE GOT THERE.
THAT'S TOO SLOPPY TO BE A KNIFE WOUND. WHAT'D THE BUTCHER USE, A SHOVEL?
IS THIS SUPPOSED TO MAKE ME A MAN?
I LIKE THE WAY YOU SHUDDER WHEN I STROKE YOUR GASH.
I DON'T FEEL LIKE A MAN.
IS HE DONE?
YES, SIR.
GOOD. WIPE HIM DOWN.

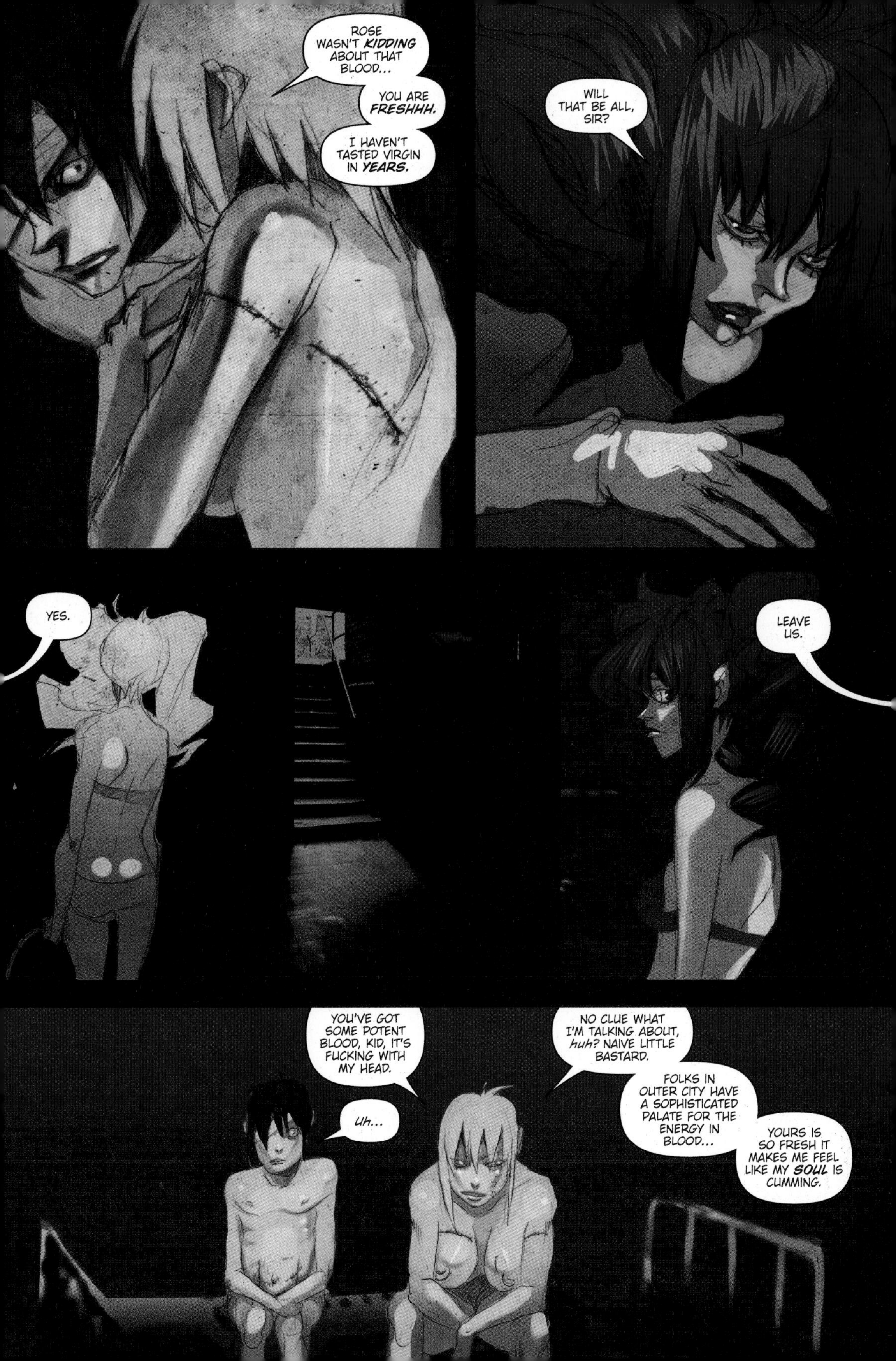
ROSE WASN'T *KIDDING* ABOUT THAT BLOOD...
YOU ARE ***FRESHHH.***
I HAVEN'T TASTED VIRGIN IN ***YEARS.***
WILL THAT BE ALL, SIR?
YES.
LEAVE US.
YOU'VE GOT SOME POTENT BLOOD, KID, IT'S FUCKING WITH MY HEAD.
UH...
NO CLUE WHAT I'M TALKING ABOUT, *HUH?* NAIVE LITTLE BASTARD.
FOLKS IN OUTER CITY HAVE A SOPHISTICATED PALATE FOR THE ENERGY IN BLOOD...
YOURS IS SO FRESH IT MAKES ME FEEL LIKE MY ***SOUL*** IS CUMMING.

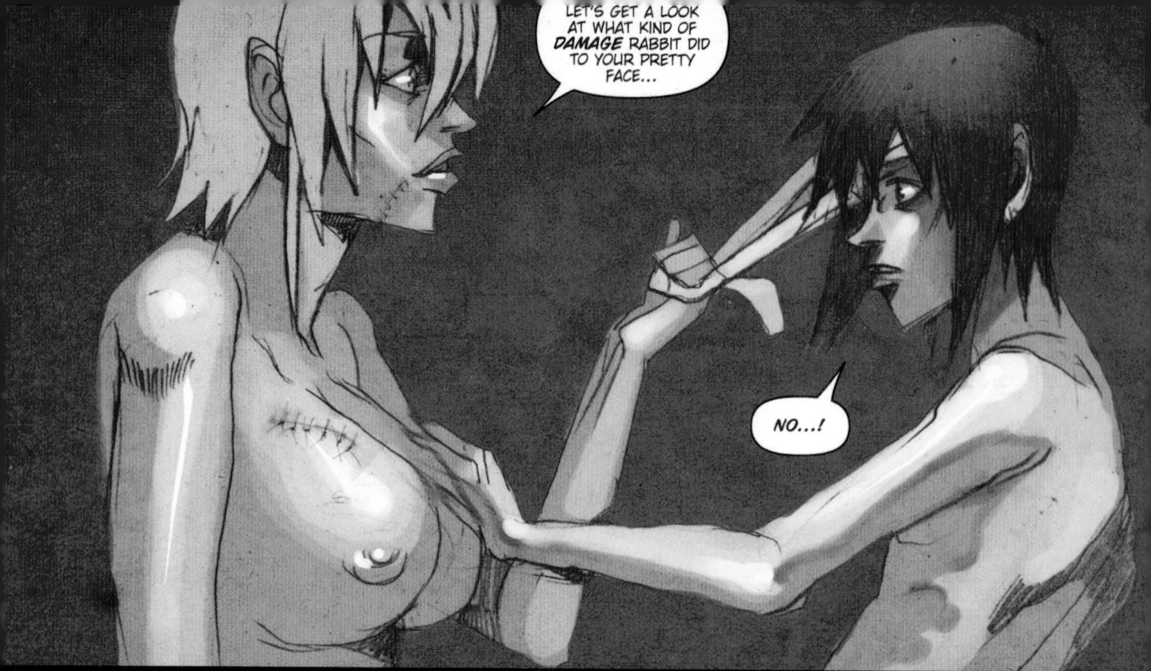
LET'S GET A LOOK AT WHAT KIND OF DAMAGE RABBIT DID TO YOUR PRETTY FACE...
NO...!

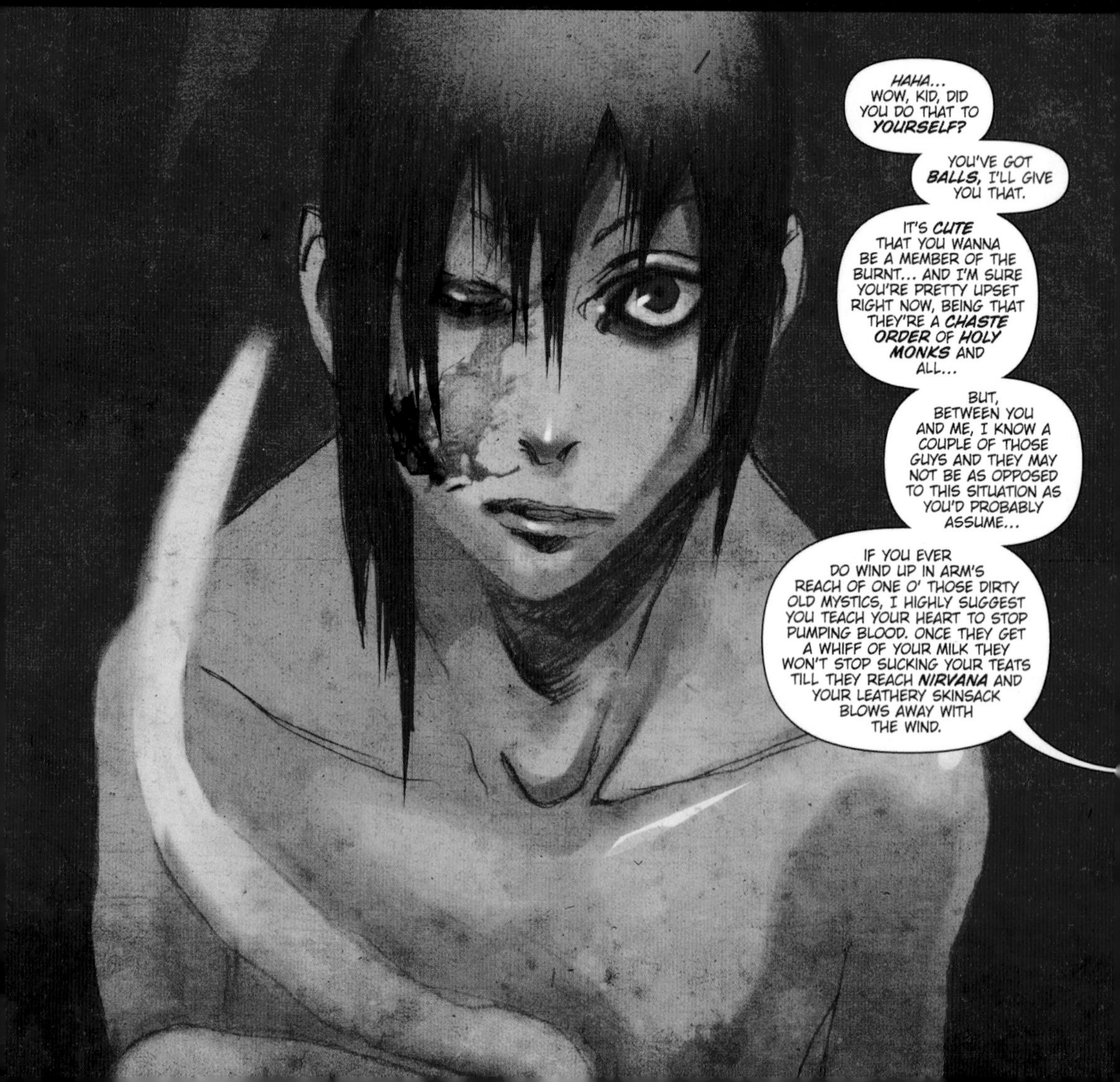
HAHA... WOW, KID, DID YOU DO THAT TO YOURSELF?
YOU'VE GOT BALLS, I'LL GIVE YOU THAT.
IT'S CUTE THAT YOU WANNA BE A MEMBER OF THE BURNT... AND I'M SURE YOU'RE PRETTY UPSET RIGHT NOW, BEING THAT THEY'RE A CHASTE ORDER OF HOLY MONKS AND ALL...
BUT, BETWEEN YOU AND ME, I KNOW A COUPLE OF THOSE GUYS AND THEY MAY NOT BE AS OPPOSED TO THIS SITUATION AS YOU'D PROBABLY ASSUME...
IF YOU EVER DO WIND UP IN ARM'S REACH OF ONE O' THOSE DIRTY OLD MYSTICS, I HIGHLY SUGGEST YOU TEACH YOUR HEART TO STOP PUMPING BLOOD. ONCE THEY GET A WHIFF OF YOUR MILK THEY WON'T STOP SUCKING YOUR TEATS TILL THEY REACH NIRVANA AND YOUR LEATHERY SKINSACK BLOWS AWAY WITH THE WIND.

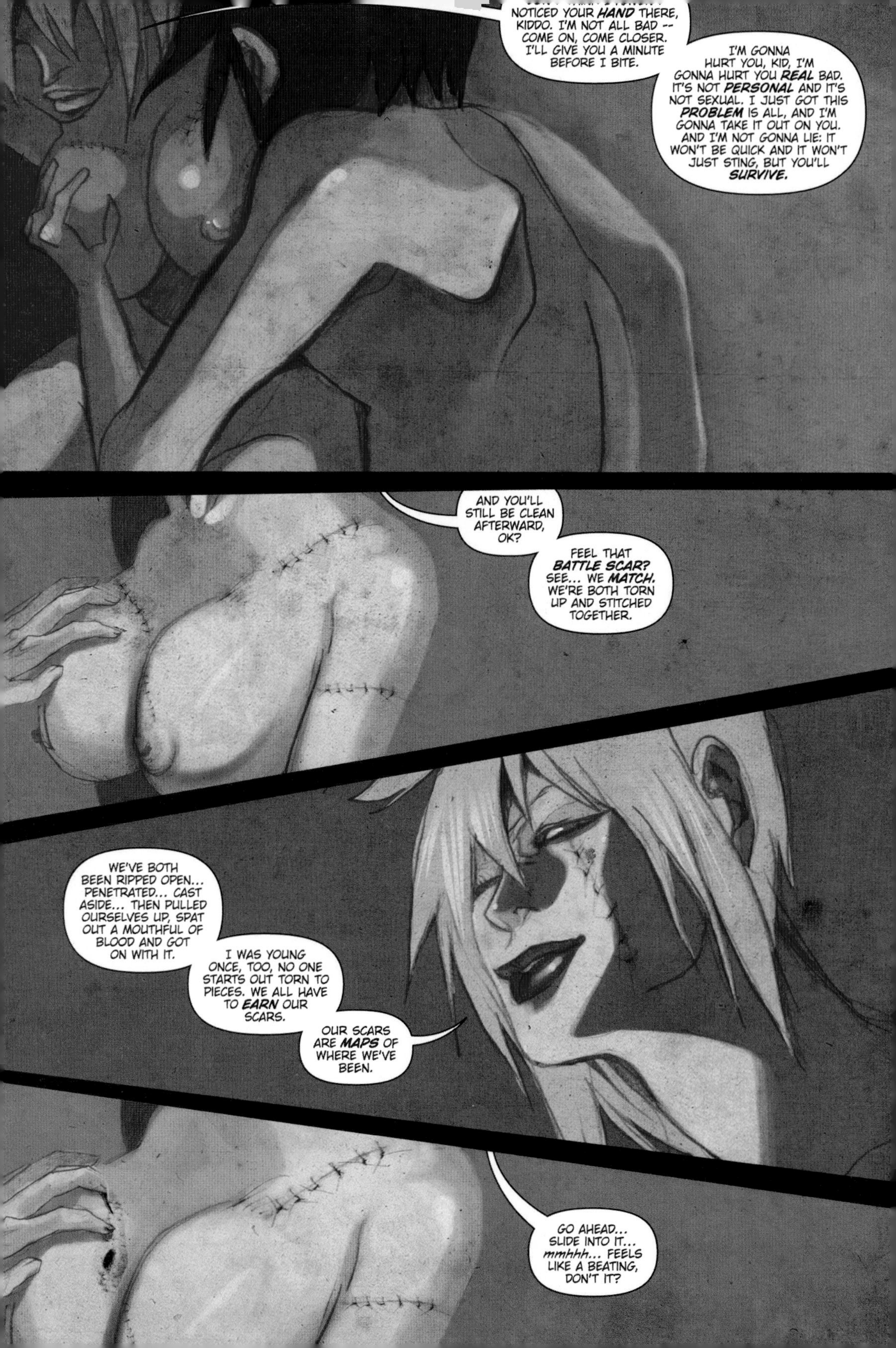
NOTICED YOUR HAND THERE, KIDDO. I'M NOT ALL BAD -- COME ON, COME CLOSER. I'LL GIVE YOU A MINUTE BEFORE I BITE.
I'M GONNA HURT YOU, KID, I'M GONNA HURT YOU REAL BAD. IT'S NOT PERSONAL AND IT'S NOT SEXUAL. I JUST GOT THIS PROBLEM IS ALL, AND I'M GONNA TAKE IT OUT ON YOU. AND I'M NOT GONNA LIE: IT WON'T BE QUICK AND IT WON'T JUST STING, BUT YOU'LL SURVIVE.
AND YOU'LL STILL BE CLEAN AFTERWARD, OK?
FEEL THAT BATTLE SCAR? SEE... WE MATCH. WE'RE BOTH TORN UP AND STITCHED TOGETHER.
WE'VE BOTH BEEN RIPPED OPEN... PENETRATED... CAST ASIDE... THEN PULLED OURSELVES UP, SPAT OUT A MOUTHFUL OF BLOOD AND GOT ON WITH IT.
I WAS YOUNG ONCE, TOO, NO ONE STARTS OUT TORN TO PIECES. WE ALL HAVE TO EARN OUR SCARS.
OUR SCARS ARE MAPS OF WHERE WE'VE BEEN.
GO AHEAD... SLIDE INTO IT... mmhhh... FEELS LIKE A BEATING, DON'T IT?

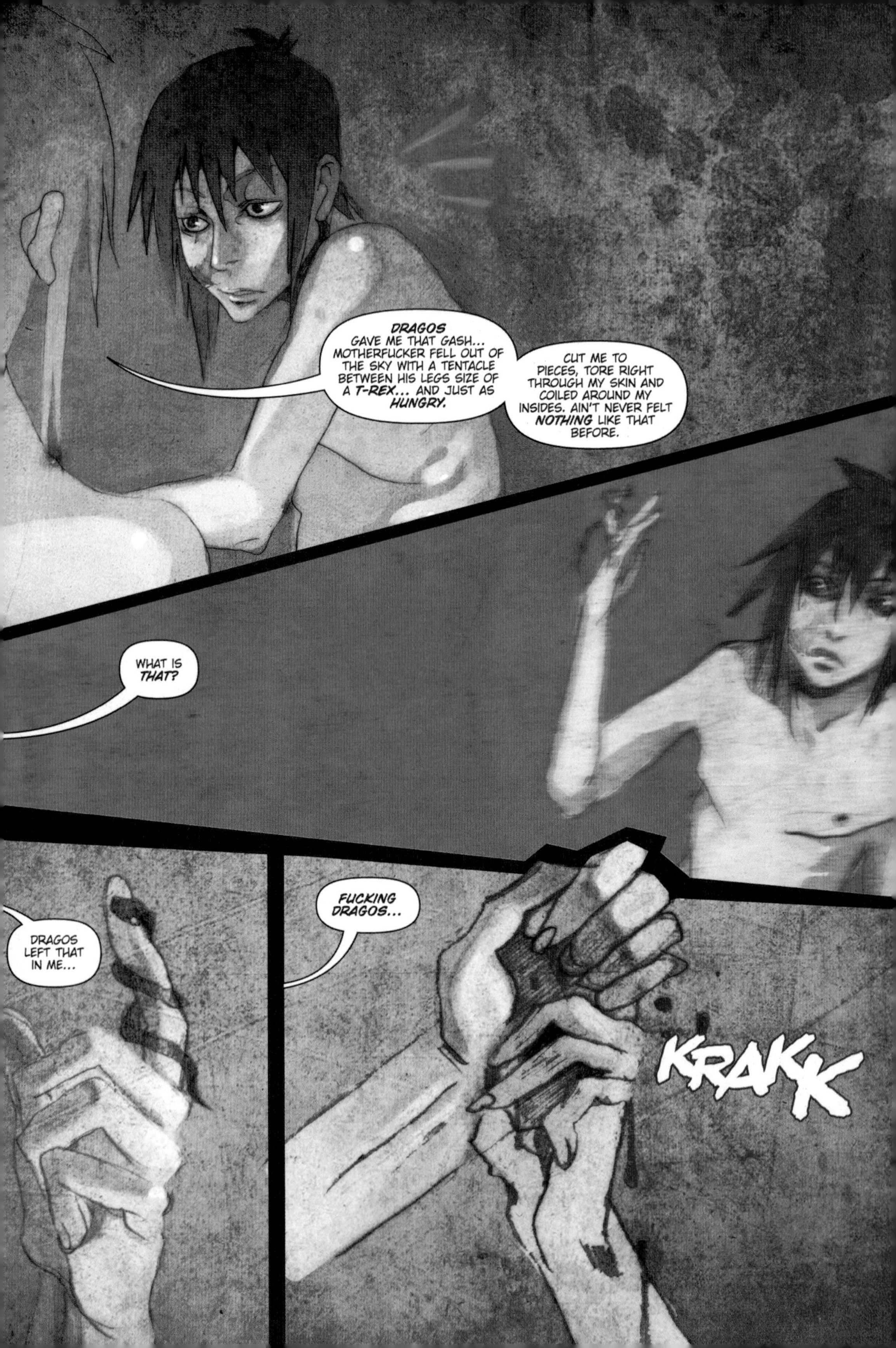
DRAGOS GAVE ME THAT GASH... MOTHERFUCKER FELL OUT OF THE SKY WITH A TENTACLE BETWEEN HIS LEGS SIZE OF A T-REX... AND JUST AS HUNGRY.
CUT ME TO PIECES, TORE RIGHT THROUGH MY SKIN AND COILED AROUND MY INSIDES. AIN'T NEVER FELT NOTHING LIKE THAT BEFORE.
WHAT IS THAT?
DRAGOS LEFT THAT IN ME...
FUCKING DRAGOS...
KRAKK

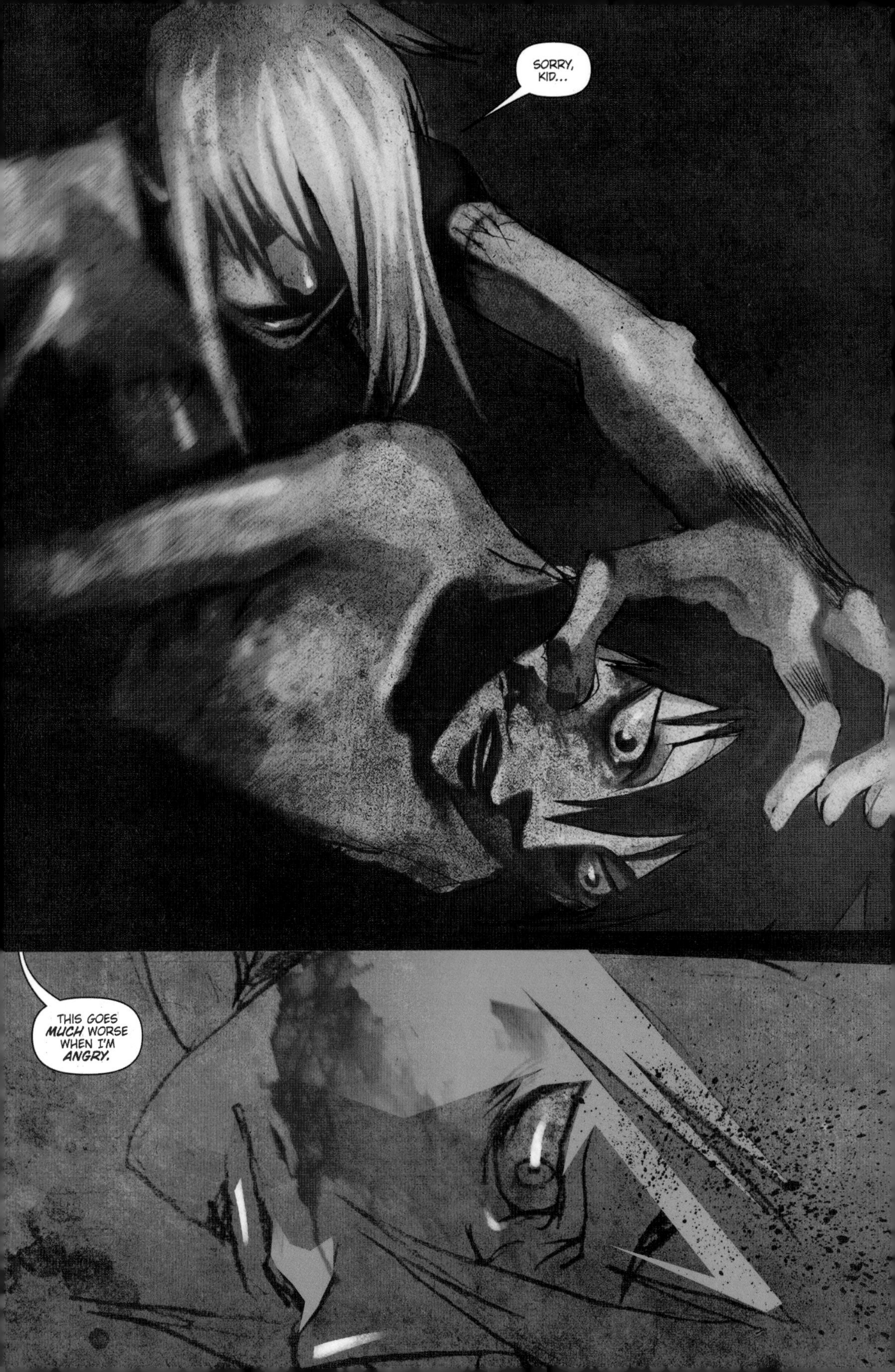
SORRY, KID...
THIS GOES *MUCH* WORSE WHEN I'M *ANGRY*.

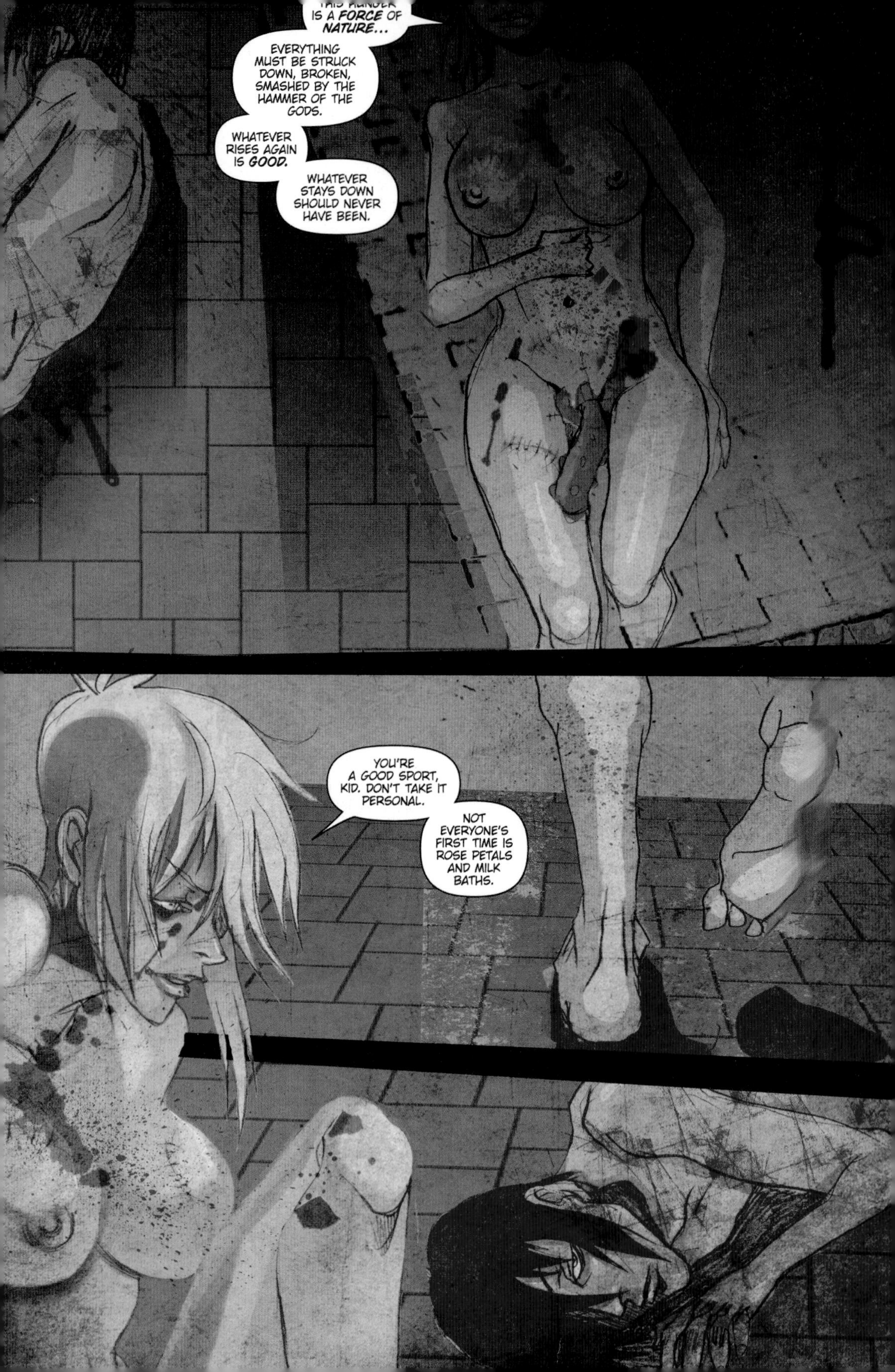
IS A FORCE OF NATURE...
EVERYTHING MUST BE STRUCK DOWN, BROKEN, SMASHED BY THE HAMMER OF THE GODS.
WHATEVER RISES AGAIN IS GOOD.
WHATEVER STAYS DOWN SHOULD NEVER HAVE BEEN.
YOU'RE A GOOD SPORT, KID. DON'T TAKE IT PERSONAL.
NOT EVERYONE'S FIRST TIME IS ROSE PETALS AND MILK BATHS.

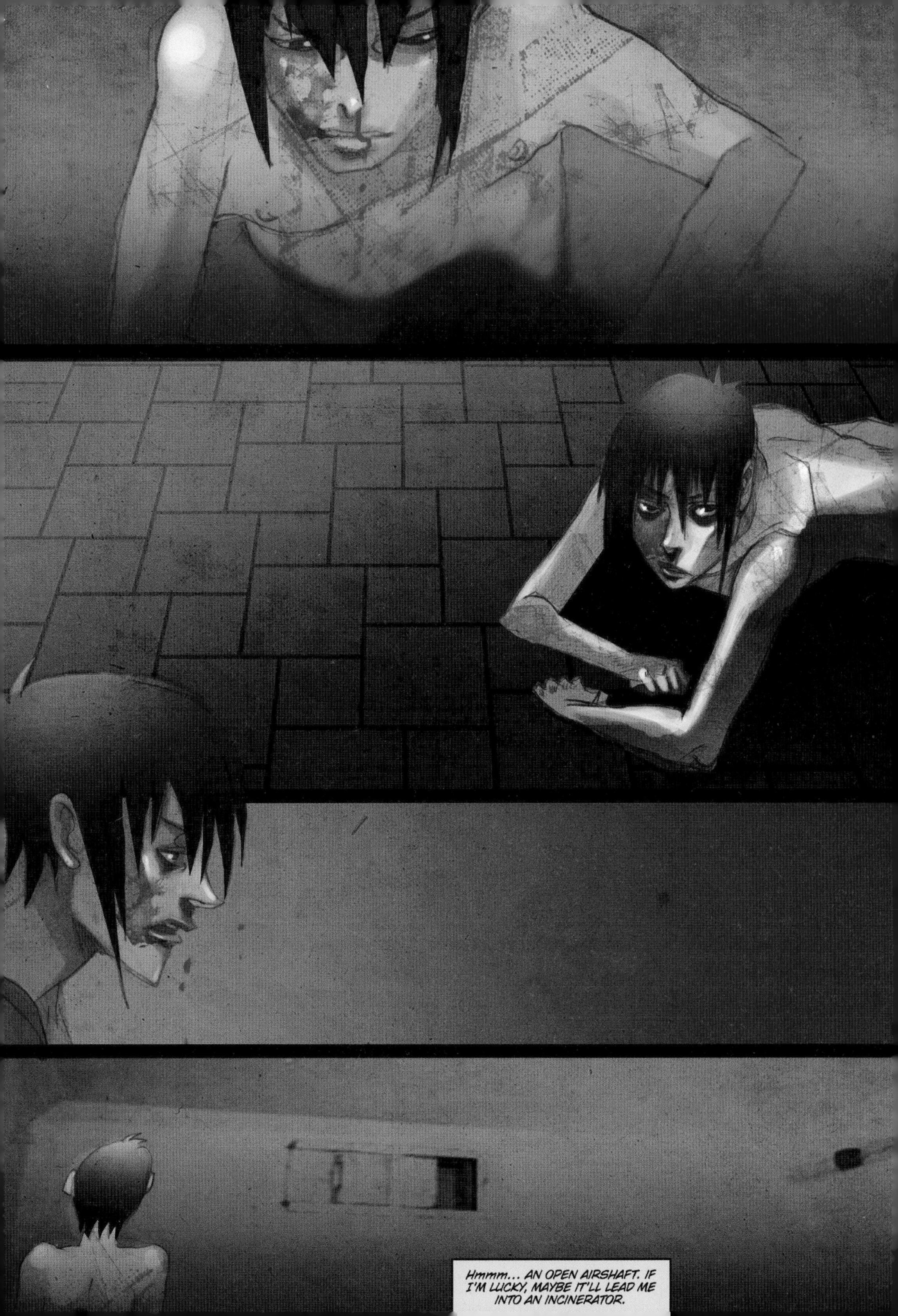
Hmmm... AN OPEN AIRSHAFT. IF I'M LUCKY, MAYBE IT'LL LEAD ME INTO AN INCINERATOR.

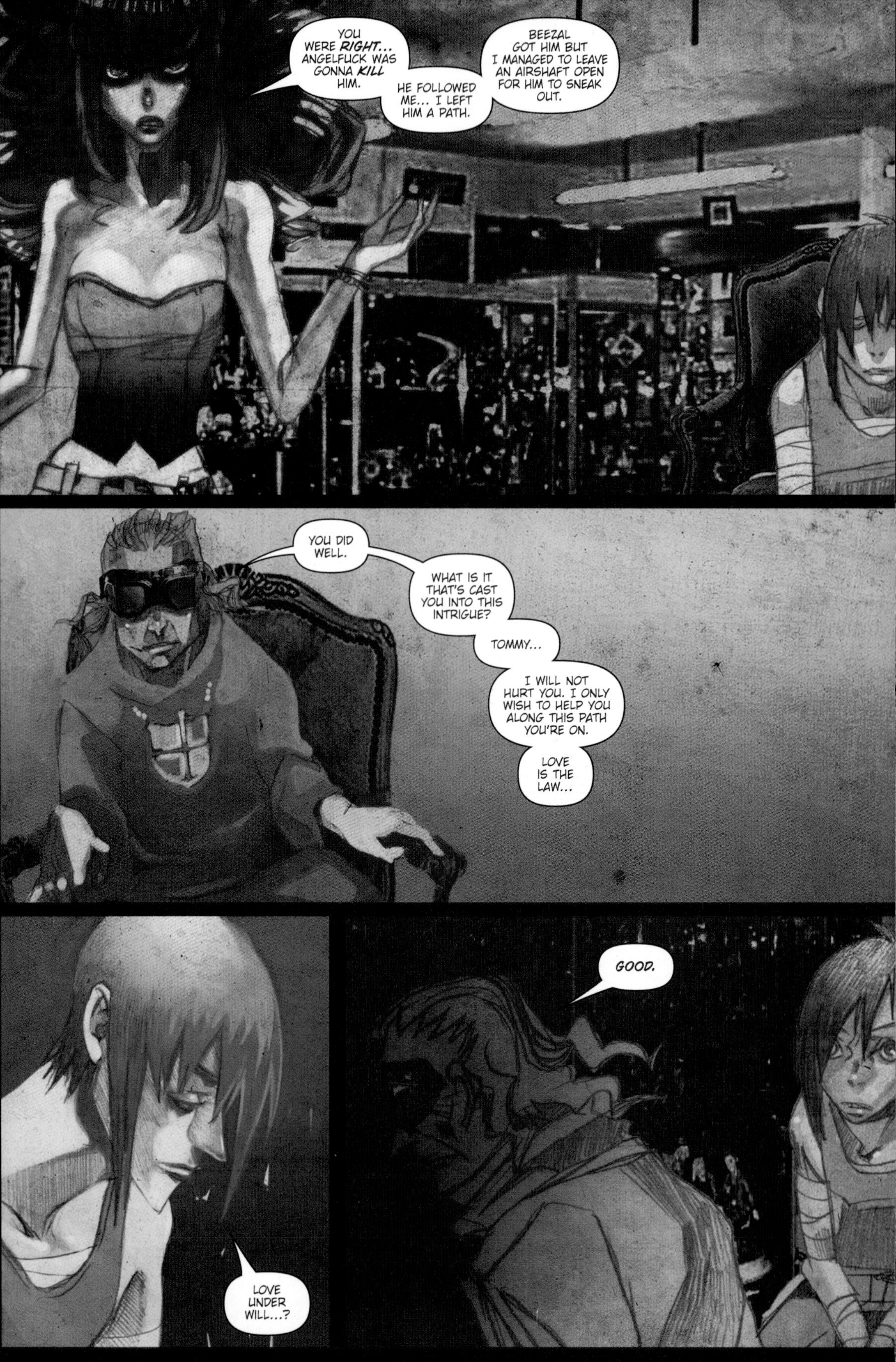
YOU WERE RIGHT... ANGELFUCK WAS GONNA KILL HIM.
HE FOLLOWED ME... I LEFT HIM A PATH.
BEEZAL GOT HIM BUT I MANAGED TO LEAVE AN AIRSHAFT OPEN FOR HIM TO SNEAK OUT.
YOU DID WELL.
WHAT IS IT THAT'S CAST YOU INTO THIS INTRIGUE?
TOMMY...
I WILL NOT HURT YOU. I ONLY WISH TO HELP YOU ALONG THIS PATH YOU'RE ON.
LOVE IS THE LAW...
LOVE UNDER WILL...?
GOOD.

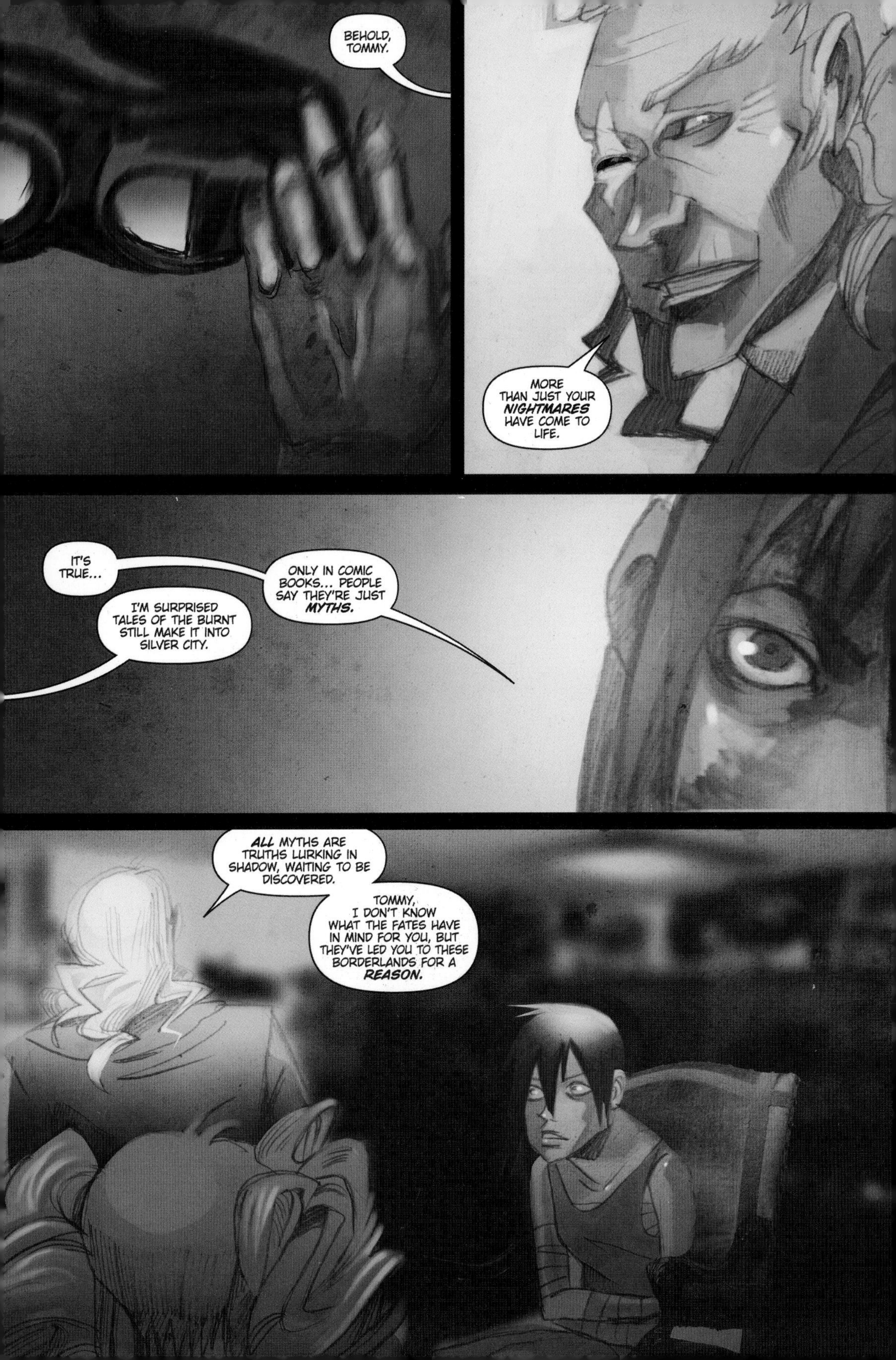
BEHOLD, TOMMY.
MORE THAN JUST YOUR NIGHTMARES HAVE COME TO LIFE.
IT'S TRUE...
ONLY IN COMIC BOOKS... PEOPLE SAY THEY'RE JUST MYTHS.
I'M SURPRISED TALES OF THE BURNT STILL MAKE IT INTO SILVER CITY.
ALL MYTHS ARE TRUTHS LURKING IN SHADOW, WAITING TO BE DISCOVERED.
TOMMY, I DON'T KNOW WHAT THE FATES HAVE IN MIND FOR YOU, BUT THEY'VE LED YOU TO THESE BORDERLANDS FOR A REASON.

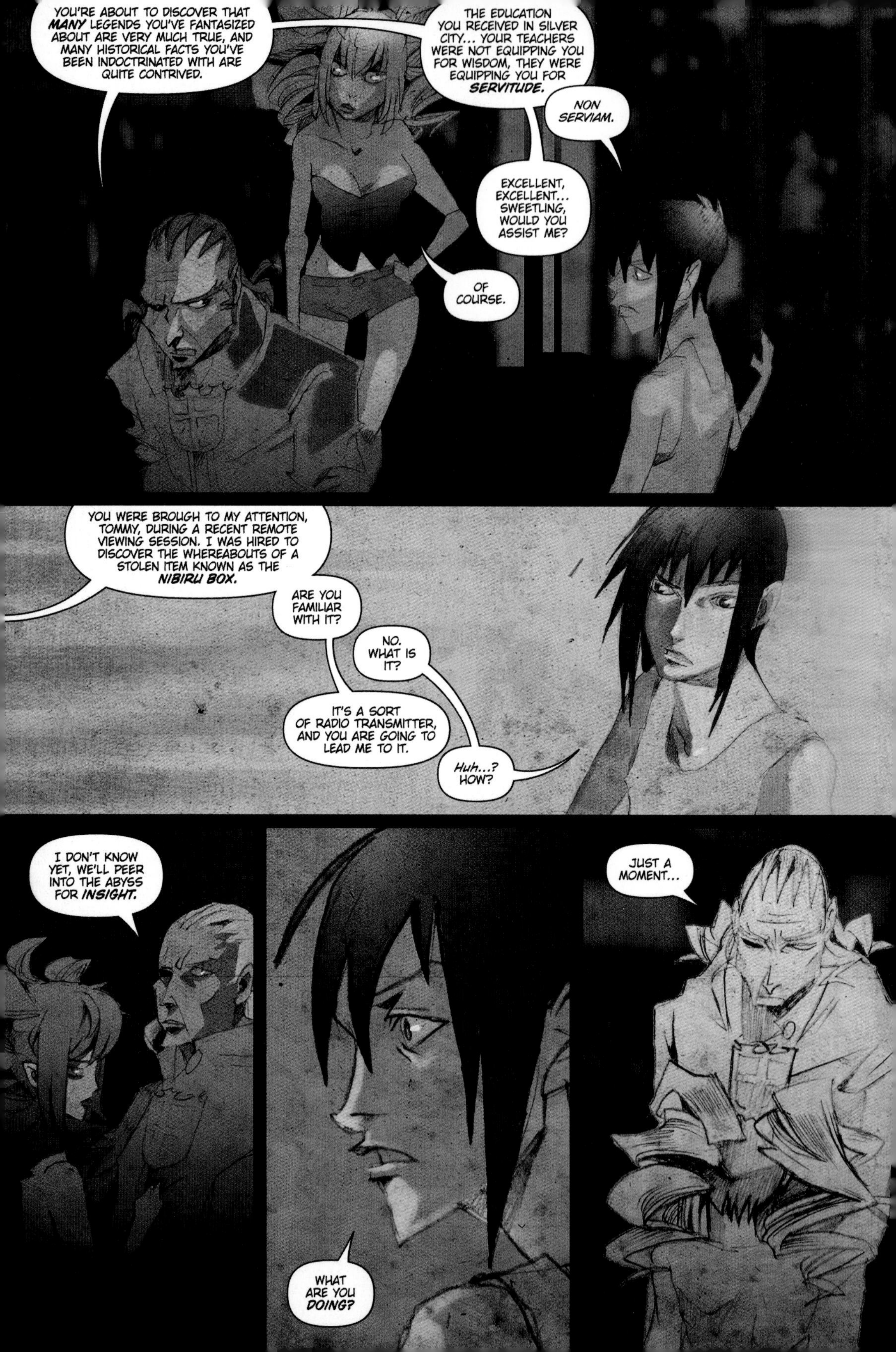
YOU'RE ABOUT TO DISCOVER THAT MANY LEGENDS YOU'VE FANTASIZED ABOUT ARE VERY MUCH TRUE, AND MANY HISTORICAL FACTS YOU'VE BEEN INDOCTRINATED WITH ARE QUITE CONTRIVED.
THE EDUCATION YOU RECEIVED IN SILVER CITY... YOUR TEACHERS WERE NOT EQUIPPING YOU FOR WISDOM, THEY WERE EQUIPPING YOU FOR SERVITUDE.
NON SERVIAM.
EXCELLENT, EXCELLENT... SWEETLING, WOULD YOU ASSIST ME?
OF COURSE.
YOU WERE BROUGH TO MY ATTENTION, TOMMY, DURING A RECENT REMOTE VIEWING SESSION. I WAS HIRED TO DISCOVER THE WHEREABOUTS OF A STOLEN ITEM KNOWN AS THE NIBIRU BOX.
ARE YOU FAMILIAR WITH IT?
NO. WHAT IS IT?
IT'S A SORT OF RADIO TRANSMITTER, AND YOU ARE GOING TO LEAD ME TO IT.
Huh...? HOW?
I DON'T KNOW YET, WE'LL PEER INTO THE ABYSS FOR INSIGHT.
WHAT ARE YOU DOING?
JUST A MOMENT...

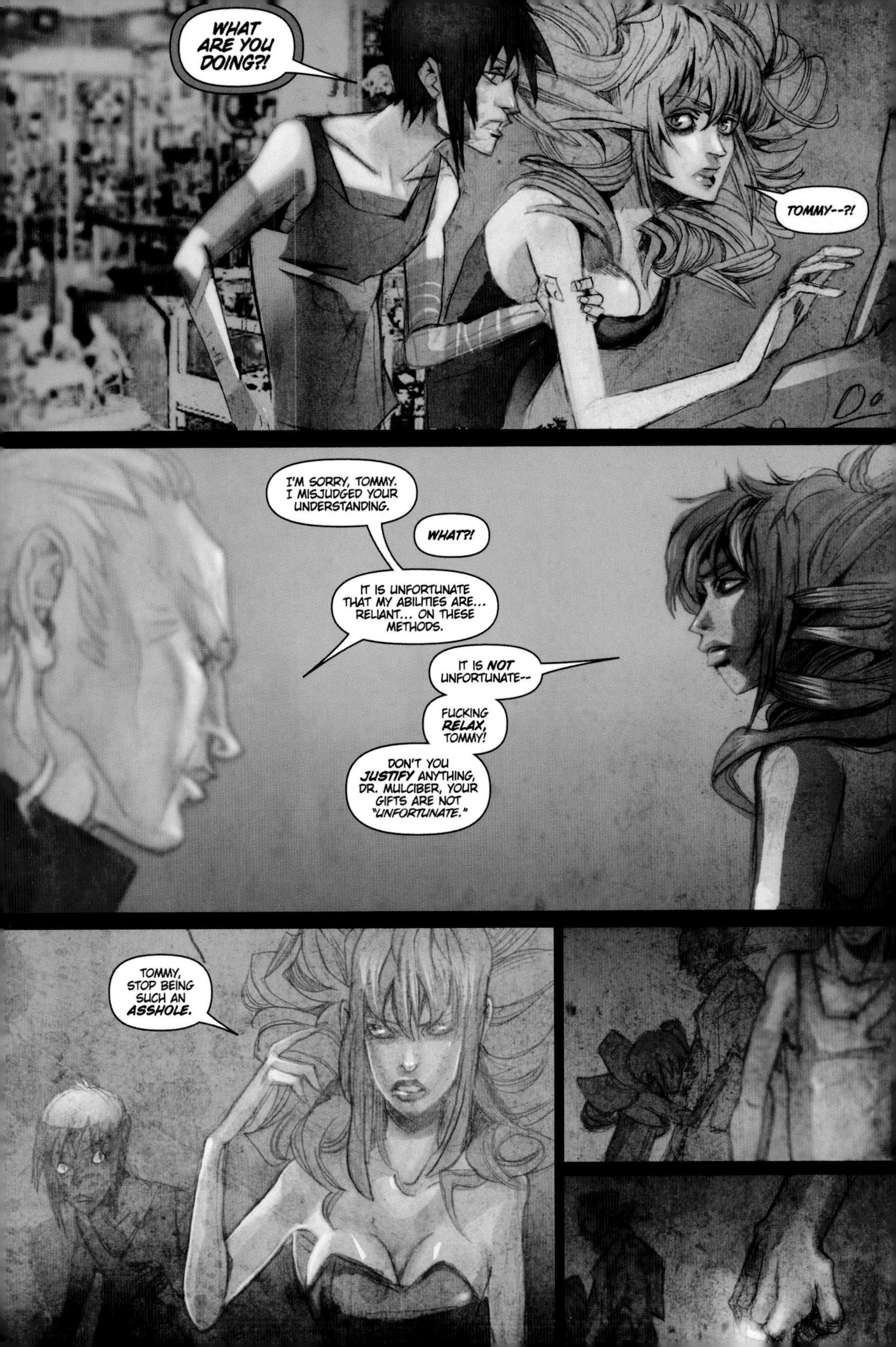
WHAT ARE YOU DOING?!
TOMMY--?!
I'M SORRY, TOMMY. I MISJUDGED YOUR UNDERSTANDING.
WHAT?!
IT IS UNFORTUNATE THAT MY ABILITIES ARE... RELIANT... ON THESE METHODS.
IT IS NOT UNFORTUNATE--
FUCKING RELAX, TOMMY!
DON'T YOU JUSTIFY ANYTHING, DR. MULCIBER, YOUR GIFTS ARE NOT "UNFORTUNATE."
TOMMY, STOP BEING SUCH AN ASSHOLE.

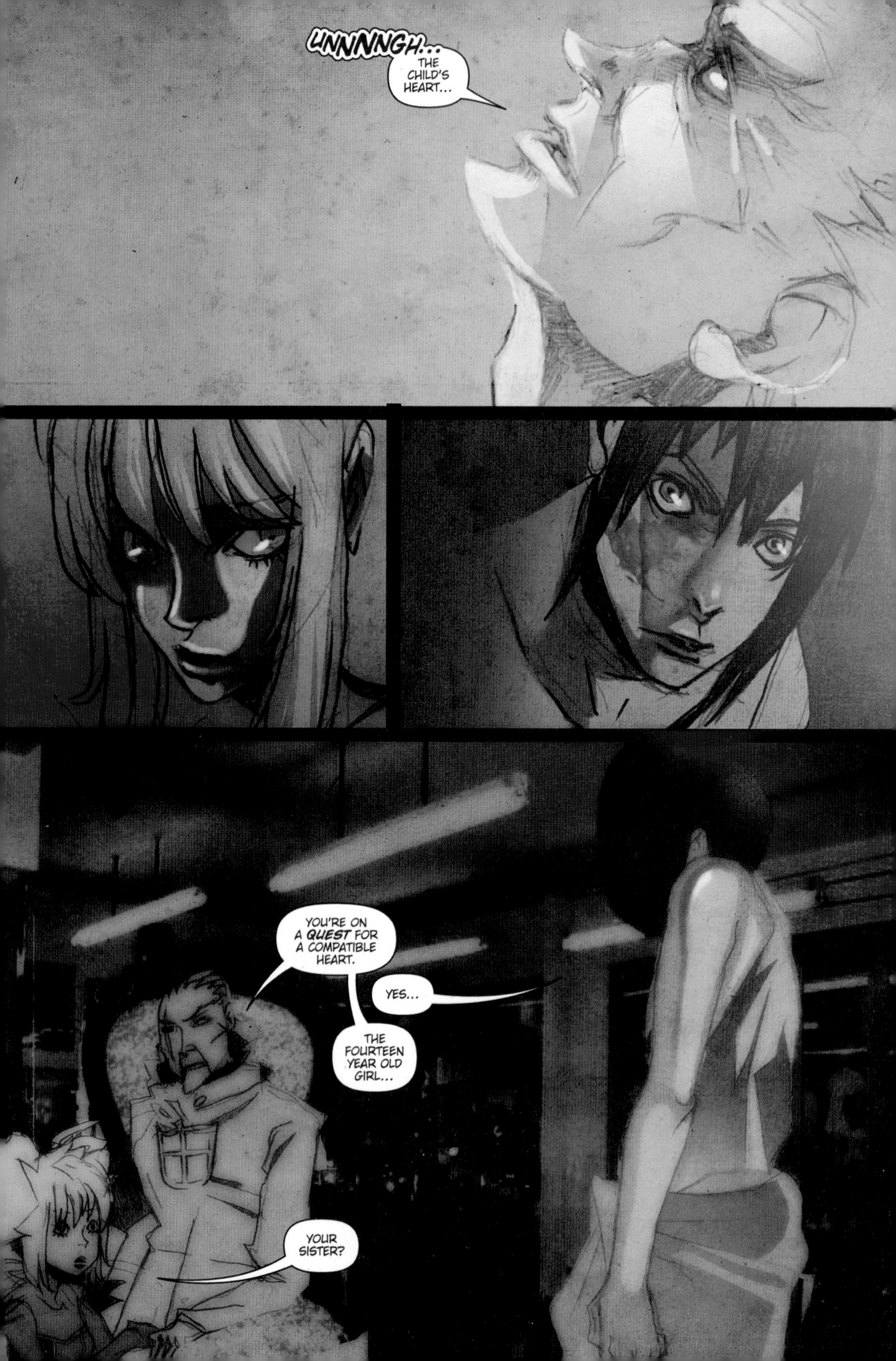
UNNNNGH...
THE CHILD'S HEART...
YOU'RE ON A QUEST FOR A COMPATIBLE HEART.
YES...
THE FOURTEEN YEAR OLD GIRL...
YOUR SISTER?

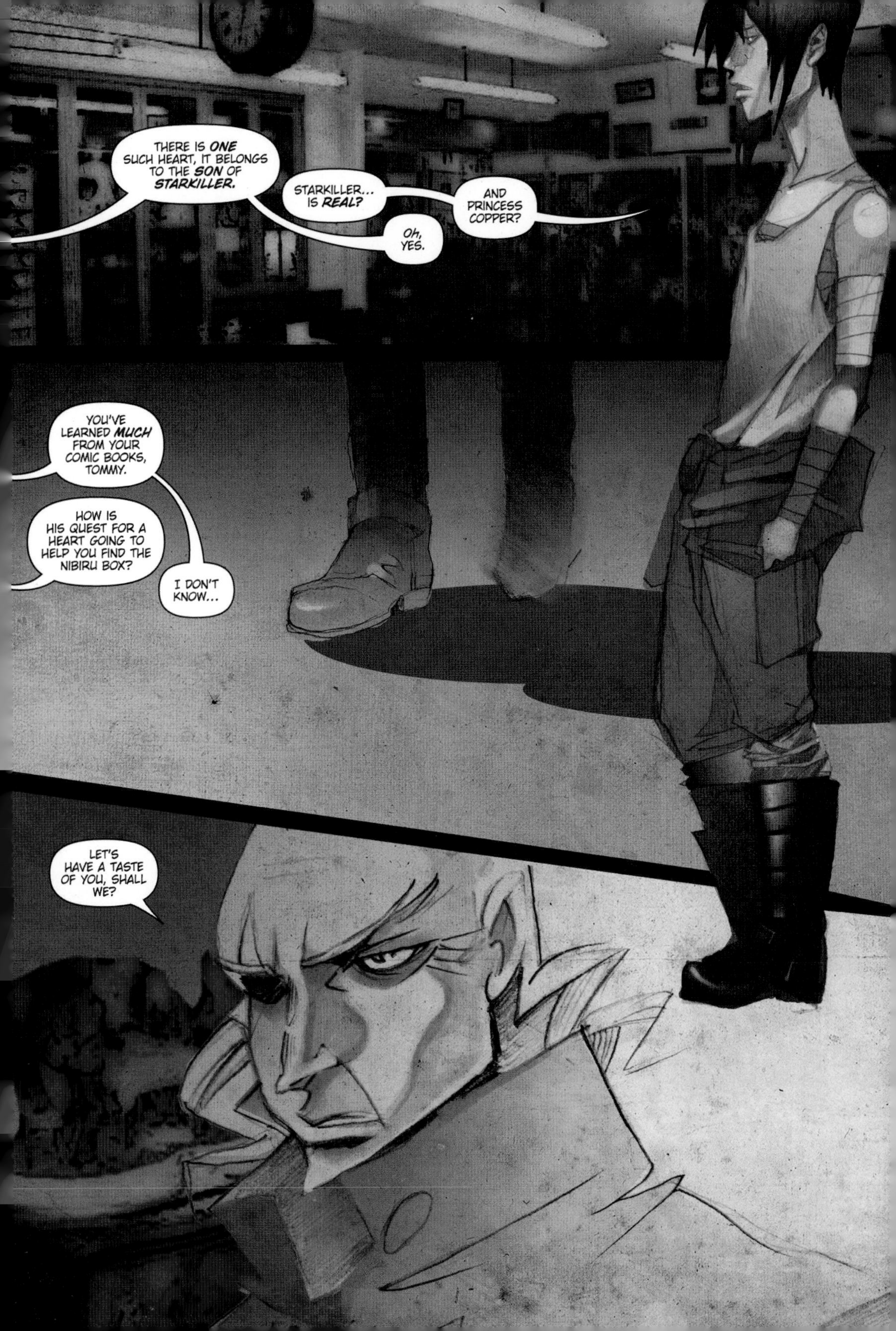
THERE IS ONE SUCH HEART, IT BELONGS TO THE SON OF STARKILLER.
STARKILLER... IS REAL?
AND PRINCESS COPPER?
Oh, YES.
YOU'VE LEARNED MUCH FROM YOUR COMIC BOOKS, TOMMY.
HOW IS HIS QUEST FOR A HEART GOING TO HELP YOU FIND THE NIBIRU BOX?
I DON'T KNOW...
LET'S HAVE A TASTE OF YOU, SHALL WE?

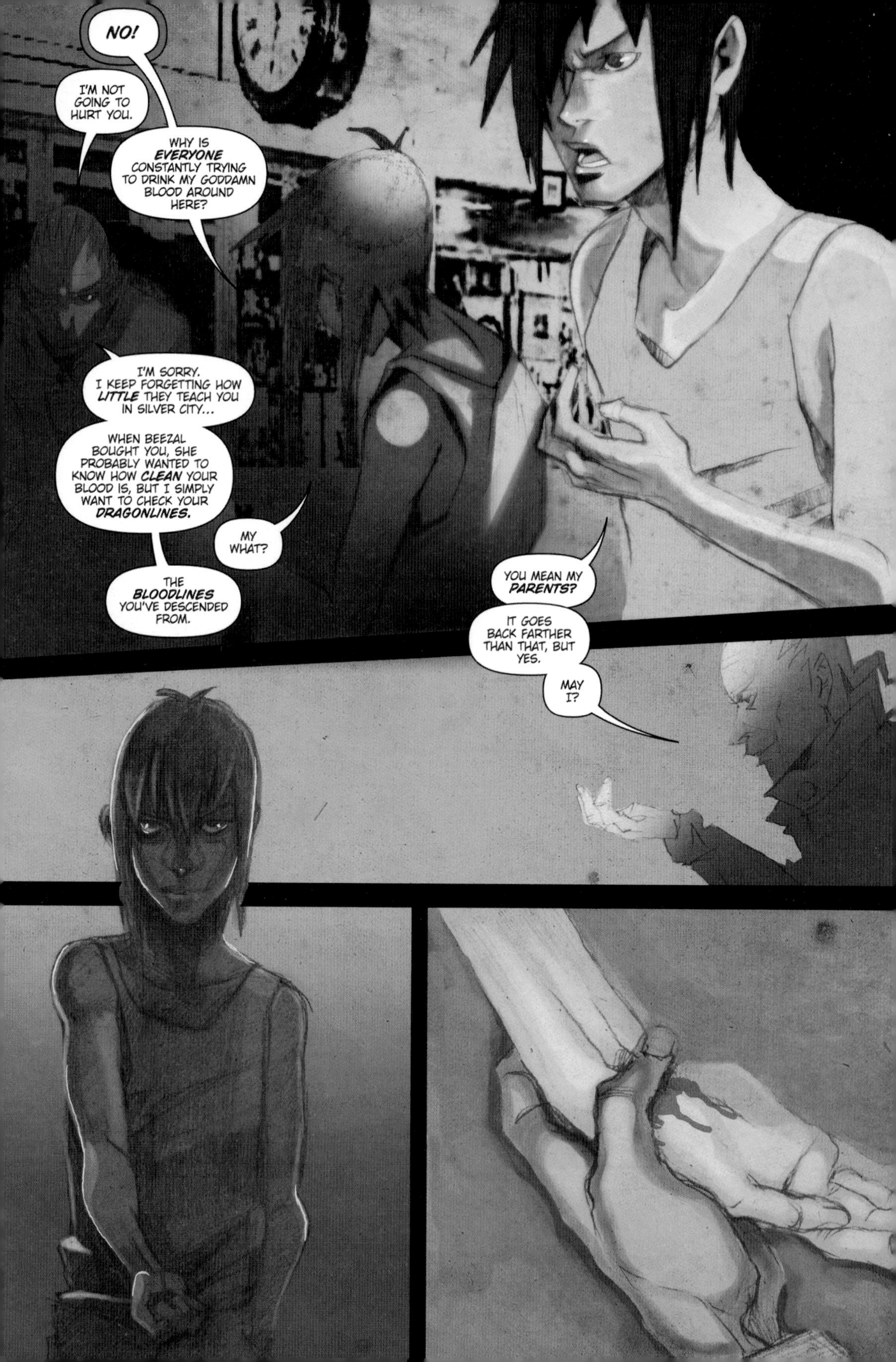
NO!
I'M NOT GOING TO HURT YOU.
WHY IS **EVERYONE** CONSTANTLY TRYING TO DRINK MY GODDAMN BLOOD AROUND HERE?
I'M SORRY. I KEEP FORGETTING HOW **LITTLE** THEY TEACH YOU IN SILVER CITY...
WHEN BEEZAL BOUGHT YOU, SHE PROBABLY WANTED TO KNOW HOW **CLEAN** YOUR BLOOD IS, BUT I SIMPLY WANT TO CHECK YOUR **DRAGONLINES.**
MY WHAT?
THE **BLOODLINES** YOU'VE DESCENDED FROM.
YOU MEAN MY **PARENTS?**
IT GOES BACK FARTHER THAN THAT, BUT YES.
MAY I?

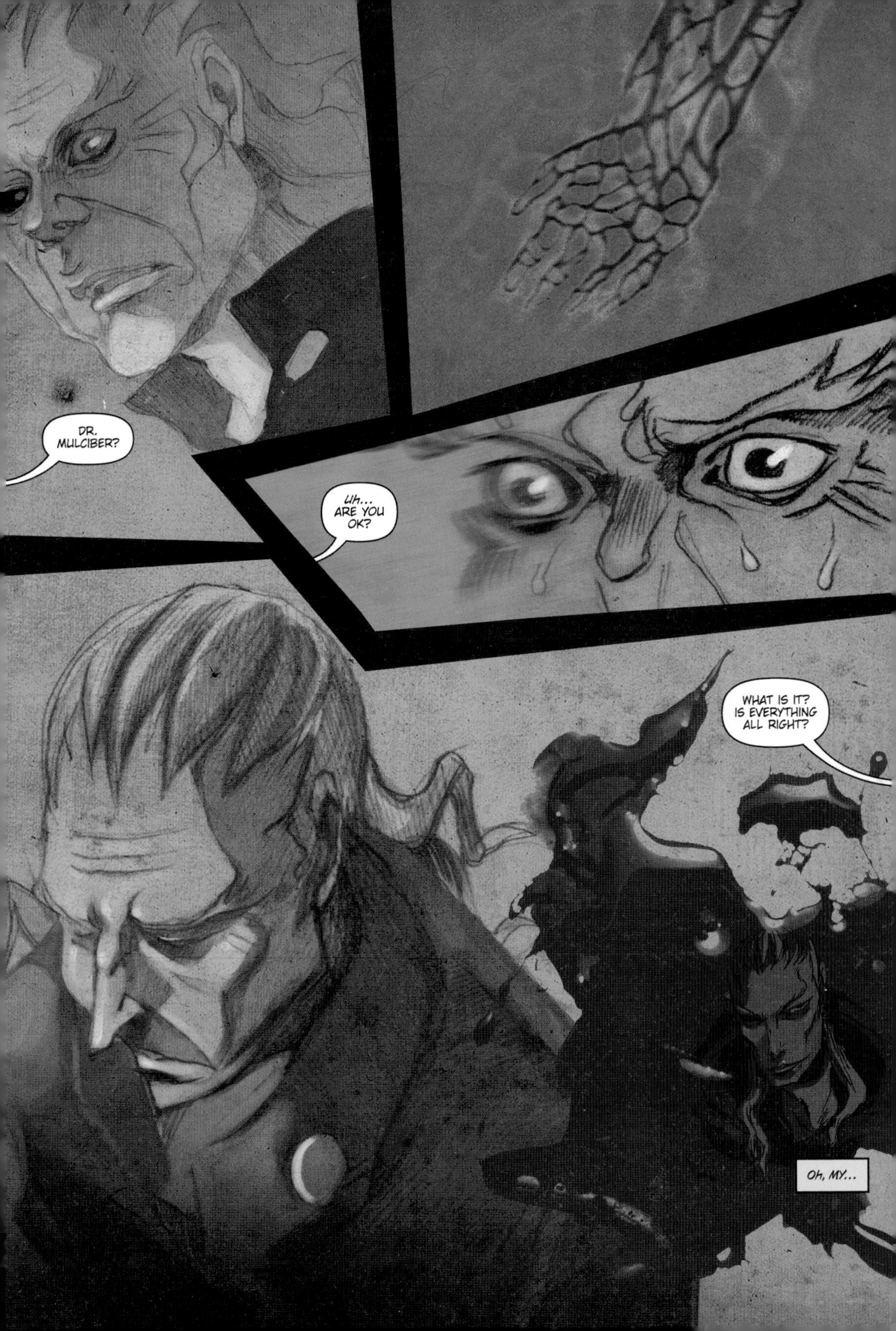
DR. MULCIBER?
Uh... ARE YOU OK?
WHAT IS IT? IS EVERYTHING ALL RIGHT?
Oh, MY...

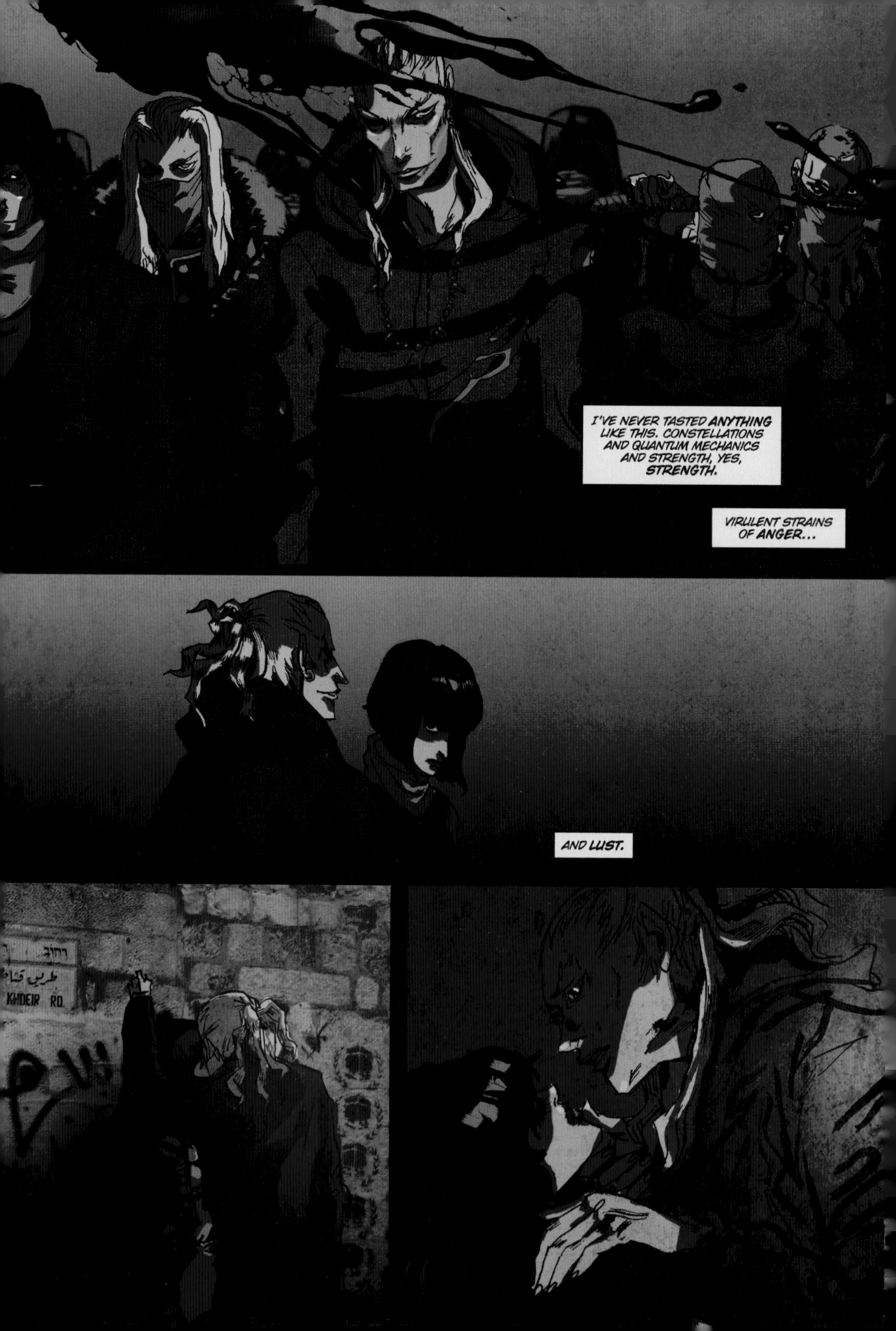
I'VE NEVER TASTED ANYTHING LIKE THIS. CONSTELLATIONS AND QUANTUM MECHANICS AND STRENGTH, YES, STRENGTH.
VIRULENT STRAINS OF ANGER...
AND LUST.
KHDEIR RD.

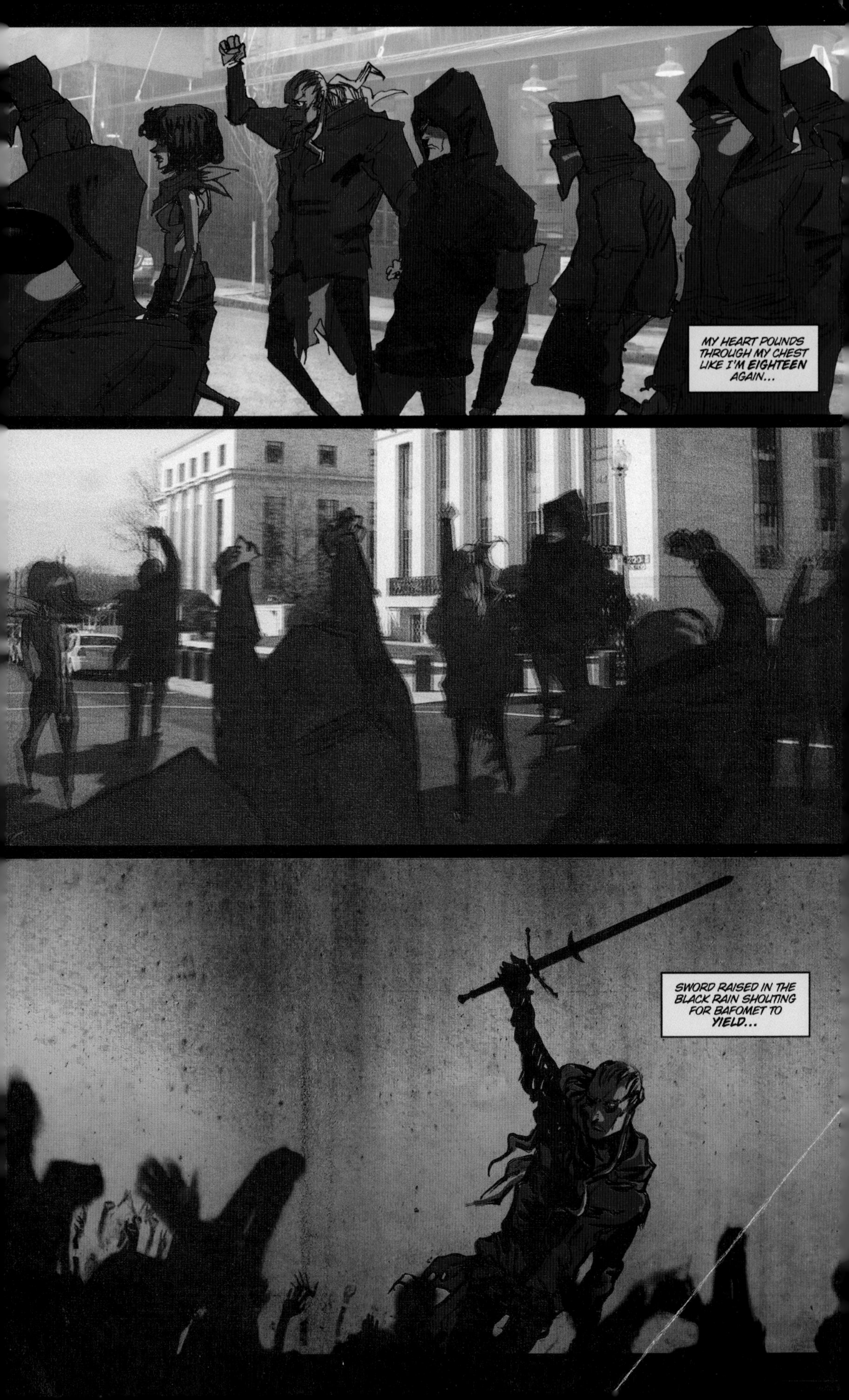
MY HEART POUNDS THROUGH MY CHEST LIKE I'M EIGHTEEN AGAIN...
SWORD RAISED IN THE BLACK RAIN SHOUTING FOR BAFOMET TO YIELD...

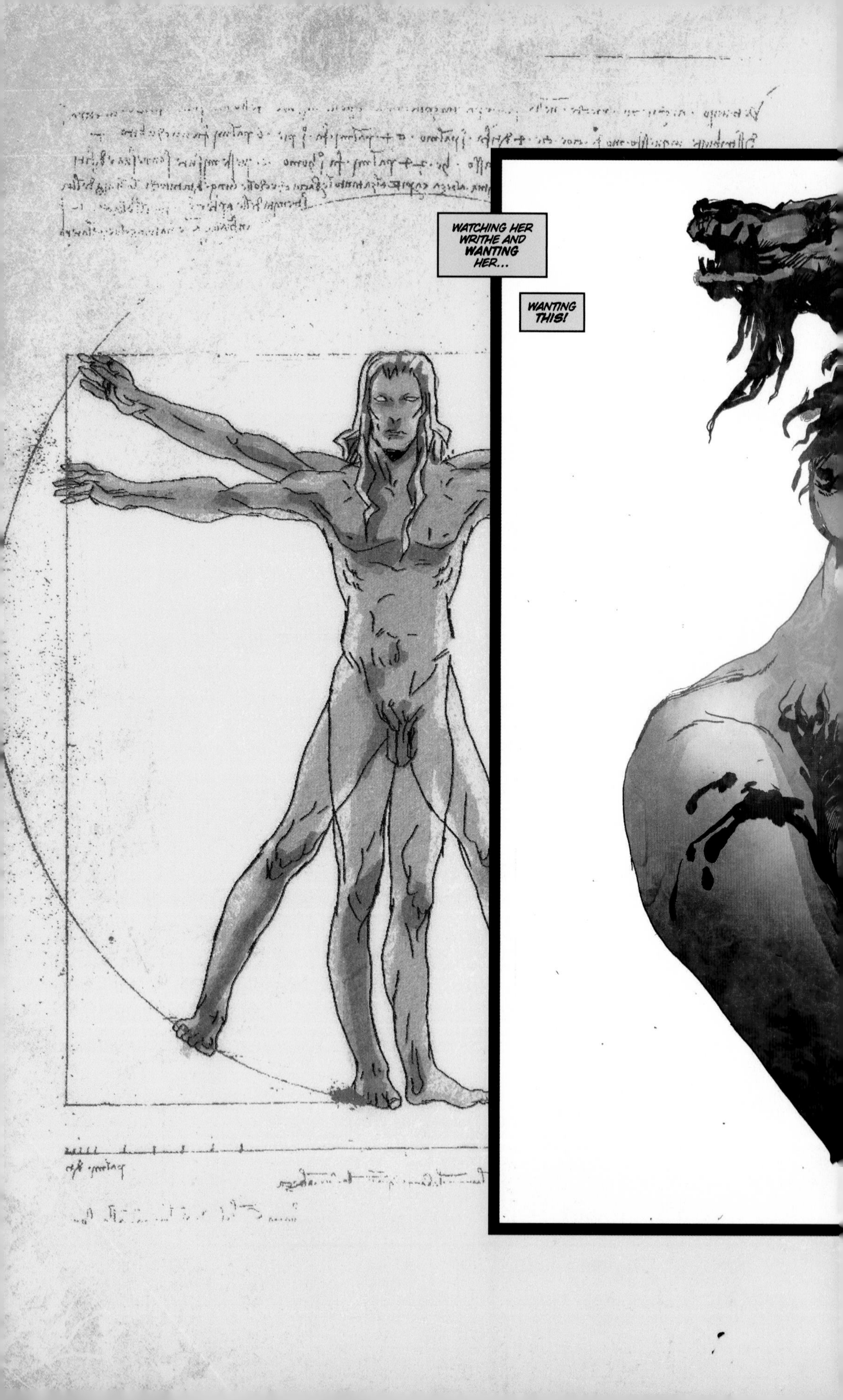
WATCHING HER WRITHE AND WANTING HER...
WANTING THIS!

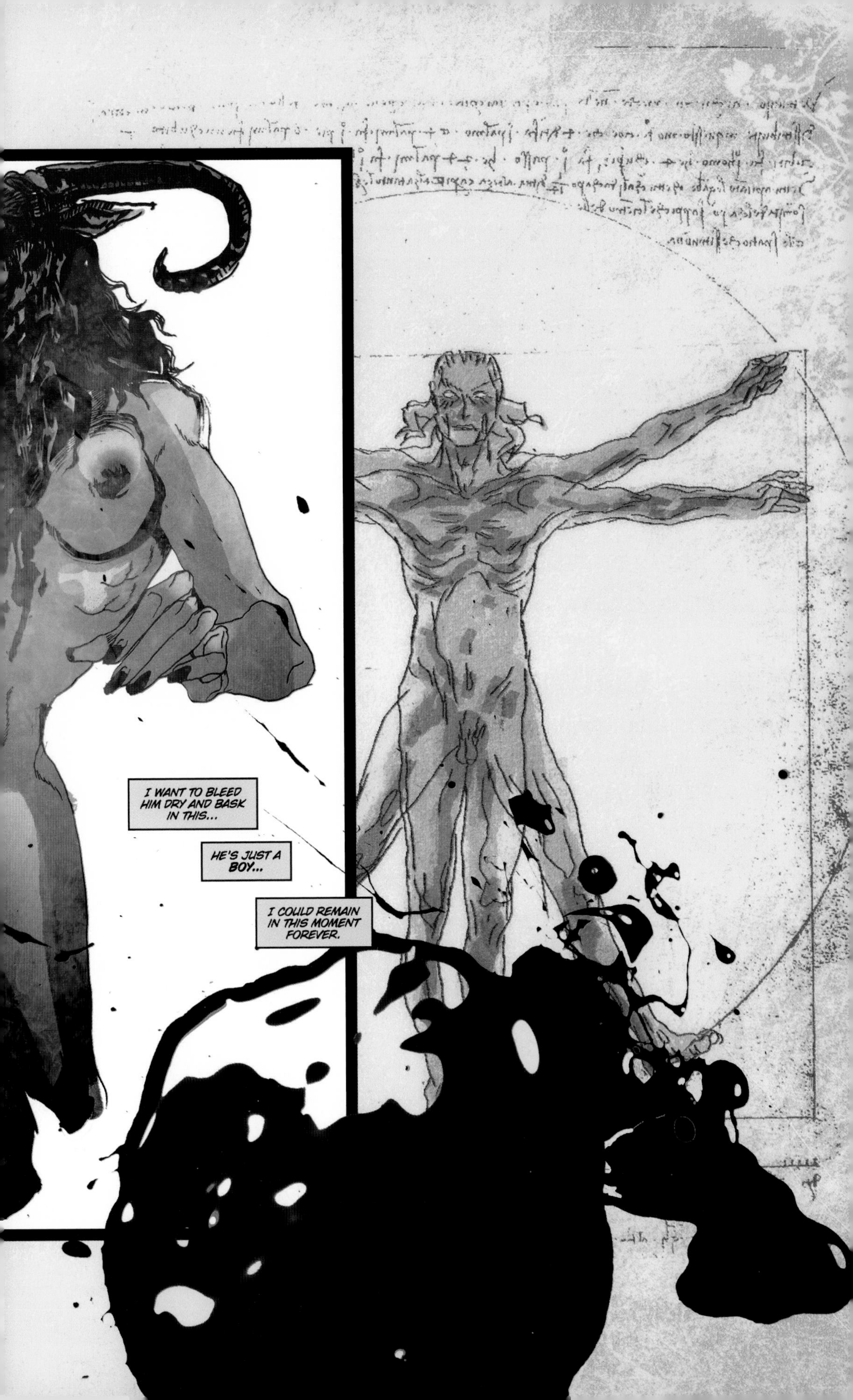
I WANT TO BLEED HIM DRY AND BASK IN THIS...
HE'S JUST A BOY...
I COULD REMAIN IN THIS MOMENT FOREVER.

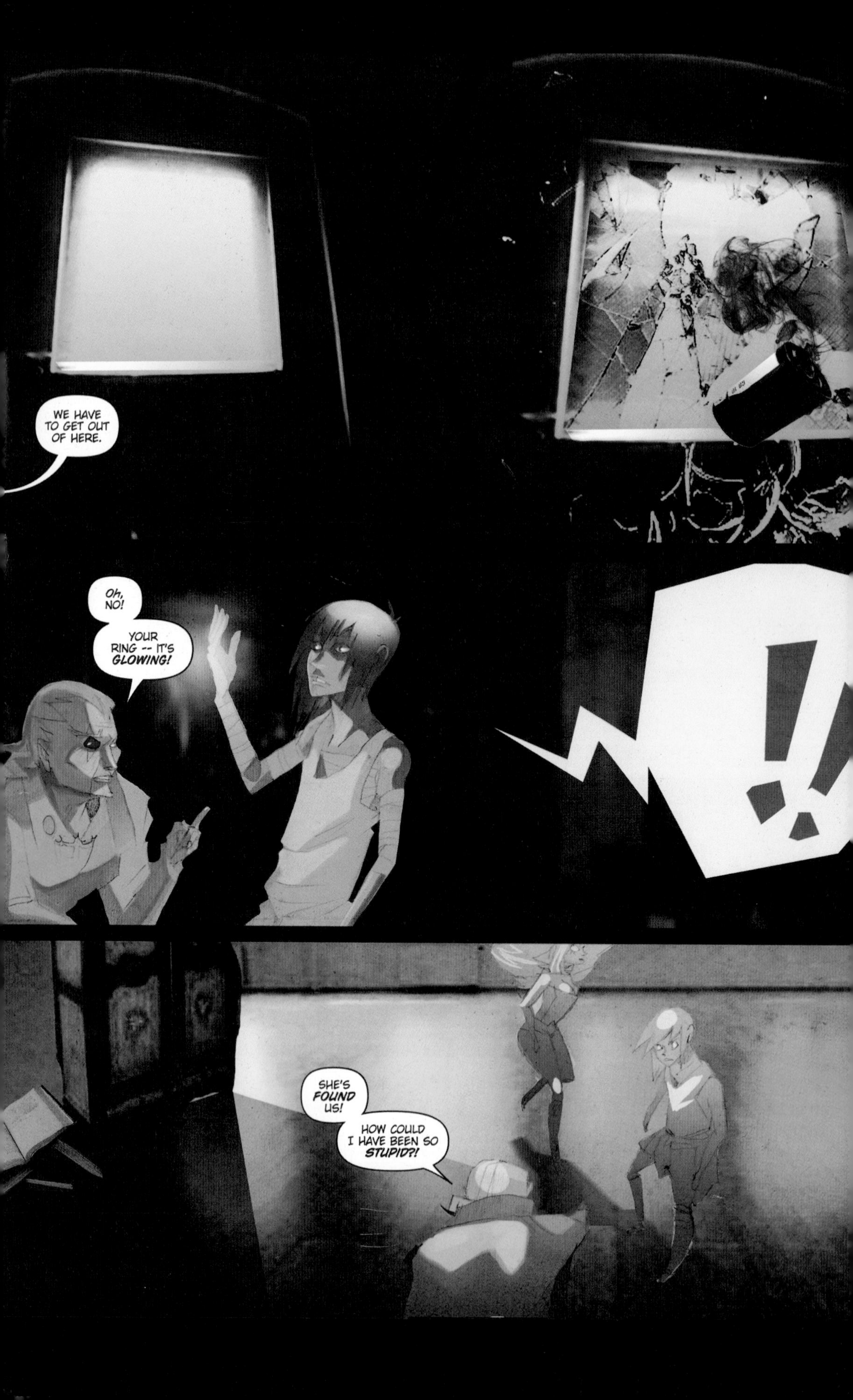
WE HAVE TO GET OUT OF HERE.
Oh, NO!
YOUR RING -- IT'S GLOWING!
!
SHE'S FOUND US!
HOW COULD I HAVE BEEN SO STUPID?!

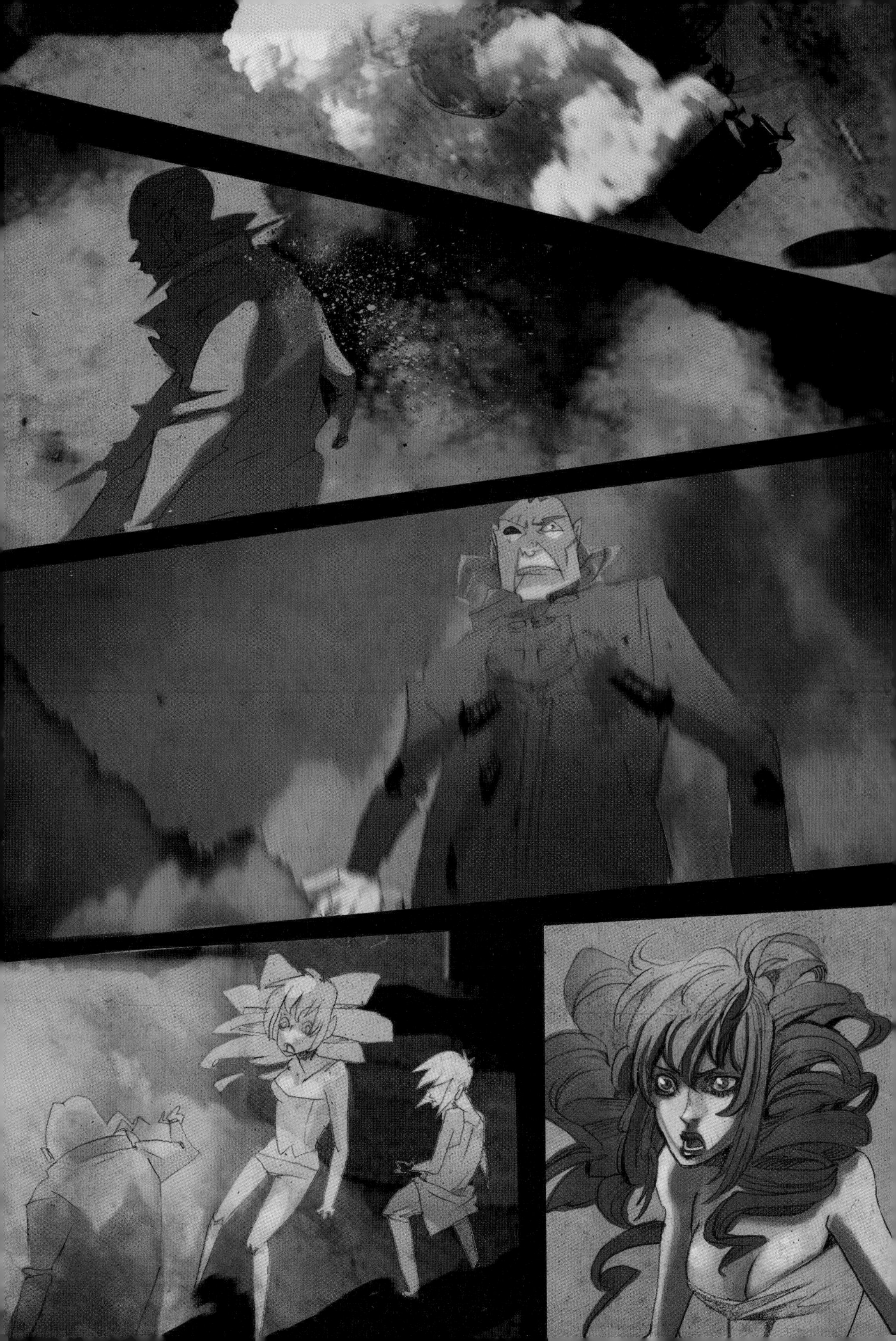

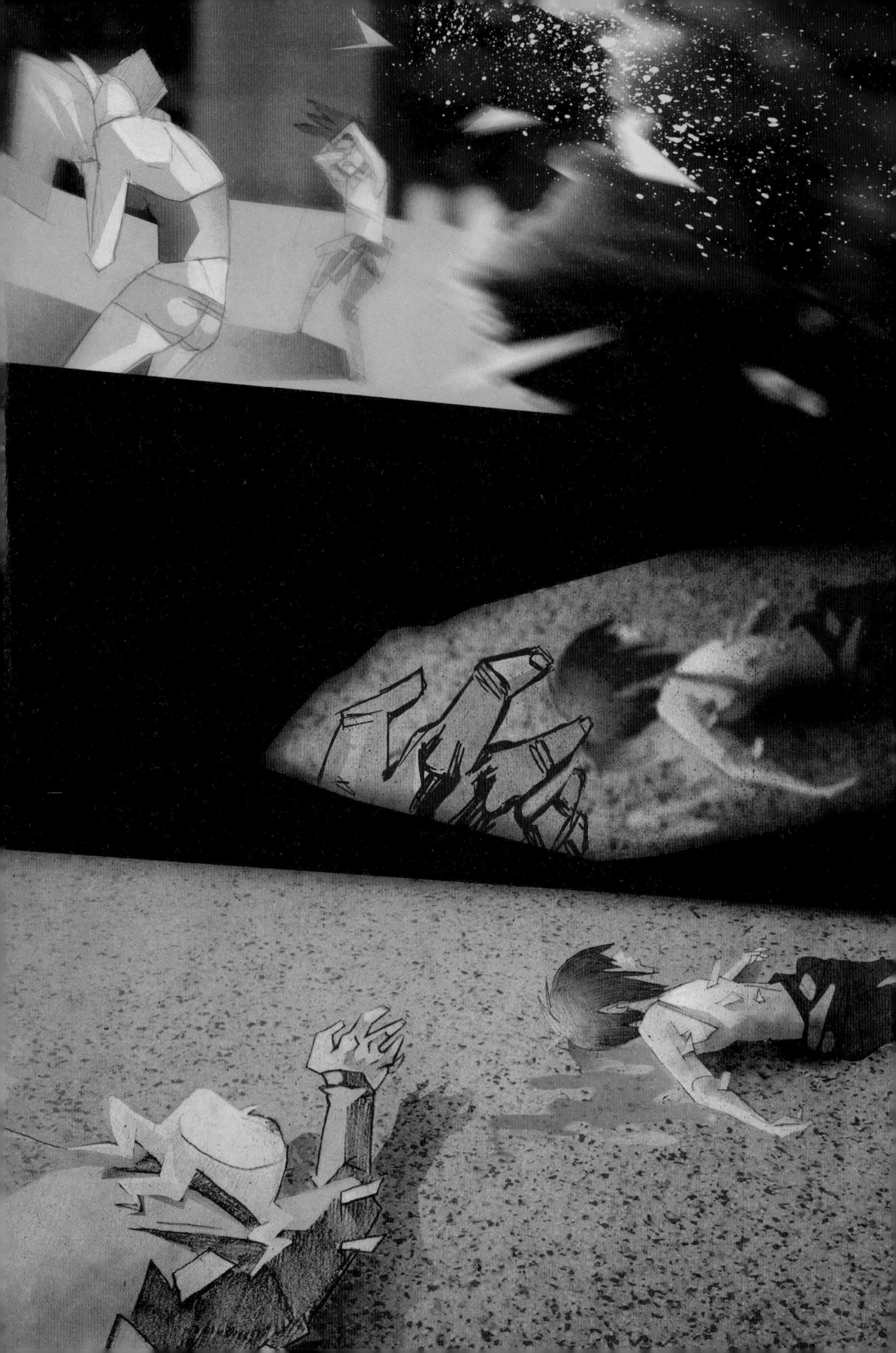

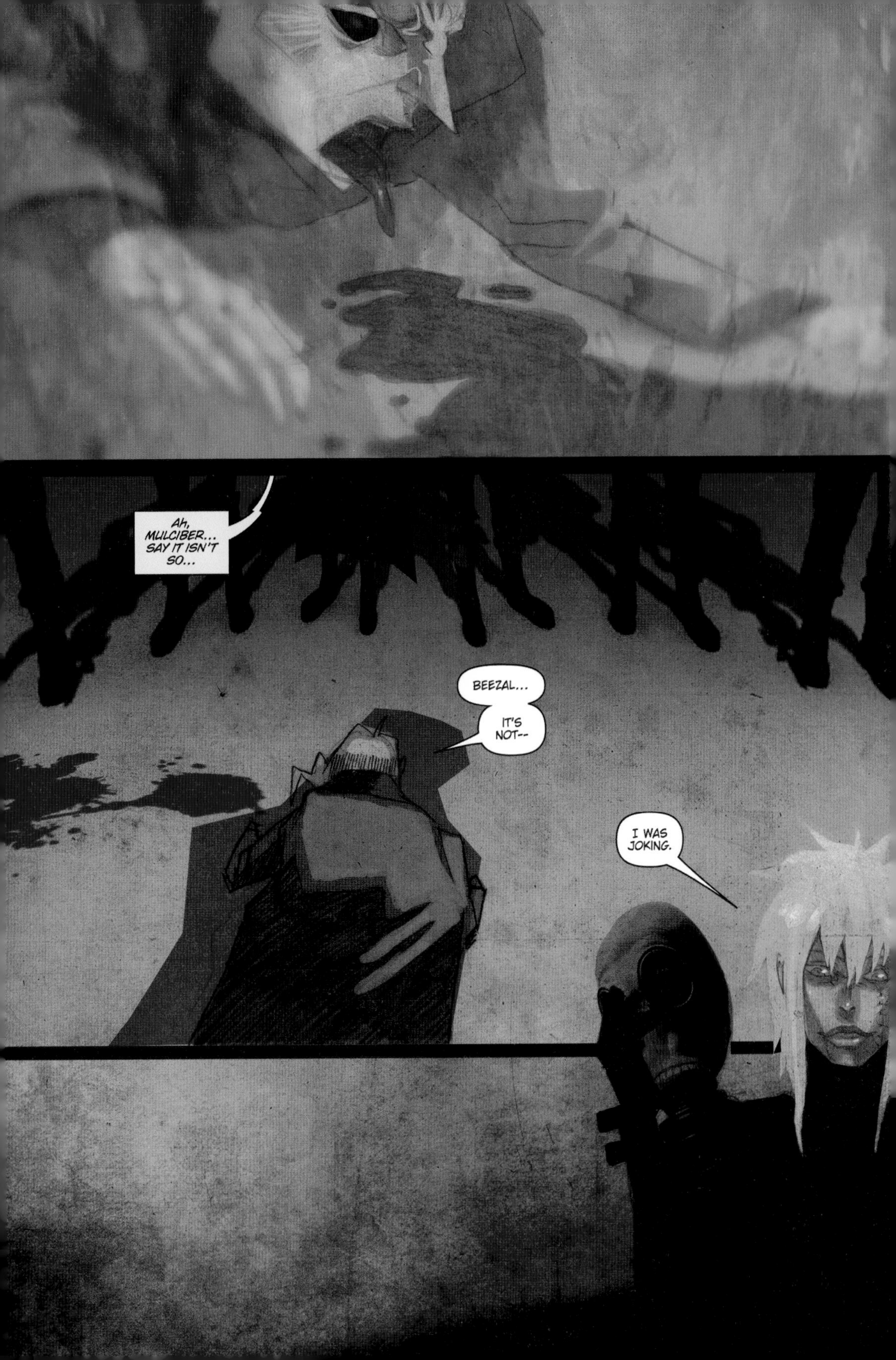
Ah, MULCIBER... SAY IT ISN'T SO...
BEEZAL...
IT'S NOT--
I WAS JOKING.

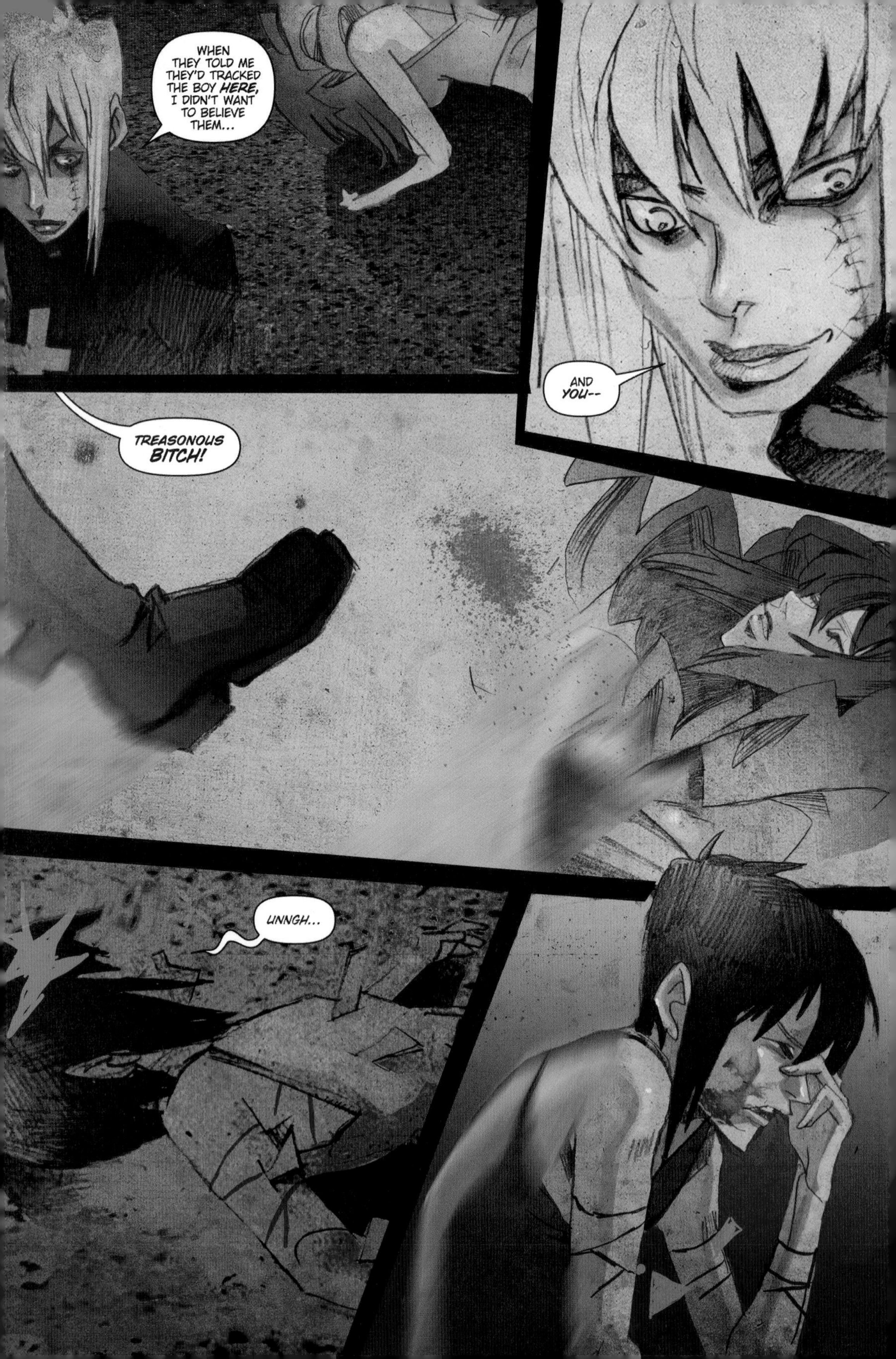
WHEN THEY TOLD ME THEY'D TRACKED THE BOY *HERE*, I DIDN'T WANT TO BELIEVE THEM...
AND *YOU*--
TREASONOUS ***BITCH!***
UNNGH...

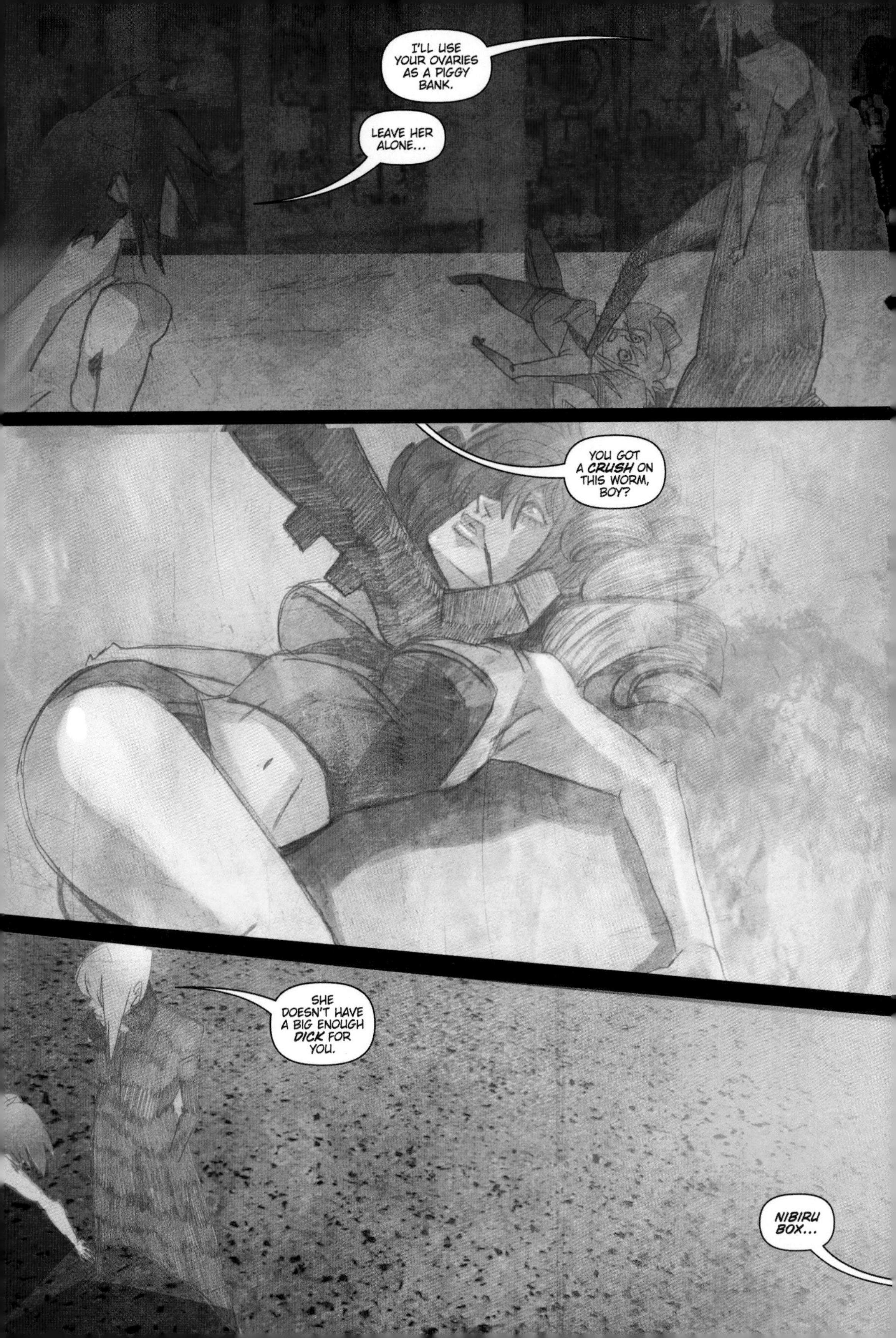
I'LL USE YOUR OVARIES AS A PIGGY BANK.
LEAVE HER ALONE...
YOU GOT A **CRUSH** ON THIS WORM, BOY?
SHE DOESN'T HAVE A BIG ENOUGH **DICK** FOR YOU.
NIBIRU BOX...

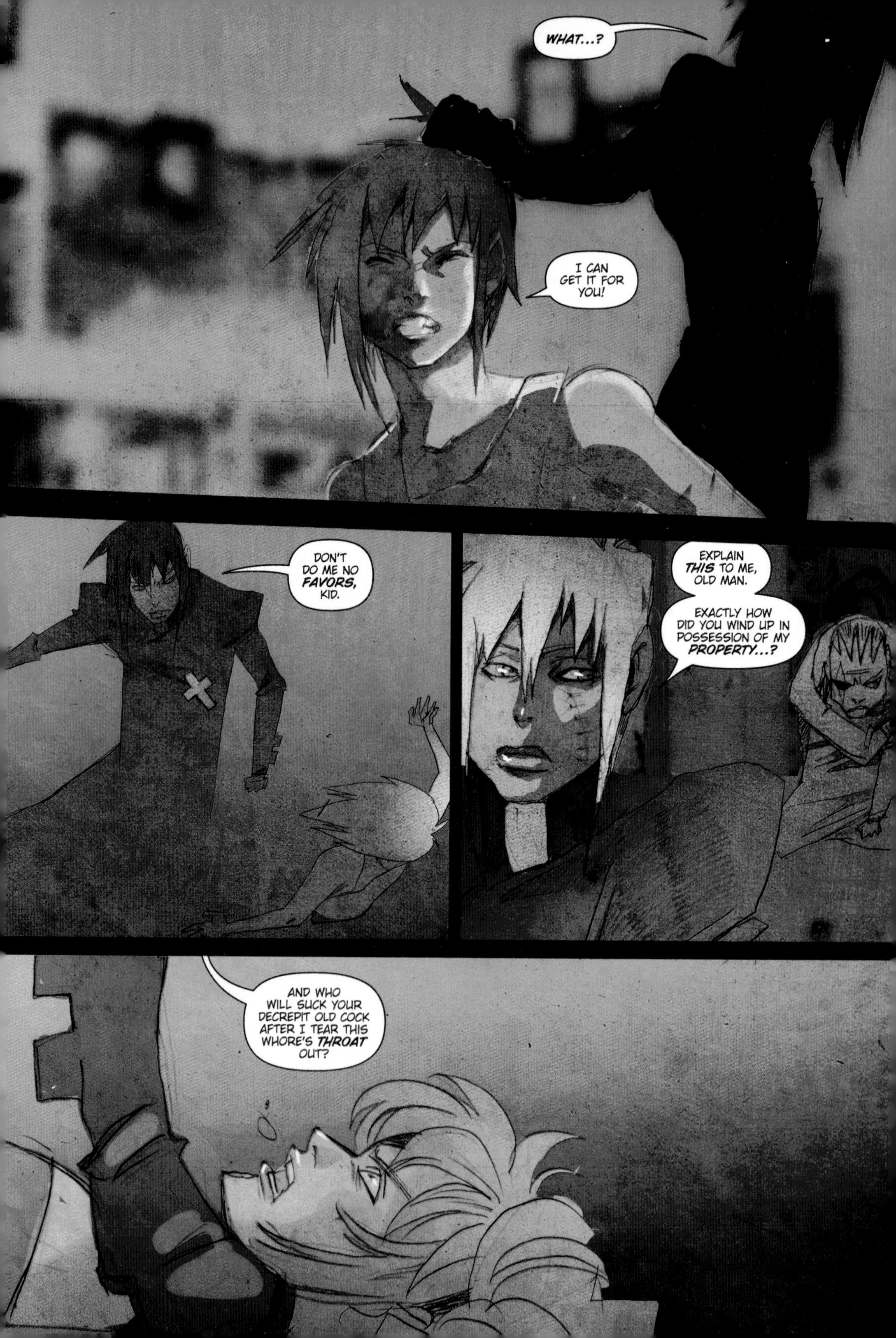
WHAT...?
I CAN GET IT FOR YOU!
DON'T DO ME NO FAVORS, KID.
EXPLAIN THIS TO ME, OLD MAN.
EXACTLY HOW DID YOU WIND UP IN POSSESSION OF MY PROPERTY...?
AND WHO WILL SUCK YOUR DECREPIT OLD COCK AFTER I TEAR THIS WHORE'S THROAT OUT?

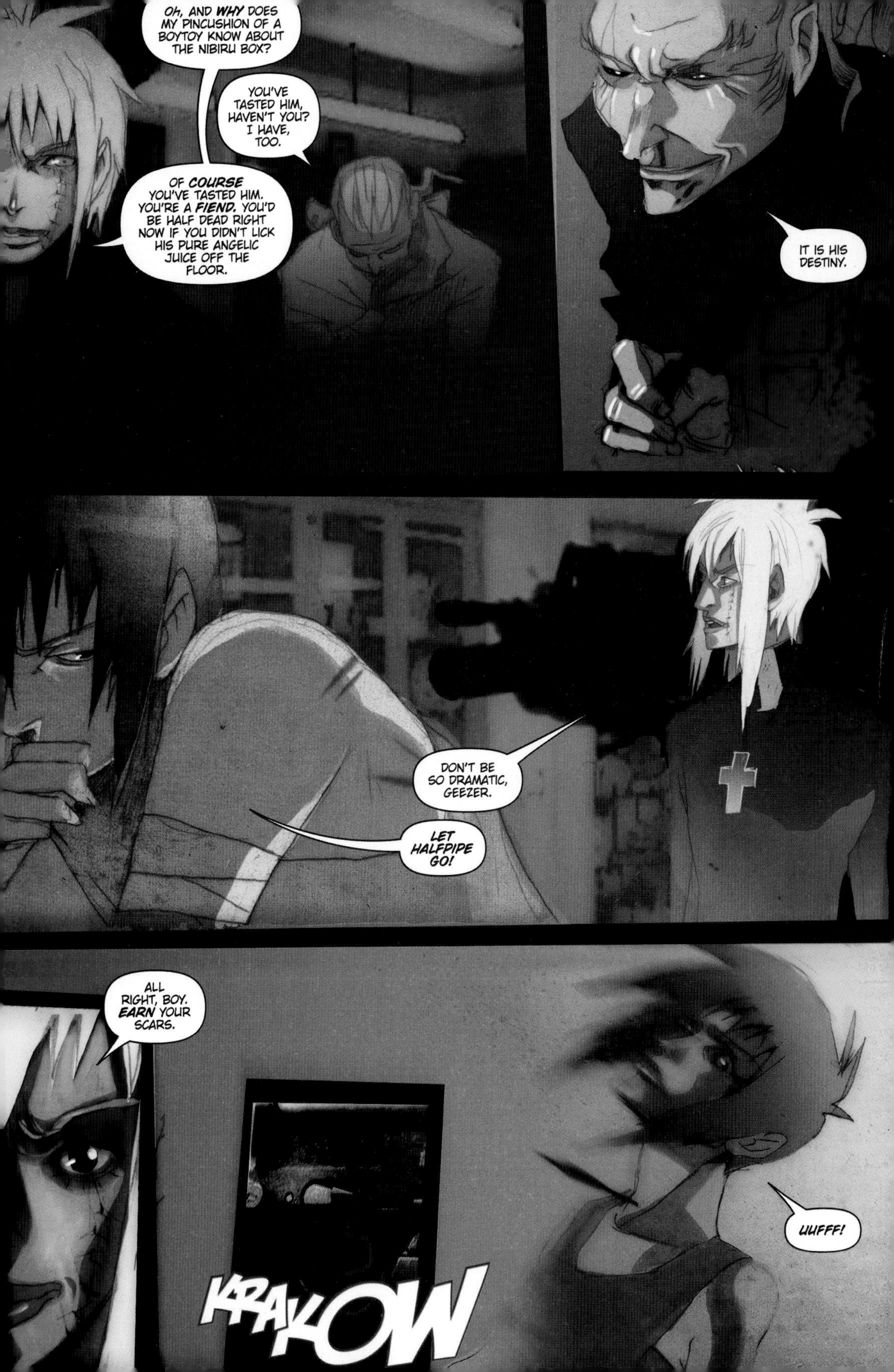

Oh, AND WHY DOES MY PINCUSHION OF A BOYTOY KNOW ABOUT THE NIBIRU BOX?
YOU'VE TASTED HIM, HAVEN'T YOU? I HAVE, TOO.
OF COURSE YOU'VE TASTED HIM. YOU'RE A FIEND. YOU'D BE HALF DEAD RIGHT NOW IF YOU DIDN'T LICK HIS PURE ANGELIC JUICE OFF THE FLOOR.
IT IS HIS DESTINY.
DON'T BE SO DRAMATIC, GEEZER.
LET HALFPIPE GO!
ALL RIGHT, BOY. EARN YOUR SCARS.
UUFFF!
KRAKOW

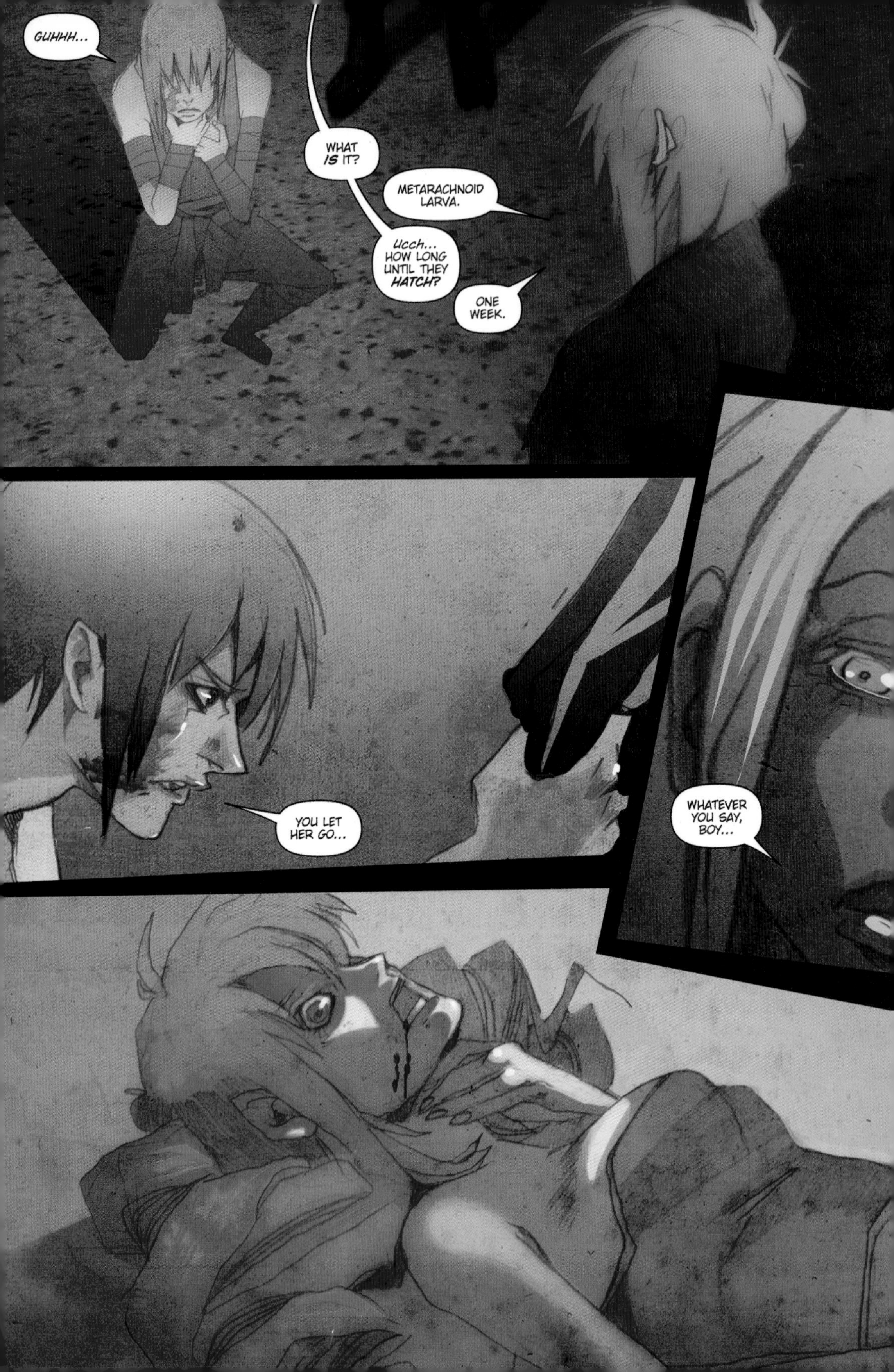
GUHHH...
WHAT IS IT?
METARACHNOID LARVA.
Ucch... HOW LONG UNTIL THEY HATCH?
ONE WEEK.
YOU LET HER GO...
WHATEVER YOU SAY, BOY...

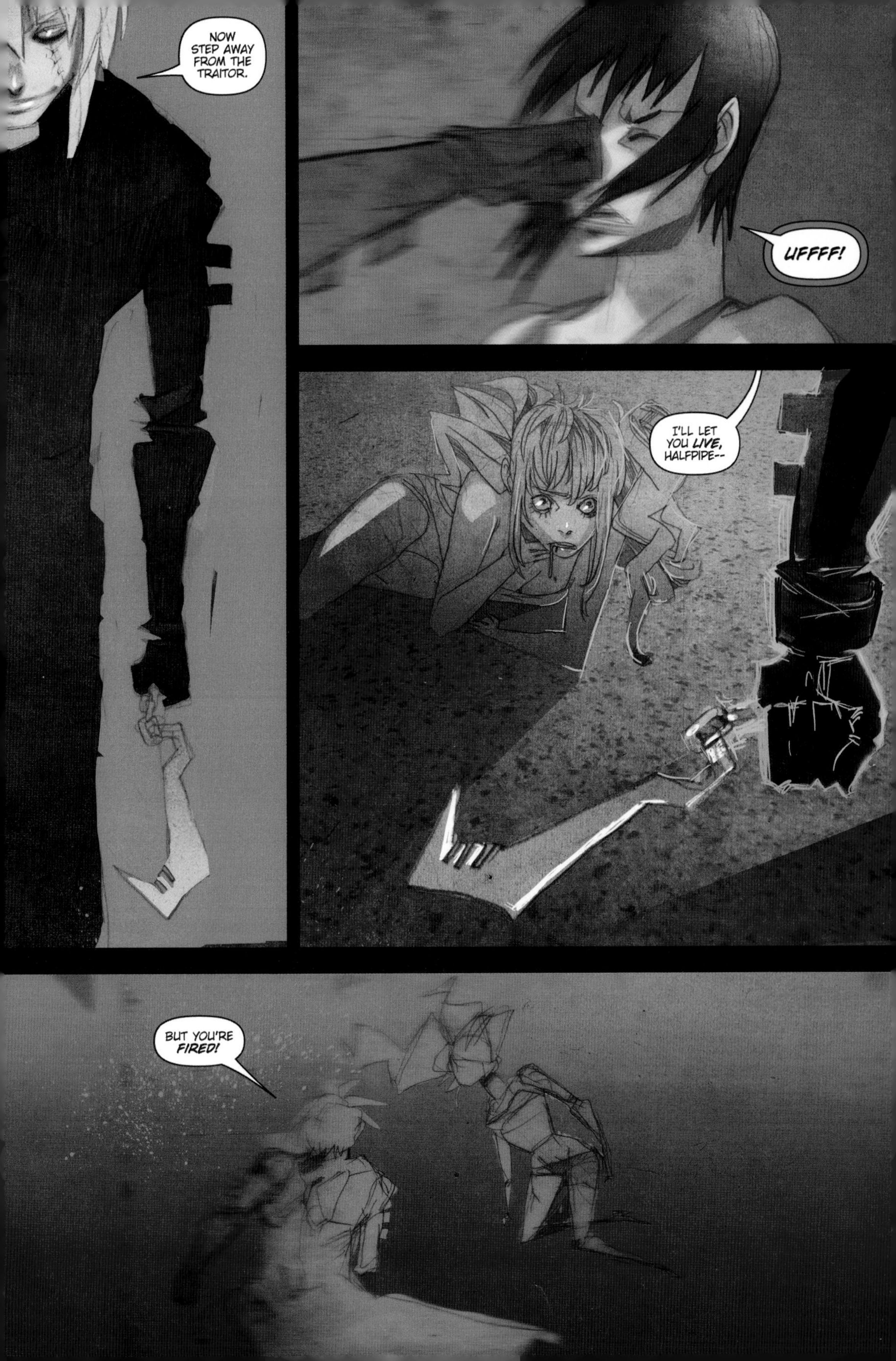
NOW STEP AWAY FROM THE TRAITOR.
UFFFF!
I'LL LET YOU LIVE, HALFPIPE--
BUT YOU'RE FIRED!

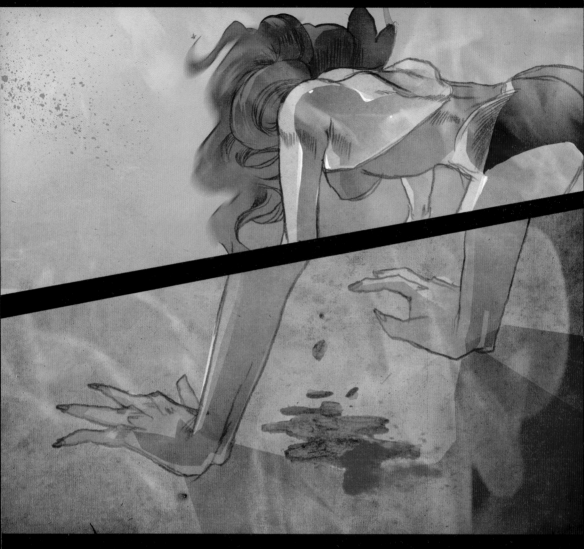

HERE'S A TIP: DRAGOS HAS IT.

I KNOW.

ONE WEEK.

Continued...

EVERYTHING
IS
PERMISSIBLE

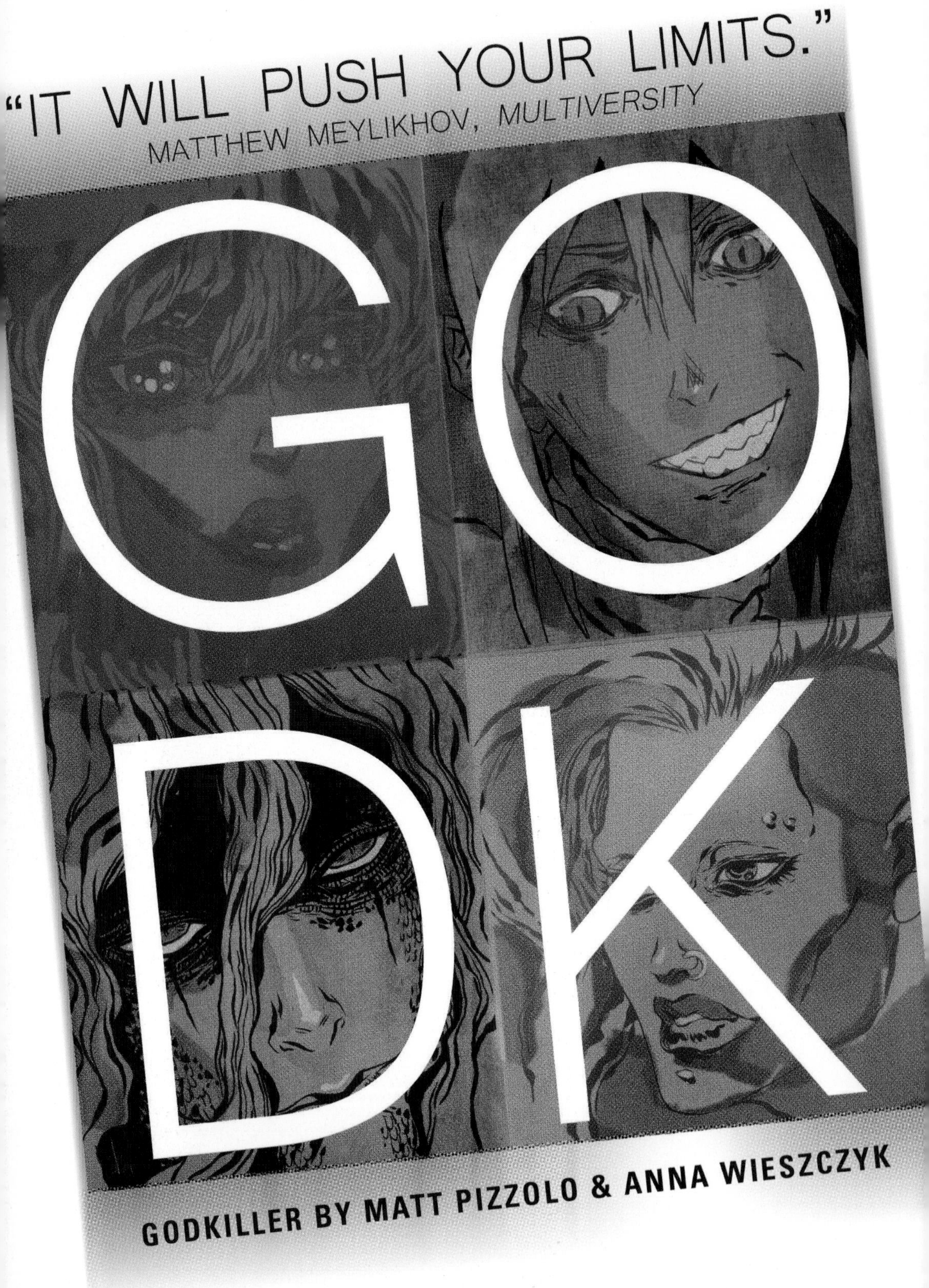
"IT WILL PUSH YOUR LIMITS."
MATTHEW MEYLIKHOV, MULTIVERSITY
GO
DK
GODKILLER BY MATT PIZZOLO & ANNA WIESZCZYK

GOD KILLER

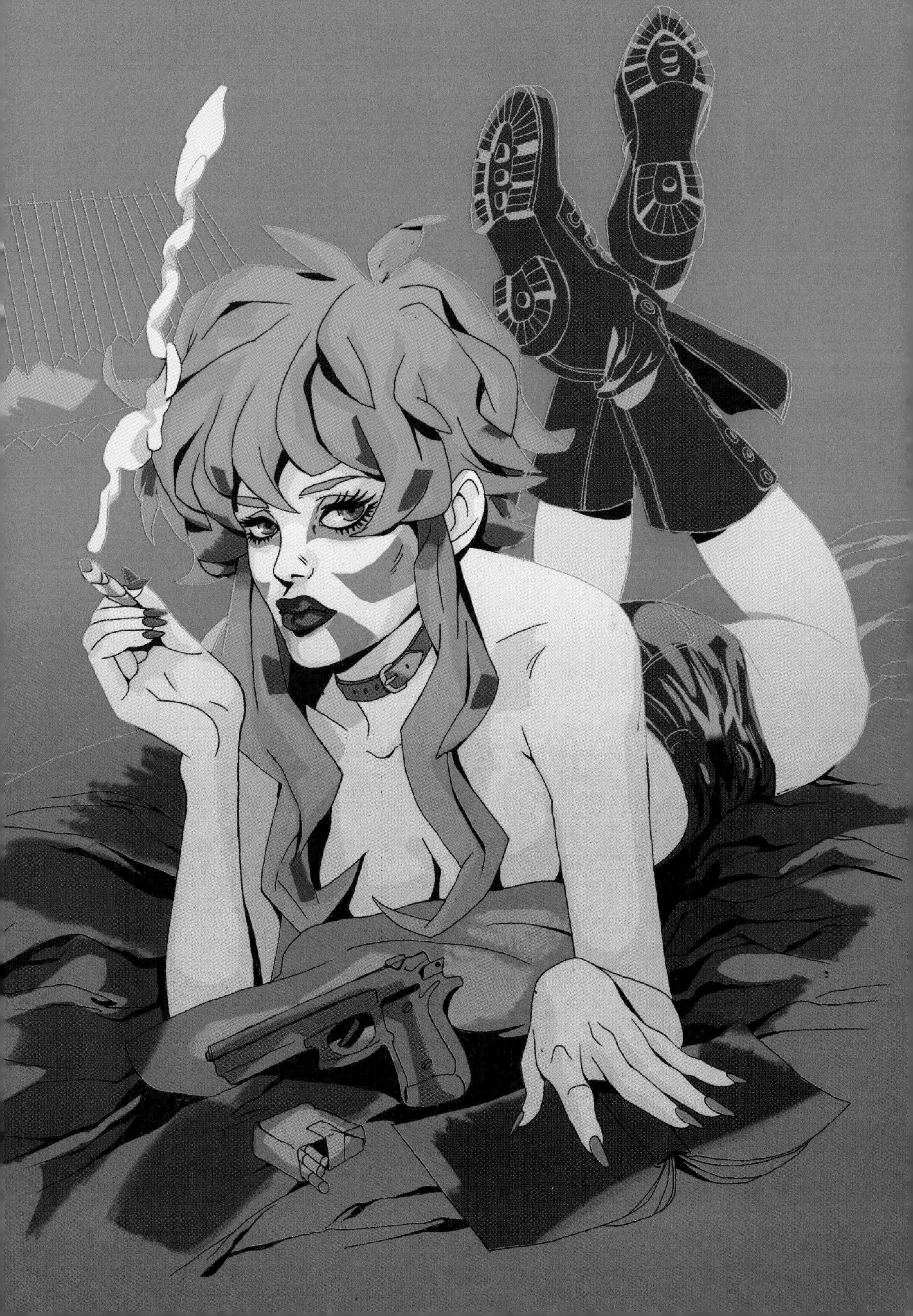

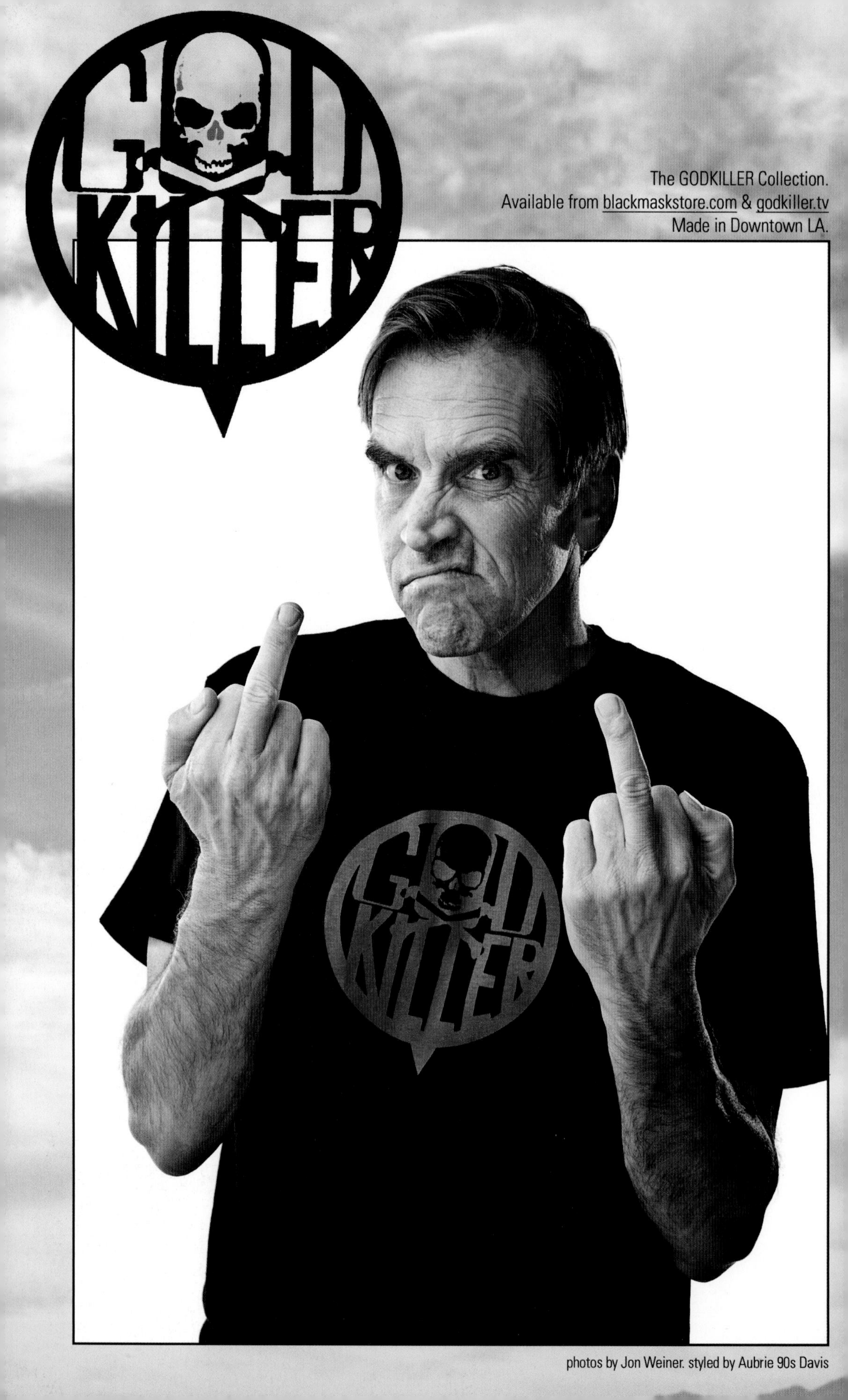
GOD
KILLER

photos by Jon Weiner. styled by Aubrie 90s Davis

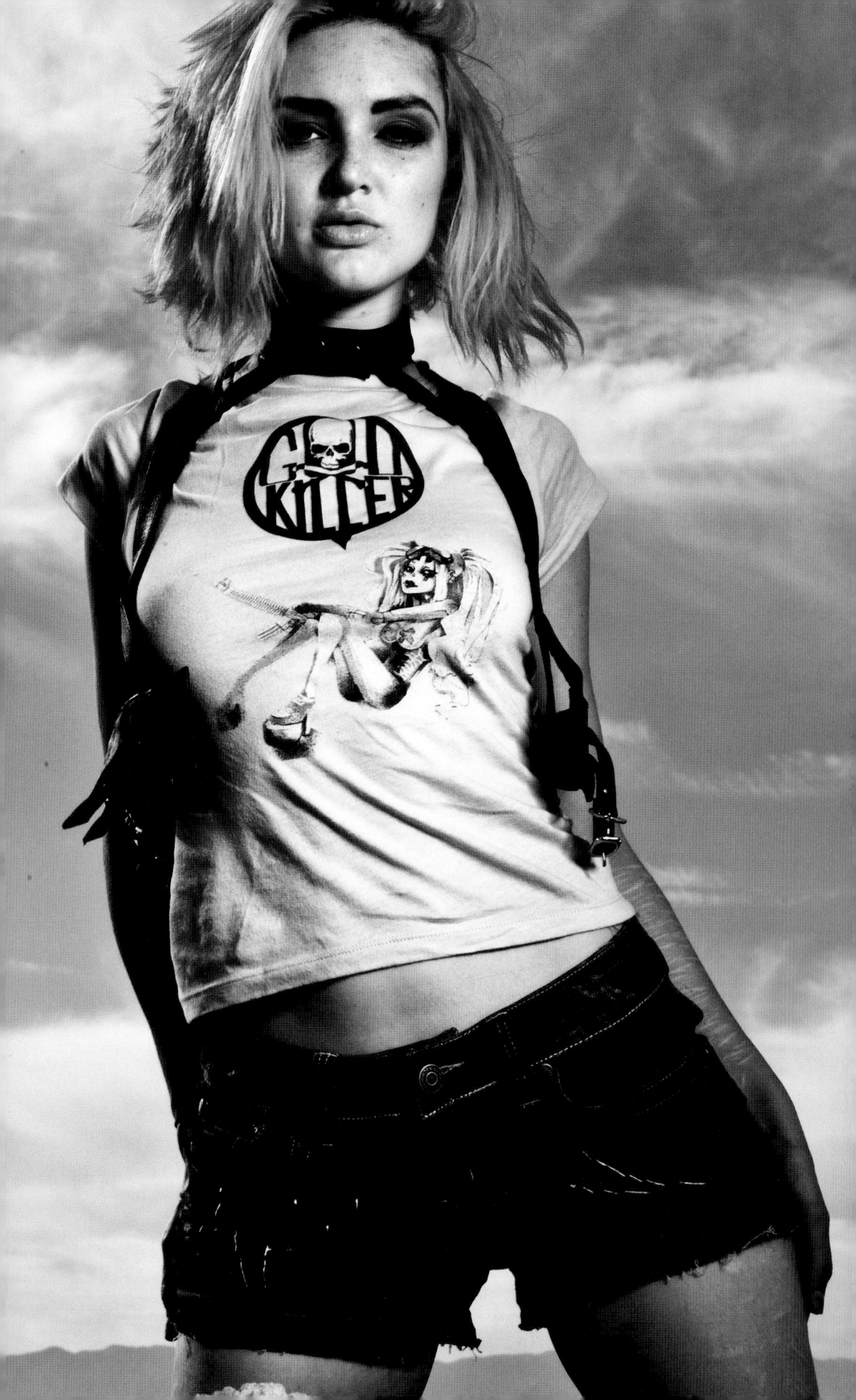
KILLER

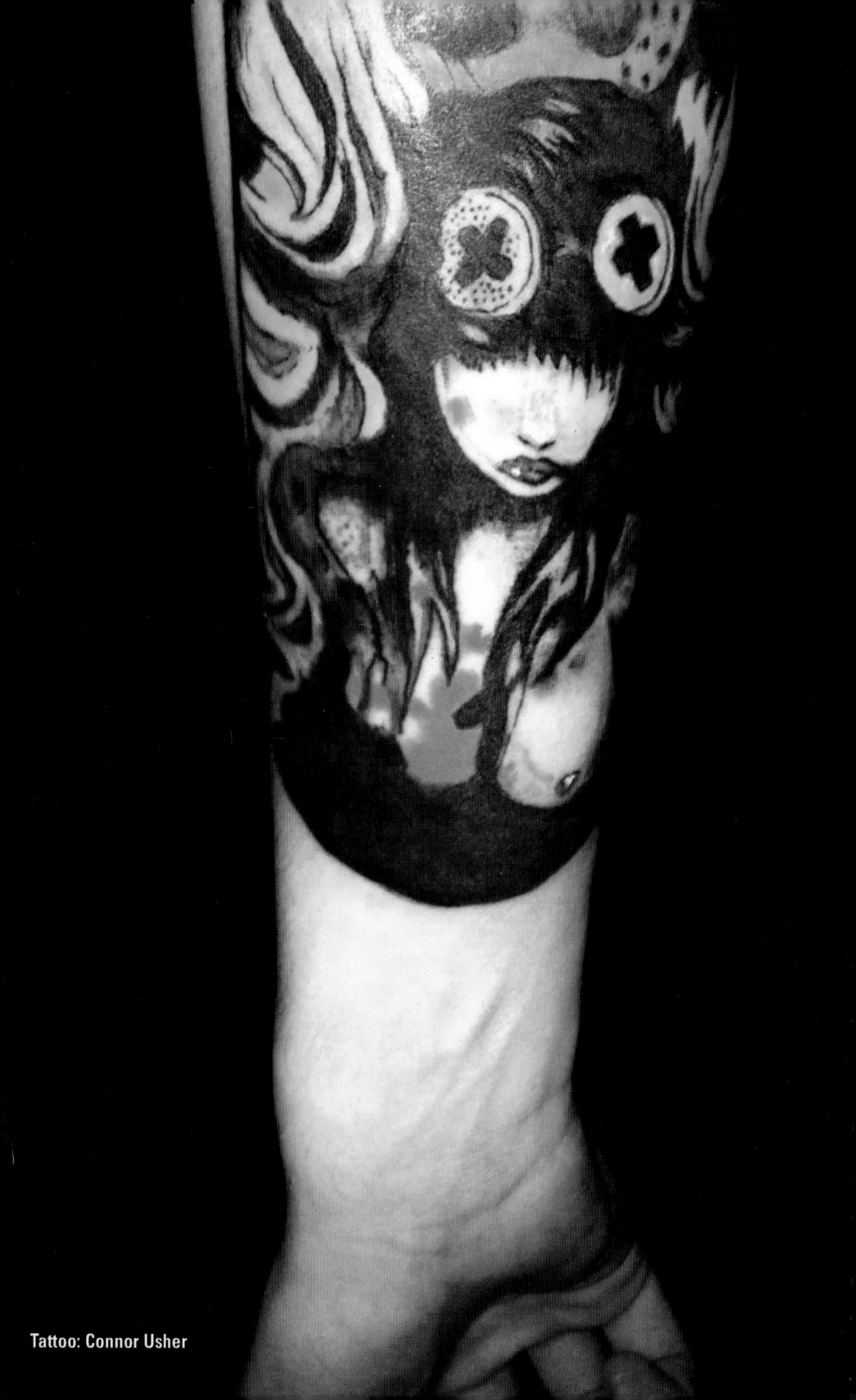

Tattoo: Connor Usher

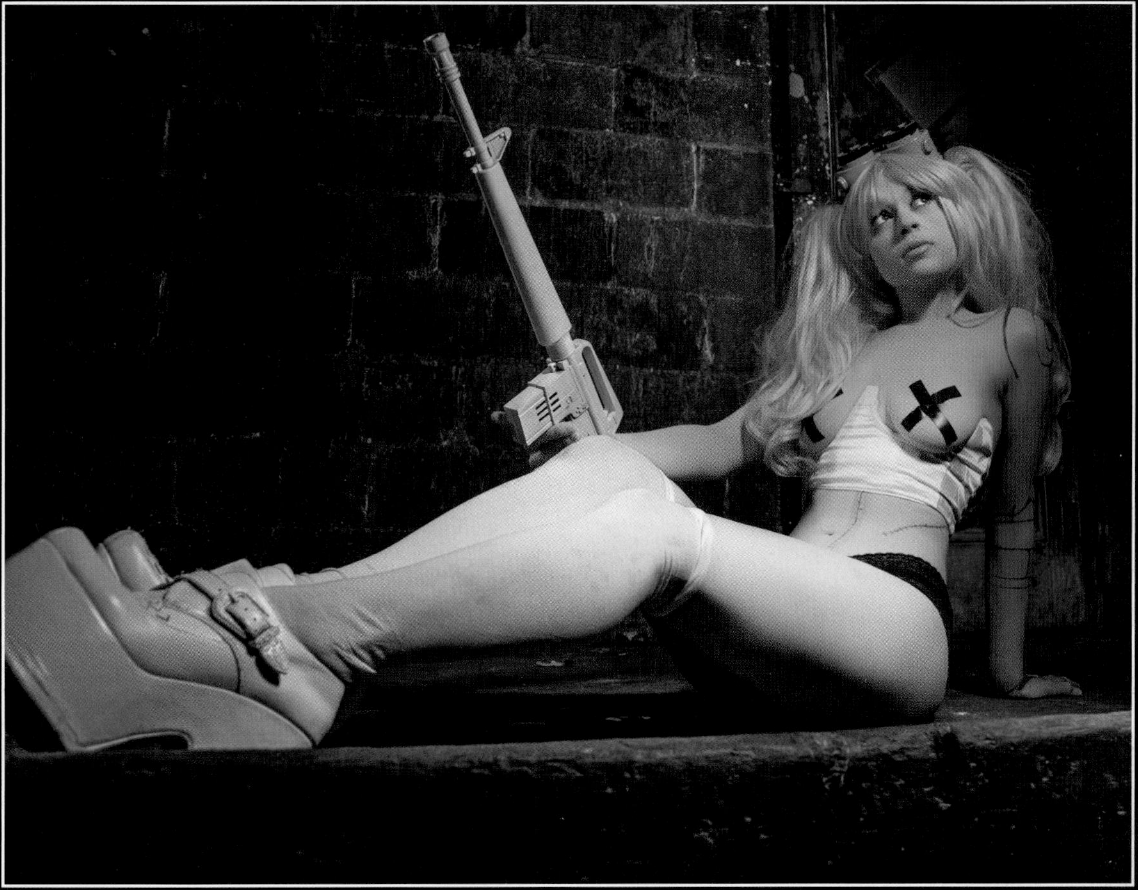

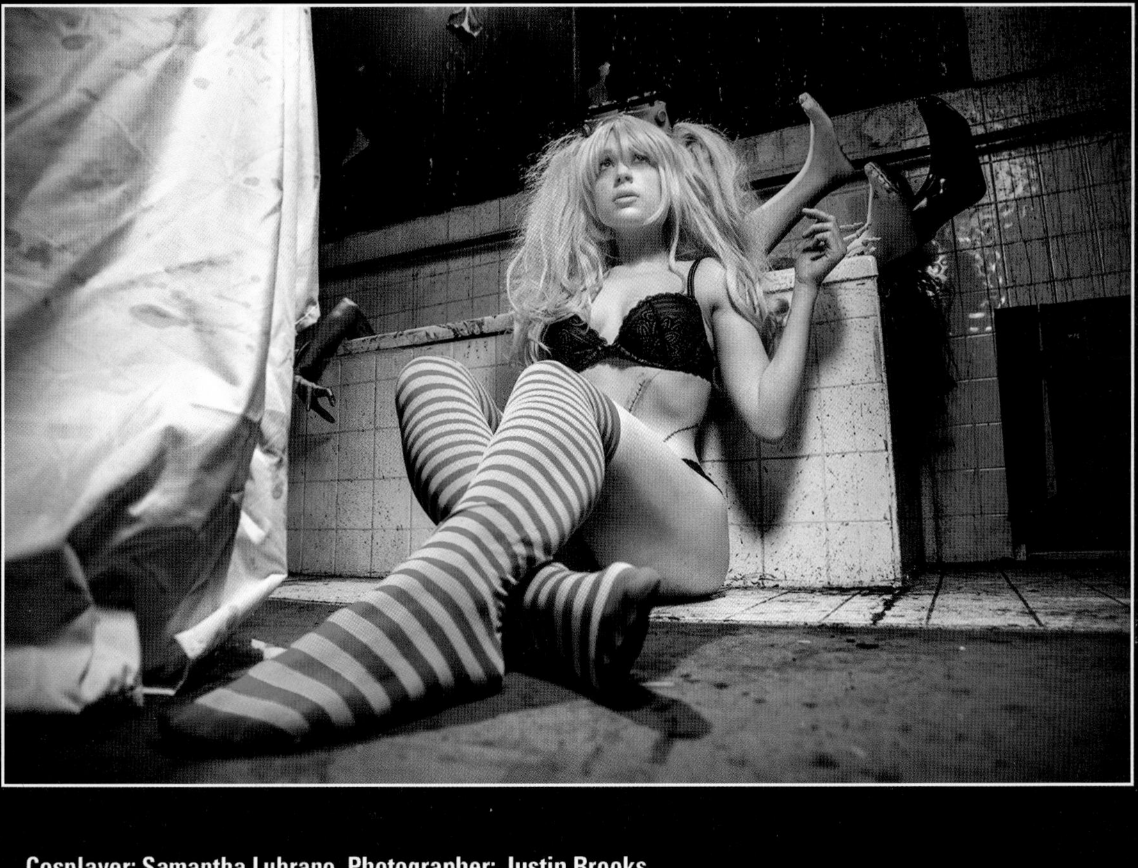

Cosplayer: Samantha Lubrano, Photographer: Justin Brooks

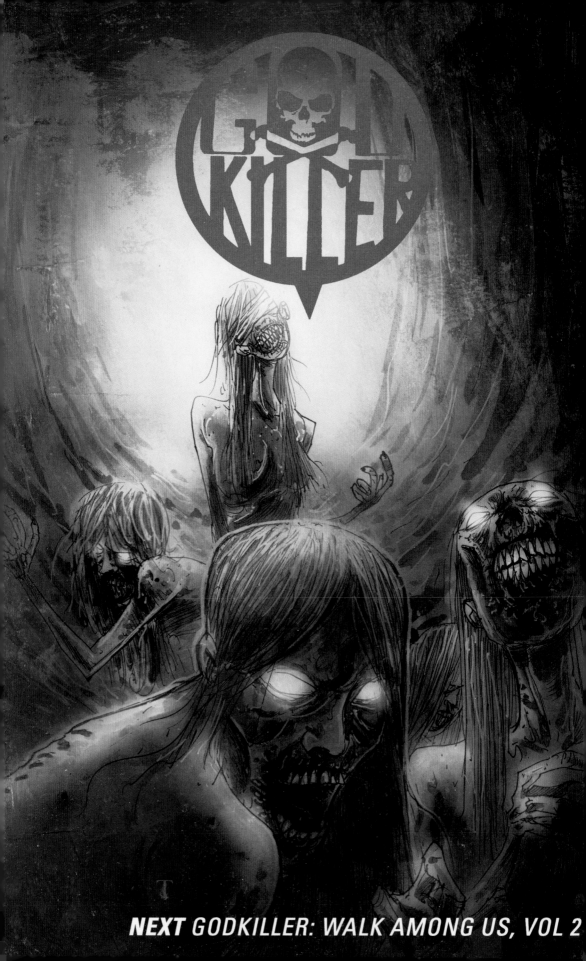

NEXT GODKILLER: WALK AMONG US, VOL 2